WITHDRAWN

# UNBREAKABLE

Also by Elizabeth Norris

*Unraveling*

# UNBREAKABLE

## ELIZABETH NORRIS

BALZER + BRAY

*An Imprint of* HarperCollins*Publishers*

Balzer + Bray is an imprint of HarperCollins Publishers.

Unbreakable

Library of Congress Cataloging-in-Publication Data is
available.
ISBN 978-0-06-210376-5

Typography by Alison Klapthor
13  14  15  16  17   LP/RRDH   10  9  8  7  6  5  4  3  2  1

First Edition

*For Dan, it was worth the wait* ♥

# UNBREAKABLE

# PART ONE

*Labor with what zeal we will,*

*Something still remains undone,*

*Something uncompleted still*

*Waits the rising of the sun.*

—Henry Wadsworth Longfellow

# 07:15:01:55

Some days are so perfect, they just don't seem real.

They're the days when you wake up and aren't tired, when the sun is shining and the breeze kicks up from the ocean, keeping you from getting too hot or too cold, and everything you do goes right. Like you're inside of a movie with your own soundtrack, where you're so happy that you can't help just spontaneously breaking into a smile. Some days are like magic.

But I haven't had one of those days in a long time.

So long, it feels like maybe I never did. In fact, when I've been up for eighteen hours, letting Cecily boss me around in an old snack bar that she converted into a kitchen—one that might be a hundred degrees—it feels like maybe perfect days are a lie.

"What are you doing?" Cecily says, scolding me. "That's never going to work."

"My idea, not work? That's shocking." I make a big show of rolling my eyes. "Come up with a better idea and we'll try it." I almost add that we don't need popcorn, but I keep my mouth shut. I can only push her so far. The wrath of Cecily when plans go awry is something I'm trying to avoid.

It's movie night at Qualcomm.

About a month ago, Cecily decided that a movie night was just the thing Qualcomm needed. It would give people something to look forward to, and with the right equipment it was something we could actually get done. She made Kevin Collins and me spend a weekend going through the wreckage of every movie theater in San Diego, looking for the right projection equipment and an assortment of movies we could show.

So now we have a little more than thirteen hundred people seated on what used to be the Chargers football field—with more watching from the seats. Blankets are laid out, people are huddled together, and Cecily has *It's a Wonderful Life* cued up on the projector. I had argued with her choice of that one—it's not like much going on around here could be called wonderful—but my arguments had gone down in flames, and Kevin didn't help matters since he had backed her up, hoping to win her over.

The only snag in her plan right now is the popcorn.

The generator let us use the microwave to pop over half of the bags we found when we scrounged around the city, but it started taking its toll on our power. Even Cee wasn't going to argue that popcorn was more important than lights. So now I'm using a couple of old pans and a wood-burning stove.

Because I'm thinking of him, Kevin pushes through the door with a wide smile for Cecily. In a surprising and I'll admit impressive move on his part, he got his GED and enlisted in the Marines a couple of months ago. "Lady J!" he shouts as a few of the guys in his unit come in behind him. "We've come for you to feed us."

I'd like to say the whole enlisting thing made him grow up, but he's the same as ever.

I ignore Kevin. I'm good at it.

Cecily, who has only her own agenda on her mind, beams at him. "Oh, you're here, perfect," she says, piling bags of popcorn into the guys' arms before they have a chance to speak. "Start with the people in the back since they're farthest from the screen. And make sure everyone takes a small handful and passes it down. We have about one bag for every fifteen or so people; no one gets their own."

One of the guys rolls his eyes—he's obviously here as a favor because poor Kevin has it bad for Cecily.

Kevin bows with a flourish. "Your wish shall be done."

I have to force myself to keep from snorting at the ridiculousness that is happening right in front of me.

Before he leaves, Kevin looks at me. "Hurry up, woman. If we have to wait for you we'll never get to see the movie."

Unable to control her laughter, Cecily pushes Kevin out the door, and the universe finally rewards me, because the popcorn finally starts to pop.

"So this thing with Kevin . . ." I say once he's gone. Every guy has a thing for Cee—even Alex had a huge crush on her. Alex, my best friend, the one who told me he wasn't going to date anyone until college because he didn't want to have to introduce a girl that he liked to his mother unless he knew she could handle it. Alex, who will never date anyone. Alex, who's gone because of me.

I swallow those thoughts down, despite the tightness in my throat, and focus on Cecily. I want her to be happy.

She blushes but doesn't say anything.

"He is pretty cute," I add. He's also immature and drives me a little out of my mind, but I can't deny that he's nice to look at.

Cecily laughs and shakes her head. "He is." Then she pauses and adds, "And he's funny, too, you know? Like super funny. Every time I see him, he makes me crack up about something. Plus, I can't help being surprised at how thoughtful he is. He always does really nice little things for me."

She says it like there's a "but" coming.

"So, what's the problem?" I laugh a little, but Cecily doesn't join in.

"This is terrible. I mean, I kind of want to like him." She sighs. "I just can't. I don't know. I guess he's just not really my type."

I know what she means. About wanting to like someone and just not being able to. Kevin's tried to hook me up with half the guys in his unit, and then of course, there's Nick. A date or even a little romance would be such a welcome distraction from everything going on, but all I see when I look at another guy is someone who's not Ben Michaels.

Since the day he left, I've been looking everywhere for Ben. Remembering his dark brown eyes; the way his hair falls in his face; the way he reached out, touched my cheek, and pulled me into one last kiss; the way he took slow steps backward toward the portal, as if he didn't really want to leave; the way he said my name and told me he loved me.

The way the portal swallowed him up and he disappeared.

But mostly I think about how he said, *I'll come back for you.*

"Okay, don't laugh," Cecily says suddenly, doing me a favor and pulling me from thoughts I should be able to let go. "But

I kind of have a thing for the bad boys, like from afar, but still. Give me a leather jacket, a devilish smile, a guy my parents wouldn't approve of, and you know, someone who needs to be saved."

Ben didn't have the leather jacket or a devilish smile. But he was definitely the kind of guy my dad would've been wary of. And he did need to be saved.

Only I'd saved him, and now he was gone.

"It wouldn't hurt either if he had nice eyes," Cecily adds.

I smile, thinking of Ben's dark, deep-set eyes and the intensity in them when he looked at me.

Every five or ten minutes, Cecily carts an armload of popcorn bags out to the field. When we finally have them all passed out, we pick through the crowd to find my brother, Jared, and Kevin and his friends. There's one extra bag of popcorn, and because we're feeling gluttonous, we keep it.

I barely watch the movie because I'm more interested in watching Jared, who can't take his eyes off the screen.

It doesn't matter that I've missed more than half of the movie. Or that it's black-and-white and from 1946. It doesn't matter that the popcorn is too buttery, that the wool blanket itches my skin every chance it gets, or even that I'm tired and sweaty from the stove.

With about fifteen minutes of the movie left, Struz finds us and sits next to Jared, whose eyes are a little watery.

And then Struz winks at me.

I glance at Cecily, who just smiles. It's a smile I know well. The one that says, *So there,* or *I was right,* or any other *I told you so* type of phrase. I give her the finger, because there's not much else to do.

She was right.

Popcorn and movie night were exactly what we needed.

Maybe this day was a little magical after all.

# 07:00:45:13

The next morning, the magic has worn off. That tends to happen to me when I have to get out of bed before the sun is up, especially on my day off. The reason I'm up is that Struz is sending Cee and me on a supply run up to Camp Pendleton. He chose us because we're charming—or, more accurately, Cecily is charming.

And it works. She manages to sweet talk everyone we run into. I'm just there to help with the heavy lifting.

We spend the drive home, with Cecily at the wheel, in silence. It's not because we're sad or even tired—despite the fact that this day has already been exhausting and it's not quite noon. This silence weighs down on us because when you do this drive, you can't deny that the world has changed.

The coast is the worst. Buildings are collapsed, homes demolished or just gone. The roof on my favorite restaurant, Roberto's, caved in, and the patio cracked and split open, putting an end to my burritos-after-the-beach tradition. Trees have been uprooted, and they lie on their sides as if they've been discarded like weeds. In my old neighborhood, the trees took out any houses that hadn't already collapsed from the quake itself. Debris is everywhere, littered across the grass and piled up on the side of the road.

But what's worst is how it feels. Before the quakes, San Diego was the kind of place that felt alive. The sun, the ocean waves, the crowds of tourists—it had personality. Now it feels empty, destroyed. Dead.

This silence is one of respect, the kind that you observe.

Because it's been a hundred and forty days since an old pickup truck hit me, and the warmth of the engine, the smell of locking brakes, and someone shouting my name were the last things I remembered. A hundred and forty days since I died.

Since my whole world changed.

Because I didn't stay dead. Ben Michaels healed me and brought me back. Because of him, I had a second chance. I don't know how it happened, but Ben changed my class schedule, argued with me in English, took me to Sunset Cliffs, and made me love him.

And then he left.

Now the whole world has changed—for everyone.

My dad died because he didn't know what kind of case he stumbled on. I solved his murder, saved the world, lost my best friend, and watched Ben walk through a portal and leave this universe.

I stopped Wave Function Collapse, but the damage was already done.

All of the natural disasters hit at the same time—and no corner of the globe was spared. Tornadoes took out the Midwest. Earthquakes leveled cities close to fault lines and also ones that weren't, like Dallas and Vegas. Tsunamis blanketed and sank low-level areas like Coronado Island, New Orleans, Manhattan, and parts of the California coast. Wildfires swept the nation in all different directions, reducing land, trees, houses—even people—to ashes.

And we weren't alone. Other countries had been hit just as hard. Some of them were just gone.

Millions of people died.

Millions more went missing.

Modern life took the biggest hit. Satellites were knocked out of position, telephone lines went dead, electricity flickered out, and running water went dry. Aftershocks took out most of the buildings that were still standing. Hospitals overflowed with people injured and dying. Medicine and medical supplies were used up. We started running out of food and water. Almost nothing survived the looting.

As Cecily drives, I lean my forehead against the window and feel the warmth of the sun against the glass. I almost close my eyes to block out the reminders, but it's pointless. I can't forget what's happened here.

"Don't do that!" Cecily says, snapping her fingers at me as we go over a bump on the uneven road. "And by *that*, I mean that weird sad thing where you go all quiet and depressed."

"I thought you knew I was lame like that," I say, but I pull my head back and sit up straight. She's bossy, but right.

Cecily smiles. "I know you better than you think, J."

"Didn't you know cheerleading is sort of a dead sport?" I ask. "I'm not sure you need to stay so peppy."

She gasps and pretends to be offended, but I know she's not. We both had a first-class ticket to seeing the world change. Well, maybe that was just me, but Cecily has seen the aftereffects up close and personal even if she doesn't know the actual cause.

I'm about to say something else when I see it.

Ahead there's a house, half standing with a sunken roof, and in front of it a few people are milling around, looking at an assortment of stuff laid out on the dead grass.

Cecily sees it too. "Oh, a yard sale! We have to check it out."

It's not that they're likely to have anything we want. These yard sales are for trades. People need supplies—usually medicine or food—and they're willing to give up other material possessions in order to get it.

Of course, not many people have medicine or food to spare. But we do. Between my connection to the FBI and Cecily's family running one of the largest evacuation shelters in the area, we have access that normal people don't. There's a case of water and an economy-size bottle of aspirin in the back of the truck. I can't give it all away, but I can give these people something.

"It looks like they have books," Cecily adds as we crawl to a stop. "Maybe they'll have something for Jared."

He needs a new book. We can only reread *Harry Potter and the Order of the Phoenix* so many times. As he's pointed out, it's the middle of the story.

I get out of the truck. A man wearing broken glasses approaches us, but I let Cecily talk to him. She's the friendly one, after all.

There are some old clothes and blankets off to the side, and then a row of DVDs. I look at them just in case there's something *X-Files*. We lost our collector's edition box set when our house collapsed. Electricity is too spotty still to play DVDs, but once it comes back, my brother will miss them.

The collection is mostly indie movies, so I head for the books. It's a lot of literary stuff, a lot of classics, and not necessarily the good stuff, in my opinion. I know I should want to preserve *Moby Dick* or *Great Expectations*, but I just can't make myself do it. Then I see a flash of a red-and-black book cover.

I reach for it, excitement making me feel giddy and light-headed. I turn, ready to call out to Cee to tell her what I've found, but I'm not looking, so I walk straight into some random guy.

He's taller than me, and my face plows into his shoulder. The soft cotton of his shirt rubs against my cheek as I stumble against him. He grunts and drops all of the books in his hands. I pause, taking a minute to make sure I have my balance before I look up. Even though it wasn't really my fault, I'm about to apologize.

Only the words get stuck in my throat.

"Sorry about that. The danger of picking up too many mass-markets," he says with a tentative smile, a smile that says he's a little embarrassed.

And suddenly everything around me stops. The sounds of the other people, the wind in the trees—it fades away, and all I see is the guy in front of me. Everything about him is the same. The wavy hair, the dark eyes, the self-conscious half smile.

I close my eyes, sure that I'm imagining this, that too much sun and not enough sleep have finally gotten to me, but when I open them again, he's still there.

It's like I've conjured him out of thin air.

"Ben?" I whisper, because my whole body feels like it's frozen, like I'm worried he'll disappear.

# 07:00:40:53

**B**en blushes, and that's all I need.

It's like he never left, like he's been by my side the whole time, like we've been sharing half smiles, stealing glances at each other, and blushing because we remember too well what it feels like to melt into each other, press our lips together, and forget how messed up the world is.

I let out a yelp and throw my arms around him. I don't ask what he's doing here or how long he's been back or even why he hasn't come to find me. I just pull him close and hold on to him with everything I've got. I revel in how real he is. The feel of him under my hands, the warmth of his skin, the muscles in his arms, the breath in his chest. He's real.

Only he's not *right*.

It's after I've thrown my arms around him that I realize what's different.

And it's not just the awkward way that he's standing limply in my arms, like someone who's been tackled by a crazy chick he's never seen before. It's that he doesn't feel right in my arms. It doesn't feel like we fit, and he even smells different—like spices and wet grass.

I know what that must mean.

Flustered, I pull back from him and start rambling. I don't even know what I'm saying, but it has to be some sort of awkward apology, because he shrugs and runs a hand through his hair, then opens his mouth to say something before shutting it again.

My heart is pounding in my ears and my throat feels thick. A wave of desperation rolls through me, stinging my eyes and carving a hole in my chest. This isn't fair.

I look at him again, and suddenly all I see are the differences. His hair is a little too short; his eyes are a little too light and maybe not sad enough; his chest is a little too broad; and he's wearing khaki shorts and an NFL sweatshirt. I fight to suck down enough air to keep from hurling all over his Adidas sneakers.

This guy isn't *my* Ben at all. He's a stranger wearing the same face.

Because there isn't just one universe, but rather many. A multiverse. There are thousands of different universes, and one theory is that they all started parallel, but when different people in the different universes made different choices, things grew outward differently.

Everyone in this world could have a doppelgänger out there—more than one. There could even be other versions of me living different lives in different worlds.

Just like there could be other versions of Ben.

Like this one.

# 07:00:38:22

I thought about *my* Ben Michaels every day.

All one hundred and forty of them.

I try to keep myself busy, and most days I can push thoughts of him to the back of my mind, but I can't forget him. I'll be doing something mundane, like teasing Jared and ruffling his hair or helping Cecily at the evac shelter, and a memory of Ben or something he said will just strike me.

Like the time Cee and I were fueling the last of the gas tanks and I told her, "I've always loved the smell of gasoline."

And suddenly I was overcome with a moment and I was somewhere else—*Ben and I standing outside Kon-Tiki Motorcycles in Pacific Beach, a breeze coming off the ocean, my skin feeling strangely empty and open. My fingers intertwined with his, I moved into his space and laid my forehead on his chest. His whole body relaxed, as if tension was rolling off his body in waves. His free hand came up and his fingers slipped through my hair before his hand settled between my shoulder blades, and I whispered his name.*

There's always a second where I'm lost in the memory and I feel light and happy. A giddy smile will overtake my face, and it will almost feel like he was just here.

Almost.

Then the heaviness of reality sets in, and I remember that I'm alone. That Ben is gone.

And it's like my heart breaks all over again.

Nights are worse. I lie awake and think of the way Ben's lips tasted against mine, or the strength in his long fingers and the way they felt against my skin. Sometimes missing him is visceral—I remember what it was like to have his arms around me, and I can feel their absence.

What I miss most is the way he smiled against my cheek.

But this isn't *my* Ben Michaels.

# 07:00:38:21

We stand there—me and this stranger—for a minute, unsure of what to say next. I still can't believe he's real. Ben told me he'd never run into a double in this world. I guess I'd assumed one didn't exist.

The guy must know I mistook him for someone else, because he says, "I just moved down here from San Clemente." He gestures to another guy behind him who is a little thinner with dark hair that's cut a little shorter but has the same curl at the ends, and he has the same deep-set eyes. He looks almost identical. "My brother and I came after the quakes took out our house. We heard there was more food down here."

*His brother—Derek.*

"It's the military presence," I mumble. Hopefully that's enough of an explanation. I can't force myself to say anything else. I'm too busy looking over his shoulder. His brother looks so much like him, just an older version. I don't ask what happened to their parents or what kind of lives they used to have. I just stare.

Finally the guy who's *not* Ben says something that's half

grunt, half mumble, then bends down and starts picking up the books he dropped.

I almost help him. I ran into him, which is why he dropped the books, but for some reason, I can't make myself help. I don't want to get sucked into a conversation with him. I don't want to know who he is or why he's here or what he's like. It doesn't matter. His similarities and his differences will both feel the same. They'll hurt.

I look over my shoulder. Cecily is handing two bottles of water to the guy with the broken glasses, but she's looking at me. I have an overwhelming need to get out of here.

So I do.

I head back to the car, grabbing Cecily and pulling her with me.

"Hey, wait, is that Ben Michaels?" she says. "Oh my God, I thought—"

"It's not him." I don't want to explain what little I know of the multiverse and doppelgängers. Not now.

"But—"

"Cee, I said it's not him. Do they have anything you want?"

Cecily shakes her head.

"Can we get out of here?"

She must see it on my face, whatever it is that I'm feeling. Or maybe it's just her good-friend instincts that let her know this is a dead topic. Either way, she nods and moves around to the driver's side. "Out of here it is."

I get into the car, my door slamming shut behind me.

Cecily starts the car and we pull away, leaving Ben's lookalike behind. I curl my hands into fists to keep them from shaking, and lean my head back against the seat.

A few times, I catch her glancing at me, and I know she wants to ask what my deal is. But she doesn't. Because that's what makes our friendship work. We tease each other—she's too high-spirited and I'm too bitchy—but we're there for each other when it matters.

Which means she knows when I need to be left alone.

I think about Ben Michaels all the time.

Sometimes I wonder if I chose wrong—if I should have asked my Ben to stay. If I had that day to do over, I wonder if I would still make the same choices.

Mostly I just wonder if I'll ever see him again.

# 06:12:21:53

Twelve hours later, I arrive at Qualcomm and see Cecily again. Her uncle ran the stadium before the quakes. Now it's the largest evacuation shelter in San Diego, and running it is a family affair.

Normally I like being here. Something about the way Cee has adopted the shelter and all its inhabitants as her personal responsibility makes things feel a little less bleak. Hanging out and being bossed around makes it seem like we're all in this together.

But not right now. This isn't that kind of visit.

When she sees me, she doesn't sugarcoat it. "There's another missing person," she says, her white-blond hair hanging disheveled from something that might have been a ponytail. Her gray T-shirt is dirty, and her jeans are ripped in a few places. If I'd ever wondered what it looked like to carry the weight of part of the city—the homeless part—on your shoulders, now I know.

Our missing person this time is Renee Adams. She's twenty-two years old, and according to the description, she's five-four and thin, with wavy, shoulder-length brown hair, and brown eyes. The only possessions she has to her name are a white long-sleeved sweater, a pair of 7 jeans, flip-flops, a last-season Coach purse, and a gold ring. She worked downtown, and before the quakes, she lived with her boyfriend in Pacific Beach. He's presumed dead now, and she arrived at Qualcomm after seeing that her apartment building had collapsed in on itself.

Assigned to a cot in Club Level section 47, one of the areas reserved for single women, Renee kept to herself, spent more time sleeping than awake, and cried a lot. She was even assigned to the suicide watch list for one of the grief counselors.

But she wasn't in her group therapy session this afternoon. And at this moment, a little past nine thirty on Monday evening—more than three hours past city curfew—she isn't anywhere in section 47. The all-call announcements in the stadium have gone unanswered. Her cot is empty.

Except for the ripped sheet and a tiny, yellowed fragment that unmistakably used to be part of a fingernail.

I hold a ruler between gloved fingers and take a picture of the measurement. The rip is four and three quarters inches long, half an inch at its widest point, and the nail looks like it might be from her thumb.

I imagine a girl pulled off the cot, reaching out to grab on to something—anything—and catching hold of the sheet. Only sheets aren't very strong, so it rips easily, and she leaves a tiny piece of herself behind.

"When did she go missing?" Deirdre asks, her voice quiet but weighed down with a sense of gravity.

I don't look at Cecily when she says she doesn't know. She's trying to look calm and in charge, trying to hold it together, but her eyes are red-rimmed, and her face has that splotchy look it gets when she's cried too much.

Deirdre has been an FBI agent for a little more than ten years. She worked with my dad for eight of them. She doesn't know Cecily like I do, but she can recognize undeserved guilt when she sees it. "Cecily, none of this is on you. The best thing you can do right now is give us information." Rephrasing, she says, "When was she last seen?"

Cecily swallows forcibly. "She missed the group meetings yesterday, too, which was why someone wanted to check on her after she missed again today. I've talked to everyone, and by everyone I mean everyone I could find, but she didn't know many people, or I guess not many people knew *her*. So as far as I can tell, the last time anyone saw her was the group therapy meeting on Friday at four p.m."

Three days.

Even though I'm in jeans and a hoodie, I shiver. My dad used to say that, in an endangered circumstance, like an abduction, if you didn't find the person within twenty-four hours of their disappearance, the chances you'd find them alive were less than 10 percent. And those chances diminished every hour.

"I'm going to talk to the counselor," Deirdre says, and I can tell by her tone that she's talking more for Cecily's benefit than mine. We've been opening enough of these files lately; we have a routine. "Finish up and meet by the ramp. Cecily, if you remember anything—"

"Of course," Cecily says, her eyes wide and eager to please. Her blond hair bounces with each nod of her head. "I'll tell you right away."

As soon as Deirdre's out of sight, Cecily's shoulders droop and she slumps into a seated position on the floor.

After I snap a few more pictures and write down the remaining details—Renee's purse is still here, overturned with a broken cell phone on the floor next to what looks like a drop of blood on the concrete—I turn and look at Cee. "I didn't know her," she says.

"There are a lot of people here." We both realize it's unrealistic to expect her to know everyone. Even someone with the social-butterfly gene like Cee can't possibly get acquainted with everyone in a stadium full of displaced people.

"But I don't know anything about her. Not really," she says, folding her arms across her chest. "Just her name and what people have said about her."

I want to say something comforting—that's what Cecily needs from me right now—but everything I think of sounds too cold. Reducing a person to a paragraph of hearsay is depressing no matter what words you use.

"Oh!" Cecily sits up straighter. "I forgot. Someone told me they thought Renee did something with computers. You know, like, for work. They weren't sure what, but something pretty badass. She'd said something about it one night, about missing her job, and how without computers she was practically obsolete."

"I'll put it in the file," I say.

Cecily laughs. The bitterness doesn't sound right coming from her. "She thought she was obsolete then. I wonder what she's thinking now."

Even though I know it won't help, I say it anyway. "This isn't your fault."

"How could she have disappeared like that?" she asks, picking at her fingernails. "How could any of them? Jennifer Joyce or Clinton Nelson or David Bonnell or—"

I interrupt her before she names all of them. The truth is that she's right. We shouldn't be losing *more* people now. But I don't say that. Instead I say, "I don't know, but these are teenagers and grown adults. You can't be responsible for them."

She looks up at me, and our eyes meet for the first time tonight.

Her blue eyes are glassy, and I want her to feel better, so I reach for something—anything—that might do it.

"Who knows, maybe they're not even missing," I say. "Maybe Renee Adams walked off." The words stick in my throat. The lie is awkward and forced on my tongue. Someone who loses half a fingernail doesn't walk off without the last few belongings to her name.

Cecily just shakes her head and looks away.

She knows what I do: that most of the people who are here have nowhere else to go.

"We haven't found any of them," she says, her voice hitching near the end of the sentence.

I press my lips and try to think of something useful to say, something to make her feel better. But she's always been far better at that than I have.

"Where are they all going?" she asks.

I don't answer, because for the life of me, I don't know.

# 06:12:14:43

Cecily and two of the evac center's armed guards escort Deirdre and me back to the car.

"Don't worry, it'll get better," I lie as I hug her.

Then Deirdre and I are in the car and driving through the maze that is the parking lot. We suffer in silence for a few minutes, Deirdre with her lips pressed together, her frown lines etching themselves more permanently into her face. I briefly wonder if she'll ever laugh or smile like she used to, and then she says what I've been thinking this whole time. "Another one."

I don't answer, because I don't have to.

My dad worked in Missing Persons—it was his first job as an analyst with the Bureau—back in the nineties. His first year, there were 67,806 active missing-person cases in the US. I remember thinking then how unfathomably huge that number seemed.

But that was when he was alive.

It doesn't seem huge anymore.

Because as of this morning, there are 113,801 missing persons—the ones not presumed dead. And that's just in San Diego County.

Renee Adams is number 113,802.

# 06:11:52:37

The interstates are cracked, collapsed, half fallen, and unstable, so we take back roads. They've been cleared, but they're not in good shape. I hold on to the "oh shit" handle as we drive to keep my body from slamming into the door. We don't talk, because the headlights only allow Deirdre to see about ten feet of road in front of her. The ride is bumpy, slow, and dark.

We pass through the first military checkpoint at Aero Drive and then the one at Balboa Avenue without incident.

Each time, Deirdre stops the car and it's the same routine. A Marine with a machine gun strapped over his shoulder shines a flashlight into the car. Deirdre holds up both our IDs, and when we're recognized, the Marine nods and waves us through.

While we drive, I avoid looking out the window. It's dark, so it's not like I could really see anything. But I know what's there. I know the Walmart on Aero Drive survived the quakes with minimal damage, only to be destroyed by the looting. It's too easy to remember the last time I was there. The crunch of broken glass under my feet, the thick smoke, the smell of fire and burning plastic, and the body of the dead pregnant woman, killed by blunt-force trauma to the back of the head.

It's much too easy to remember. Every time I close my eyes, I wish I could forget.

Around Balboa, there are some houses still standing and some that are at least inhabitable—but for the most part, everything is different. It doesn't hurt any less to drive by neighborhoods that are flattened, to see debris where there used to be structures.

It hurts to think that I can hardly remember what it looked like before.

I keep my eyes closed and try to think about nothing—absolutely nothing. I will my mind to keep itself blank. But it's black, like a black hole, like a portal, and suddenly I can see Ben, his dark eyes and his soft brown hair. I can see the look on his face when he said, *"I'll come back for you."* When he took one more step back and promised. When he stopped, said my name, told me he loved me, and then the portal swallowed him into the blackness.

Aching and a little breathless, I press the heels of my hands into my eyes hard, as if that will somehow get rid of the memory.

# 06:11:37:11

The third checkpoint is at Clairemont Mesa Boulevard. We pass two flares and a Marine with a machine gun to signal the upcoming stop. Deirdre slows the car until it jerks to a standstill, then rolls down her window and holds out our IDs.

But instead of waving us through, he holds on to them, examining their every corner with the flashlight.

My first reaction is to be annoyed. I'm so exhausted my whole body aches with a heaviness that makes me feel sluggish and irritable. We're supposed to be on the same team—the good guys—and here we are being detained by some overeager hero wannabe.

But when he still doesn't give the IDs back, a trickle of fear moves through me like a chill. I shiver a little and sit up straighter.

Something's not right.

He looks up and says, "What's your business on the road?" His voice is deep, and I don't recognize it. He's either new to this checkpoint or new to the night shift.

My heart speeds up, pumping a little too fast.

Deirdre has the patience of a saint, so she doesn't snap at this guy. Instead she quietly explains, "We've just come from Qual-comm. Another missing-person case, endangered, class two."

*Endangered* means it looks like an abduction scenario, rather than someone who's run away or someone who hasn't been found and is presumed dead from one of the disasters. Class two means it's someone between the ages of sixteen and twenty-four.

"Can you step out of the car, please?" he says, and my breath feels shallow.

Deirdre must be feeling like me because she says, "Seriously?"

He waits for us to get out. I force my breath to stay even and my hands to relax. Clenched fists don't exactly say cooperation.

Deirdre opens her door and glances at me. I'd have to be blind to miss the pointed look she gives me. It says, *Don't cause trouble.* I don't need the reminder. Before anyone declared martial law, people sometimes fought the military—there were even a few cases of leftover entitlement after it was official, people who didn't want to believe the world had changed, people who refused to give up their liberties.

Those people ended up dead.

I bite back the spike of fear that shoots through my chest and open my door.

Getting out of the car, I immediately raise my hands and intertwine my fingers, locking them behind my head. I exhale evenly and tell myself that I know this drill. That I will cooperate and that this is routine.

In a few minutes we'll be back on our way.

Two Marines in full camouflage step out of the darkness. One trains his gun on me.

# 06:11:33:28

The other Marine adjusts his gun so it's behind his back as he says, "Do you have any weapons on your person?"

"No, sir," I say.

He nods and begins patting me down.

I almost tell him my gun is in the glove compartment, but then I don't.

For one, he didn't ask. And I'd rather he not know it's there in case I need it.

My whole body is tensed, poised for something—fight or flight, I'm not sure. Maybe I'm also just inherently resistant to some guy with a gun feeling me up. I see two Marines search the car, and I hear the muffled sounds of Deirdre's voice, though I can't make out the words.

I force myself to let go of my breath and relax a little.

The Marine feeling me up straightens. He's young and makes me think of Alex—not because they look anything alike, but because four months ago, this guy could have been in high school.

"You can put your hands down," he says to me, adding louder, "we're clear."

Not for the first time, I wonder if Alex would have enlisted if he hadn't died out behind Park Village. The wave of guilt and sorrow at that thought roils through my body, leaving an ache in my chest and a bitter taste in my mouth. I made so many mistakes, and Alex paid for the worst of them.

I hear Deirdre open her car door. "Janelle, get in."

I don't hesitate. I jump in and shut my door in one movement.

My leg bounces a little while I wait for Deirdre to start the car. Her movements are slow and purposeful, so it doesn't look like we're running away. Even though I understand the psychology of it, I feel a panicked urge to reach over and do it for her.

I keep my face blank while the engine roars to life. As we start to drive away, slowly leaving the flares and guns behind, I realize I've been holding my breath.

"We're fine," Deirdre says, her shaking voice the only thing that tells me she's trying to convince herself as much as me.

"I know," I say, so she doesn't worry, but then I lean my forehead against the cool glass of the window, feeling my pulse ring through my ears.

Either she's unconvinced, or talking it out will help her calm down, because she continues, "They stopped a driver, alone, fifteen minutes before us. He had no explanation for being out after curfew, and when they asked him to get out of the car, he abandoned the vehicle, disarmed one of the Marines, and gave the guy a bloody nose. They lost him in the dark."

"He got away?" I ask, because I'm surprised. The checkpoint

Marines are well trained and heavily armed. Probability would suggest running from them would mean injury or death.

Deirdre nods. "The suspect was male, approximately six feet in height, and in his twenties with shaggy dark hair, blue eyes, and light facial hair. He was dressed completely in black with boots that looked military."

She stops, and I wait for her to keep going. There's obviously more.

But she doesn't say anything else, so I look over. Her face is a mask as she stares out the windshield, but then she presses her lips together, slows the car to a stop, and looks over at me.

She repeats the description, though she doesn't need to. "Sound like anyone you know?"

I look away. Of course it does.

It's exactly how I would have described a certain agent with the Interverse Agency, the agency that polices the multiverse. An agent who infiltrated the FBI when he was trying to stop Wave Function Collapse. An agent that I don't have a stellar relationship with.

Taylor Barclay.

# 06:11:27:56

I don't say Barclay's name out loud, as if speaking the words could somehow make them more likely to come true.

Deirdre adds, "They sent out a search team, but it's like he disappeared."

Chills move over my arms and down my neck. These days, *disappeared* has a new meaning to me—for several reasons. First, because we have so many people just dropping off the face of the earth. But also because I've seen people vanish right in front of me.

I've seen black holes that open out of nothingness, circular portals to other worlds, seven feet or taller, like some kind of big vertical pool of tar. I've *felt* the temperature drop as the air around me suddenly took on a different quality and smell—wet, never-ending, open. I've had to watch people get swallowed up by portals and leave this earth.

And it's not the first time I've wondered if the disappearances in my world and the portals are somehow connected.

People disappearing into thin air shouldn't be this common.

# 06:11:20:45

**W**e don't have any answers—just too much speculation—
when we finally pass through security at Miramar and pull
into the on-base housing.

"Do you want to tell him, or should I?" Deirdre says before
we get out of the car. I know she's still mad that I never told her
anything this past fall until it was too late. I know it was careless
to keep everything to myself. As soon as we uncovered what was
happening with the portals, Alex wanted me to tell Struz what
was really going on, and I didn't.

And I know that's probably the main reason Alex is dead.

I have to live with that.

"I'll tell him," I say.

Deirdre nods, and we get out of the car. She heads to her
apartment and I head to the one I share with Jared and Struz. It's
a two-bedroom and military furnished, which means everything
is taupe and gently used, but it's dry and sturdy and we have
cases of bottled water stacked up in every closet, which is more
than a lot of other people have. For the past hundred and fifteen
days, we've been calling it home.

"Dude, I'm starting to feel like a neglected housewife," Jared says with a smile when I get inside. The room is dark, but he's got a paperback in his lap and a candle lit on the corner table next to the La-Z-Boy that he's started to refer to as *his chair*. Electricity is scarce; brown-outs are common, and as a result everyone is only supposed to use it when they have to—luckily the base has a wood-burning stove.

"Did you make me dinner, at least?" I say, joking right back, even though the irony of the situation twists a little like a rusty knife in my gut. After I tried so hard to keep him from having to grow up too fast, the past few months have forced it beyond my control.

"There are cold SpaghettiOs on the counter."

Food is rationed and handed out once a week, one of my many jobs. Right now we're dealing with nonperishables, because that's all we've got. Things like fruit, vegetables, dairy, and meat are already all gone. Anyone on a farm is working to rebuild, but I don't know how long that will take. And I'm not sure we have a plan for when the nonperishables run out.

Water is the worst. Anyone with a well can boil water to purify the effects of the wildfires, but tap water in most of Southern California is undrinkable. The military has been doing supply runs, bringing in cases of bottled water that had been stockpiled by FEMA. Struz keeps saying things will get better, but they'll get worse before they do—the rest of the winter will be hard, harder for people in colder climates, harder for people in poorer communities. It's a different kind of aftershock.

"Gotta love SpaghettiOs," I say with a sigh. I'm hungry, but I go to Jared first and ruffle his hair. "Did you get enough to eat?"

He picks up his book and rolls his eyes. "Don't even try to

give me your dinner again."

I don't respond, because that's exactly what I'm trying to do. Instead I say, "How was school?"

"Lame," he answers. "I don't know who decided it was okay to have school on Sunday, but they should be abducted by aliens."

Schools shut down when the quakes happened, but they've opened up again—large, auditorium-style, and organized by accessibility instead of grade, and they're open every day. Jared walks to the old Mira Mesa High School each morning with the other kids who live on the base. Grades seven and up have classes in the gym, and everyone else is in the cafeteria. I went the first few weeks, but Jared's right, it was lame.

The truth is, organized school keeps kids out of trouble. It's a mild sense of normalcy to hold the hysteria at bay. That's why there's school on Sundays. Instead of that, I say, "Got to make up for that lost time."

Jared frowns, but he doesn't bother voicing his opinion about my absence at school. It's a discussion that was considered closed a long time ago.

I put in to take my GED and effectively graduate early. So did most of the people I knew from Eastview. A lot of them got involved with the Red Cross to help the reconstruction effort. That's what Kate and Nick are doing. Anyone a little more hard-core took the ASVAB, the military entrance exam, and joined the military.

I got where I am now because of Struz. After I "graduated," I went one step further with the tests and firearms qualifications. Then Struz signed off on my employment with the FBI—so I'm essentially a cross between an apprentice and a temp. He paired me with Deirdre because of her experience and told me he expects me to pick up and go to college once things get back to normal.

We have no idea when that will happen, though, and I don't know what else I would want to do with my life, anyway. I didn't really ever have concrete plans, but I wanted to go to college, travel, and study abroad. I wanted the chance to figure out what my dreams were. Alex wanted to follow in my dad's footsteps. With both of them gone, I feel like I owe it to them to do what they can't—to fight the bad guys and all that.

Jared's stomach growls but I ignore it. "How's the leg?" I ask.

"Fine," he says, but his face scrunches up a little and I know it's not. He broke it during the quakes, and even though it's healed now, it's not as strong as it was before.

I lean into him and remind myself it could be worse. Deirdre's son lost his arm, and her daughter hasn't spoken since the world changed.

"What are you reading?" I ask, but focusing on the book makes me think of Ben's lookalike and how maybe I should have helped him pick up the books I made him drop—maybe I should have talked to him—and I have to shake him from my head.

Jared's eyes light up. "It's super cool. Struz found it somewhere. Some of the pages are water-damaged, but it's all still readable. It's about this guy who just got out of prison and goes hiking up in Alaska and he finds this downed airplane that had the president's wife on it, and she's dead."

"Because of the crash?"

"No way, people totally murdered her," he says, standing up. "I'm only like fifty pages or so in. It's pretty awesome. You'd like it." Then his face gets serious. "You're really not hungry? Because if you are, you should eat, but if you're not . . ."

I shake my head. "Go for it. Struz out back?"

"Yeah, he's doing the whole walkie thing."

I nod and head out through the sliding glass doors to the porch and the five square feet of lawn that we call a yard. Struz is sitting in one of the two folding chairs and his legs make him look like he's too big for the chair, like it's a kiddie chair or something. He doesn't pay me much attention as I shut the sliding door behind me. He's got a walkie-talkie to his ear and a high-powered flashlight trained on a map of San Diego on the patio table.

"President's new orders," a voice crackles through the walkie, followed by a bitter chuckle, and I wonder what orders these are. And what part of the conversation I've missed.

Struz sighs and says, "I'll see what we can do."

The real president, the one who was elected and in office when the world changed, is in a coma, and the vice president is dead. The speaker of the house is now the president, and apparently he's sort of a joke. It's supposed to be an election year, which means that in less than a year we could elect a new president, but that would require getting voting methods under control before then, and I doubt that's going to happen.

It doesn't matter, though. The government we had doesn't work for this kind of large-scale crisis. If San Diego had been the only city affected, or even if it had just been California, the rest of the country would be sending us aid and going on with life as usual.

But everyone was affected. No one—no matter who they were or where they lived or what they believed in—was spared.

The first thing the acting president did was suspend *habeas corpus* and declare martial law. Since then he's passed temporary acts to give the military the power to absorb every able-bodied member of local law-enforcement agencies in order to keep peace and maintain some sort of structure.

Struz looks at me and says, "False alarm?" There's hope on his face, like every time he's asked, but I don't think it's as real as it used to be. He's still *hoping* but he doesn't believe in it anymore.

I shake my head.

"You should go to bed. Early day tomorrow. I'll check out your report in the morning."

"What about you?" I ask, because now he's as bad as my dad was. He hardly ever sleeps, and when he does, it's sitting up with his walkie next to him in case something happens.

"It's going to be a long night," he says with a shake of his head.

I know better than to argue so I turn to go back inside. As I open the door, I hear a grainy voice over the walkie-talkie say, "Hey, Struz, we've got reports of another one out in Poway. I've got a team en route."

*Another one.* I don't need anyone to spell out what that means. It's always the same thing—more abductions.

More people missing.

## 06:11:01:03

I head upstairs and slip into my bedroom. The room smells like evergreen trees. We didn't have a tree for Christmas this year—obviously, since there aren't exactly trees to go around—so Jared and Struz dug up some old evergreen-scented candles and lit them all over the house.

I light the candle on the nightstand and peel off my jeans and change my T-shirt, then reach under the bed for a manila folder before crawling under the covers. The file is worn and a little frayed from overhandling, but that doesn't stop me. It was already overhandled before it was passed to me.

Lying back on my pillow, I look at her name—Emily Bauer. The blue ink is faded, as if time is trying to erase her existence completely. For a minute, I imagine what Emily was like, if she was anything like I am now. I wonder where she'd be and what she'd be like if she hadn't gone missing seventeen years ago.

Then I open it up—the one case file of my father's that I refused to throw away.

I don't even need to read it—every word has been burned in my memory at this point.

The file is an unsolved case from 1995, from one of my dad's first years on the job, back when he worked missing persons—ironically, the same job I'm working right now.

A seventeen-year-old girl—captain of the swim team, with an academic scholarship to USC, a boyfriend, friends, the perfect family with a dog and a white picket fence—went missing from her bedroom. All her possessions were untouched and in their rightful place. No forced entry, no signs of a break-in, no one who heard or saw anything unusual—it was like she just disappeared.

Except for a bloody partial handprint on her wall.

I know the case is cold now; it's been cold for the past seventeen years while it sat on my dad's desk, and now that the world is changed, I know there isn't any hope of solving it. But this case isn't that different from the ones we have now. Maybe something will help me solve them. Besides, if my dad were still here, he would still be looking over the file every night, still looking for something he missed.

Once, when we were twelve, Alex asked my dad why he held on to the case. He said, "Why haven't you given up?"

It was a Saturday in the summer. We'd just played in one of those coed Little League softball games, and we were sweaty and starving, and my dad was pulling pizza leftovers from the fridge. But when Alex asked that, he stopped and turned around. His face was so serious that, even then, I knew whatever he said would be something I never forgot.

And I haven't.

He said, "Giving up on something is like admitting you never wanted it in the first place. I won't ever give up on that girl. I'll always be looking for her. Even if everyone else in her life has moved on, I won't rest until I figure out what we missed and we've gotten her back. Until she's safe."

He's not here to look for her anymore, but I am, and I'm not going to give up on her either.

Who knows—maybe something will help me with the people going missing right now.

Or that's what I tell myself. The other reason I reread this file every night is because I need something to focus on right before I go to sleep—something to think about—because that's the moment when my mind is at its worst, when if left to its own devices, it won't stop remembering.

*The gunshot, Reid's and Alex's hands on the gun, blood pouring from the hole in Alex's neck, his eyes glassy, my hands covered in blood.*

I can't shake these images. I see them every time I close my eyes. I dream about that night almost every time I fall asleep. In the dreams, I try to make different choices, but the end result is always the same.

My dad is still dead. There won't be any more *X-Files* marathons or bad Syfy movies. Alex is still dead—his blood still staining the ground just outside Park Village—and he's never going to drag me to another terrible action movie with no plot. He'll never have the chance to defy his mother and go to West Point instead of Stanford. He's never going to follow his dreams.

And Ben is still gone.

# 05:17:37:43

The next morning I'm up early and then gone all day, delivering rations from the base to different neighborhoods. When I get home, Struz is out. Jared launches into a story about his Monday before I even get inside, something about a guy diving out of a skyscraper or something. I know I'm not hearing him right, but all day this terrible feeling has been welling up inside me, the kind that reaches through your veins and down into your bones. My whole body is practically vibrating with it.

Like my body knows something bad is about to happen.

"Dude, if you're not going to listen to me . . ."

"Jared, I'm sorry, I spaced out."

I look at my brother—he's got Monopoly set up, and he's playing against himself. He sees me looking and says, "I set it up so you could play with me when you got back, and then I got bored. But we can set it up again."

"Sure, that works," I say. I suddenly feel like I'm too old. Not physically, but just that I'm too tired, too stressed, and too anxious. Even though there isn't any danger of Wave Function Collapse and there's no Oppenheimer counting down to the end

43

of the world, it's like I'm waiting for something else to go wrong.

I sit on the floor with him, and he launches into a story about his class field trip to the movie theater down the street from the school. "It was so cool. Mr. Hubley totally broke into the theater and we went in the biggest one, and he had the other teachers all sit with us while he set up a projector and we watched *Mission Impossible 4*."

I'm not sure if it's considered breaking in now that the theater has been abandoned, although I guess it's still private property. "How was the movie?" I ask, even though I'm sure it was just as bad as the first three.

My eyes burn with that thought, because it's something I would have said to Alex.

"It was so awesome. There's this really cool part where Tom Cruise flies down the side of this building. Maybe Cecily can get that for the next movie night?"

"I'll ask her," I say truthfully, as we clear the houses off the board.

"What's for dinner tonight?" Jared asks. "No spaghetti, right?"

We try to have something special on Mondays. I'm not sure if it was Struz's idea or mine, but we all eat together then too. It's nice. "I was thinking a feast of macaroni and cheese, and canned peas and chicken."

"Canned chicken?" Jared makes a face.

"I imagine the canned sardines are worse," I tell him.

"Why can't you just lift something better from the commissary?" Jared asks.

I don't tell him there is nothing better. Instead, I say, "Wow, Jared, I don't know, maybe because that's stealing?"

"Whatever, plenty of people steal stuff." Jared begins listing all of his friends and the amazing things they've gotten to eat recently.

There's a knock at the door.

"I bet Struz forgot his keys," Jared says, bouncing up from the floor.

"I can assure you if Victor Le says he had filet mignon last night, he either has cattle in his backyard or he's lying," I call after him.

I hear my brother say something muffled, and then there's a slam as someone kicks open the front door.

I have a split second to consider a strategy, but I don't know what I'm up against, so I jump up and step into the hall.

In my doorway is the outline of a man, standing behind my brother. Based on his height and build, I know it's not Struz.

It feels like all the air has been sucked out of the room. I have absolutely nothing to defend myself with, and this guy has my brother.

But when he uses his foot to kick the door shut and the light adjusts in the room, I realize it's Taylor Barclay.

"What's the matter, Tenner? You look like you've seen a ghost," he says with a smile.

# 05:17:21:49

I relax for a second. My whole body feels a little like Jell-O, and I reach out and put my hand on the wall. Though I'm sure Barclay in my world is a bad sign.

He's got one hand on Jared's shoulder. I don't like that.

Barclay must see the shift in my position. "Why don't you head upstairs, kid?"

Jared looks at me, and I nod. The last thing I want is him getting dragged into whatever has Barclay showing up at my door. We both watch him as he leaves the room.

"Tenner, relax." He raises his empty hands and smiles. "Just here to talk. I didn't mean to startle you."

His smile is disarming. It's light and casual, like we're long-lost friends and he's happy to see me.

"So you come to my home and scare my brother?"

Barclay shrugs. "I knocked."

"What do you want?" I ask, because let's face it, he wants something.

His smile disappears and his eyebrows draw together, a flicker of annoyance on his face. "I need your help. I need you to come with me."

He pulls a quantum charger from his pocket—I'd recognize one of those anywhere—and I shake my head. I remember how much it burned the last time he dragged me through a portal, and that thought sparks one that's worse—all our missing people. What if that's why Barclay is here? What if I'm next?

"I'm not going anywhere." I bite my bottom lip and debate what to do next.

"We don't have time to argue right now," he says. "I'll explain everything once we're out of here."

In hand-to-hand combat, I don't stand a chance with Barclay unless I can take him by complete surprise and knock him out. I'm sure he has a gun on him, and I don't. He also has a quantum charger and as a result he has access to *anywhere*—any universe. I can't possibly keep him away from us.

Which means I need to hear him out.

"If you want me to go somewhere with you, you can explain it right now," I say, pulling back. "I'm not about to just blindly follow you through a portal."

"Fine, you want to have a chat, Tenner? Why don't you have a seat," he says as he sits down on our taupe couch with that stupid, arrogant smirk on his face.

I move into the living room and sit down on the couch as far as I can physically get from him. "So what is it?"

"We have a problem."

"*We?*" I ask. Because there's Barclay, and then there's me. There's no *we* at all.

He turns his blue eyes to me and stares for a second. Then he says, "It's Ben."

My heart might actually stop. "What about Ben?" My voice is too breathy, too quiet. It doesn't sound like my own.

Barclay sits up straighter. "Have you seen him?"

I swallow. Hard. "No, he's back in his home world."

Barclay nods. "If you have—"

"I haven't," I insist, and I hate the fact that I've had to say it again.

He nods. "A couple months ago, I stumbled on a case. It's big, Tenner," he says, rubbing his hands together. "People from different universes are disappearing. They're being kidnapped."

*Kidnapped.* As in abducted.

He has my full attention now. I can feel my pulse all over my body, even in the tips of my fingers.

"Everything I've uncovered points to a complex organization, one that's avoided getting caught for a long time," Barclay continues. "Someone has set up the ultimate human-trafficking ring. They're going into different universes, kidnapping people, and then selling them into slavery on other earths."

"Human trafficking? Like sex slaves?"

"It's bigger than that," Barclay says with a grimace. "Think about the overall picture. Stealing people from other universes, especially universes that don't have interverse travel capabilities. No one's going to come looking for them, and they don't have anywhere to go. No escape.

"And if there's no fear of getting caught, someone could turn a huge profit by selling house slaves to the wealthy in every different world. Slaves for cheap labor, slaves that could be soldiers in a war you're waging, and yes, slaves for sex, too."

*No one's going to come looking for them, and they don't have anywhere to go.*

I can't help be stuck on that. I see what he's saying—that makes it the perfect crime—but there's something in my brain that's having trouble computing. How selfish and depraved does a person have to be to put something like this together? I wonder if they watch people and pick them out with a purpose, or if they just grab them at random and figure it out later.

I think of Renee Adams, and I wonder what kind of slave she is right now. The thought makes me want to throw up.

"So that's what's happening here—why we have so many missing people?" I ask, even though I already know the answer.

"What?" Barclay asks, before he nods and says, "Oh. Yeah. Any world that has low technology capabilities would be a huge target. A world that's just gone through a disaster or a war, or any kind of devastating event, of course would become a likely target. More people can be abducted in a shorter period of time before authorities catch on."

Something in the matter-of-fact way that he says this makes me realize that's not why he's here. He doesn't care about Renee Adams or any of the other *hundred thousand* missing people we have in San Diego.

"So why are you here?" I ask.

"I need to find Ben," he says. "And you're the only one who can help me."

"I haven't seen him, Barclay," I repeat, and I feel my throat tightening and my eyes burning as I have to admit *again* that he hasn't come back.

"I know," he says. "But you can still help me."

"I'm not going to talk him into doing anything dangerous, if that's what this is about," I say, although from the look on Barclay's face, I can tell that's not it. "Besides, what does Ben have to do with a human-trafficking ring, unless . . ."

*Unless he's missing.*

# 05:17:11:02

I can't bring myself to even voice the possibility.

Barclay shakes his head. "It's complicated. Like I said. This is a big case. Missing persons was never even really on my radar—until a few months ago."

"And what happened then?"

"The details aren't important, but I started looking into a standard missing-persons case as a favor to a friend, only it turned out not to be very standard. It's big, Tenner. A major interverse trafficking ring."

This all makes sense, but . . . "I still don't understand what this has to do with Ben."

Barclay hesitates. He looks at his hands for a second, and I notice he's biting the inside of his cheek. I've never seen him agitated quite like this.

"Tell me," I say, even though I'm afraid to hear it.

Then he looks up with pity in his face. "Someone with unique abilities—like the ability to open portals and travel universes at will—would have an easier time getting around the strict interverse travel regulations the IA has in place."

My mind jumps to the logical conclusion, but it takes my heart a minute to catch up. Because I don't want to believe that it's a possibility. "Ben can't be a suspect. He—"

"You know what Ben can do," Barclay says. "He's the *prime* suspect."

"But he's home—"

Barclay shakes his head. "Tenner, Ben hasn't been in his home world for almost three months."

# 05:17:09:58

I can't breathe. For a minute, I'm not sure what I'm more upset about—the fact that the IA suspects Ben of human trafficking or that he isn't at home and he hasn't come back to me. Where else would he be? The whole reason he didn't stay here was because I told him to go home—to his family.

"Look, I know Ben isn't responsible. That's why I need your help," Barclay adds.

That makes me remember what I know of the IA and I realize that if Ben is the prime suspect, they probably have a shoot-on-sight command, and I focus on that.

"Ben would never do this," I say. "You know him enough to know that."

Barclay nods. "I've said as much, but none of my higher-ups will listen."

"What do you need from me? To testify or something?" I ask. Character witnesses don't count for much, but I know Ben. I know him better than anyone else. I know what kind of person he is, the mistakes he's made, and the things he's done to make up for them.

Barclay shakes his head, and something about the look on his face tells me whatever his plan is, it's bigger, more dangerous, and maybe even less legal than something like testifying. "I need you to help me find him."

I almost laugh. "If he's not at home and he's not here, I've got no other ideas. You have resources I can't even imagine. How can I possibly help you? Besides, did you look around on your way in? My world is trying to rebuild. I need to be here."

He shakes his head. "I'm not on the case anymore."

"What do you mean?"

"Exactly what I said." Barclay sighs. "I've been taken off the case because I have too many ties to it. They think that I'm personally invested since I know all the main players involved."

He doesn't have to say that he thinks it's bullshit. I know he does, and he's right. Sure, he worked a case that ended up involving Ben, but Ben was a target in that case, and if he were a suspect now, any agency would want an agent who knew the suspect to help out.

Agents are taken off cases for one reason: when they've become a liability.

Barclay didn't seem to *dislike* Ben—once he decided not to shoot him, at least—but he didn't have any real personal ties to him, either. If Ben did something wrong, Barclay wouldn't hesitate to do what was needed. It's the one quality he has that I actually respect.

Which begs the question: Who thinks he would be a liability, and why?

"What about Eric?" I say. Eric Brandt is another IA agent and Barclay's partner. "You said he was your mentor. He could talk to someone."

Barclay shakes his head, and when he speaks again his voice is thick. "Eric is dead."

## 05:17:04:14

"What?" My voice is breathless. "How?"

"Officially, it was an accident," Barclay says. "He was home alone, taking a shower. He slipped and fell, pulling the shower curtain down with him, and knocked himself out. The shower curtain clogged the drain and he drowned."

And in case I hadn't heard the skepticism in his voice or seen it on his face, he adds, "But it wasn't an accident. Someone murdered him."

I don't disagree. It sounds like a scene from one of those bad *Final Destination* movies—too many coincidences lining up to equal an accidental death. Instead, I get to the point. "Who would do that?"

"I don't know," Barclay admits.

I open my mouth to offer my opinion, but then I stop and look at Barclay. He's looking at me, waiting—expectant even. He obviously has a theory, and he wants to know if I'm going to come up with the same one.

I take a deep breath because I know that if I'm right, I might be about to dive into something huge. "When did it happen?"

"Both Eric and I wrote up our reports as soon as we realized this was human trafficking, not just one missing person," Barclay answers. "Then we were excused from the case. I fought it. This case was huge for me, a career maker, but Eric told me to lay off the information, that he'd talk to the higher-ups."

"And he did," I say. I don't like where I think this is going.

Barclay nods. "Two days later, Eric was dead and a report he supposedly signed with 'proof' against Ben was on the server. The order to find Ben and bring him in was issued."

"That means . . ." My heart hammers in my chest, and I can't say what I think out loud.

But Barclay knows what I mean. "Someone in IA is involved."

Which would also explain the liability issue—Barclay was taken off the case because someone above him doesn't actually want it solved.

Because Ben is a convenient scapegoat.

# 05:17:01:46

I listen to everything Barclay says while I fight to keep my breathing even and my hands still.

I'm tempted to run upstairs, change my clothes, give Jared a hug and tell him I'll be back, and bolt through a portal with Barclay—charge off and rescue Ben from these false charges. This is *Ben*. He saved my life, and I would do anything for him.

This is Ben—and I love him.

Even though I don't trust Barclay himself, I trust his motives. This is Barclay wanting to do the right thing—get the right guy—and it's him wanting to do the right thing for his career. Plus he and Eric were partners, and there's an unwritten rule in law enforcement that says when your partner is killed, you do whatever it takes to nail the guy responsible.

But for me there's still one very important thing to consider.

"How can *I* possibly help you?" I ask.

Barclay purses his lips, and I know he must have a well-thought-out reason. He strikes me as a guy who hardly ever asks for help, and I doubt I'm his go-to person. But whatever it is, he's hesitant to tell me.

"I'm serious," I add. "Even without IA resources, you're still way more equipped to handle this alone. At best, I'll slow you down. At worst, I'll get in your way."

He doesn't say anything—he looks like he's trying to weigh his words before speaking. Given his ability to offend me pretty easily, I can't say I blame him.

"Don't underestimate yourself," he says finally. "I did that, and you almost shot me."

"That's different. We were here." I shake my head. "How is me traipsing through different worlds with you going to be helpful? Plus, I have my brother to think about and a world to help rebuild."

He rolls his eyes. "My plan is a little more sophisticated than that, Tenner."

"So what is it?"

He doesn't say anything, and that's when I have my answer. I'm not going to blindly leave my world and put my life in Barclay's hands, when I can't think of anything that would actually help me find Ben or prove him innocent. "My answer is no."

"You can't say no. I—"

"This isn't about you," I say over him.

Barclay stands up and begins pacing around the room in front of me. "This is important. You need to come with me—I can't find Ben without you."

"Tell me your plan, and maybe I'll reconsider."

He shakes his head.

*Stupid prick.* "Then get out of my house," I say as I stand up. I've had enough.

I'm halfway to the stairs when Barclay says, "You're in danger, Tenner."

I stop and turn to him. His expression is blank, his blue eyes just staring at me, without betraying whatever it is he's thinking.

I don't get a chance to ask him why. Because right then, as I'm halfway up the stairs, the front door flies open and Deirdre is there, gun drawn, with about a dozen Marines at her back, screaming at Barclay, telling him to put his hands on his head and get down on the ground.

# 05:16:53:35

"I can't fucking believe this shit," Barclay says as he raises his hands.

From the stairs, I yell that it's okay, that it's just Barclay, but no one listens.

The Marines move into the apartment, sweeping into position to cover any possible escape and to make sure no one else is here. Their guns are pointed at Barclay, their eyes only on him.

Deirdre shouts at Barclay and advances on him swiftly but cautiously. The look on her face is absolutely feral—this is Deirdre Rice, FBI agent, and Deirdre Rice, widow and mother of two kids, all in one. Deirdre, who's not about to lose anyone else. If I was Barclay, I'd be scared.

As she moves in, Barclay keeps his hands raised. He's relaxed, but with a clear look of annoyance on his face, as if this is inconvenient for him.

He doesn't even flinch as Deirdre moves in and disarms him, taking a gun from the base of his spine.

"Do you have any other concealed weapons on you?" she says, her voice thick with venom.

"Gun at my left ankle," he says.

Without taking her eyes off him, she bends down to retrieve the backup gun, and once she has it, orders a Marine to move in and frisk him.

I can't help holding my breath. I'm worried Barclay has another weapon. He's the kind of guy who would have a backup for the backup *and* the kind who would keep something to use to escape. Plus, with the technology he has access to, he could have something innocent looking like a pen that's actually a lightsaber.

The last thing I want is for anyone to get hurt—Deirdre, the Marines, even Barclay.

"Can we put some of the guns away and maybe sit down and have a rational conversation?" I say.

Deirdre doesn't turn to look at me, but I can see the anger sweep across her face. I know how much she blames Barclay for everything that's happened—because he betrayed the Bureau, because he lied, because he was, in a lot of ways, too late.

"Taylor Barclay is wanted for questioning," she says. "And I plan on doing just that."

I nod because I know it's true, and if Struz were here, I'm sure he'd be going through the same precautions.

"Cuff him," Deirdre says to the Marine who's just frisked Barclay and come up empty.

I hear a creak from the hallway upstairs and look up to see Jared. "You okay?" I whisper.

He nods. "Are you?"

I couldn't be more proud of him. Deirdre and the Marines are here because Jared used the walkie-talkie in Struz's bedroom to get in touch with them. Jared reacted, even though no one told him to, and now he's watching me with fierce protectiveness.

It's a little like looking in a mirror.

"I'm good, I'll be up in a minute." Again he nods, and he goes without having to be asked twice. He's going to be a great man someday—he's going to be a lot like our dad.

When I look at Barclay, Deirdre is maneuvering him to the couch. His hands are behind his back, and he's not actively working against her, but he's a pretty solid guy, and he's not exactly helping her either.

"Where have you been, Taylor?" Deirdre asks.

He snorts. "Not anywhere you'd be familiar with."

"So you just went home to your own universe and left us to clean up the mess you left behind?" she asks.

Barclay's eyes shoot to mine, and I see the flicker of surprise, like he'd assumed I'd kept the multiverse and everything that went with it to myself, before he covers it with a shrug of feigned indifference. "Wasn't exactly my mess."

"And whose was it?" she asks, even though I told her—several times—the same story I told Struz. She knows it was Reid.

Barclay smiles. "That's classified."

I'm not sure why he's trying to piss her off, but when she backhands him across the face, he must know it's working.

# 05:16:21:57

The rest of the interrogation is painful to watch. It's not like on television. There's no soundtrack to manipulate your emotions, no music to muffle the shouted questions and answers, the sound of skin hitting skin, and the anxious breathing of everyone stuffed into too small a room. The air is tight and smothering, with fear, anger, and egos threatening to strangle us all. It's too hot, and the sweat beading on my skin only seems to emphasize the way my pulse is pounding underneath.

Deirdre's questions are focused and specific. She asks Barclay about everything from his life in his universe to the recent disappearances here in ours. She's unyielding and determined—even I feel a little off guard at the way she fires questions at him.

But Barclay doesn't once seem fazed. A few times he lets out little quips or snide remarks. Once he answers her question with, "That's a little above your pay grade." But mostly he's just silent, wearing a heavy-lidded expression of smugness with his lips curved in an arrogant smile.

He doesn't flinch the couple of times she slaps him, but his lip is bleeding when Struz finally comes home. He opens the door slowly and scans the room without a single expression coming over his face. His eyes meet Deirdre's, and after whatever silent communication passes between them, she nods and steps aside.

"Take him to a secure location and confiscate everything he has on his person," he says to the Marine in charge. "Keep three people on him at all times. Someone has to take a piss, they radio for someone to cover for them first."

"Yes, sir," the Marine says.

Two of them haul Barclay up, as Deirdre whispers something to Struz. He nods.

As they're pulling him out the door, Barclay turns back and looks at me. "You're smart, Tenner. Just like your father. You know you should come with me."

My face feels hot at the mention of my dad. I wonder what he would think of all this.

But Barclay has no right to bring up my dad. If Barclay had just come clean with him, maybe my dad would still be here. Which means I'm not about to feel bad for Barclay.

I take a deep breath and remind myself that he didn't want to tell me his plan, and I wasn't going to blindly follow him. I remind myself I can't do anything to help.

"You should come with me," Barclay repeats. "We don't have a lot of time."

What he means, though, is Ben.

Ben doesn't have a lot of time.

# 05:16:19:03

When the door shuts, Deirdre slumps onto the couch, and Struz watches her, then turns to look at me. "Someone want to tell me what the hell is going on here?"

"That asshole has come back to tear more shit apart," Deirdre says, and I'm a little surprised. She isn't the kind of person who swears. "What more do we need to know?"

"Where the missing people are going," I say without thinking. Because it's true. If nothing else comes out of this night, now we know why people are being abducted.

For a minute it feels like the air has been sucked out of the room. Both Deirdre and Struz freeze with their eyes on me. My heartbeat throbs in my chest.

"Barclay is investigating a human-trafficking ring," I say. Then I tell them about Barclay following me today, surprising me before I got home, and about Jared opening the door for him.

Struz turns to Deirdre. "Get everyone here in the next fifteen minutes. I don't care what else is going on." She nods and grabs the walkie-talkie, and Struz puts a hand on my shoulder.

He squeezes lightly, and the look on his face is my undoing. His eyes are soft and the lines on his face express concern and worry—they say, *Are you okay?* I struggle to keep my emotions under control, keep the sting in my eyes from turning into tears. The truth is, sometimes it all feels like it's too much, like I can't take it anymore, like I don't know how to keep living like this.

Struz can either tell how close I am to losing it, or he just gets it, because he pulls me into a hug. "It'll be okay, J-baby."

I know that's not true, but it still makes me feel better.

When everyone is here—everyone being fifteen other FBI agents, most of whom I know from when they were part of my dad's team—I start over. They all seem to be aware of what happened four months ago, so I start with the missing-persons cases, the ones Deirdre and I have been working on over the past couple of months. I tell them what Barclay told me.

The only thing I don't tell them is that Ben is a suspect.

I don't care where he is or what he's doing. I won't let myself think about why he didn't stay at home with his family or why he hasn't come back. No matter how much it's eating at my insides, the facts are that he's not there and he's not here. But I know he has nothing to do with a human-trafficking ring, and I'm not about to make him a suspect here.

I tell them what Barclay told me about the human trafficking and that the missing people—our missing people—are being abducted for who knows what and pulled into some other universe where they can't get back, and we can't go rescue them because we don't have the technology.

When I finish, no one says anything. A few people exchange

looks, but Struz is clearly thinking something through, and no one else is about to jump in. I start to count the seconds as they pass, and it's a full minute before anyone speaks.

Then Struz says, "Well, fuck me."

"So we need to figure out how people can combat that," Deirdre says. "The first priority has to be that we can't lose more people. Then we can figure out how to get back the ones we lost."

Several agents jump in and start talking over one another. There's mention of the Multiverse Project, something Struz has started. The goal is to prove that the multiverse exists and to figure out interverse travel. Struz recruited a few renowned scientists in Southern California and gave them the necklace Barclay told me I could wear to portal safely as well as a few other things he left behind.

A couple of agents are intent on brainstorming ways to fight against the portals. Someone says they need to tell the public. Make some kind of announcement. Explain to people.

At that, Struz shakes his head. "I've already violated a presidential order by telling you what Janelle went through in September. And I've just violated it again, by having her share this new information."

One of the agents I don't know laughs bitterly. "Who cares? That guy's not our real president, anyway."

"Wait, we still have a government?" another guy says.

"Let's save the jokes for later. We can't make an announcement until we know how people should keep themselves safe," Deirdre says.

Struz nods. "We'll only create more panic."

"We should change curfew," I say. The side chatter stops. I

feel everyone's eyes on me and even though I don't know what I'm doing either, I'm bolstered by the respect most of these people have for me. "All of the abduction cases so far have been people grabbed when they were alone. The night curfew could still be in effect, but we could push it up an hour or two to make people feel better, while at the same time saying that no one should be alone. Institute a buddy system."

A couple of people nod. The guy who doesn't care about our president shrugs. "We could work with something like that."

They continue talking about it, but I've had enough. I excuse myself and head up to my bedroom. No one minds since we're beyond my realm of usefulness anyway. I can't stop thinking about Ben. Not just because of what Barclay said. But because he's out there and maybe in trouble. What if he's stuck somewhere— or what if he needs me?

I think of the way my skin tingled when his fingers touched mine, the way I felt warm from the inside out when he wrapped his arms around me, the sense of calm that was impossible to ignore when my head was against his chest, the soft thump of his heartbeat under my cheek.

The intensity of missing him is so strong, it's physical. It starts as an emptiness in my chest and radiates outward until my hands are shaking and I feel like I'm gasping for air. I have to put a hand on the wall to keep my balance.

I wonder if I've made the right decision.

Barclay wanted me to go with him. I haven't changed my mind—I still don't understand what I can do to help. And I still don't think that following Barclay blindly without knowing his plan is a smart thing for me to do. I'm *not* Ben. I can't portal around on my own. He wouldn't want me lost in some other world.

But even knowing all that, even repeating it to myself, I can't silence the thoughts that say: *Maybe Ben needs me.*

*Maybe I should go.*

# 05:05:23:13

I wake with a start, drenched in sweat, my heart racing. A shadow is looming over me, a hand heavy on my shoulder. For a second it reminds me of the first time I really noticed Ben—when I came back from the dead to see his silhouette leaning over me. I open my mouth to say his name.

But the fog of sleep disappears, and I recognize Deirdre's blond hair.

"What happened?" I ask. "Is Jared okay?"

"He's fine," Deirdre says. "But there's been a distress call. We need to go to Qualcomm."

I nod and roll out of bed automatically. My jeans are in a pile on the floor. I put them on and grab my hoodie and my gun and am out the door just seconds after her. Deirdre hasn't said what the distress call is for, but she doesn't need to.

Qualcomm, the middle of the night. Another missing person.

When we're in the car, I pull my hair back into a ponytail. My watch says it's 3:38 a.m. We're the only people on the road except for the Marines at the checkpoints. They check our IDs and wave us through, their faces pulled into tight expressions.

I think about Qualcomm, about Cecily and how she's going to take this. I never told her about the multiverse, not because it sounds crazy—between her obsession with all things science and her love for anything new and different, Cecily is probably the one person who would believe me without a doubt—but when I was with her, I was trying to hold on to the aspects of my life that were almost still normal. Telling her about the multiverse, about the portals, about Ben leaving me for his world—it would mean thinking about it. Hanging out with Cee is one of the only times I'm distracted enough to relax.

But now she's getting dragged into it anyway. I'm going to have to tell her so she can do something to help protect people at Qualcomm.

I wonder who will be missing now—and what kind of slaves they're going to become—and it makes me feel sick. Other than a buddy system, I can't even begin to think of a way to combat more abductions.

I need to see Barclay.

I almost say it aloud, to Deirdre, before I stop myself. She might not go for my plan. She might not see the logic in it because it will mean letting Barclay go. I'll talk to Struz when we get back and ask him to make some kind of deal. If Barclay can give Struz something concrete that people can do to arm themselves against traffickers, or some way for us to track them when they disappear, or something, I'm sure Struz will let him go back to Prima.

We need to be working with Prima—with IA—not against them.

Because I know who would win, and it wouldn't be us.

When we get to Qualcomm, Cecily's aunt is awake to meet

us, her eyes bloodshot and her face red and splotchy. The stress is obviously getting to her, too. "Thank God you're here," she says, and as soon as we're close enough, she pulls me into a hug.

I cover my surprise by getting down to business. "Two people are missing?" I ask.

"Yes," she says, as she pulls back. "Jack Wright. He's eleven."

I can feel the bile moving around in my stomach.

"Where did this happen? Was he alone?" Deirdre asks.

Cecily's aunt nods. "Both his parents were killed in the quakes, so we've housed him with the other kids who are alone now. Cecily and some of the girls have been taking care of them."

No wonder she's so upset. This is going to be hell on Cee.

"He'd gotten up to go to the bathroom in the middle of the night," she adds. "He was gone a little too long, so Cecily and Kate got up to check on him."

I glance off to the side and see Kate, a blanket wrapped around her. She's shaking a little with her head down, as if she's crying into the blanket. I've finally gotten over the way she turned on me and traded our friendship for popularity. We're not exactly friends again, but I've let go of the hate.

I look around for Cecily, since she is usually quick to comfort anyone who's crying, and a shiver moves through my body. I don't see her anywhere, and when I look back at her aunt, the question almost freezes in my throat.

"And the second?" I ask.

Her eyes water and Deirdre says, "Please tell us it's not another kid."

It's not, but for me, this answer is worse.

"It's Cecily."

# 05:05:02:35

I first met Cecily my sophomore year. She was the only freshman in AP Chem, and when it came to answering questions and playing teacher's pet, she gave Alex a run for his money. She sat up front with a crisp notebook and eight different-colored pens, and she practically fell out of her seat with enthusiasm every time Mr. Easterly asked a question.

She was blond, bubbly, and far too excited to be at school. She was perkiness personified.

Alex had a huge crush on her, and I hated her a little on principle.

Then I got stuck with her for a lab partner.

Alex was at some special "best students in California" weekend up at Stanford, and Easterly was trying to discourage Mason Rickman from coasting through class by letting Cecily do all the work, so he stuck me in a threesome with the two of them, knowing I'd badger Mason into doing his fair share. The lab itself was essentially analyzing a few different chemicals in commercial bleach. My plan was to just get it done—even with Mason slowing us down, it would be an easy one.

But then Mason spilled some of the bleach and Cecily said, "God, Mason, just because Janelle is here doesn't mean you have to get all weird. Stop letting her make you nervous. It's like you have a crush on her or something."

Mason snorted. "Well, I certainly don't have a crush on you."

"Thank goodness. I don't need another stalker. I mean, it's hard enough to leave my house as it is."

Mason looked at me and rolled his eyes, but the smile never left his face.

"Don't worry, Janelle," Cecily said to me. "He's a little funny looking, but I promise you he's pretty harmless. In fact, if we let him, he'd probably just go to sleep." Then she handed me a beaker. "Here, fill this before he manages to spill it and get it all over our clothes."

I realized Cecily was funny. She made fun of Mason—and me—constantly. And she loved it when we managed to think of something witty enough to make fun of her right back.

She was smart and hard-working—like me, if I was less serious and more friendly. When Alex came back, she and I stuck him with Mason on most of the labs and worked together. Though he hated working with Mason, he loved the attention he got from Cecily as a result.

I've already lost Alex. Cecily is the only friend I have left. I can't lose her, too.

I try to listen to Cecily's aunt as she describes what happened. Kate and some others heard Cecily shout, "Fire!"—it's the one thing you can shout and guarantee that people will come running—and got up and ran to the hallway in time to see her disappear through some kind of black hole. But there's something wrong with either my ears or my focus—or both. I feel like I'm caught in some kind of air tunnel and the wind is roaring in my ears.

We're on the first floor of Qualcomm, where the small children and families with young ones are staying, where the crime took place. Despite the time, handfuls of people are standing around watching Deirdre and me.

And I can't stop staring at them, memorizing each one.

Their faces all ask variations of the same question: *What are you going to do about this?*

A young boy is missing, which is tragic enough as it is. But Cecily is missing too—the girl who kept this place together, the girl who gave people hope. Underneath the lines of anger on their faces is a desperation—you can see it in their eyes. Because without Cecily, how will they keep going?

The faint singed line of a burn on concrete—what I now know is the mark of a portal flaring to life and disappearing quickly—draws my eye, and I squat down to touch the end of it with the tips of my fingers. It doesn't feel any different. There's nothing about this soft mark to suggest that two people were just ripped from this world.

I look a hundred feet south, toward the bathroom. In my mind I see Cecily in pink sweatpants and her I ONLY DATE NINJAS Teenage Mutant Ninja Turtles T-shirt coming out of the room where she sleeps and heading toward the bathroom. Her white-blond hair is mussed, probably from tossing and turning, and she has circles under her eyes from not actually sleeping.

I see her stop and her head swivel at a sound—maybe a shout or a yell, maybe just something unusual and therefore alarming—and then I see her take off running toward us, toward an eleven-year-old boy with sandy-brown hair struggling against one or both of his captors. She shouts for them to stop, and one of them turns to her, grabbing her when she gets close, deciding that taking her is far better than leaving a witness. A girl who just turned sixteen, a girl who's petite, and thin, with blond hair and innocent doe eyes—she'll be easily placed as a slave.

She shouts, "Fire!" as one of the abductors covers her mouth and jabs her with a syringe. Then they're vanishing through the portal.

# 05:03:08:12

Struz is awake but still home when I get there. He's drinking coffee, black and probably drowned in sugar, one of the few luxuries he's made sure we still have.

He opens his mouth, probably to ask about our newest case, but I don't let him get that far.

"Don't leave yet," I say, walking past the kitchen and toward the stairs. "You and I are going to see Barclay."

Deirdre calls after me as I run upstairs, but I don't stop. My plan has changed slightly, but the dynamic here is still the same. I need Barclay, and I don't need Deirdre trying to step in and stop me.

When I get to my room, I move straight for the closet and reach toward the back, grabbing my backpack from the floor. The clothes I'm wearing—jeans, T-shirt, hoodie, and sneakers—are going to have to be good enough, but I can't walk blindly into whatever Barclay's planning. I grab my dad's old hunting knife, his backup gun, and all the ammo we have for it and stuff them into the backpack. And I take my leather jacket because who knows how cold it will be where I'm going.

With everything in the backpack, I put it on.

I get up and leave the room without looking back, because it would be easier to stay here and just be upset than try to do something about it. I need to hold on to my anger—I need to wrap myself up in it, in the injustice of everything that's just happened, and keep it close. I can't lose my resolve.

I peek into Struz and Jared's room before I head downstairs. My brother is still asleep, tangled up in his covers like he fought them into submission, his brown hair sticking out in odd places. I think about before the quakes, when we went to Disneyland and I knew it might be our last time together if the world ended. I remember how much he smiled then—how much he still manages to smile now, despite everything.

This is my brother, the only member of my family I have left. I have to stop these abductions before they get worse, before these guys start grabbing people out of houses instead of just shelters. I have to do this to get Cecily back and to keep my brother safe, so that I don't have to worry if he'll be next.

I move into the room and touch his shoulder, his skin warm from the blankets. I sit carefully on the edge of the bed. His eyes flutter open and he groans a little, pulling himself tighter into a ball.

Brushing my fingers through his hair, I whisper, "I love you, Jared," and then, because I know it's an *X-Files* quote he'll understand, I add, "'Even when the world was falling apart, you were my constant. My touchstone.'"

A muffled, "'And you were mine'" comes out from under the covers. From the sound of his voice, I can tell he's smiling.

He'll be mad when he fully wakes up and finds out that I'm gone, but if this is the last conversation we're ever going to have, it's a good one. One that's true—and worth remembering.

After kissing his forehead, I get up and head downstairs.

Both tense and red-faced, Struz and Deirdre pause what is clearly an argument and turn toward me. Again, I don't give them a chance. I just look right into Struz's blue eyes.

"I need you to let Barclay go," I say. "Because I need to go with him."

# 05:02:57:43

Deirdre reacts first. "He can't let Barclay go." Her face flushes a shade slightly darker, and her voice, stern and loud, escalates as she keeps talking. "And you certainly can't go with him. Go where? In the middle of all this?"

Struz doesn't say anything yet, so I don't either. I stand still and straight, with my lips pressed together in a hard line. I let my body language and facial expression tell the complete truth. I let them say that I've thought this through, that I can do this, that it's the only way.

Struz takes a slow sip from his coffee mug. Then he looks at me. "You're not going anywhere. And I can't just let Barclay go. We need to know more about what happened this fall. And if what he's said is true, we need to know what we can do right now. After we've gotten information, we could let Barclay take a team of trained agents with him if he needs help and can't trust his own people."

"You think we can really afford to wait that long?" I ask.

"Struz," Deirdre says. "You can't possibly . . . Where the hell is she going to go? We can't trust him!"

He doesn't answer her. "It doesn't have to be you," he says to me.

But he's wrong. It *does* have to be me. I think of Ben and Cecily and know that it does.

It has to be me.

I don't say a word because my face says that I am my father's daughter. That I'll do this with or without his help.

Because I will.

Even if Struz doesn't want me to. I can't sit around and wait for someone to figure out how to get Cecily back. And I can't sit around wondering if Ben is dead because of my inaction. Doing that last night was enough.

And Barclay isn't going to take a team of FBI agents or Marines and go through a portal into Prima and shake things up with the IA. He isn't even going to hang out and let himself be detained very long. If they've still got him, it's only temporary—maybe even because he's waiting for me.

When Struz pours the rest of his coffee down the sink, I know I have him.

"J, come with me. Let's talk to Barclay," Struz says. To Deirdre he adds, "Call another meeting for an hour from now. We need people to be prepared and not panicking. We need a way to fight this."

"Struz—"

"D, we've got enough shit to deal with without people disappearing right and left." He looks at me. "Let's go."

# 05:02:03:15

When we first come in, Barclay is silent. The holding cell is cleaner and *whiter* than I expected. The floors, walls, ceiling, even the bars are white. There's a small metal sink and toilet on one side and a small cot on the other. The bed is untouched, the blanket and sheets unwrinkled as if Barclay hasn't slept. He's sitting on the floor, his head against the wall, his eyes closed, his hands now tied together.

He doesn't even look up when the door opens and he doesn't acknowledge it when Struz says he's come to talk.

When he adds, "And I brought someone with me," *that* makes Barclay react. He smiles.

"I knew you'd change your mind, Tenner," he says.

I sort of want to smack the smugness right off his face.

Struz frowns. "We need information."

Barclay doesn't answer.

"We need to know everything about Prima, the portals, this human-trafficking ring, and exactly what part you played in the events that happened a few months ago," Struz says.

Again, Barclay doesn't answer, but he looks at me like he's a combination of annoyed and surprised that I gave up information about what happened.

"Don't be an asshole," I say. "We don't care about your problems as much as we care about ours." It's not necessarily true, since I care a lot about Ben and Cecily, and someone dirty in the IA has the potential to be a huge problem, but I have to say something.

"It's against IA regulations to discuss the multiverse to persons in a world that isn't part of the Interverse Alliance," he says.

"Seriously, you're going to spout that at me?" I fold my arms across my chest. "I seem to recall you've already broken that one."

He knows I'm referring to the information he told me before the quakes—and what he told me yesterday.

"Look, the sad fact is that you need me," I say, even though I'm not a hundred percent sure why yet. "I'm not going to help you for nothing. So you need to talk to us and give us answers."

Barclay's eyebrows draw together and I'm pretty sure he's clenching his teeth, but he gives a quick nod and then says, "What are your terms?"

I take a deep breath. "My friend Cecily has been taken. So I'll go with you—"

Struz clears his throat. "Actually, I'll go with you. Janelle will stay here."

My mouth falls open, though I'm not sure what I'm about to say. I can't tell myself that it's surprising that Struz would go in my place. But I just hadn't seen it coming.

Barclay shakes his head. "No deal. I don't need you. I need her. She knows about the IA and they know about her. I can bring her in under the guise of questioning her and no one will think it's off. If I brought you in, it would draw attention to us."

Struz looks like he's about to argue, so I put a hand on his arm. I don't know why Barclay needs me, but I believe him. And I also know I need Struz to take care of Jared while I'm gone. To make sure he's safe.

"I'll go with you," I repeat. "On two conditions."

"That we get your friend back?" he asks.

"Yes. And that you tell Struz how to fight this stuff."

"What about Ben?" Barclay asks.

My stomach drops and I feel short of breath, like he just punched me. "What about him?" I'm not about to tell Barclay that I've been lying awake at night waiting for Ben Michaels to walk back into my universe while he's been running around and getting himself in trouble with IA and who knows what else. I need to make sure he's safe, but the most important thing is to get Cecily back. That's what I need from Barclay right now.

"Fair enough," he says with a shrug. The corners of his lips turn up, though. Like he doesn't quite believe me.

The truth is there's actually not a lot Barclay can tell us that will block the portals. If we had hydrochloradneum, we could use it. Apparently in New Prima, the capital city where Barclay lives and IA is headquartered, there are buildings with the chemical compound in their foundations, and it acts as a shield to prevent portals from opening inside those buildings.

We don't have that, though. And even though Struz has given information to scientists, there hasn't been much advancement in the Multiverse Project, not that anyone can blame them, given the state of the country right now.

"Can't IA track these guys through their quantum chargers or something?" I ask.

He shakes his head. "No, that's the problem. They're either

using black-market chargers or they've dismantled the tracking chips." Barclay sighs. "If it was that easy to track them, Tenner, we'd have shut them down."

"Well, can't you track the activity or something?" Struz asks.

"Not likely. Every universe has soft spots. They're spots where travel between universes is easy—or easier, at least. Those spots don't register activity unless the portals are unstable, unless they're creating some kind of bigger disturbances between universes." Barclay shifts on the floor and looks directly at me. Ben's portals were unstable. That's why we ended up with so many problems.

"Where are the soft spots?" Struz asks.

Barclay chuckles. "We're in a big soft spot. It's called San Diego."

# 05:01:44:59

Barclay looks at me. "You think it's a coincidence that your boyfriend and his friends got dumped here? They opened a portal with no direction, so it chose the closest soft spot, and here they were."

"Why the ocean, then?"

"Because that's the thinnest part," Barclay says. "This whole area is a soft spot, but some areas are thinner than others—some more conducive to portals."

"So we're looking for the thinnest soft spots where someone could portal in and do some reconnaissance, and areas that are highly populated," Struz says. "Dammit."

I look at him. I'm not sure what he's on to.

"We need to break up the evac shelters. Think of how many disappearances there have been from Qualcomm alone."

"Oh, God," I breathe. "Even all the people in the beginning that we thought might have abandoned the shelter because it was too crowded . . ."

Struz nods. "I'll get our people on it while you're gone." He looks at Barclay. "Are there any spots that are . . . whatever you'd call it, thick?"

"Downtown," Barclay says. It's a mess downtown, not exactly habitable. "It would be the last place I'd want to portal in if people were looking for me. The veil between the universes is thickest there, and portaling in would register a certain level of activity."

I look at Struz. He certainly has his work cut out for him.

# 05:01:42:58

After Struz gives the order for the soldiers to release Barclay, he drives the two of us to where La Jolla Village Drive turned into North Torrey Pines Road. It's what used to be the southwestern tip of UCSD's campus. Now it's just uneven land, downed buildings, and cliffs that drop straight down into the ocean.

Between the quakes and the tsunami, the California coastline retreated anywhere between two hundred feet and a couple of miles. Here in northern La Jolla, the ocean starts about two thousand feet inland of where it used to.

According to Barclay, this is a good place for us to disappear.

When he parks and turns the engine off, Struz says, "Barclay, a word."

The two of them get out of the car and head about ten yards away. I'm not sure what exactly Struz has to tell him, but I imagine it's something along the lines of, *Make sure she doesn't get hurt.* Not that Barclay could guarantee that—not that he would, either.

When I get out of the car, my shoes hit the dry, scorched earth and kick up some dust. The wind doesn't help, and I have to close my eyes for a second to keep them from burning. It's not quite sunrise yet. If I look back toward the way we came from, there are orange and pink streaks in the sky, and I imagine the sun will be up soon. But in front of me the sky is still dark, and even though I can't see the ocean, I can hear the waves sliding out to sea, curling and cresting, then crashing against the side of the cliffs.

Apparently done with threats, Struz walks back over to me. He puts one of his giant hands on my shoulder and squeezes—almost too hard. His eyes are closed and the lines on his face are deeply etched—stress leaving its mark. When his voice comes out, it's strained, and I appreciate how much restraint he's capable of. I wouldn't be able to just close my eyes and let *him* leave *me*.

And I know it's not easy for him.

It doesn't matter that it's the right thing to do or that he can't be the one to leave. It doesn't even matter that I'm technically an adult and he's not really related to me. We've been tied together by our love for my dad for a long time, and now the ever-present ache that stems from my dad's absence and our love for each other makes us family.

It's the two of us against the rest of the world—I can see that in the way he bites his cheek and in the tension of his body. I can feel it in the rising lump in my throat and the way my eyes burn.

There are no words of advice. He doesn't tell me to be safe or to be careful. There are no words of encouragement—serious or comical. He doesn't tell me to bring Cecily back, to save the day, or to stick it to the bad guys.

He just says, "Come back."

I nod first because I can't answer. Something's blocking my

throat. I lift my eyes to the black, cloudless sky to keep from crying, and I memorize how this feels—the cool desert breeze, the middle-of-the-night silences, the hard earth of my universe underneath my feet, the burned smell of smoke lingering everywhere, the taste of sweat on my skin. And Struz—the warmth of his fingers digging into my shoulder, and the deep breath he takes to keep his shit together.

I resolve to keep from losing this. It might be filled with problems, and it might take us years to solve them, but this is my world—my universe. I belong here.

No matter what, I promise myself I'll come back to my family.

# 05:01:37:26

I touch Struz's hand on my shoulder. I squeeze it with my own and whisper, "I will."

I almost add something snarky—I almost tell him I'm not that easy to get rid of. But I don't. Because I'm about to follow someone I don't trust through a portal and into another universe. I'll be in a different world, facing a human-trafficking ring, a potentially corrupt international agency, and technology I can't fathom.

Nothing about this is going to be easy.

"Here," Barclay says, handing me a necklace identical to the one he's wearing, identical to the one I wore the last time I moved through a portal, when Ben and I were coming back here. "Put this on."

It's a metal necklace, the one all Interverse Agents wear. It looks like it's just braided wire, but it has an electronic charge that allows it to travel through the activated portals without being affected by the radiation.

Barclay watches me, our eyes meet, and he holds my gaze.

I think about how it felt when he pulled me through my first portal a few months ago, when one of the quakes was about to bring Ben's house down on us—the way it felt like fire was moving through my veins, liquefying me from the inside out, like my skin was melting off my bones. Barclay injected me with something then, to keep me from dying from the radiation.

I crack a couple of knuckles to keep my hands from shaking.

"Do I need another injection?" I ask. I'd rather take the shot first and avoid feeling like that than wait until afterward.

Barclay shakes his head. "You only need those about once every six months."

I nod, take a deep breath, ignore the pounding of my heart, and tell myself that I'm ready.

From his pocket, Barclay pulls out what looks like a complicated cell phone—some kind of cross between an iPhone and an old Palm Pilot. It's his quantum charger, another thing all IA agents have. They activate and open portals, like a navigation system that uses coordinates to pinpoint the exact spot in any given universe, so an agent knows where he's going. And it stabilizes the portal when it opens.

Struz steps back and I want to turn around and say good-bye one more time. Because what if I don't make it back? What if this is the last time that I see him? I want the moment to matter.

But I don't look because I don't want him to be able to see how scared I am. Instead, I just watch Barclay as he presses a few buttons on the charger. He points it at the ground in front of him.

I hear that electrical sound—the sound of something powering up.

And then the portal springs open.

It's a perfect circle, pure black like oil, with a diameter of a little more than seven feet, and it's in front of Barclay, backlighting him, giving his silhouette some kind of otherworldly glow.

The temperature drops, the wind picks up and moves through my hair, goose bumps spring up on my neck, and the air smells like we're in that moment right before a storm sets in.

I shiver.

Not just because it's cold.

Barclay turns around. His eyes look impossibly blue in this light, and I have the urge to back out. I can't help but feel like I'm about to violate every law of the natural world.

He must know I'm struggling, because he says, "This is the right thing to do, Tenner."

Our eyes don't break contact as he takes a step back into the black hole that is the portal. I watch as the blackness seems to grab hold of him and pull him deeper—until it swallows him, and he's gone.

I could leave him. I could let the portal just fade out of existence and I could stay here.

But I can't, and Barclay knows that—he knows I'll follow him. For Cecily.

And for Ben.

The sky is red and orange. The clouds look almost gray, with glowing white outlines. The sun is rising, a golden globe peeking over the eastern horizon, lighting up a world that almost ended.

I take one last look around my universe at the cliffs under my feet, not so different from the cliffs where Ben and I watched the sun set, where we shared burritos and our first kiss. I listen to the ocean waves beneath me and think of the cold sting of the salt water, of the way my arms and legs burned every time I swam. I memorize the feel of the sun, the way my skin warms as the light touches me and chases back the shadows.

Then I glance back at Struz, too tall and lanky, blond hair and grayish blue eyes, the lines on his face clearly giving away how helpless he feels. "Keep Jared safe," I say.

And I follow Barclay through.

# PART TWO

*When we two parted*

*In silence and tears,*

*Half broken-hearted*

*To sever for years,*

*Pale grew thy cheek and cold,*

*Colder thy kiss;*

*Truly that hour foretold*

*Sorrow to this.*

—Lord Byron

# 05:01:37:14

Heat courses through my veins, my body flooding with fire, my fingertips and toes tingling with the sensation. But as soon as it starts, it's already over, and I'm lying on my side, cold and wincing at the way my left arm and hip throb from how hard I just hit the ground.

The earth underneath me is cold, and I can smell the wet grass as if it rained recently. The air is still and unmoving, and all I can hear above me is the sound of Barclay's breathing. The grass I'm lying in is long and overgrown; huge trees shoot up to the sky and block out the sunlight; and everything I see is green and brown.

This doesn't look like the Prima I remember. We're more likely in a jungle than we are in a capital city. "Where are we?"

"This is Earth 06382," Barclay says. "It's been uninhabited for the past two hundred years or so. Don't worry, we're not staying here." He looks down at his quantum charger and begins typing things in.

I can't help but groan a little when I stand up. If I'm going to make portaling into different worlds a habit, I really need to figure out how to land. Barclay is standing casually next to me, quantum charger in hand, so there must be a less traumatic way to do this.

I take a deep breath, and it's like I can smell the earth. It's that deep, woodsy smell sweetened with pollen. But there's something not right about this place. In the distance there's a cabin. The overgrowth has sprung up around it, and it's slumped on its foundation. I can't picture anyone ever living here. Not even two hundred years ago.

Because even though it's green everywhere and I can hear the rustling of the leaves as the wind moves, there's a creepy stillness around us.

I can't *hear* anything. No birds, no animals, nothing. That's what's wrong with this place.

"What happened?" I ask.

Barclay looks at me, his eyebrows raised, his lips pursed together. It's an expression that says, *You don't really want to know.*

"No explanation, that's shocking." He should know by now how much I hate secrets.

He sighs. "They were actually the first world, we think, to discover interverse travel. We're not exactly sure what happened, but the scientists who've studied this world think no one controlled the portals. People opened them and started going in and out, without any kind of regulation. Maybe they had too many portals opening and closing. Maybe they didn't have the technology to keep the portals stable. Whatever it was, a radiation virus swept through this world and killed everyone."

Everyone. If IA doesn't know what caused this, there's nothing to say it couldn't happen again.

"So why are we here?"

"We can't just portal into New Prima directly because I don't want anyone in IA to know we're there. So we certainly can't just portal into my apartment, like we did last time. We need to muddy our trail a little just to make sure there's no energy signature that will trace us back to your world. Then we need to enter Prima through a soft spot in a remote location."

I know he's trying to keep things under wraps, but I didn't expect all this secrecy.

"Tenner, the situation is a little worse than I let on," he says. He looks guilty, which is a bad sign. "What we're doing is directly against IA orders. I was actually sent on a completely different mission, and I'm ignoring those orders."

"What mission?"

He shrugs it off. "It's stupid and I'm not doing it, so it doesn't matter."

"Couldn't you, I don't know, get fired or something for ignoring orders?" If he loves anything, it's his job. I'm surprised he'd be careless like that.

"Worse," he says. "This is why we're running low on time. I could be tried and thrown in jail, even executed for treason, if they find out, which means we have to do everything under the radar."

I let that sink in. For a second, I'm glad the stakes are high for him, too. Not only are we on the same team, but this is about more than just glory for him. It's personal. Then reality sets in. What am I doing on some unnamed, unoccupied world just now finding out about this? "What else is worse than you've let on?"

His jaw clenches, and I know there's something. So I wait.

Barclay's voice is quiet but firm. "Government officials in Prima have put out bulletins to all the worlds that are part of the Interverse Alliance. If Ben doesn't turn himself in by nine a.m. on the thirty-first, they're going to execute people he cares about."

The air comes rushing out of my lungs like I've been hit, as I think of his parents—of his brother—and of Ben, of how much his family means to him. He just got them back, after being gone for seven years. He can't lose them now. Not again.

"By the thirty-first?" I say, trying to do the math in my head. I count the days several times, hoping that I've made a mistake somehow. But I haven't. "That's in five days."

Barclay nods and glances at his watch. "Five days, one hour, thirty-seven minutes, ten seconds."

"Shit." What else is there to say, really?

"They've already got all the remaining members of his family in custody," Barclay adds.

Ben's family. He told me about them after the first earthquake, when we sat under our table in Poblete's English class. His mom the scientist, and his dad the traveling salesman. His older brother Derek.

*We had these miniature car kits. They were like toys, but you built a car that was about two feet long from scratch and it was real, like with an engine and everything. But they were really expensive, so when my mom bought Derek a new kit, she used make him let me work on it with him. Then we'd take turns with the remote, racing the car down our street. We chased the dog a lot.*

I take a deep breath. I can't let anything happen to them. When we were in New Prima, Ben could have gone home to his world, but he came back with me to mine, to help me find my brother and stop Wave Function Collapse.

But this isn't going to be easy. And now there's a deadline—one that doesn't leave us much time. We only have five days. Less than a week. "What's the plan?"

Barclay grunts. "We need to find Ben, prove him innocent, and figure out exactly who's behind this."

And we need to find Cecily.

It's a tall order for only five days.

I take a deep breath. "How do we find Ben?" That's the first step, and we don't have time to waste.

"We have to talk to the one person who knows Ben better than you," he says.

I don't have to ask who *that* is, I already know.

Elijah.

# 05:01:09:07

A half hour and four portals later, we're finally in Prima, and I'm flat on my back and aching. I try not to think about how badly bruised I'm going to be from all the falling down. Instead, I focus on New Prima and how it doesn't exactly remind me of the brief memory I have of looking down on the city from Barclay's window.

For one thing, the stench is awful. It's some dreadful combination of burning rubber, week-old garbage, and warm sewage. I wrinkle my nose at Barclay and look up.

The sky is the same iridescent gray that I remember, something that would be beautiful with all the different shimmering colors if it wasn't crowded by thick, stormlike smog clouds hanging heavy in the air.

We're in some kind of alley in what must be New Prima's red-light district. Instead of the crystal skyscrapers, there are dark, graffiti-covered buildings with neon signs for alcohol, drugs, gambling, sex toys, and hotel rooms by the hour. The skyscrapers must be up there somewhere, since the sun is completely blocked out. It might as well be dusk or early evening.

But it's morning, and no one seems to be around—probably because they're still asleep from whatever they did last night.

"Did anyone see us portal in?" I ask anyway, since that could potentially blow our cover.

Barclay shakes his head. "I don't think so. But if they did, it wouldn't matter. No one down here would give a shit."

I push myself to my feet and hug my jacket a little closer around me as I realize the building across from us has a number of floor-to-ceiling windows that only make sense if they're lit up and showcasing someone stripping.

"Pull your hood up," Barclay says. "We're safe from being recognized for the moment, but we need to get to my apartment without being seen."

He pulls a beanie from his coat pocket and puts it on his head. "Stick close to me; keep your head down. Don't talk to anyone, and whatever you do, don't look up."

I follow his orders and stay close to his left shoulder as we walk through the alley. Underneath the neon lighting and the flashy signs, the filth matches the smell. There's trash piled up next to the sidewalks and blocking the gutters, and old rainwater and possibly human waste sits puddled around the trash since it has nowhere to go.

We turn the corner and head down another alley, through a layer of foul-smelling steam that's rising up from under the street. Barclay walks fast and keeps his head down, and I find myself almost running to keep up with him.

Whatever part of Prima this is, it's not one I want to be hanging out in by myself.

After a couple more turns, we pass a stand in the street with a sign that says OPEN-AIR BODEGA, but really it's just a guy grilling some kind of meat that looks burned and smells unclean. My stomach shifts uncomfortably as I try not to wonder what kind of meat it actually is. There's a bulky guy next to the grill, watching a couple of people nearby approach. He's clearly some kind of guard to make sure no one steals the mystery meat. He catches me looking at him, and his eyes rake over my body while his lips curl into a smile. A shiver moves up my back.

"Walk faster," Barclay says without turning around.

For once, I listen without question.

We make another turn and pass a homeless guy sleeping on a pile of trash. Next to him, an old metal trash can is smoking from a fire about to die out.

He lifts his head as we pass him. "How much for your girl, man?"

I almost expect Barclay to make a joke about selling me to the homeless guy if I don't follow his orders and cooperate with him, but he doesn't. And I'm glad.

Finally we get to a metal building that at least seems well kept. Two guys who look like some kind of cross between military and police are standing guard next to the door. They're wearing dark fatigues, bulletproof vests, and black boots, and carrying machine guns. As we approach them, their bodies visibly tense, and they adjust their grip on their weapons.

"I'll do the talking," Barclay whispers. I've got no problem with that. "And remember to keep your head down."

When we're a little less than five feet away, with guns trained on us, one of the cops shouts, "Hold it right there. Let's see your tags."

# 05:01:05:31

We stop, and Barclay says in his most polite voice, "I'm going to reach in my back pocket and grab my face tag." But he doesn't make a move yet. He waits for the approaching cop to nod, then reaches in his pocket and pulls out a black wallet. From it he hands over something that looks like the most glamorous driver's license I've ever seen.

I shift on my feet. I can't help it. My body feels tense and a little too warm, and I'm not sure how this is going to work.

The cop examines Barclay's ID, tilting it to see a hologram, and then runs it through a scanner. While he does so, we don't say anything. I'm not exactly sure what the card says. A face tag sounds like some kind of ID, only any form of identification announces, "Hey, this is Taylor Barclay, the guy who's supposed to be on some kind of IA mission, and guess what, he isn't," which, as far as I know, wasn't the plan.

This is worse than the checkpoints I go through with Deirdre. For one thing, I know I'm on the right side of the law at home. Feeling guilty means we're more likely to look it too. For another, I know Deirdre will fight for me. Barclay, on the other hand, will serve his own ends. He might need me right now, but if it looks like we're in trouble and it's him or me, I know I'll be on my own. Plus I don't have any kind of identification on me, at least not any that would make sense to these guys.

I shift my glance to Barclay to see if he's giving me any kind of sign. If we want to get past them, and he can't get us through by talking, we're going to have to storm the entrance by force. The two of us might be able to take out the guy in front of us with the element of surprise, but we'd be dead before we got to the door.

It doesn't matter, though, because Barclay is relaxed and patient, waiting for the cop to give him his ID back.

"Tomas Barclay, sir," the cop says as his stance shifts a little. "I apologize for the delay, but I'll need to report what you were doing down here."

Barclay offers him his most dazzling smile. "If possible, I'd love to keep this off the record," he says. "You see, my wife's sister . . ." He gestures toward me. "She's had a rough go of it lately, and I had to come get her. It's not going to happen again."

The cop doesn't say anything, and Barclay apparently takes that as an invitation to pay him off. He pulls several bills from his wallet and passes them to the cop. "For your discretion?"

I can barely breathe as I wait for the cop to decide what he's going to do.

If he declines the money, I don't know what our backup plan is, which puts me at a disadvantage if we have to put that plan into action. I can follow Barclay's lead, sure, but I'm going to be slow.

And sometimes, being slow is how you end up dead.

But right when I think he's going to decline, the cop takes the money and puts it in his pocket. "I'm sorry for the trouble, sir. Right this way." Then he escorts us to the door.

When the door opens, it's an elevator, and it's clearly the cleanest thing in this part of town. I follow Barclay in and avoid eye contact with the cops.

I let out a breath when the doors close and the elevator comes alive.

"Taylor and Tomas?" I ask.

"Later," Barclay says.

As we rise, I can smell the difference in the air with each level we ascend—cleaner, sweeter. In the silence, my mind goes to Ben and his family. He spent seven years trying to get back to them—to his parents and his brother. I remember the first time he told me about them. It had been so long he was having trouble remembering their faces.

I conjure up an image of Jared in my head, with his hair that needs to be cut and his dimpled smile, and I think of the lengths I would go to in order to keep him safe.

Right now Ben is either plotting how he can get his family back or he's planning to turn himself in.

Either way, we have to find him first. And we have barely five days to do it.

The elevator dings and opens to a shiny white-and-blue outdoor platform. A crowd of people in business suits and an array of high-end coats are standing around. Some of them have tablets like iPads, only they're completely clear, like they're made of glass.

Barclay leads me off the elevator into the crowd. People move easily to make way without paying us any real attention, and I try to do the same. Marveling at all the differences between their world and mine would make me look like a tourist or someone out of place, and that's going to attract attention.

But I can't help gasping when I see the sky. Iridescent gray with shades of blues, pinks, and purples and streaks of silver, and it's right in front of us.

At the end of the platform, there's a railing separating people from a drop that has to be at least six stories off the ground.

Barclay pulls me against him and puts his arm around me. "If you don't relax, you're going to get us shot."

As I nod, I hear the train approaching. I turn and look, even though I know I shouldn't. I'm glad I do. It's silver and sleek, like a bullet train, only it doesn't run on actual tracks. It hovers above them.

Stars cloud my vision, and I feel light-headed as the gravity of where I am sinks in. I wonder if Ben felt like this in our world—or if this is what he felt like when he went home.

I'm in another universe—a place I don't belong. I'm here, interfering with the laws of this world and the laws of physics as I understand them.

And the only person I know is Barclay. Which means I'm completely alone.

I wish Alex were here. I wish he could see this, but even more than that, I wish he could tell me what he thought of all this.

Because I'm in even more over my head than usual. I'm going up against serious criminals and an entire law-enforcement agency. And I'm in a strange world that isn't mine.

# 05:00:06:31

When the noise from the train is loud enough to muffle our voices, I ask, "So, Tomas?"

"My brother," he says without looking at me.

"Those cops—their whole demeanor changed when they ran his ID."

Barclay smirks, but it's not exactly friendly. "He's a big shot in the corporate world. I lifted his face tag a few weeks ago, before he left town for a conference on global warming or something. He's one of those environmentalists."

"One of those?"

"Saving-the-world-by-doing-everything-green-and-organic types. His wife is too."

The train hovers to a stop in front of us and the doors open to reveal a clean and almost empty car. Barclay's hand on the middle of my back guides me onto the train and toward a corner in the rear of the car as everyone else crowds on. Floods of people move from the platform into the train and Barclay holds my arm to keep me next to him.

I can't help wondering why whoever designed this city chose

an aboveground system instead of a subway like my New York has.

And suddenly something occurs to me. Something I should have thought of before. "Why is Elijah on New Prima?"

Barclay shushes me. "Not now."

"You suck at working with someone," I say, because it's true.

Barclay leans into me. "There are cameras all over the city." His lips brush against my ear as he talks, and I hold my breath, partly because of what he's saying and partly because he's a little too far into my personal space. "They'll pick up noise and chatter, and a program will pull out any designated words. We don't want them to know we're here."

I nod and he pulls back.

If there are cameras and what he's saying is true, he's absolutely right, but there's a bad feeling in the pit of my stomach. I can't imagine why Elijah would ever come to Prima of his own volition. In fact, I know he wouldn't.

Which means that if he's here, someone made him come here.

I can think of only a few reasons they would do that.

And none of them mean anything good.

"He's been detained by IA for questioning," Barclay whispers once the train starts moving. "The detention center is here in New Prima. They're not going to release him anytime soon, which means we need to get to him."

"IA has Elijah?" I ask, that sinking feeling in my stomach getting worse. I think I know, but I have to ask anyway. "Why?"

Barclay grits his teeth and doesn't answer.

And it hits me that I'm right.

"Because he's someone Ben cares about . . ." For the first time, it actually sets in what that might mean for *me*.

# 04:23:55:49

"Not exactly," Barclay says.

"Not exactly *what*?" I hiss in his ear. I'm surrounded by people I don't know, suffocating on a train that smells like a mixture of cleaning products, perfume, and detergents. If Barclay's going to do the whole vague thing, he can get someone else's help.

He grabs my shoulder and whispers, "Elijah's been detained for the past few month or so, and I'll be happy to explain more later, but we can't just hang out in the middle of the city and wait to get caught, Tenner. Use your head."

He doesn't elaborate on why. And I get it. He can explain all this at his apartment. Except I don't want to go to his apartment. I don't want to go anywhere. Every alarm in my body is blaring right now, and all I want to do is go home.

He must sense my panic, because Barclay grabs my arm. "Come with me," he says, pulling me along to emphasize his point. When we get to the back of the train car, Barclay opens the door and pushes me through, shutting it behind him.

The air around us is deafening. I'm not sure I realized wind could be this loud. We have to be moving at almost ninety miles an hour. Barclay will have to scream for either of us to hear anything.

"When we got back, Eric and I wrote up a report about what happened!" he yells. "A few months ago, Ben and Elijah were both detained. I'm not exactly sure why they were really brought in, but they were held in connection to illegal interverse travel and trafficking, and at some point, Ben either escaped or was let go, and now the order is out that he needs to be brought back in, dead or alive."

I look at Barclay's face. His jaw is tight, and he looks a little worried.

"In the write-up you did." I can barely hear my own voice. "Did you mention my relationship to Ben?"

He doesn't look at me and that's enough of an answer in itself. The hood up, the avoiding the cameras and not speaking, it takes on a whole new meaning now. "So they might actually be thinking of grabbing and executing *me*?"

"It is a possibility," he says, but I can tell from the look on his face that's not what he means. It would be more accurate if he just said, "Yes."

And he brought me here.

# 04:23:41:45

The train slams to a stop and I lose my balance, crashing into Barclay, my face colliding with his chest. His arm goes around me, holding me up to keep me from falling again. He smells a little like the ocean—like portals.

I push myself back from him. "What part of your brilliant plan includes getting me executed for something Ben didn't even do?" It comes out louder than it should, but yelling at Barclay isn't exactly something I'm about to start scolding myself for.

"Would you relax!" he hisses at me.

"How can I relax?" I suck down air and try to get a hold of myself. We only have four days.

Four days to rescue Cecily, find Ben, save his family, and stop the traffickers. And IA is looking for me. Which means that in four days, I could be dead.

Barclay still hasn't answered me. When I look at him, he jerks his head to the left and I can see a camera tracking people who are moving from the platform onto the train. We're far enough away and there should be enough background noise to cover us, but I understand. As pissed off as I am, this conversation can wait a few more minutes.

I wait quietly, though not patiently, as we travel two more stops. When Barclay nods toward the platform, I follow him off the train and from the platform to a long window-covered hallway. We're still high up, walking on some kind of elevated pedestrian bridge between buildings, and when I glance out the window, all I can see is sky, crystal buildings, and a city that looks like it's been built on the clouds.

If I weren't suddenly worried about ending up dead, I would think that New Prima was just a little bit beautiful.

But I *am* worried. And I'm terrified.

About Ben and his family. About Cecily, wherever she is. And now I'm worried about myself, too, because I promised Struz and myself that I'd come back. I mean to honor that.

The walkway takes us directly to what must be Barclay's apartment building, because he unlocks a door that leads us to another elevator.

We get off on the thirty-fifth floor and head down a hallway of apartment doors. I remember the last time I was here and suppress a shiver. One moment we were in Ben's basement, facing off against each other, the next an earthquake hit and the house was starting to collapse. And after that, Barclay opened a portal and pulled us through into his living room.

I think of how it felt like my insides were melting as I traveled through the portal for the first time, and I'm glad that at least this time I'm not going to need a sedative.

Hopefully I'll make it home alive, too.

Barclay unlocks his door and lets me in the apartment.

Once we're inside, he pulls off his hat and sets the alarm over his apartment door. I drop my backpack on the floor, peel off my jacket, and throw it on his couch. Then I fold my arms across my chest and wait. Because we're not doing anything else until I get some answers.

"I'm not exactly leading you into this blind," he says, turning to me. "You think I want to see you executed?"

"Please, I know I'm just collateral damage to you."

"Let's get one thing straight, Tenner. We're both using each other. I came to you and asked for your help. But you want help from me, too. That puts us on even ground. It means you aren't collateral damage, because I need you, so stop making me out to be the bad guy. We're on the same team."

"Fine." He's right. We're on the same team, not because we like each other or because we want to be stuck together, but because everyone else is on the *other* team. Fighting with each other is stupid, and it's going to get one of us killed—probably me. "So what's the plan?"

"Here's the deal. I can't talk to Elijah because I'm not on the case," he says. "The clearance level to talk to a prisoner charged with unauthorized interverse travel, conspiracy to commit treason, and human trafficking is way above my pay grade."

"So how are we going to talk to him?" I say. But as soon as the words are out of my mouth, there's a sickening feeling in my chest. Because I think I know what he's going to say.

"You're going to have to talk to him," he says, putting a hand through his hair. Something about the gesture tells me he's not happy about what he's about to say. "You were right. IA is looking for you. You're important to Ben, and they know that."

That hits me harder than it should. The air seems to get

siphoned out of the room, and I take a step backward as if I've been pushed.

IA is *already* looking for me.

So there's no turning back. Even if I wanted to go home now, I can't. I have to see this through. I have to solve this thing. Or someone from IA is going to portal into my earth and snatch me out of my bed and bring me back here to be executed.

They're just as bad as the traffickers. I wonder if that irony is lost on Barclay.

"The plan is that I'm going to bring you into IA to be detained," Barclay adds. He speaks slowly, his words come out even and soft, as if he's expecting the worst from my reaction. "You'll get put in the same cellblock as Elijah, the same cell if we're lucky."

"And then what?" I'm not about to let him leave me to rot in some prison cell.

"Then, with my help, you and Elijah break out."

# 04:23:05:17

I stare at Barclay. I don't move, not even a twitch or a change of my facial expression. It's like I just freeze while my mind replays our conversation. We have four days to find Ben and solve this case before the IA executes people he cares about—including me. The only way to find Ben is through Elijah, who's in a secure IA prison. Which means I have to give myself over to them and then somehow get him out.

But I can't.

I'm one of the most confident people I know. Alex always used to tell me it was the thing he loved most—and the thing he loved *least*—about me. Because I'm confident to a fault.

And of course, that's what got Alex killed. My overconfidence.

But I'm also one of the most realistic people I know. And what I've got right now is clear-cut logic. Four days to go into a prison, break out, search the multiverse for Ben, and take down the largest human-trafficking ring Barclay's ever come across.

There's just no way. There's not enough time. I don't have enough of the right skills. I'm not sure what the hell is wrong with Agent Taylor Barclay, but I can't believe he's managed to trick me into coming here with him and thinking there was something I could do.

We're going to fail and I'm going to end up dead.

Barclay sees something on my face. "Don't overthink this just yet. Hear me out."

I don't have a choice.

After all, if I don't do this, it's likely IA will find me and bring me in. Cecily will be sold into slavery, Ben will be found guilty of human trafficking, and I'll be guilty by association.

If I don't do this, I'm likely to be dead in four days.

# 04:23:02:33

" I have a plan," Barclay says. "I've got everything under control. I'll be able to talk you through breaking out. It'll be almost easy."

"Almost?" If tone of voice could kill, I would have just cut Barclay into ribbons. And I'm glad, because he deserves it.

"Tenner . . ."

"No, Barclay, this is nuts," I say. "What were you thinking? I don't have any kind of tactical training or anything that would be remotely helpful for someone who needed to break out of a prison!"

"I know you think I'm crazy, but—"

The anger in my chest blossoms. "You're out of your mind."

"I'm serious about this. I know exactly how you can escape once you're inside," he says. "Look. I've spent the last six weeks trying to figure out this case and all its details. Every waking minute, I've been devoted to this. Even when I'm asleep, I'm dreaming about it. I've come up with a good plan. I can get you out.

"But more than that," he adds, "this is the only way. There's not a single other option that's less dangerous and has a chance in hell of working."

This isn't just about this case, and it isn't just about Ben, or even Cecily. If we don't solve this, the IA will be after me the rest of my life. I'll never be safe.

As a drop of sweat rolls down the back of my neck, I realize my skin feels flushed, and it's suddenly too hot in this room.

"Are you okay?" Barclay says.

I shake my head. As much as I want to find Ben—want to see him again and feel his arms around me—we don't have much time, and a prison break seems counterproductive when we need to be going after the traffickers. The words try to stick in my throat but I force them out. "Maybe we don't need to find Ben."

"I thought about that," Barclay says. "But Ben is missing for a reason. Whoever is in charge of the trafficking ring, they clearly want him dead. He must know something."

I open my mouth to talk, but I have no words. How could Ben know something about a human-trafficking ring? He should have been at home with his parents and his brother. That's why he left. Not so he could get mixed up with traffickers and put his life at risk. I take another breath. My lungs feel like they're on fire—like I just swam too far and too deep, like I'm drowning somehow.

Barclay reaches for me but I flinch away. "Sit down," he says. "I promise it's not as bad as it sounds."

I move toward the window. My hands shake as I lift them to the glass. The way the sun is coming through the clouds, the sky looks purplish blue. Hundreds of skyscrapers made of crystal, like ice castles, loom in front of me, and the streets below are hidden from the smog. It's like something out of a movie or a dream, only there are people down there in the streets I can't see—people who want me dead.

I've been in over my head before, but this is worse. Because this time I'm alone. This time I don't have my dad or Struz, or even Alex or Ben, to lean on—to ask for help. I don't even have Jared beside me. Right now, I'm in a strange world and the only person I can depend on is me.

Eating canned SpaghettiOs, drinking bottled water, playing board games by candlelight, reading the same books over and over again, watching old movies, even handing out rations—I miss it all so much. The longing for my own world, even broken as it is, pierces my chest so deeply and so suddenly that I lean on the window for support.

The glass is cool against my forehead, and it gives me perspective. This is what I have to do in order to get back home. To bring Cecily home.

I can picture her, just the other night when we were watching *It's a Wonderful Life* with all those people seated on what used to be the Chargers' football field. Blankets were laid out and people were huddled together. There was an excited anticipation in the hushed tones everyone used to talk to one another. Not because of the movie but more because they were excited to do something. Anything was better than sitting around and thinking of what they'd lost.

I barely watched the movie because I was more interested in watching Jared, who was clearly captivated by the magic of black-and-white films, his eyes watery.

When the movie was about to end and Struz came in and winked at me, it was almost a perfect moment. I was surrounded by friends, by people I care about, and for a minute, I forgot about everything that was wrong—with the world and with me.

Cecily did that. She gave people something to look forward to—something to remind them they were alive.

That's why I have to do this. To make sure the people I love are safe. It's terrible and frightening and too much.

But I have no choice.

I push back from the window and look over at Barclay.

"It's a good plan, Tenner, I swear."

I look back toward the window. But instead of the unfamiliar city in front of me, I see my fingerprints on the glass, and they remind me I've overcome insurmountable odds before. I solved my father's murder, I stopped Wave Function Collapse, and I lived to see my world survive through the quakes.

I walk back to the kitchen table and sit down. "Okay," I say, my voice sounding less steady than I want it to.

Barclay nods like he's thankful I'm finally going to play along. "All you have to do is listen to me and convince Elijah to come along."

"Why can't Elijah just portal out?" I ask.

Barclay sighs, like my stupidity is annoying him. "The building is portal resistant. It's a defensive measure in the event that a world with the ability to portal chooses not to be a part of the alliance. No one can portal in and out of certain buildings here. This is one of them."

My turn to sigh. The building is portal resistant. Of course it is.

"You need to get out and get at least ten feet from it before he might be able to portal you out."

"Might?"

122

Barclay stands up and moves into the kitchen. "I don't know how injured he is."

I follow him and try to ignore the sinking feeling in the pit of my stomach.

"That's why we have to have a plan B in place." He grabs some rolled-up papers from behind the fridge.

Standing across from Barclay, in front of the kitchen table, I take a deep breath and pull my hair back into a ponytail. "Okay. Before we tackle plan B, how do I get Elijah out of his cell?"

"Good, okay," he says as he rolls out the paper in his hands. It stretches across the entire table.

Blueprints of the prison.

# 04:22:41:19

Barclay does have a plan. And he wasn't lying—it's detailed. He's clearly thought of this from every possible angle. It's not exactly comforting, but it certainly seems like this is a prison break that could work.

The blueprints are faded, poster-size papers that take up Barclay's entire kitchen table. There's one page for each level of the prison, and while there are twenty-four levels, Barclay is pretty sure we won't need to be familiar with anything other than levels one and two.

According to him, I won't be housed in any of the cellblocks on the first floor with the regular prisoners. Instead I'll be put in a cell one floor up in the solitary block. Those are the cells that are supposed to be reserved for the worst kinds of criminals, but also house the people IA doesn't have any reason to hold—the people they want everyone else to forget about. It's where Elijah is.

The plan is that I need to get out of my cell, get Elijah out of his, and get us both to the infirmary one level down and in the opposite wing of the prison. There, we'll be able to escape through a grate in the floor that leads to the sewers.

I try not to think about how hard this will be, about how many things have to go right in order for us to escape without getting caught. I try not to think about what the consequences will be if we don't make it. And I try not to think about the fact that I'm in this alone. Elijah won't know the plan and he might be injured, and he's never been my biggest fan anyway.

No matter what Barclay says about us being on the same team, if I don't get out, he's got to cut his losses and leave me there. The whole *never leave a man behind* thing doesn't apply here. To have any hope of solving this case, he would have to preserve his cover—or whatever you'd call it. Which means if I can't do this, I'll be stuck in prison, counting down the minutes until I'm executed.

But I can't focus on that, because I have no choice. This is the only way, and we have to make it out.

"What's your problem now?" Barclay asks.

I'm about to respond with something caustic when there are two soft beeps. They could be anything—the microwave, some kind of electronics, even Barclay's cell phone. But instantly I know they're not.

They're something worse.

Because Barclay freezes for a split second, his lips slightly parted with surprise, and then his eyes, wide with fear, flick to me.

"What is it?" I whisper. I'm aware of my pulse in my ears, the dryness in my mouth, and the fact that I don't know what to do with my hands. Because fear is contagious, and I can't think of a single instance I've ever seen Barclay afraid.

He doesn't answer me. Instead, he bolts up and with one

hand grabs the blueprints, with the other grabs me, and before I have a chance to understand what's happening, he's pulling me into his bedroom.

"It's an alarm. Someone is coming," he says, shoving me into the walk-in closet.

"Who?" I ask, my voice breathless.

Barclay's eyes meet mine. "IA."

# 04:21:52:30

Maybe Barclay is paranoid. Maybe it's a UPS guy or some-thing.

Or maybe that's my own wishful thinking.

Whatever's been going on with him lately, clearly something made him set this up. He's not exactly an alarmist. And if he was, he'd have a right to be. If IA is after me, it's only a matter of time until they're after him, too.

Or it might not be IA. It might be worse—it could be the traffickers.

I don't have time to say anything anyway because Barclay presses down on two of the floorboards until there's a click, and they pop loose. He pulls them up to reveal a hidden compart-ment about two feet deep.

"Here, get in." He steps down into the hole in his closet. The floor comes up to his knees.

Looking at it, I'm confused. I don't know how I'm going to fit in here. Even if I crouch down, he won't be able to get the floorboard over my head, and he certainly won't be able to get in there with me.

"Hurry up, Tenner!" Barclay takes my hand and pulls me toward him.

I step in, even though I'm not sure where I'm going to go, only once I put my foot down, I realize it extends underneath the floor. I can lie down flat and the board will be able to go over my head. My body flushes with heat as Barclay pushes me down. I stretch my body out the length of the compartment.

As I lie down, my hands quiver against the wood. My chest is tight, my breaths shallow.

The compartment is the size of a coffin.

"I can't do it," I say, pushing against Barclay and trying to get back up. I'm not claustrophobic, but I've never had to fit into such a small tight space. A space that will effectively trap us here.

"You have to," Barclay says.

"We should run." My legs twitch at the thought.

"There's nowhere to go," he says. "Just for once, do what I tell you."

He knows this apartment—and this world—better than I do. I suck in a deep breath, my lungs burning.

I'm almost completely prone when I pause and sit back up. I brought more evidence of my existence here than just myself. "My backpack, the coats!"

"Fuck!" Barclay says, jumping out of the hole. "Lie down and leave as much room as you can. I have to get in there with you."

He rushes out of the closet, and I lie down, flat on my back. I cross my hands over my chest, like a dead body, but I can't breathe right in that position. I switch to my side, and even though I don't know where to put my arms, I tell myself this is better. If I press my back up against the side of the compartment, we'll have more room for him to be in here with me, though not much.

I hear two more beeps, and Barclay is back. Out of the corner of my eye, I see him put my backpack up on the top shelf, then throw both our coats in the hamper. Then he's climbing into the hole with me.

He pulls a string connected to the floorboards, and they fall over us, snapping back into place. We're lost in almost complete darkness, and Barclay lies down on his side facing me. I put my hands against his chest, and he drapes an arm over me and turns my face into his collarbone.

"Don't make a sound," he whispers. "Don't even move. If they find us here, we're as good as dead."

I don't know what I'd say to that if I had the chance, but it doesn't matter, because at that moment, I hear the front door click open and someone says, "Hey, anybody home?" followed by a thick chuckle. Like this is some kind of game, like it's funny.

The door slams.

A different voice says, "You want his neighbors to narc on us when he gets home?" It's gruff. Annoyed, even.

There's an exchange of words, but they've lowered their voices and it's too muffled to hear over the pounding of my heart.

I need an escape strategy. That will calm me down. How will we get out of here if we're caught? Maybe there's just two of them. I hope. Maybe Barclay has his gun on him and another one nearby. If they do find us down here, we'll have to come out swinging. So far they're at least both male—I can come up with a strike to the balls and maybe somehow get the upper hand and get away.

At least that's my plan right now.

If these guys are IA like Barclay thinks, and they find us, there's only one place I'm going—prison, to be detained and then executed. Barclay would be going there too, and since we're hiding with the blueprints to the prison, there's no way we'd be able to escape.

I remember what Barclay said about Elijah. *I don't know how injured he is.* I wonder what they did to him, and what they're likely to do to both of us, if they find us now. Maybe being executed in four days wouldn't even be the worst of it.

"Let's just hurry up and get this done," someone says. I think it's a different voice than the first two, but I can't be sure.

I close my eyes. My left leg twitches again, and I can feel my calf starting to cramp up. Barclay shifts slightly next to me and my left knee slides in between his. I can feel the soft cotton threads of his shirt under my fingertips, the tense muscles tight underneath the fabric. And I can feel his heartbeat thumping in his chest.

Outside dishes clatter in the kitchen, drawers open and slam shut.

I wonder if the IA will trump up fake charges to put on my execution papers or if they'll be honest and cite that I'm a means to an end, something that doesn't matter. I wonder if they're allowed to just dispose of me since I don't live here.

In the living room, I hear books being pulled off shelves and dumped onto the floor, while Chuckles gives a soft running commentary of what he thinks of Barclay's reading selection and laughs at his own jokes.

"Don't dump them on the floor," Gruff Guy says. "Check the pages."

My hands curl into fists and I hold on to Barclay's shirt so tightly, they start to shake. I want to let go of him, but my brain doesn't seem to be listening. I try to take a deep breath, inhale from my mouth, but I hear myself wheeze.

"Relax," Barclay whispers into my hair. He rubs a circle on my back, but then he stops because the fabric of my shirt rustles against his hand.

I try to count his heartbeats. Eighteen beats in the span of six seconds. It means his heart rate is 180. I used to finish ocean swims with a lower pulse.

Paper crackles, and fabric tears. They're looking for something, something Barclay has hidden and doesn't want them to find. I wonder what's so important that they'd break into his apartment, that he'd hide us under the floor of his closet in order to keep it from them. I wonder what's turned them against him and what they would do if they found us.

"Got it," the third voice says, and fingers clack against a keyboard.

Beneath my hands, Barclay's chest expands and his pulse speeds up. He's holding his breath.

The noise goes on—the rustling of paper, the books thumping against the ground, the drawers opening and shutting, things being moved around, the shuffling of footsteps, the murmur of voices—I'm not sure how long. Sweat beads on my skin, and droplets slide from my neck down the curve of my shoulder.

It feels like we've already been here forever. I try to count the seconds, but Barclay's pulse against my skin keeps messing me up, and I keep losing count somewhere in the forties.

Heavy footsteps enter the bedroom.

Another set follows.

"Check the drawers, I'll look in the closet," Gruff Guy says.

My breathing comes too fast and too loud, and it doesn't matter how much I tell myself to calm down and *shut up*, I'm not seeing any results. Barclay's arm tightens around me, and he pulls me closer to him.

The bulb in the closet flicks on and threads of light shine through the floorboard.

Heavy footsteps thump right above us—military style boots. They step into the closet, and I'm paralyzed, waiting for him to notice the difference in sound from where he steps. Wire hangers scrape against metal as he moves Barclay's clothes around.

There's a thud, like he just dropped to his knees. I hold my breath and refuse to breathe. His hands slide around the floor right above us.

I wonder if the heat of our bodies will tell him where we are.

"Yo, I found something in here," Chuckles calls, and Gruff Guy stands up.

# 04:21:39:34

I feel like I'm made of liquid, or like I'm melting somehow.

Another set of footsteps comes into the bedroom. "That's just an old charger," Third Guy says.

"You don't think we could trace where he's been?" Chuckles asks.

"What good is that going to do if he hasn't used it in months?"

There's movement and rustling, and someone comes back to the closet. He reaches up and feels around the top shelf, pulling things down. My backpack falls heavily to the floor and I flinch from the sound.

"I don't think there's anything in here," Third Guy says, stepping out of the closet.

"We can't go back empty-handed," Gruff Guy says. Something in the way he says it catches my attention. There's an undercurrent of fear in his voice, like he's a little afraid of whoever sent him here.

All three sets of steps come to the edge of the closet. They're so close, I can smell the polished leather of their boots.

"If it was my house, I'd have hidden it under the floor in

my kitchen," Chuckles says. "There's a tile that comes up easy. That's where I keep all the good stuff."

"What have you got to hide?" Third Guy says. "You don't even have enough cash to do laundry."

There's a sweeping sound, like fingers sliding against the floor.

They're so close. We're only separated by thin pieces of plywood.

"There's something weird about this floor," Gruff Guy says. His fingers feel along the edges of each of the floorboards, and he grunts as he tries to pull them up.

Any second now, they're going to realize we're underneath them. Barclay presses his lips down into the top of my head, his arm around me tightening even more.

I taste salt on my lips. I hadn't realized I was crying.

"Hey, is that a safe?" Third Guy asks.

Gruff Guy stands up and shuffles something around in the closet.

"Oh hell yeah," Chuckles says.

"Get me something to get it open," Gruff Guy says.

They move around, someone says something I don't hear, the floor above us shifts. Through it all, I try to hold my breath.

After what feels like an eternity, there are several beeps and a click, and Chuckles laughs in celebration of whatever they've got. More shuffling, as all three of them crowd into the closet.

"Is that it?" Third Guy says.

"Of course it is, what else would it be? And there's at least twenty grand in here."

"Let me see it," Third Guy says. "Not the money."

I hear pages flipping against each other, and then there's a pause. I can hear someone, probably Chuckles, shuffling through the closet still. And there's a sharp intake of breath as Third Guy confirms, "This is it."

"Good," Gruff Guy says, taking a step back. His heel comes down right above us, and the floor gives in slightly and clicks. "Take the gun and the money too," he adds, as Barclay's hand shoots up and grabs the string.

"And grab anything valuable on the way out. If we're lucky, when he gets back, he'll think it was random."

They shuffle around, the closet light flicks off, and the door shuts behind them. Still holding on to the string, Barclay's arm starts to shake under the stress.

"Think Wonder Boy will come back empty-handed?" Chuckles asks with his signature laugh.

"Doesn't matter," Gruff Guy says. "We know where to find her."

# 04:21:07:11

After the front door closes, Barclay lets go of the string and the floorboards pop up. A rush of cool air hits my face as I sit up and scramble out of the compartment. I can't get out of there fast enough. And I can't seem to get enough air. My breaths are harsh and loud.

"Are you okay?" Barclay asks as he sits up and cracks his knuckles.

"What were they looking for?"

"I don't—"

"Don't give me that, what was in your safe?"

"Tenner, it's not important," he says, pulling himself out. "It's all over, we'll—"

I shake my head and slide back as he approaches me. "What was the mission IA gave you, the one you ignored?" My voice rises. "What were they looking for, what did they find in your safe, and if you come back empty-handed, what does 'we know where to find her' mean?"

I push backward with my feet again, and this time my back hits the wall.

On his knees Barclay crawls toward me, reaching his hands around mine. His eyes are closed. "Janelle," he says quietly. My first name sounds strange on his lips. "IA sent me to your world, to bring you back here. That was the mission."

"Because of Ben?"

Barclay's hands squeeze mine. He nods. "It was also a test, for me. To see how dedicated I still was after Eric's death."

They sent him after me. I don't know why, but I can't believe it. Even knowing that they were looking for me, knowing that Ben's family is in prison, it's like I can't reconcile my notion of law enforcement with the truth. "So why—"

"I deleted all the files," he says.

"What?"

"Before I left, I deleted all the files that referenced your world. Everything that Eric and I found out while we were there, all of the addresses and the names. I deleted everything."

For a split second, I'm almost moved. I look at Barclay, kneeling just a few inches from me—this guy who's the youngest agent in IA. He's smart and determined, and he's not above being a complete asshole to get his own way, not above doing whatever needs to be done in order to solve the case and make his superiors proud. And he deleted my file in order to protect me.

"There's no written record of you."

But there is, and as I realize that, I'm over my awe of him. There's a hard copy, and they have it now. When Elijah and I escape from prison, they're going to be able to use everything I care about against me. Jared and Struz. They're not safe. How could I have not realized IA would come after my family if I did this?

Ben, the guy who brought me back to life—IA is after him.

They threw him in prison, and when he escaped they grabbed his parents, his brother, and his best friend. They grabbed the people he cared about.

"Oh my God, we have to go back." I struggle to get to my feet, but Barclay pulls me back down. I pull against him. "Barclay, my family—my brother!"

He pushes me against the ground and leans into me. "Listen to me." I try to push him off me, but he's too heavy. "Janelle, I took care of it!"

I relax for a second, and his hands come to rest on either side of my face. "I took care of it," he says again, his forehead against mine.

I'm not sure if I believe him. "How?"

"The file is a fake," he says. "Someone in IA, someone high up, doesn't trust me. With good reason," he adds darkly. "When I erased the files, I doctored them first, printed out a fake one to leave here, just in case, and then I deleted them all. So even if they recovered the information, it would be wrong."

I nod against him, but he must not be convinced. "No one is going to find Struz or your brother. You might not think that much of my word, but I swear to you, on everything I've worked for, no one will ever find them."

I take a minute to absorb that. *No one will ever find them.* There are thousands of universes out there and billions of people still on mine. But there's nothing now—no record of me or my family or where we lived.

Thank God.

"Thank you," I whisper, closing my eyes. This right here is the treason he was talking about. He erased IA files and destroyed evidence. This is what he could lose his life for. He couldn't have done this *just* for me. His job and the IA are everything to him. I know it must be killing him that there are people high up who are dirty. I know what my dad thought about cops who were dirty—they were the worst kind of bad guys. Because they were supposed to be good guys and they changed teams for money.

But at the same time, sitting here in the corner of Barclay's closet, leaning my forehead against his, his hands holding mine, I know he *did* do this for me.

I don't even care if he did it as some kind of leverage to somehow get me to help him. It's done now, and no one can undo it.

His thumbs sweep under my eyes, wiping the tears away.

"Are you okay?" he asks again.

I nod and open my eyes. And I realize how close together we are. Barclay is practically sitting on top of me, and our faces are touching. "Get off of me, will you?" I say, trying to ignore the fact that I can feel myself blushing. "Haven't I been through enough today?"

"Whatever you say, Tenner," he says as he stands up, and for a reason I can't explain, I'm glad he's back to using my last name.

I push myself off the floor, and because I need to acknowledge what he's doing for me, I add, "We're going to win."

"You bet we are." Barclay smiles, and for the first time the arrogance in his expression doesn't bother me. "We're going to take them down."

He doesn't say *we have to*.

He doesn't need to.

"We need to get out of here," Barclay says when we make it out into the living room. The bedroom is messy. His drawers have been emptied onto the floor, and his things carelessly strewn about. But they did a number on the rest of his apartment.

The flat-screen TV is gone, the living-room lamp is overturned, and papers from Barclay's desk are everywhere. The couches where Ben and I watched the collapse of my earth have been gutted and there's stuffing everywhere. Something like Coke has spilled and splattered the rug with brown stains. In the kitchen, all of Barclay's cabinets and drawers are open, their contents now shattered in a mix of glass and ceramic on the floor.

"Here, put these in your backpack," he says, handing me the blueprints.

I fold them carefully and do as instructed. "I'm not exactly a fan of the need-to-know basis," I call after him as he slips into the bathroom.

"If I were you, I'd say that's shocking," he says.

I just stare at him. "Where are we going?"

The bathroom door opens, and I look away as he tucks in his shirt and then buttons up his jeans. "Take this too," he says, handing me a gun. It's a 9mm, black and stainless steel, and just a few pounds in my hand. It looks a little like the HK that Deirdre carries, only instead it reads HM USP. It has a compensator on the end that makes the barrel longer, but I know from Deirdre that this is only a stylish way to weight the barrel, reduce the kickback, and make the gun more accurate.

My heart beats a little faster as I turn it over in my hands. This is a gun that means business.

"We're going somewhere else to study the blueprints and crash for the night."

He doesn't have to say any more. He wants to get out of his apartment, sleep somewhere else tonight. I don't blame him. I'm not anxious to stay here any longer than I have to, and I certainly don't want to hang out here alone while he does whatever it is he's got to do.

"Not a problem. Let's go."

I follow him to the door, but before we head out, he turns to me. "Same rules as on the way here. Keep your hood up and eyes down. Stay quiet and stay by my side."

I pull my hood up and follow him through the hallway, down the elevator. But instead of getting off at the lobby, we go ten floors down to P10.

"Are we taking your car?" I ask. I don't add that I think that might tip off some of the city cameras, but it's on the tip of my tongue.

Barclay shakes his head as the elevator doors open to a very empty and dimly lit parking garage that smells like mildew and looks like it hasn't seen use in at least five years. We exit into the alley at the back of the building. It doesn't exactly have the red-light vibe of the alley we portaled into, but in a way it's worse.

This is what anyone would call the slums. Graffiti-covered buildings seem to droop rather than stand. There are broken windows, collapsed doors, boxes piled awkwardly and adorned with thin blankets to make some kind of tentlike structure. We walk at a brisk pace, not fast enough to call attention to ourselves, but not slow, either.

The smell of burning rubber and cigarette smoke hangs in the air. It reminds me of old New York, from before Giuliani, when the city was covered in graffiti, drug needles, and worse. When the crime rate was the highest in the country and no one felt safe walking alone. It's the New York from *Taxi Driver*.

It doesn't take much for me to realize the glitzy buildings near Barclay's apartment in New Prima are hiding a lot of the same problems that are a big deal in my world—poverty, drugs, organized crime. I'm surprised. I thought they were more advanced here, smarter somehow. If they're policing the interverse, surely they should be able to create better lives for their own people.

# 04:20:00:29

We turn a corner and Barclay leads me down a set of stairs and into an underground subway that smells like urine and worse. I stick close to him even though there's no one else on the platform with us.

When the downtown train comes, it's only three cars that look like they should be out of commission. The windows are broken or just gone, and when we get inside, most of the seats are cracked, stained, or falling apart. I follow Barclay's lead and sit down next to him on one of the cleaner seats. I'm already looking forward to a shower.

There's one other guy in the car with us, slumped in a seat at the opposite corner. From the color of his skin and the smell, he's either passed out or dead. I look at Barclay, about to ask if there's anything we should do, but he shakes his head.

At the sixth stop, Barclay stands and nods his head toward the door. I get up, following him out, with one last glance at the guy we're leaving behind. I might die tomorrow in an attempted prison break, but I still can't help feeling like I'm better off.

We come aboveground into another alley that looks like it's

straight out of a movie where the naive girl gets off at the wrong subway stop and ends up dead. We're facing the back of a line of abandoned row homes that look like they were boarded up years ago and forgotten about.

"Where are we?" I ask.

"Home sweet home," Barclay says.

I look around.

Barclay smirks. "I grew up here. This neighborhood is called the underground."

"How come?"

He glances at me with a smile. "About thirty years ago, the city had a huge crime problem. They didn't want to lose jobs and people to the suburbs, so they put in the monorail a hundred feet off the ground. Developers built up—higher buildings, better views, enclosed access to the monorail. If you have enough money, you can spend your whole life a hundred feet above everything.

"And if you don't . . ." He shrugs and gestures around us. "You live in the underground."

# 04:19:32:58

We've barely gone a block and a half when a siren goes off.

The screech of it is almost deafening.

But Barclay's reaction is worse.

He grabs my arm, fingers biting into my skin, and his voice comes out low but urgent. Above him, I hear something that sounds like a helicopter in the distance. "I need you to run," Barclay says.

And I do. We both take off, Barclay with his death grip still on my arm as he pulls me to keep up with him. I match him step for step, running at full speed, my lungs and muscles burning from the strain, as the sirens wail and spotlights flood the alleyways around us.

I don't know what I'm running from—what *we're* running from—but I can guess. Either someone has seen us, which is unlikely, or someone has reported something else. It doesn't matter, though—if we're caught by law enforcement, we'll be turned over to IA and we're as good as dead.

But I'll be damned if we're going to get caught by accident. Not when so many people need us.

We take a left, then a right, and then two more lefts in a row. We run behind a building and across a lawn. I'm concentrating so hard on keeping up with Barclay that I can't be sure at all where we're going. I'm just hoping we can get somewhere before I collapse from exhaustion.

When we're about to turn down an alley, Barclay grabs me and pulls me against him, and we crouch behind a Dumpster. A split second later, a floodlight shines down on the alley in front of us. We're still surrounded by the darkness, but only an inch or two separates us from the light.

I scrunch my knees closer to my body, and my chest heaves as I try to catch my breath, to rest while I have the chance. I count the seconds as the light moves up the alley and then back toward us. Next to me, Barclay's breaths are as heavy as mine, and he's close enough that I can feel the pumping of his heart through the warmth of his skin.

Barclay leans into my ear, his lips tickling my skin. "There's a diner with good coffee two streets over," he says, and I manage to hear him despite the continued wailing of the sirens and the motor of the helicopter.

# 04:18:47:12

We wait almost fifteen more seconds, then the spotlight moves on. Barclay darts up and runs down the alley. I follow on his heels.

When we make it into the diner, we slow down like two normal people. There's a handful of patrons inside. None of them look over when we come in. As the door jingles shut, I've never been so happy to be inside a crumbling diner in a shady part of town. Barclay heads up to the counter to order and I hang back.

Standing still, with the sirens muffled, all I can feel is my pulse pounding through my body. I've never run from the cops before, not even because a party got busted up or anything. It's not exactly something I want to ever experience again.

But I can't help feeling like this is what I have to look forward to.

It makes me wonder where Ben is, what he's doing right now, if he's running constantly, if he's hiding in the shadows, breathing quietly and looking over his shoulder to make sure that no one's behind him.

I think of how we held each other the night Elijah got shot—the night it rained and Ben came to my house with blood on his clothes. The world might have been ending, but it didn't feel that bad because we had each other. It doesn't feel right that this time we're alone. It almost makes me mad, not at Ben, but just . . . mad at the world. Ben, my dad, Alex—it isn't fair how much I miss them or that they've left me here to carry this burden alone.

Dizziness makes me sway. If I don't sit down soon, my legs are going to give out.

"That was good," Barclay says as we slide into a booth to sit and wait. "I didn't think you'd be able to keep up," he says, gesturing outside.

"I'm pretty fast, for a girl." I ignore the way the sweat is cooling on my skin.

He smiles, and I laugh a little, though I don't know how I'm able to. The adrenaline running through my body makes me feel light and a little giddy now that I don't need it.

It's not like we're out of danger—I know that—but for the moment we're safe.

"No, I'm serious, Tenner," Barclay says. He's stone-faced, his skin shiny with sweat, his eyes ocean blue. But it's his voice that makes me shiver. It sounds like truth. "You're good at this."

I think of what my dad would say about that, and smile. Barclay and I both know we have to be good at this. We know what the stakes are. If we aren't *good*, people will die.

"What is *this*?" I say, even though I know.

"I'm trying to compliment you," Barclay says. "Can't you just say thanks?"

I shake my head. "Too stubborn to accept compliments."

The waitress comes and brings us two cups of coffee and a slice of the pumpkin pie to share, on the house. Her eyes are on Barclay the entire time she talks, and I'm pretty sure the pie is for him.

I'm about to comment on it once she's gone, but Barclay's face loses its humor and he leans closer to me. "After this is over, you should think about joining IA."

I don't know what to say, so I just stare back at him.

"You wouldn't necessarily have to live here," he says, cracking a smile. "IA has a presence in almost every universe."

I bite my lip. It isn't about moving to Prima, not that I have any desire to do that, either. But joining IA is something I've never thought about. I didn't realize it was an option, but I can't think of a single reason I'd want to. The IA is threatening Ben, and *me*, pretty violently. Why would I ever want to be a part of that?

I don't say that out loud. Because for whatever reason, IA means something to Barclay.

But he's waiting for me to say something. "It's just, with all the corruption," I say, carefully. "How can *you* even want to be part of IA anymore?"

"It wasn't always corrupt, and that's why we're doing this," he says, taking a sip of his coffee. "Just think about it. You'd make a good agent. I'd help you."

I stare into the black abyss that is my coffee, and I wonder what Alex would say about this—if he'd jump at the chance to run around the multiverse and fight the worst kind of bad guys. With how smart he was and how hard he worked, Alex would have made a great agent.

"One of the first things I learned was observational survival," Barclay says.

I dump a packet of sugar into my coffee. "Care to elaborate?"

His eyes don't leave mine, not even for a second, and he says, "There are twelve people in this place, counting us. Six are other diners, then there's the waitress, two line cooks, and a manager in the back office. He's probably got a gun tucked in a safe, but the biggest threat is the guy alone in the booth behind me. He's not much bigger than I am, but his worn-out boots are military issue and he's still sporting the standard army haircut. He's probably not a soldier anymore, but he looks like he wishes he was.

"But no one in this place is even close to being as dangerous as you and me. We could take everyone out without a problem if we needed to." He pauses, searching for something in my face. "You do it sometimes too. You analyze the situation and calculate the best escape routes and chances of survival. I don't know if your dad taught you or if it's some kind of instinct, but being aware of your surroundings is the most important thing anyone can ever teach you in this line of work."

Barclay leans back against his seat as I think about his words. I can't actually remember my dad ever specifically telling me to analyze a room, but I know he used to do it all the time. And I know I do it—especially when I think there's going to be trouble.

But I didn't do it when we walked in here. I skimmed the patrons to see if there were any cops, but that was it. If we did have trouble, it would be too late.

Barclay nods. "Tomorrow, when we're separated, analyze every situation you're in. Always know who else is around you, who's likely to be the biggest threat, what your escape route would be if you needed one."

I nod. I'm not exactly looking forward to being anywhere without him right now.

"Think of it like a chess game."

"Stay at least one step ahead of my opponent?" I ask with a smile. Even though it's not funny.

"Absolutely," Barclay says. "We have to win."

I'm not as confident as he is, mostly because I wasn't a very good chess player.

But also because this isn't a game, and I have a lot to lose.

# 04:18:12:49

After we leave the diner, I follow Barclay to the subway. The sirens are off, and there are no helicopters or spotlights to worry about.

I look back. In the window, the pink lights that read HOT COFFEE flicker. For a moment, surrounded by coffee, Barclay, and the illusion of normalcy, I had felt almost calm, like I wasn't wanted by IA or in a strange different world—like I wasn't alone.

Then it hits me that this is it. I need to find Ben.

It's not that he can bring me back from the dead and heal my scars, it's not that he can hack into a computer system and change my class schedule, and it's not even that he can kiss me breathless.

It's that I want to go to another diner. I want to go inside, slide into an uncomfortable booth, grab a cup of bad coffee, and split a piece of pie. I want to watch the waitress flirt with the guy I'm with and then laugh about it when she leaves.

And I want that guy to be Ben.

I turn to Barclay. He's got his hat on and his hands shoved in his pockets, and he hasn't noticed yet that I'm not right behind him. I could probably add up the minutes we've been forced to spend together and it would be less than a full day, and here I've thrown my future and my life into his hands.

And right now, it's possible that *this* moment is the one that says there's no turning back—the one that changes everything forever.

Because I know exactly what I'm fighting for.

# 04:18:11:20

I keep close to Barclay as we walk underneath the bridge and past a row of bars and restaurants. The graffiti isn't as bad, and neither is the smell, but I still wouldn't want to be alone.

There's a bodega on the corner and some store called Kings Superhero Supply, and Barclay turns down a dark and sleepy side street where there are rows of old townhouses. He leads me to the last building on the block, and I follow him around it to a side door.

"Whose house is this?" I ask when he reaches under the mat and grabs a key.

"Relax, Tenner." Barclay chuckles as he slides the key into the back door. He jiggles it a little and the door pops open. "This is my mother's old house. No one will be here."

He holds the door open for me and I follow him inside.

The house looks lived in, but it's quiet. In the living room, the tan rug is plush and soft and the light-blue couches look comfortable. There's a flat-screen TV on one wall, like the one Barclay has in his apartment, and a row of bookshelves on another. I'm surprised by how normal it all seems. This is a house I could have grown up in.

I'm just about to sit down on one of the couches and rest my legs when I hear something. It sounds like the ceiling just creaked, the way it would if someone were upstairs.

I freeze and look at Barclay, who holds up one finger and signals for me to follow him. We move through the living room to the kitchen. Barclay grabs a stainless-steel pan from the counter and we crouch behind the island in the center of the kitchen. He holds the pan at an angle where we can see a distorted image of the stairs.

We'll be able to see whoever it is before they come down.

We wait in silence, and I have a moment to wonder if we actually heard anything at all, when I spot something reflected in the pan. I see the sneakers and the black leggings first, and I'm sure it's a woman.

And she has a gun.

# 04:18:09:04

I suck in a breath and wonder what could possibly go wrong next when Barclay leans in to get a better look and then shakes his head.

"Hayley," Barclay says, standing up. "You scared the crap out of me."

I stand up as well, because the last thing we need to do is startle her while she's holding a gun. Better to lay our cards on the table up front.

"I scared you?" she says, not lowering her gun. "You just broke into my house!"

"You're not supposed to be here," Barclay says. "I thought you were on assignment."

"I got back this morning. What's your excuse?" Then she looks at me. She's pretty, with dark caramel skin, dark eyes with long eyelashes, and shoulder-length black hair. Whatever she sees in my face, she forms some kind of opinion because she adds, "Never mind."

Barclay doesn't tell her who I am.

But we might not need an introduction because she looks at

him and says, "I can't believe you're trying to bring this down on me."

"Hayley, I—"

"I don't even want to hear any of your sorry-ass excuses," she says, holding up a hand. "Let me pack a bag. I'll spend the night at the office. I don't want any part of whatever this is."

When she disappears upstairs, Barclay relaxes. "Don't worry, we can trust her."

I don't say anything, and he must not think I'm convinced.

"Hayley was a year ahead of me at North Point. Right now she's still stuck doing a lot of analyst work, and some shadowing with a mentor."

I don't ask him who she is to him, but he tells me anyway.

"We dated a few times, but you know, it just didn't work." He sounds a little embarrassed about it, and I wonder if he's still carrying a torch for her, especially if she's living in his mother's house. But it's not really my business, and we've got more important things going on than trying to fix Barclay's nonexistent love life. It's not like Ben and I are ever going to go out with Barclay and his girlfriend on some kind of double date.

"How much does she know?" I ask instead, since that's the important question.

Barclay shakes his head. "Not much. I told her about some of it, about Eric and about Ben and the human trafficking. About you."

"That sounds like all of it," I say.

"No, I mean, she knows the backstory, but she doesn't know anything about what we're planning." He opens the fridge. "It's not that I don't trust her, it's more that I don't want her to go down if . . ."

He doesn't finish the thought, but he doesn't need to. He's protecting her in case we don't make it.

He offers me a beer, but I shake my head. That's the last thing I need tonight.

Hayley comes downstairs again, this time with a duffel bag slung over her shoulder. She looks at Barclay, her mouth open to speak, but then turns to me. "Make sure he calls me if he gets into a jam."

I don't know what constitutes a jam—I mean, a couple of guys from IA were searching his house today. Does that count? But I just nod. There may come a time when we need her help whether Barclay wants her involved or not.

She seems satisfied with our girl moment and looks back to Barclay. "Return Tomas's calls, will you? He's harassing me about it."

She doesn't wait for a response, she just heads out through the kitchen.

"I've got nothing to say to him," Barclay says. Then he adds, "Don't work yourself too hard," and Hayley is out the door.

"You don't talk to your brother?" I ask.

Barclay shrugs, but the way his body tenses and the corners of his mouth turn down a little, I can tell there are some serious bad feelings there. "If Tomas had his way, we'd shut down interverse travel completely, heal up the soft spots, and destroy anything that can be used to open a portal."

"Shut down IA? Why?" I ask, before the second half of what he just said hits me. "Wait, you can heal up the soft spots? How?"

"I'm not a scientist, Tenner," he says, taking a deep swig from his beer. "I don't exactly know how he plans to heal all the soft spots, but he thinks there's a way to do it." He gestures to the kitchen. "Come here."

I do, but I'm not about to let this line of questioning drop. "But if we could heal the soft spot in San Diego, we could keep people from being abducted."

Barclay shakes his head. "As I understand it, it's not that simple. It wouldn't be a viable long-term solution for anyone unless we completely stopped interverse travel."

I don't care if we stop interverse travel, but I say, "If we get through this thing, I want to talk to your brother. I want to know what we can do to protect ourselves."

Barclay opens his mouth, and from the look on his face I know he's about to say something snarky that's going to piss me off, but then he surprises me, and his face changes a little. It softens, like he's actually thinking about what it's like to be in my shoes for once.

"You help me get through this, and I'll make sure you meet and talk to anyone you want to," he says. "You know, there have got to be people who can help with all the rebuilding and the resources. All that."

My shoulders relax, and I feel so much lighter, I'm almost dizzy with relief. With Prima's help, my world could eventually go back to normal. We could have food and medication and clean water. We could get electricity back up and the roads paved. Jared could go back to school and polo practice. Cecily could go back to cheerleading and asking obscure questions in science class. The enormity of hope that swells inside me makes my eyes water, and I look down at the wood floor to keep my emotions to myself.

After a deep breath, I look up to see Barclay sitting at the kitchen table. He lays out the medical supplies in front of him, then looks up and nods toward a chair. "Here."

I don't have a good feeling about this.

I sit across from him and he takes my left wrist in his hand and swabs it with rubbing alcohol. "I promise to make this as painless as possible, but it's going to hurt. Probably a lot."

I swallow the urge to pull my hand back. "Please tell me I'm going to get a better explanation than *that*."

He smirks. "You and the humor." He pulls something small out of his pocket. At first glance it looks like a transparent piece of paper, but on closer inspection, I can see something in it, something like digital code, and that's when I realize it's a microchip. He opens up the plastic casing and holds it close enough so I can see it. "This is a watch. It's high tech, undetectable without an MRI or a body scan, and it can be programmed with multiple alarms and even a countdown."

I don't ask what he's going to program it with. I know the answer. If I want to avoid the cameras in prison, it's going to be infinitely easier if I have a watch or some kind of stopwatch to keep track of the time.

I also know the answer to the question I do ask. I'm hoping I'm wrong. "And where does it go?"

"I have to insert it underneath your skin."

Not wrong at all.

I look at the microchip again. This little thing is how I'll be able to time everything. How I'll be able to keep track of things. This might be the difference between getting out alive and getting killed. Which I guess is why I can stand to let Barclay perform minor surgery and insert it under my skin.

"I've programmed it so it will beep once at the minute mark and the numbers will light up five seconds before the EMP is scheduled to go off," Barclay continues. I swallow hard. The EMP—an electromagnetic pulse—will shut off the power, which will turn off all the security cameras and give me a good head start. "Then it'll convert to a stopwatch. It'll look like you have green glowing numbers under your skin."

"That sounds awesome," I say. I do need a way to keep track of time, but I don't exactly want some microchip inserted under my skin. "And the EMP won't affect it?"

"Nope. EMP-proof."

I didn't know that was possible, but Prima is obviously doing some pretty amazing things where technology is concerned. "Why does something like this even exist?"

"Back when IA first started, you couldn't take metal through the portals. The hydrochloradneum shots hadn't been perfected, and skin exposed to metal would have a bad reaction. But a watch was a must-have. No one had a quantum charger, and the portals were opened and closed through IA headquarters in New Prima. Anyone who went through had to be back at the extraction point by the deadline or they were assumed lost."

It makes sense, then, why this is important, although I can't imagine I'd be about to have it surgically put under my skin if it was just for the sake of adventuring into the unknown multiverse.

I tilt my head to the side until my neck cracks and I grit my teeth. I'm going to need all the help I can get. I look at Barclay and the metal instrument in his hand—it looks like a laser pen.

Somehow, I'm sure this is going to be pretty awful.

I conjure up an image of Cecily the time she dragged me out to Scripps Pier. I'd been in one of my "moods," as she calls them—basically I was pissed off at the world and maybe even a little depressed. So she made me get up at sunrise and drove me to the beach to try to brainwash me with her positive thinking. She went on about the golden sky, the smell of salt water, the sound of the waves, and the magic in the air. The sunlight lit up her hair like some kind of strange white halo, and she screamed out into the ocean, yelling at the universe like it might change something. Then she made me do it too.

She was right in the way that only Cecily could be. Maybe the world was still the same after I screamed my problems away, but when we walked off the pier, I was slightly different—lighter, somehow.

And then I think of Ben. He sat next to me in those few weeks of APEL, close enough that sometimes our arms brushed against each other. Whenever I looked at his face, those dark eyes were glancing back at me from behind his brown curls, and he'd offer me a sly sort of half smile, like we were both in on a secret. And I suppose we were.

I need to save them.

And that's what I hold on to when I brace myself and say to Barclay, "Do it."

# 04:11:47:08

**B**arclay makes me spend most of the evening reciting prison-break plans back to him. Every time I make a mistake, he has me start over.

It's a little like when my dad quizzed me on spelling words when I was in third grade, only a lot more intense. Barclay would make a tyrannical parent.

When I finally get it all right, I'm dismissed for bed. Wearing a pair of Barclay's sweatpants and an oversize T-shirt, I lie in his childhood bed and stare at the ceiling.

I try to sleep, but instead, my mind wanders and I think of Ben.

I think of how he walked into my AP English class, sat down next to me, and turned out to be a lot smarter than I thought he was.

*"So your perfect proposal, what would it be?"*

*"I don't know. It would just be the two of us, and I guess I'd want him to say something honest, not overly romantic, not something that would make a great story to tell his friends. I'd just want him to lean over . . ." As I say it, I lean slightly toward Ben, close*

*enough that I can feel the warmth of his body radiating into the empty space between us, and drop the volume of my voice. ". . . and say, 'Janelle Tenner, fucking marry me.'"*

I wonder what he's doing right at this moment—if he's lying in bed and remembering APEL and Charles Dickens and me dropping the F-bomb in the middle of class. I wonder if he's scared like I am.

But mostly, I wonder where he is.

I know that's not going to get me anywhere except feeling sorry for myself, so I shut my eyes and will myself to fall asleep. It's dark, cool, comfortable, and quiet, the noise from the streets below blocked out by the thrum of the fan. And I'm exhausted. Even my hips hurt.

But the minutes just tick by and I can't make myself lose consciousness.

When I can't stand it anymore, I get out of bed and head to the living room. From the doorway, I can see Barclay on the couch, wrapped up in a comforter, his eyes on the TV.

"What are you watching?" I ask.

He flinches and there's a harsh intake of breath. Apparently, I surprised him.

"What's wrong?" Barclay asks, sitting up. His blanket slips and reveals his bare chest. I can see the curve of each of his muscles. It makes me think of when I was pressed against him, and heat floods my face.

"Nothing," I say, looking away. I'm not sure why I'm so embarrassed. "I just feel restless."

He nods and leans back. "I always get that way before a big mission."

"Really?" It's not easy for me to see him as nervous or sleepless.

"How about some tea?" he asks, turning off the TV. "That always helps me."

"Sure," I say, even though it's hard to imagine Barclay drinking tea. He seems more like the sports drink kind of guy.

But he heads into the kitchen like hot tea is a normal thing.

For the millionth time I wonder what I'm doing here and how so much has managed to change in my life since that day I died on Highway 101 next to Torrey Pines Beach. How did I go from being just an average teenager with messed-up parents, scheduling issues, and a mean-girl problem to who I am now? I'm someone else now—someone who's traveled through portals, watched people disappear, seen worlds that aren't my own—someone who has four days to break open a human-trafficking ring that spans multiple universes, or die trying.

It doesn't feel like it should be possible.

"Did I ever tell you about my first assignment with IA?" Barclay asks when he comes out of the kitchen with two mugs. He hands me one and I can smell the cinnamon from the tea. It's amazing.

"I was just a newbie," Barclay says. "I'd just graduated top of my class from North Point—which is like your West Point. My assignment was supposed to essentially just be research."

Barclay takes a sip of his tea. I take a sip of mine. It's like drinking warm liquid cinnamon. I smile at him.

"This assignment, my first mission," Barclay says. "It was essentially a test. I had to research an area that had reported interversal disturbances—"

"English, please?" My tone comes out a little sharper than I intended. So I add, "You know, since I don't know a lot of this stuff."

"You know a lot more than you give yourself credit for," he says, but he explains anyway. "Basically it's a natural phenomenon that could be caused by instability in another universe. I had to research events that had been reported, find one I wanted to take on, go in and investigate what was happening, decide what might be causing it, and then write up a report proposing the action that needed to be taken. If I did well, I'd be given a mentor and be inducted into the IA training program. If I sucked, then they'd tell me to go find a different career path. Everyone who falls in the middle gets stuck with desk duty and paper pushing.

"I wasn't about to blow my chance in IA or end up as a paper pusher."

"Shocking," I say. Clearly anyone who's ever met Barclay knows he's an ambitious guy.

He smirks. "Right, so when I was researching, I found that on Earth 16942 there were rips in the fabric of the universe—"

"Rips?" I don't ask about Earth 16942, because that will just open up a million other questions I have about how many earths there are and how Barclay seems to know so much about each of them. I'll never sleep if we get on that topic.

Barclay adjusts his position. "Okay, so with this," he says as he picks up his quantum charger, "I can program a destination and open a portal. Portals are like wormholes that allow people or objects to pass through from one world to another. It doesn't matter how far apart the universes are, people can move through a portal easily."

I think of Ben and how *not* easy it was for him to get home.

"Some universes have soft spots like the one in San Diego," he explains. "But other universes have what we call pressure points, which are areas where the veil between two worlds is so thin that sometimes it overlaps. Which can cause disturbances."

"Disturbances?" I ask. I'm assuming the distance between universes is based on the fact that they started as parallel and separated when people in the different universes made different decisions. A "close" universe would be one that was really similar.

"It could be anything like weird weather or earthquakes, or there have even been cases where someone or something accidentally slipped through the veil and ended up in another universe," Barclay says.

"Like some poor guy could be driving his car and suddenly be in a completely other universe and not know it?" I can't imagine how scary that would be. At least Ben knew he went through a portal.

"Like some poor guy could drive home for dinner, show up at his house, and he's got two sons instead of three daughters, and another version of himself is sitting at the table."

I raise my eyebrows, and Barclay nods. "It was a case I read about at North Point. The veil had gotten so thin that there was a very small point where it actually intersected and sometimes people would just slip right through.

"Anyway, in my case, the disturbances were bad electrical storms, and witnesses had reported that the storms had a magnetic pull. Like this one woman was washing dishes when the storm rolled in. She had her kitchen window open, and the magnetic pull was so strong that all of her metal silverware was yanked from the sink, through the window, and up into the storm."

"Creepy." I have a talent for understatement, but it makes Barclay smile.

As he talks about the intricacies of electrical storms and a lot of science that goes over my head, I drink my tea and study the way his face has changed. He's still smiling, and his eyes are alive with the excitement of the story. This is the first conversation we've ever had where I haven't wanted to punch him and he hasn't been arguing with me about something.

"So what was causing the storms?" I ask when I can get a word in.

"Well, that's just the thing. The magnetism was being caused by field distortions between universes, which always means some powerful science at work."

I don't exactly grasp what Barclay is talking about. I probably won't ever grasp it. His understanding of the natural world is just way different than mine. But I get the important thing—this was a man-made event, not something that was just happening on its own.

"So who was the bad guy?" I ask. Because isn't it always about a bad guy?

"I did some research and a lot of math to trace the magnetism back to this man who was essentially a reclusive mad scientist working out of his garage," Barclay says. "He was trying to contact his doubles in all the other universes. We think he had some kind of plan for them all to work on together, but he never got that far."

I can't help laughing at the image of Barclay apprehending this guy without a gun or credentials. "What did IA say? I mean, they essentially let you take on a real case rather than just some research assignment."

He nods. "That's how I am where I am, baby."

Oh yeah, the smugness is back and it's bad. "Seriously, what did they do?"

The smile falls a little. "They gave me Eric as a mentor and let me tag along on all his assignments. With him I was in the middle of all the biggest cases."

"He was a big agent?" I ask, trying—and failing—not to think about the fact that he had a lot more experience than we do, that he'd been trained to handle people like human traffickers and I'm not. And now he's dead and we might be next.

"The biggest," Barclay says, running a hand through his hair. "He was a legend, the kind of guy who gets a monument named after him for all the shit he's accomplished."

"So IA has high hopes for you then?" I'm trying to get him in a better mood. Smug Barclay is slightly better than depressed Barclay.

But he doesn't bite. "They might have had at one point. I doubt now."

I roll my eyes. "I didn't realize this was a pity party." Please, like I'm not in a worse position than he is. I'm the one on the hit list.

Barclay is quiet for a second. He sets his empty mug on the coffee table, and while he's looking down, he says in a quiet voice, "There's a monument built for Clyde Tolson. He's the guy who founded IA. It's near here. I used to walk by it every day on my way to school when I was a little kid.

"He accomplished so much, Tenner. For the world, not just Prima. I mean, the whole multiverse is different because of what he discovered and because of the legacy he left behind. Eric was on track for that. He'd made an impact."

"I get it," I say. And I do. I don't exactly have dreams like Barclay—I don't even know what I want to do with my life. But I want to have an impact, and I get *that*.

I reach for Barclay's hand and give it a squeeze. "You're doing the right thing *right now*. It's hard, and it sucks—it's even dangerous—but you're doing it anyway. That counts for something. Remember that."

He nods, and I feel him squeeze my hand back. Slowly, a devilish smile spreads across his face. Then he glances up at me. "Think if we pull this off, it'll get me a monument?"

I don't say my first thought. Instead, I smile back and say, "This is epic monument-style shit we're in."

But what I think is, *I just want to make it out alive.*

# 04:10:01:45

Later, after the tea has made my arms and chest feel heavy, I leave Barclay on the couch and get back into bed.

I think of Ben and Cecily and how different things were when the three of us and Alex were a tetrarchy in AP Physics. After that first lab where Cecily made Ben carry everything out to the field and answer all her questions to make sure he was smart enough to work with us, we sat at our back table, ate Cecily's candy, and listened to the science that's the foundation for what I'm living through right now. Science that brought Ben and me together.

I picture Cecily, her blond ponytail swinging with the breeze, her hands on her hips. *"Okay, I have one more question, and it's the most important one."*

Ben, rubbing his hands together like he's getting ready. *"Hit me."*

*"Who's your favorite superhero?"*

*"That's easy. Wonder Woman. A girl saving a guy is hot."*

I saved him when we were ten. Last fall we saved each other. I wonder who's going to do the saving this time around. I say a silent prayer for both of us, and then I lie back and close my eyes.

In less than ten hours, I'll be at IA headquarters, and they'll take me to prison.

In less than twenty-four, I'll be trying to break out.

# 04:01:00:00

**W**hen the clock radio comes on in the morning, I get up and turn it off without hesitation. I pull on my clothes and pack my backpack.

In the living room, Barclay is waiting for me. He has a fire going in the fireplace, and when he sees me, he hands me some kind of protein bar. "It's gross, but it will keep you from getting hungry."

I nod and hand him my backpack. He's warned me against eating any of the food they give me once I'm in the prison. He doesn't think they'll actually lace my food with drugs, but he knows they've done it before to try to get people talking or even just to keep them subdued.

I carefully open the protein bar, tearing the wrapper down the seam.

Barclay is going to leave my backpack here. He'll take me in to IA headquarters and stay with me as long as he can. At some point, he'll be dismissed and head to the office. He'll file some paperwork about where he found me and what deal we made.

It will all be lies.

When the day is over he'll come back here, pick up my backpack and the portable EMP that he has. He'll go to eat at a diner near the prison. He's already paid off the prison doctor so she'll make herself scarce when the time comes. Then he'll drive to our rendezvous point to wait for us.

Because of the watch, he'll be able to track my location in the prison. He'll hack into the prison mainframe and unlock my door just before the EMP goes off.

And the rest will be left to me.

He's set everything up, and he'll be waiting for me. But on the inside, I'll be alone.

"Are you afraid?" he asks.

I am.

I would be an idiot if I wasn't. I know how much is at stake: Ben and his family's lives and Cecily's freedom and the freedom of who knows how many other people who, like Renee Adams, have gotten pulled from their world. And I know this is the hardest thing I might ever have to do.

When we needed to stop Wave Function Collapse, it was just one thing. Sure it would have ended the world, but it was just one person who was opening unstable portals. That's what we had to stop.

This is different. There are so many variables.

But I don't say any of that.

Instead I think about the time when I was a little girl, maybe four or five, and my parents took us to visit my dad's parents in Ohio. They had a basement that was only partially finished where they did the laundry. It was dark and damp, and it smelled weird. It terrified me. I didn't ever want to go down there. I was too afraid.

My dad told me fear was just an emotion, something we felt when we thought someone or something was dangerous. He said it was as empty as the air, and the only way to deal with it was to confront the danger with a plan to minimize it.

He asked me what about the basement I thought was dangerous. Like any other five-year-old I was afraid there was some kind of monster down there, and I told him that. He gave me his dad's old baseball bat and told me that one good swing would take down even the worst monster. I took a few practice swings, and then he made me walk every inch of that basement, bat in hand, until I wasn't afraid anymore.

Later, when I was older, Alex asked him what kind of parenting philosophy he subscribed to, sending his daughter into the basement with a baseball bat to fight off anything dangerous.

Dad told us it was the same thing he told guys on the job. He'd been with the Bureau a long time, and he'd seen too many guys get injured or lose their lives. And he chalked most of those incidents up to a guy's inability to control his fears.

I find Barclay's blue eyes, and as much as he pisses me off sometimes, I know why he's a good agent. I know why I like him—and I do like him despite whatever I thought before. He doesn't get scared. Things might scare him initially, sure, but he comes up with a plan, and he gets the job done. It makes me wish he did work for my dad.

And because he'll get it, I tell him the truth. "Fear kills swifter than bullets. My dad said that."

"I liked your dad," Barclay says with a nod.

I can't help but smile. Everyone liked my dad, but the more I get to know Barclay, the more I think my dad would have liked him, too.

"Let's go," Barclay says.

I take one last look at the blueprints burning in the fireplace, and I follow him out to the backyard.

I hold my hands in front of me, and Barclay fastens the plastic restraints around my wrists. Then he pulls out his quantum charger and I hear the electronic sound of the portal powering up.

And there it is—a huge pool of black ink standing in front of me. The smell of salt water, open space, and endless possibility emanates from it, and cool air moves over my skin. I wonder if I'll ever get to a point where these things lose their magic and just seem mundane.

"Try to relax this time," Barclay says. He holds on to my restraints with one hand and puts the other on my back, and together we step through the portal.

This time I don't hold my breath. Cool air moves through my lungs, and I can feel it move through my body. For a second, I feel frozen from the inside out, then heat replaces the cold, and my extremities tingle with the sensation.

And then we're stepping out of the portal on concrete. I start to lose my balance, but Barclay pulls me next to him and keeps me on my feet.

"Here we are," he says. "IA headquarters."

In front of us are a dozen concrete steps, leading up to a tall glass skyscraper. This one is simpler—a big glass rectangle rather than the intricate designs I've seen on the others—yet it's more impressive. Rather than having a cool crystalline finish, the glass looks like someone painted it in oil. From one angle, it makes the building look dark, but when the sun hits it a certain way, it's a rainbow of color.

Barclay must sense what I'm looking at. "That's the hydro-chloradneum that shields the building," he says. "It's in the foundation and the glass so that no one can portal inside."

Which means once I'm inside, there's no one who can save me.

I take the first two stairs, Barclay at my side, and I glance back at what I'm leaving behind. The crystalline city of upscale Prima life, and below that the dark smog clouds hiding the underground beneath us.

I remember what Barclay said—about people living their whole lives a hundred feet off the ground.

He tugs on me a little, and I know it's time to go. We head up the stairs, Barclay pulling me by my restraints for effect. Right before we reach the doors, he whispers: "Try not to trip the alarm."

He doesn't have to specify that he's talking about tonight. I roll my eyes. "Obviously."

"No, I forgot to tell you. If you trip the alarm and they know you're headed for the sewers, they can use the flush system."

"Fantastic," I hiss. One more thing to worry about. "So we'll be flooded and drown."

Barclay shakes his head. "No. The flush system is fire."

# 04:00:43:06

With its marble floors and granite surfaces, the lobby of IA looks like we could be in any upscale corporate building. The only difference is the airport-style security complete with body scans, metal detectors, X-ray machines, and armed guards.

The watch is supposed to be undetectable by a body scan, but Barclay isn't a hundred percent sure if it actually will be. We're hoping someone in IA wants me bad enough that no one will make me wait in line.

Barclay pulls me past the civilians waiting to get through security and we approach one of the guards. "I have a code eleven nineteen," he says.

I keep my head down, and I imagine what this was like for Ben and Cecily—someone restraining them and taking them somewhere they didn't belong.

The security guard hesitates. "The director is out of the office for an emergency meeting."

"Surely someone can handle an eleven-nineteen." The

condescension practically drips off Barclay's voice. If I didn't know the plan, I wouldn't know that we'd hit a snag. He was expecting the director—and looking forward to it. The director's reaction to me might tell us a little about where his loyalties lie.

The guard radios to someone, repeating the code.

We're in the enemy's headquarters. Any of these people could want Ben dead, or at least be involved in the human-trafficking ring. Any of these people could know where Cecily is. As a result, I'm hyperaware of my blood as my heart pumps it through my veins.

"The deputy director will see you," the guard says, and he lets Barclay pull me under the security rope, and two armed guards accompany us to the elevator.

I glance at Barclay to gauge whether that's good or bad for us, but his attention is somewhere else. On a tall blonde walking toward us. She's attractive, probably in her thirties, and for a split second I want to elbow him—it's not exactly like we have time for him to take a mental detour and stare at some hot woman. But then I see she's flanked by several broad-shouldered men in matching black suits and black ties. At first they look like they could be businessmen who work out, but as they get closer to us, I can see the clear earpieces they're wearing, and the way their left pant legs bulge over the backup guns strapped to their ankles. They're security guards disguised as suits.

Whoever she is, she's obviously worth paying attention to.

"Taylor," the blonde says, her voice husky, like she smokes too much or works as a lounge singer. "I heard you were out of the office. How are you?"

Barclay smiles as she approaches us. "Governor, it's lovely to see you as always."

I stifle the urge to start coughing. *She's* the governor? I examine her a little more closely. With long hair, smooth skin, and perfectly sculpted facial features, she looks more like a distinguished supermodel.

"What are your plans for lunch?" the governor asks. "You must let me take you to the new café at the top of the tower. It's supposed to be the best air in the city."

"I would be honored, Governor," Barclay says, and I can tell he means it. I'm not sure if it's because he respects her or if he just thinks she's hot. Either way, I'm annoyed. I'm going to be in prison and he'll be on a lunch date enjoying the "best air in the city"—how is that fair?

"Splendid," she says, reaching out to grasp his free hand. That's when I notice her hands. They're thin, wrinkled, and bony with loose skin—hands that belong to a sixty-, seventy-, maybe even eighty-year-old woman. Hands that don't match the rest of her. She's either had extensive plastic surgery or she's some kind of ageless vampire, and let's just say I know which is the more likely possibility.

She's like some creepy old cougar.

And she's hitting on Barclay.

She leans into him and lowers her voice, but I still manage to hear her. "I'd like to do something for Eric's family, and I was hoping to run it by you."

I resist the urge to roll my eyes as Barclay nods. Clearly, he respects her. Creepy old hands aside, she must deserve it.

"Gentlemen," she says as she pulls back. "Keep up the good

work as always. We appreciate everything you do for our fine city."

And then she's gone.

I bite my lip and watch as the glowing numbers above the elevator descend toward the lobby floor. The elevator dings and opens, and all four of us crowd inside.

# 04:00:42:03

Once the doors close, one of the security guards claps Barclay on the shoulder. "Damn, Wonder Boy, lunch with the governor."

Barclay shrugs, and each guard offers his two cents about Barclay and the governor's lunch plans. It's obvious they're jealous and trying to make him uncomfortable. I don't think it's working—after all, we have a lot more to worry about.

Suddenly Barclay clears his throat. "She introduced herself to me after my first mission." And here I thought he was going to be typical Barclay, just shrug and be silent and let everyone come to their own conclusion. I think this is for my benefit. "She and Eric used to have lunch periodically . . ."

His voice trails off, and the guards each add their condolences about Agent Eric Brandt and fall silent.

The elevator climbs and no one says a word. Like a weight, the gravity of the moment sinks deep into my bones. This is life or death. Everything that comes next depends on what happens right now.

The higher we rise, the more afraid I feel.

I think of my dad. I picture the strong lines in his face, the wrinkles in his forehead and at the corners of his eyes, his hair starting to thin and speckled with gray, his five o'clock shadow. I remember how serious he was when he looked up, his eyes meeting mine.

*Fear kills swifter than bullets.*

I repeat it to myself like some kind of mantra. Because I need to stay strong to get through this. We have so many plans riding on what happens right now.

The elevator dings again at the twenty-seventh floor and the doors open. The armed guards exit first and wait for us, then the four of us walk down the hallway.

I can do this. Not just because I have to but because I am my father's daughter, and I'm not going to give up on the people I care about.

We pass three offices before we reach the double doors at the end. One of the guards opens them, and all four of us move inside. The carpet is gray and looks relatively new, maybe only a year old.

I look up.

And say out loud, "You've got to be kidding me."

Barclay coughs and then says, "Deputy Director, I have an eleven-nineteen. This is Janelle Tenner, subject 2348739 from Earth 23984. She's surrendered herself to IA custody in connection with case BM132."

That's not really who I am, subject whatever from Earth 23984, but we're still playing the game that's supposed to keep my family safe.

"Also," Barclay adds, "she's familiar with your double in her world."

I look at Barclay—I don't care where we are. I can't believe he managed to leave out this detail. But he's looking straight ahead, eyes on the deputy director.

Who is none other than Struz.

# 04:00:39:53

I've known Ryan Struzinski, aka Struz, for as long as I can remember. He grew up in Orange County, went to school at USC, then put in for the FBI as soon as he graduated. He passed the tests with flying colors and went to work as an analyst for my dad in San Diego.

I think it took a week before my dad brought him home and adopted him as part of the family.

When I was fourteen Struz and my dad were part of a Joint Terrorism Task Force going after a group of extremists who were suspected of terrorist activity. I only know some of the details because Struz took a bullet and was laid up and out of the field for a few weeks. He spent those weeks on my living-room couch babysitting Jared and me while our dad was undercover. We ate ice cream for dinner, watched R-rated movies, and stayed up until two in the morning debating who was the best supervillain.

In the end, my dad got the bad guy, came home, and told Struz he was a terrible babysitter, then we all went out for pizza.

Struz is six feet seven and lanky, with a superhero complex.

He's the kind of guy who dresses up as Superman for Halloween every year and wears the costume with the foam stomach muscles built in. He's also the kind of guy who can manage to hold the world together when earthquakes, a tsunami, and a rash of wildfires take out electricity, running water, and any semblance of civilization.

He's the best guy I know.

# 04:00:39:52

Struz 2.0, the Prima version, is apparently the deputy director of IA, and after listening to Barclay, he nods at the armed guards. As they leave, he points to the chairs and gestures for us to sit down. There's a suaveness to the gesture that's completely alien on his body.

I can't take my eyes off him. His hair is shorter. He obviously cuts it himself or has someone keep up with it regularly. He's clean-shaven, and his clothes fit. The shoulders are the right width, the arms the right length, the material something expensive. He looks really good.

If I get home, I'm making it a mission to buy my Struz some nice clothes. We might manage to find him a girlfriend yet.

"Good to see you, Barclay," he says as soon as the door shuts and we're alone. He smiles as I sit down in my chair. It's a smile that's a little too big for his face, and it's never looked so good on him. "Glad you're back."

"Thank you, sir," Barclay says with a polite smile.

I feel a little like I just fell into *Invasion of the Body Snatchers*.

"Now, forgive me, but how is Miss Tenner connected to case

BM132?" Struz 2.0 asks. He's all business, which shouldn't surprise me. But this guy is so important to me in my life, it's hard to process and accept that I'm so absent in his.

Barclay gives a rundown of my involvement with Ben. It's weird to hear someone reduce the intensity of what I feel to just a few sentences. Where we met, the days and times we interacted, the things we told each other—it sounds sterile.

There's nothing in his report that's wrong, it's just that there's nothing in there that's right either, nothing that suggests he's talking about *my* Ben, the guy who fixed my schedule, pressed his finger to mine and healed a paper cut, inserted himself in two of my classes, brought my favorite food to a picnic dinner at Sunset Cliffs—the guy who saved me from death. Nothing that says since the day he left, I've been daydreaming about his face, his dark brown eyes, his lips, the way his hair falls in his face, the way he reached out, touched my cheek, and pulled me into one last kiss, the way he took slow steps backward toward the portal, as if he didn't really want to leave, the way he said my name and told me he loved me, and the way the portal swallowed him up and he disappeared. The way he said, *I'll come back for you.*

When Barclay finishes, Struz 2.0 looks at me and then touches his computer screen. "Good work bringing her in, Barclay." He frowns, and the emotion that flickers over his face suggests he's not happy about something. "It looks like the director wants her questioned and detained."

Maybe he doesn't want to send me to prison to await my execution. Or maybe that's me and my wishful thinking again.

"Yes, sir," Barclay says.

"I can take it from here. You'll file your report?"

"Yes, sir," Barclay says, then gets up and leaves the room

without so much as looking at me. As he's leaving I have a moment of panic. What if this has all been some elaborate trick and there isn't going to be any escape? What if this is it—if I just turned myself in to the enemy?

But I swallow any hysteria down and remind myself that Barclay didn't need to convince me to come, insert a microchip in my arm, make me memorize prison blueprints—he could have just portaled in and grabbed me when I was sleeping.

It's not exactly comforting, but it's all I've got right now.

I'm alone with Struz 2.0. When I look at him straight on, that's when I realize deep down that this isn't Struz at all There's something about Struz 2.0, the fact that he's so similar, yet just slightly different, that's alarming. He has the same face, the same eyes, the same voice, the same everything. But there's so much that *feels* different. And it's more than just the way he's sitting with his legs crossed, the matching socks, the polished shoes.

It's like whatever made the Ryan Struzinski in my world into a guy that would go by "Struz," this guy doesn't have it. And I don't know what that means.

The realization has a sinking effect on my heart, my eyes get a little watery, and an overwhelming feeling of desperation wells up inside me. More than anything I just want to go home—I want to hug my brother and tell Struz I'm sorry for all the stress I cause him. I want to see them again before it's too late.

"This should go relatively quickly, Miss Tenner," this guy who's not Struz says. "We just have a few questions."

I look around the room, at the wall behind him, the door, the ceiling, anywhere but at the man in front of me, and I try to concentrate on my breathing. I take long, decisive breaths, inhale for a full five seconds, exhale for another five.

"I've met a few doubles in my time," he says, his voice even and soft, and I can't help looking at him. "It's unnerving at first, but you just have to keep reminding yourself I'm not the man you know. We might look a lot alike, and we maybe have a lot of similarities, but we are completely different people with different experiences that caused us to lead different lives."

I nod as my eyes fall on a picture frame on his desk. It's next to his monitor, a thick silver frame, well polished and dust free. Inside it are two smiling faces, a boy and a girl with bright blond hair, deep blue eyes, fair skin, and wide smiles. The resemblance is undeniable.

They must be his children.

I shift my eyes to this Ryan Struzinski, and he's looking at me expectantly.

I think about what Barclay told me—I should answer truthfully as much as I can. Short, concise answers.

My breathing has slowed, and I'm as ready as I'll ever be.

"Okay," I say, keeping it brief.

"Excellent. Now, when's the last time you had contact with Ben Michaels?" he says, sliding a picture of Ben in my direction.

# 04:00:32:46

For a second, I can't breathe. I just stare at the picture.

It's a candid shot, taken without Ben's knowledge. He's wearing a faded blue grease-stained button-down shirt that says WAKEFIELD AUTO over one breast pocket and BEN over the other. He's not looking at the camera, he's looking somewhere off to the side, his eyes down, his mouth parted slightly as if he's talking to someone. His hair is slightly longer than when he lived in my world, and it flops over his face, partially obscuring his expression.

"Miss Tenner?"

I look up. Deputy Director Ryan Struzinski is sitting with some kind of clear glass iPad and pen. He's not looking at me.

This man is not the Struz I know. And it's not just that he's more put together. Despite the fact that he seems to have wayward morals, he works for the IA and they are threatening people's lives—Ben's, his family's, and mine. He's either okay with that or he's okay with the fact that it's just the way things are done.

I breathe out. "About four months ago, that's the last time I saw him."

He nods and presumably jots down what I just said. "And what was the circumstance?"

"We drove to an abandoned house and confronted two of his friends," I say. "We knew one of them was opening unstable portals. Agents Barclay and Brandt arrived shortly after us. They sent Ben back to his world."

"And by his friends, you mean Reid Suitor, now deceased, and Elijah Palma," he says.

I answer, even though it's not a question. "Yes."

His eyes flick toward mine. "And you haven't seen Ben Michaels since that day?"

I hate that this answer is the truth. "No."

"Have you had any contact with him?"

I shake my head. "No."

"No emails, letters, texts, nothing?"

"Is that even possible?" I ask, because if it is, I'd like to know for future reference.

He leans back. "I just need you to answer the questions."

I roll my eyes. So much for trying to be nervous and diminutive. "No, I haven't heard from him at all."

"Well, thank you for answering my questions. We're going to need to detain you until this matter is settled," he says, looking down at his paperwork, and I don't know why I can't follow directions, but something in this moment makes me have to say it. Because it's the truth, and this man right here, wearing the same face as the man I trust and love more than anyone, he should believe me.

"Whatever you think he's done, Ben is innocent. He would never hurt anyone."

Deputy Director Struzinski looks at me, with the corners of his mouth downturned, his chin tucked in, and his eyes soft—full of pity. And he says, "There's a lot of evidence against him, but when we bring him in, we'll make sure he gets the chance to prove himself innocent."

I almost say, "What about me?"

Because I'm innocent—though I won't be at this time tomorrow. But right now I am, and yet he's willing to detain me and file the paperwork for my execution in less than four days.

# 03:22:56:02

Two armed security guards pick me up from the deputy director's office and take me to a back exit where a van is waiting. They load me in and strap me down. If there's paperwork to be done or any kind of processing for prisoner transfer, it doesn't require my involvement.

The windows are blacked out, and I can't tell if it's night or day.

I think about Ben. Wherever he is, he must have some sort of plan—to save his family, to prove his innocence. I just hope we can find him in time.

And I think about Cecily and where she might be. If it's somewhere without any light, if she's been bound with restraints this whole time, if she had to be sedated after going through the portal, if she cursed and screamed at whoever took her, if she's hurt and scared.

I try not to question if she's already a slave—or if she's still alive.

My breaths are shaky and my eyes burn. None of this is right. Cecily should be at Qualcomm, planning the next movie night and organizing more team-building exercises. And IA should be trying to find her. Instead they're threatening my life, locking me in prison, and throwing away the key.

This isn't just about the traffickers anymore. Because there's a deeper problem in the fabric of IA, and we need to fix it.

I understand that people in law enforcement sometimes make hard decisions in order to get the bad guy and save the day. I understand that sometimes the greater good requires sacrifices. I even understood four months ago why Barclay's orders were to sacrifice my entire world—to blow it up, demolish it—before Wave Function Collapse destroyed two worlds and adversely affected a number of others.

I didn't like it, but it made sense.

But what the IA is doing right now—detaining people Ben cares about and planning to execute them if he doesn't turn himself in—it's not right.

Even if Ben really was the bad guy, it still wouldn't be right.

And it doesn't necessarily mean everyone in the IA is evil, or that everyone there is involved in the trafficking ring. It takes a different kind of corruption to actually get involved with a criminal organization as opposed to going along with something that's not a good policy. But it means the underlying morals of the IA, as an organization, have gone astray.

Somewhere in its history, someone crossed a line and other people went along with it. And now, instead of using resources to find the bad guy, they're threatening him to get him to come to them. And they're willing to throw away innocent lives to do it.

My dad and I watched the first few seasons of *24* when it came out. I loved the show. Jack Bauer was like a superhero for the modern world, but eventually my dad stopped recording it, and it became one of those shows we just didn't watch anymore. When I asked him why he said he didn't like the message the show sent. I pressed and found out it was specifically the torture that bothered him.

What I loved about Jack Bauer was that he would do anything to save the city. He would torture the bad guys if he needed to. He would get the job done. But that was exactly what bothered my dad, because if the good guys are going to cross that line and torture someone, what is it that separates them from the bad guys?

I didn't have an answer then, and I don't have one now. But the question I'm asking myself, as the armed security guards unload me from the van and walk me through the prison's front doors, is this—if IA is willing to execute me to draw out Ben, what separates it from terrorists?

# 03:22:08:38

The prison is called the Piston because it's visible from the city center of New Prima, and it looks like a grotesque black cylinder that clashes with the rest of their buildings.

The guards parade me inside, past the inmates in cellblock A. They're two to a small cell with bunk beds, a toilet, and sink, and there are eight floors of them. It's not much different than any prison I've imagined or seen on television.

But the fact that I'm here, in restraints, about to be put into a cell, makes my skin feel cold and clammy.

A few inmates call out to me as we pass, a few more whistle, but it doesn't matter. I won't be housed with the general prison population. I'll be in a solitary cell, where they keep the worst kind of prisoners, the ones who are a danger to others, and the ones they want to forget.

We go up one flight of stairs and turn the corner. We're heading down a long hallway toward cellblock S, the solitary cells, and my shoulders relax just a little. Every small thing that goes right means I have a better chance of getting out of here.

According to Barclay, solitary confinement is small. There

are sixteen cells, eight on each side, with low ceilings and thick black walls. There are no bars because there are no windows.

When we turn into cellblock S, I see that Barclay is right.

I also see that we're not alone.

# 03:22:05:08

The fifth cell door on the left is ajar. The opening is blocked by a man who isn't in a guard uniform. He's wearing jeans and a drab olive button-down shirt. His haircut is military, high and tight. A tattoo of black barbed wire peeks out from his shirt collar and climbs up his neck.

A shiver moves through my body and air seems to get caught in my throat. His shirt is spotted with dark blobs.

Something inside me wants to stop, to dig my heels in and refuse to get any closer.

Then I hear the muffled sounds of a struggle coming from inside the cell, and I realize the dark spots on his shirt are blood.

My heart pounds harder in my chest. I don't want to be anywhere near this man.

"Hurry up," he says to whoever's in the cell. "Get him out."

That cell shouldn't be Elijah's. Unless he's been moved? No, why would they?

My guards continue to push me forward, and the man with blood on his shirt turns to watch us approach. His eyes linger on me, and I have to fight to keep from looking away. The bitter smell of urine hits me like a wall, and fear slithers through my veins until I'm dizzy with it. Then comes the rusty, damp smell of blood.

The man is still studying me, his face passive and emotionless, and it feels like with one look he's seen more about me than I want him to. The hallway is tight and he doesn't move, so we have to squeeze by him. The whole time he's watching me.

One of the guards says, "Excuse me, Mr. Meridian," as we pass.

I steal a glance inside the open door and the whispered word slips out with my breath before I can stop myself. "Ben."

He's inside the cell. His hair is matted against the side of his face with dried blood, his cheek is bruised and swollen. My breath catches in my throat, and I refuse to move forward with the guards. There are too many emotions rolling through me to try to process them all. They've beaten him—I don't want to know how many times—and then just tossed him back in his cell to sleep it off. But he's here. I can try to get him out with Elijah.

But when he raises his head and our eyes meet, I realize I'm wrong. This isn't Ben. He has the same dark hair, the same bone structure, the same deep-set eyes. But this guy's face is just slightly different.

Ben's brother, Derek.

He grunts and says something. We've never met, and I've only seen his doppelgänger, but I know that it's him. He's Ben, a few years older, swollen and beat up, in need of a shower and a shave.

The guard to my right squeezes his fingers into my upper arm and pushes me forward. I twist around and try to see behind me, but the guards block my line of sight, pushing and dragging me to the cell that will be mine—the last one on the right. Behind me, Derek says something. Then I hear a groan, labored breathing, and the sound of someone's feet dragging on the floor.

As the guard opens my cell, I realize what Ben's brother said to me.

He said, *"Run."*

# 03:22:04:29

I can't breathe. It feels like the walls are closing in on me, like the ground is moving underneath my feet. My face is too hot, my body is too cold, and my insides are flipping around. That was Ben's brother, with dried blood caked onto his clothes and bruises over his face and arms. Who knows where they're taking him now—and what they're going to do to him.

My body starts to shake, and I try to suck air into my lungs.

When I break out in eleven hours, I'm supposed to leave him here.

# 03:20:17:25

My cell is small and dark, just large enough for the thin cot on one side. Instead of a toilet, there's a dark hole in the floor in one corner. The weak light bulb on the ceiling flickers a little, giving the room a horror-movie type of feel. The fact that everything smells like bleach, but I can't get the scent of blood and urine out of my nose, doesn't help either.

I'm lying on top of the cot in the standard light-blue cotton prison jumpsuit.

But I can't will my body to relax or my mind to stop spinning long enough to even have a fitful nap.

I hear faint screams coming from somewhere else in the prison and I'm not sure if they're real or part of my overactive imagination. I can't leave Ben's family in here. I have to get them out, but I don't have the codes to open their doors—only Elijah's—and I don't know how to contact Barclay.

My legs shift a little. They're restless, and I stand up to pace around the tiny room.

No matter what, I can't stay here. Every time I hear a noise outside, I worry Meridian is coming for me. I'm worried about

Elijah and about everything that could go wrong tonight. What will I do if he's too injured to walk?

My hands shake as I pace, and I press them to my forehead. I have to relax and stay focused. Falling apart now won't help anyone. I force myself to take a deep breath. There must be a way to save Ben's family.

I shouldn't let my legs get too tired so I climb back on the bed, close my eyes, and think of Ben. I see him, wearing one of my dad's old T-shirts and a pair of his sweatpants, freshly showered, smelling like my shampoo, the night Elijah got shot. I remember how he reached out and grabbed one of my hands. Our fingers intertwined and those dark eyes looked straight into mine, lying next to each other in my bed, holding on to each other before the world fell apart.

*You're strong and smart, and you never put yourself first. You don't let anything get in your way, and you're beautiful.*

I can almost feel the heat of his body next to mine, the strength of his arms around me, and the way he made me feel like no matter what happened, we wouldn't give up, we would fight for what we wanted up to the very end.

I hold on to that memory. It's easier to keep fighting if I don't feel alone.

# 03:11:20:57

I lie on the cot, flat on my back. I've got nothing.

I haven't come up with a single viable plan to get Ben's brother—or anyone in his family—out of their cells.

And I'm running out of time.

I'm going to have to leave them. The idea settles over me like a lead blanket. I think the words—*I'm going to have to leave them*. It leaves me tingly and a little sick—it's the same feeling I got when I had to tell Jared about Alex, news I didn't want to admit in case it made it more true, and news I wasn't quite sure how he'd react to, just that the reaction would be bad.

Tonight at midnight, during the guards' shift change, Barclay will hack into the security system, my cell door will open, and he'll set off an EMP. Then he'll wait just outside the grounds.

When the EMP goes off, it will knock out all the power in the prison. It'll take about thirty seconds for the backup generator to power up and then another twenty for the computers and security systems to reboot. I need to get to Elijah's cell, open his door, and get him out, and then we need to make it through the prison and down to the infirmary without being seen by the cameras.

I recite the numbers of the door codes out loud and visualize each step of the plan. If I get one code wrong, it'll trip the alarm.

I suppose I'm glad now that my dad quoted movies and *The X-Files* and forced me to do the same if I wanted to keep up. I should thank him—and my mom, since I had to always keep a step ahead of her to stop her from drinking or hurting herself somehow. They both helped prepare me for this in their own way.

Although I'm wishing I had Cecily's photographic memory. That girl could picture and recall anything she wrote down in her own handwriting. If she wrote it down once, at the snap of a finger, she could recite it back to you. If it had been that easy for me, I could have just written the plan down and followed the map in my mind. As it is, I'm stuck repeating everything over and over again so I don't mess up.

I'm thinking of Cecily when the watch under my skin beeps and comes alive.

And the numbers start counting down.

00:05:00

# 03:11:05:00

This is it. My life-or-death moment. I take a deep breath and jump up off the cot.

*4*

I only have one chance to follow all of Barclay's instructions. If this doesn't work, and I'm still *alive*, I'll be stuck here.

*3*

Barclay won't be able to do anything without going against orders.

*2*

If this doesn't work, if I don't get us out, I could end up being beaten and tortured for the escape attempt, and Barclay will most likely leave me here.

*1*

I'm standing in front of my door, muscles tense and ready to spring, my fingers ready to pry the door open as soon as it unlocks.

The sound is audible. It's the sound of electronics powering off. The sound of silence.

And the lights go out.

# 03:11:00:00

I hear something click inside my cell door. My heart pounds in my chest as I push through. The door gives easily as if it was never locked, and I'm in the hallway. I move steadily north, staying along the right side of the hall just in case the cameras come back on early. My heartbeat and my feet hitting the floor as I run are the only things I can hear.

I try not to look at the doors I'm passing by. I know there's nothing I can do, but my insides twist anyway. I hate that I'm leaving people behind.

As I run past Derek's door, I pound on it with my palm and yell, "I'll come back for you," because if we make it out of here, I'm not going to forget what this place is like.

Then I keep running.

I slam into Elijah's door, cell number thirteen, and I key in the code burned into my memory.

*4-0-7-5-2*

The door swings open, and I gasp.

Even in the dark, I can see he's been tortured. The left side of his face is swollen and distorted. Blood and dirt are caked on his face mixing with the bruises. It looks like he hasn't showered in a month or more—his reddish-blond hair looks brown. He's thin, bony in places, like he's lost fifteen, maybe twenty pounds. His mouth opens when he sees me, but no sound comes out. I'll be lucky if I can get him walking. I grab his empty food dish and use it to prop the door open, then I run to him and pull him off the ground.

"Elijah, I'm going to get you out of here," I say. "You have to follow me."

He nods and I can feel him pull himself together to support himself. "You look good." His voice cracks, another sign he's delusional.

I sling his arm over my shoulder to help support him, and we move to the cell door. I hold the edge of it just barely open, kick his food dish out of the way, and look down at the numbers on my skin.

*00:14:70*

We don't have much more time. If we're caught by the cameras, we might as well just head back to our cells.

I throw open his cell door and pull Elijah through, then hobble, half running and half dragging him down the hallway. His breathing is labored, and there's a definite hitch in his step like he can't put much weight on his left leg. Which means most of his weight is on me.

But we get to the stairwell, and as I'm pushing through the door, dim overhead lights start to click on.

The backup generator.

"I need you to hurry," I grunt, pulling him down the stairs. My pulse pounds in my ears, and the muscles in my arms are shaking under Elijah's weight.

"If you get us caught, they'll probably just kill us," Elijah says with a cough.

"Stop trying to be helpful." I almost smile. This is the Elijah I know. They haven't broken him yet.

We hit a landing, the halfway point, and I adjust my grip and keep pulling him with me.

We have to get through the infirmary to the medical bay—where dead or severely injured prisoners are taken, operated on, or even transported to the morgue. There's a grate down to the sewer system. With the code, I'll be able to deactivate it, and Elijah and I will go through and down into the sewers. We'll make our way through the tunnels and come up where Barclay will be waiting for us. He's apparently already gone through them from the outside to make sure they lead the right way.

We hit the bottom of the stairwell, and I punch in the door code to let us onto the restricted basement level floor.

*3-5-1-1-7*

The door opens and I push Elijah through.

Barclay and I were hoping the power outage and any general confusion during the shift change would give me enough time to get to the infirmary, down the grate, and into the sewers without being seen by the cameras and setting off the alarms.

But when I glance at my skin and see that I'm at fifty-three seconds, I know I'm too slow.

We're going to get caught on camera.

I grit my teeth and try to move faster.

The infirmary is in the opposite wing of the prison, and as long as Barclay's directions are correct, we should make a right at the end of this hallway, then a left at the end of the next one, and it will be in front of us. If we flat-out sprint, maybe we'll be able to make it.

We turn right.

I'm dragging Elijah down the corridor as I run. I don't have to glance down at the numbers counting down on my skin—I know we're not going fast enough.

We're about to take our left and turn the corner toward the infirmary when a door at the end of the hall opens, and a guard shines his flashlight on us.

I make eye contact with him, and I see the surprise on his face as he fumbles for his weapon.

"Hurry!" I say to Elijah, because I can't keep supporting him and get both of us out alive.

Only my voice is drowned out by the gunfire.

# 03:10:58:49

My reaction is automatic. I duck and throw an arm over my head out of some primal instinct. And I keep running.

Elijah must have the same instincts because he manages to pick up his pace.

We turn the corner.

I can see the door to the infirmary. It's maroon, like Barclay described, the door code panel right next to it.

The code is 12386.

Time seems to slow.

I can still hear the echo of the gunfire, and even though I know it isn't a direct threat since the guard is still around the corner, I'm still holding my head, and my breath, waiting to get hit.

But I can also hear my feet fall against the concrete floor. Every step reverberates through my legs, matching my heart rate.

I don't slow down as we approach the door.

I run full speed, right into it.

It hurts like hell, but if I live until tomorrow, the bruises will be so worth it.

My fingers find the door code panel, and I punch the numbers in.

*1*

The alarm kicks on above us, red lights flash, and a siren wails through the walls.

*2*

I glance behind me in time to see the guard turning the corner.

*3*

There's a loud pop behind me—the sound of gunfire.

*8*

I flinch as a bullet lodges itself in the concrete less than an inch from my hand.

*6*

The door clicks, and I turn the handle.

As I move through the door, I see Elijah fall against the wall. My throat closes a little, and it feels like some kind of weight has knocked into me. I grab his arm and pull him into the room.

He stumbles, and a hundred and sixty pounds crashes into me. We fall backward and I slam into something sharp and cold. I hear glass breaking.

But we're safe for a moment.

We're here—the infirmary.

Only one step left before we can get out of here.

Elijah groans. "There's something wrong with my leg."

I reach down and my hand touches something warm and sticky.

Blood.

# 03:10:58:36

My dad got shot on the job three times. The first time, I was a little girl, maybe two or three, and I don't have a memory of it. The second time, I was eleven, and he got hit in the arm, just above his elbow. It was a through-and-through. He only took a day off from work.

The third time, he died.

But before he did, he told me when you first get shot, you don't feel anything. It isn't until you look down and see the blood that your body lets your brain absorb the pain.

# 03:10:58:35

I check myself. My eyes sweep over my arms and legs, my hands feel my stomach and back. The only blood seems to be coming from Elijah. From his calf.

I don't know how bad he's hit. The bullet could be still lodged in there. It could have punctured something important. I haven't taken anatomy so I don't know if there's an artery that could be counting down the last few seconds of his life. But it doesn't matter. I know I have to somehow stop the blood flow. And I know I don't have much time.

Because that guard is coming down the hallway right now.

I grab my sleeve and start to rip. Then I hand the material to Elijah, who's pushed himself into a sitting position against the wall. "Tie this above the wound. As tight as you can. I don't care how much it hurts."

"Shit, J," he says. "You got me fucking shot."

"Be pissed off about it later. We still have to get out of here."

I look at the door. We don't have enough time to disable the grate and get down into the sewers with the guard behind us. I'll have to take him out somehow.

When he comes in, the door is going to swing open. If he's been trained at all, he'll lead with his gun as he opens the door. He'll come in slow, looking for us. If he hasn't seen much action, he'll be nervous and holding the gun out in front of him like some kind of shield.

I take a deep breath and I think of Cecily who needs me to do this. I tighten my hands into fists and then release them.

We can still get out of here.

Elijah is seated diagonally across from the door, which means he'll draw the eye of the guard. If I stand behind the door, I'll have an advantage. I can knock the gun out of his hands then gain possession. I can come at his wrists with something heavy where the bones are fragile no matter the size of the person. I'll have about a second to disable him.

But I need something—a weapon—first.

There's a shard of glass on the floor. It's from a mirror that I broke when Elijah and I came barreling in here, and it's a thin triangle, the size of my forearm. But it's not going to be enough to disable him.

Then I see a fire extinguisher on the wall. It will be heavy, unwieldy, but it might just work. I grab it, position myself behind the door, and then flick off the light switch so the light from the hallway will give me another advantage.

And I wait.

# 03:10:58:10

The red lights flash, the alarm blares like a siren, and Elijah moans in pain, but over all of it, I can hear the pounding of my heart.

I keep my eyes down, staring at the light under the door. When the shadow of the guard crosses through it, I tighten both of my hands around my makeshift weapon and try to steady my breaths.

This is my only chance.

I can't hesitate. It doesn't matter that this one guard isn't necessarily my enemy. It doesn't matter if he's not the guy who threatened me or tortured Elijah. It doesn't even matter if he doesn't know who I am or what IA wants to do with me.

It matters that he's shooting at us—that he shot Elijah. It matters that Barclay is waiting for us—that Ben and Cecily need us. That the traffickers are out there and we need to stop them.

It matters that in three days, ten hours, and fifty-eight minutes, we could all be dead.

I take another deep breath. Right now it's him or me.

My life depends on what I do in this next moment.

I hear the click of the lock, and the door handle turns.

# 03:10:57:24

The light from the hallway casts a glow against him, outlining him so he stands out in our dark room. I can easily see that his left hand is on the door, his right on the gun.

With both hands tight around the fire extinguisher, I lift it over my head, and with as much force as I can possibly muster I bring it down on his wrist.

He screams. It's a terrible sound.

The gun clatters to the floor and skids away from me.

The guard pulls his arm into his body, cradling it against his chest, and the door slams shut, blocking out the light from the hallway.

It takes a split second for my eyes to adjust to the darkness.

The guard is disabled, but he knows where I am now and his gun is too far away for me to get to it first.

With only one good arm, he rushes me. I swing the fire extinguisher again, but this time he expects it and his left hand grabs it before I manage to hit anything. The misstep throws me off balance, and he pushes me, knocking me into an empty hospital cot as he twists the fire extinguisher out of my grasp.

I slam a heel onto one of his feet, and he grunts, dropping the fire extinguisher. It thuds heavily against the ground, and I lift my other knee to strike for his balls, but he's faster than I expected, and the blow glances off his thigh instead. My ankle turns awkwardly, pain shoots through my leg, and I feel myself going down.

As my back slams into the ground, a hand tightens on my throat, crushing my ability to breathe. I try to thrash away, but a knee presses into my chest.

I'm trapped.

# 03:10:56:58

My dad always complained about how feminism told us that women were equal to men. Not because he was sexist or anything, but because he firmly believed in realism.

Fact: The average man is five and a half inches taller than the average woman, and he outweighs her by twenty-six pounds.

Fact: A woman who weighs 150 pounds still has only 70 percent of a 150-pound man's strength capacity.

As a result, straight strength against strength, a man is going to overpower a woman.

That's why I'm not about to throw my strength at someone bigger and heavier than me. I'm smarter than that.

Nose, throat, groin, ears, and eyes are weak spots for everyone.

# 03:10:56:57

I go for his eyes.

I reach up, my fingers touching the slippery, sweaty skin of his face, and I press my thumbs into his eye sockets.

I try to ignore the sick feeling in my stomach as the rubber elasticity of his eyes gives under my thumbs. I think of my dad, standing in our backyard with me and Alex and teaching us basic self-defense, telling us we had to mean it, that we couldn't be squeamish about hurting someone who was attacking us.

I press harder, reaching and straining off the ground. My neck squeezes into the hand against it, until it feels like my windpipe might collapse. Stars corner my vision, but I keep working—struggling to do what my dad taught me.

Until something gives way under my right thumb.

The guard jerks back with a grunt, releasing just enough pressure on my throat to allow me to gasp for air, and my left hand slides down his nose.

Air fills my lungs, and my vision clears to see blood rolling down his face from his left eye.

Teeth bite into the soft skin between my thumb and forefinger, and my scream is swallowed by the fingers that tighten around my throat and push my head against the concrete.

Pain explodes from the back of my head, and for a second the whole world is black. I feel an overwhelming heaviness, and my hands drop uselessly to my sides.

That's when I touch it.

Something cold and sharp under my right hand.

The broken piece of mirror.

I feel around for the widest part and curl my fingers around it. The jagged edges bite into my palm, but the sharp pain helps clear my vision and give me a moment of clarity.

I remember the kill zones my dad taught me, and with every ounce of strength I have left, I drive the pointy end into his neck, right under his chin.

Blood rushes out of the gaping hole, onto my hands and chest. It's warm and thick. The pressure on my throat lets up as he reaches for his neck, trying to stop the blood, trying to hold on to it somehow, but he can't. I've hit an artery—the carotid, I think—and he'll bleed out in a matter of seconds. He looks at me, brown eyes wide with surprise as he begins to lose control of his body. The strength in his legs gives out and he starts to slump to the side.

I force myself to keep looking at him—he's in his late twenties–early thirties with short blond hair, a strong jaw, and a crooked nose—while the life leaves his eyes.

My chest feels tight.

I've just killed a man.

# 03:10:54:58

I tell myself I had no choice, but as I look down at my hands, covered in his blood, I feel nauseous. They don't look like they could possibly be mine. As they start to shake, I drop the piece of glass.

Behind me, I hear Elijah's labored breathing. I will my hands to stop shaking, and I lean down and wipe my hands on the dead guard's jacket. Not all of the blood will come off. Then I pretend this isn't me—I didn't kill this man, I'm not escaping from prison, and I'm not running around in an alternate universe trying to save my friend from human traffickers. This life belongs to someone else—I'm just acting it out.

"Are you okay?" I ask Elijah. "Did you get the tourniquet tied?"

"I'm fucking shot," he says. His voice is calm, quiet but annoyed, like he's telling me he forgot his homework—like he didn't just watch me kill someone. He shrugs. "How is that 'okay' to you?"

I drop down to look at his leg. "You know what I mean. We can't just sit here and wait for more guards." I'm relieved when I realize the bullet must have hit his calf muscle and gone straight through. The bleeding hasn't stopped, but it's slowed, and he's not in danger of dying on me just yet.

Now we just have to get out of here and meet Barclay before we run into more trouble.

I find the grate in the back corner. It looks smaller than I want it to be, but Barclay assured me he could fit through it, and he's bigger than both Elijah and me. The grate itself is a complex grid of blue laser beams that will cut right through my skin if I touch them.

On the wall above the grate is a keypad. I key in the code I memorized.

*8-4-3-1-6*

And the lasers flicker out.

There's a problem, though. We've tripped the alarm, and I can see now what Barclay meant by the flush system being fire.

It's everywhere, the heat of it coming up through the grate and making me sweat. For a second I think about the extinguisher but quickly dismiss it as something we could use. The volume of the flames is just too great.

As I'm looking down into the sewer, I see the water—and I'm saying *water* because I don't want to think about what it actually is—but the fire floods the path we need to take in order to get there.

The fire must be coming from pipes in the walls, like a complex system of blow torches, a lot of them going off at the same time.

I count how long the flames seem to last and how long the break is between them. It's not long. We're going to have to jump through the fire in order to get out of here.

There has to be a way for us to go through without getting burned. I look back at the room.

The cot.

I run to it and pull the sheets off, then I move to the sink and crank the water. When the sheets are fully soaked, I wrap one around my shoulders and the other around Elijah.

I drag him to the grate.

"You should have fucking left me in that cell," he says when he sees the flames.

"You need to trust me," I say. "And you need to hold your breath."

I have Elijah go first because we don't have long before guards come barreling through this door, and he's not going to be able to defend himself if he's alone. I push him so he's seated on the edge of the open grate with his legs dangling over the fire. The fire blares for six seconds, and then there's about a two-second respite from the flames, which means he can't try to climb down quickly. He's going to have to jump through the tunnel, and he's going to have to *start* the jump while the fire is on its last second, or else he'll get caught in it when it comes back on.

"My feet are fucking burning," he says, and I can see his Adam's apple move as he swallows.

"Actually, they're not yet," I say. "Fold your arms across your chest, tuck your chin, and close your eyes. When I tell you to hold your breath and go, you have to do it. You can't wait."

"Fuck you," he answers, but then glances at me, presses his lips together, and adds, "Don't you dare get stuck up here." His voice is serious and raw, and I think if we make it out of here, we might actually be friends.

"Stay underwater," I say.

He grunts in acquiescence and looks down, tucking his chin. The flames die out.

"On six," I say.

The flames come back on.

"One . . ." I whisper. "Two . . ." I keep my voice as even as possible. "Three . . ." I put my hand squarely on Elijah's back. "Four . . ." I hope this works. "Five." And as soon as I say it, I give him a push.

I scramble into his position as he disappears, and I hope he remembers to hold his breath. I see the splash right before the fire flares back up again, and I repeat my count.

*One.*

My feet are dangling toward the fire.

*Two.*

I cross my arms over my chest and pull the wet sheet around me.

*Three.*

I tuck my chin, look down, and fight to ignore the panic welling up in my chest.

*Four.*

Sweat drips down the center of my back.

*Five.*

I take a deep breath, close my eyes, and throw myself down into the sewers.

And I scream.

It's unbearably hot, almost like the first time I went through a portal. Just the heat in the air singes my hair and burns my skin.

Then something cold and grimy hits me, and I realize I've made it. I'm underwater. I open my eyes and see something dark that I'm hoping is Elijah. I reach for it, grabbing it. It's an arm, and it's warm, which I suppose is a good thing. He moves and his hand squeezes my arm before he starts to swim to the surface. But I grab him and hold on tight. He can't go up just yet.

Pulling him with me, I try to swim forward.

And when it's just about time, I jerk him up, and our faces break free. The stench of burning is everywhere—burning plastic, burning hair and skin, burning sewage.

"Another big breath!" I say, glancing around to make sure we're moving in the right direction. We are.

Elijah takes a huge breath, and we both plunge back into the sewage. The fact that I'm pulling him, that we're both in our clothes, moving through sludge—it all makes us too slow. We need to hurry. As soon as they realize where we've gone, they'll turn off the fire and head into the sewers to try to find us.

I can feel the moment the fire is shut down. The temperature immediately drops about ten degrees, and even though the air is still thick with the burning smell, it's easier to breathe.

Pulling Elijah up, we break the surface and I yell, "Swim as fast as you can and follow me!"

Because they've found us.

# 03:10:46:02

I hear voices in the tunnel behind us. Because of the poor acoustics, I can't make out what they're saying—their voices bounce off the water and the closeness of the walls—and I only know they're far enough that they can't see us.

If they could, they'd be shooting.

I put my head down and swim. With every pull, I reach out and grab the water and try to push it behind me, kicking double-time and hoping Elijah can just hold on.

The tunnel splits off into different directions, but in front of us is a ladder that leads up into another tunnel, a vertical one, and above that, as long as he's kept his word, is Barclay.

"Go first," I say, pulling Elijah from the water. His hands shake as he starts to pull himself up, but his legs are worse. One is messed up from who knows what, and the other is just dead weight from being shot. I slip underneath him, so his body is resting on my shoulders. He grunts in protest, but we've got no other options.

I grab the metal bars and start climbing. All Elijah has to do is keep from letting go.

I keep climbing, driving us into darkness toward a little sliver of light at the top of the tunnel, and I pray that Barclay really is up there. Because if he's not, I don't know where to go from here.

"I see something," Elijah says. Then he grunts, and there's the screech of metal grinding against metal.

Elijah's weight is pulled off me, and I quickly climb the last few rungs.

"Hurry up or we're never going to make it out of here before they spot us," Barclay says.

Elijah has collapsed onto the ground, coughing. "Did we make it?" he says.

"Almost." I look at Barclay, and I've never been so glad to see him.

He pulls me the rest of the way out of the sewer tunnel, and we both grab Elijah.

Barclay has my backpack on his back and he pulls a quantum charger from his pocket. He's apparently already set the destination, because he presses one button, and I hear it power up.

The portal opens in front of us, and something in my chest lifts as the cool air and the smell of the sea whips around us. Holding Elijah by the arms, I nod at Barclay, and all three of us step through.

# 03:10:45:38

We end up in a heap on the ground, chests heaving. My body aches, my skin feels raw, like I have a really bad sunburn, and my mouth is so dried out it hurts.

I glance around, but it only takes a second for me to realize we're in the same abandoned world Barclay took me to on our way here.

Which means we're safe.

My eyes burn, and warm tears roll down my singed skin.

Once the portal shuts behind us, Barclay grabs me by the shoulders and turns me to face him. "Are you hurt?" he asks, pulling my wet clothes aside to check for blood.

I've never been so glad to see his face in my entire life. Those blue eyes, high cheekbones, and strong jaw. He's the most beautiful thing I've ever seen. I want to wrap my arms around him, bury my face in his shoulder, and never let go.

At least, I do for a second, then I remember this is Barclay and this was his plan in the first place, and that helps me get over it.

"Janelle, are you hurt?"

His grasp digs into me, and the pain shoots through my shoulders. I shake my head and try to push him away, but he's holding on too tight.

"What happened?"

"It's not my blood," I say, finally succeeding in getting him off me.

But that reminds me. I look down, and all I can see is blood. A lot of it's been washed away, but it's still in my hair and under my fingernails. Even my hands look stained.

"Whose is it?" he says, looking to Elijah.

"A guard," I say, even though I can't believe these are my words. "I killed him."

As I say it, it really sinks in. This past fall, I saw someone die right in front of me, and I thought that was bad enough. But now I've killed someone. With my own hands, I shoved a jagged piece of metal into his neck and I felt his blood wash over my hands, soak itself into my skin.

I think about his face, and my stomach heaves. I turn away from Barclay, bend at the waist, and vomit acid and protein bar onto the grass.

"Is she okay?" Elijah asks, as I heave again. "The guard, he fucking shot me. Did he get her too?"

"She's okay, just shock," Barclay says. He rubs a hand on my back and says, "Don't worry, this always happens the first time, it's normal."

I can't imagine those words have ever made anyone feel better.

And if it couldn't possibly get any worse, he adds, "It gets easier."

I have just enough breath to say, "God I hope not," before I deposit the rest of the acid from my stomach onto the grass.

# 03:10:37:14

Barclay checks out Elijah's wounds and gives each of us a change of clothes from my backpack.

Then he crouches next to me. "He's in bad shape," Barclay whispers. "I think the bullet was a through-and-through, but I can't be sure there's not a fragment of anything in there."

For a second I just stare at him. I'm not sure what he wants from me.

Barclay must sense that because he adds, "He needs a hospital."

I nod. Right now, I feel like I might need a hospital too.

"I know a good one," Barclay says. "It's a world similar to your home one, where there's no interverse travel and not a lot of disturbances. We'll be safe there as long as we don't stay too long."

I don't say anything, and Barclay grabs my shoulders and gives them a shake. My gaze falls on his neck and for some reason, I imagine the mirror sliding into his neck and blood pouring out.

"Look at me," he says, his grip tight on my shoulders.

I lift my eyes to his.

"Whatever happened, it was not your fault," he says. "After

this is over, you can cry, but right now, I need you to snap out of it."

It's not a great pep talk, but it gets me moving. I don't have to think too hard to remember we've only got three and a half days left to take down a trafficking ring and save everyone I care about.

# 03:10:29:57

The hospital is in a seedy section of town—wherever we are—that Barclay calls Little Beijing. The waiting room is filled with kids with runny noses and coughs, and a guy who has pinkeye.

As we approach the reception desk, the woman behind it blushes, her ivory skin turning bright pink as she sees Barclay and then drops her eyes. She can't suppress the smile already forming on her lips.

Barclay leans into her, speaking fast in a language I don't recognize. It might be Chinese or it might be something else entirely. I have no idea.

But it works.

She stands up, gestures to Elijah and me, then escorts the three of us back into an empty room.

A doctor comes in, and the receptionist speaks to him in the same language I can't understand, then he gestures for Elijah to lie back on the bed. The doctor flicks the extra overhead light on and starts examining his leg.

I try to think about Ben and what it's going to be like when

I see him—how he'll wrap his arms around me and everything will make just a little more sense.

Only, every time I picture his face, it's not Ben I'm seeing. All I can see is the guard I killed, his one eye messed up, the jagged piece of mirror sticking out of his neck, and the blood coming like a wave over my hands.

He could have children who love him more than the world. Maybe they quote movies or TV shows to each other and maybe he doesn't know how to cook or can't ever seem to remember to lock the front door.

My hands are still stained. His blood, now turning black, is under my fingernails and in my cuticles. Looking at them, I know deep down that it doesn't matter how many times I wash them. Even when the stains come out, my hands will never be the same.

Someone taps my shoulder and I turn around to the receptionist. She's offering me a tube of something.

"Anti-burn cream," Barclay says, coming up next to me. "Try not to use too much. They can only afford to give us one."

I take it from her.

Elijah groans. I step forward, but his bullet wound is already clean and bandaged. The doctor is working on his bad leg.

The leg is twisted, like it was broken and didn't heal right.

I feel sick to my stomach. This is the kind of injury that says, "Your life will never be the same."

Elijah will probably never walk right again. There will always be a hitch in his step. He won't run as fast and he won't have the same kind of balance. The leg will have to be rebroken and reset.

But not tonight.

As if he knows what I'm thinking, Elijah gives me a wry

smile. "Having regrets?"

"Don't be stupid," I say automatically. Because I'm glad we got him out of there.

The doctor says something to me, and though I don't know what, I can tell he wants me to back away, so I do. I'm not willing or ready to see the damage I've done to myself in a mirror, but I open the tube and apply some of the cream to my face while I'm standing there. The cooling effect when it hits my skin makes me sigh, even though it stings a little.

"Here, take this too," Barclay says as he hands me two pills. I put them in my mouth and struggle to swallow them. It's hard without water, and when they go down, they leave the nasty taste of medicine in my throat.

"You should sit down," he adds. "We need to rest."

I know I should tell him that we don't have time to rest, that Ben's family and whoever else they're holding in the Piston are still there, that we need to get them out. But for some reason, the words don't come to me. Instead, Barclay and I stand side by side in silence for a long time. Elijah has several open sores on his body, wounds that never healed and have been gathering bacteria and festering for who knows how long. The doctor cleans and disinfects them, bandages or stitches them up. He hooks up an IV with fluids and painkillers, and Elijah passes out, probably his first real rest in weeks.

At some point the receptionist brings in a chair for me, and I sit down.

Barclay puts an arm on my shoulder, and I yawn, leaning on him for support.

Somewhere along the line, I'm tired enough that I fall asleep.

# 03:02:29:57

I wake up in my clothes, facedown in a pillow. The scratchy sheets are pricking at my skin, and my whole body is stiff and sore all over, like I ran a marathon.

Or like I escaped from a prison. The memories from last night rush back. After the hospital we came here and passed out for the night. We're in a standard cheap motel room—two beds and a coffee maker. Elijah is on the other one. My backpack is on the floor between us, and Barclay is nowhere in sight.

I get up and move into the bathroom. I don't look as bad as I'd expect.

There's a nasty—and sore—bump on the back of my head and a ring of bruises around my neck, and most of my skin is red, like a bad sunburn.

I shed my clothes and turn on the shower so the water is cool but not quite freezing, and I stand underneath the faucet with my eyes closed and let the water beat against the top of my head and soak into my skin and hair.

I broke Elijah out of prison. But I also killed a man.

The guilt is so strong it's suddenly hard to breathe. The

overwhelming desire to hug my brother, thank Struz for everything he does for me, let Cecily boss me around—to be home—washes over me like a wave, and it's like a dam inside me breaks. My eyes sting and my whole body shakes with sobs.

I killed a man. I stabbed him with a sharp piece of glass and watched his life drain away. Getting home can't come fast enough.

When I get out of the bathroom, Barclay is there, and Elijah is awake. "How are you feeling?" Barclay asks.

I shrug.

He pulls something out of his backpack and hands it to me. When my fingers feel the metal, I know exactly what it is. The HM USP Match—the gun he gave to me when I first got to Prima. I try to shake my head and give it back. The last thing I want right now is a gun—not when all I can think about is the dead guard and how I was responsible for that—but Barclay won't take it back.

"I need you to have my back," he says, his voice quiet but firm.

I don't know if I'll be able to point the gun at someone, to pull the trigger if I need to.

Barclay steps closer to me, his voice low. "A human-trafficking ring is out there right now, snatching people—including your friend. They've bought their way into IA, and we're the only ones trying to stop them. If you give up now, they win."

I take a deep breath. I know he's right. I don't have time to fall apart or worry about what I've done. I think of Cecily and what she must be going through, pulled from our world, jabbed with a syringe, and taken through a portal. Barclay is her only hope of getting home. If something happens to him or even Elijah because I can't get my shit together, I'll have more deaths on my head.

Seeing my resolve, Barclay leaves the room. Elijah limps after him, but when he gets to the door, he looks back. "You did what you had to do," he says.

I don't exactly believe him, but I nod.

We head to a Seattle's Best coffee shop. Barclay was right. This world is a lot like mine—or a lot like mine used to be.

"What are we doing here?" Elijah asks as we sit down at a table on the outside patio.

"I'm starving," Barclay says as the waitress comes over. She speaks a different language, so Barclay orders for all of us. When she's gone, he adds, "And we need a quiet place to talk."

Elijah nods and looks at me. "So is Ben meeting us here, or are we meeting him somewhere else?"

I'm so thrown off guard, I feel like I've been punched.

"Somewhere else," Barclay says, and I can't tell if he's actually not thrown by the question or if this is another one of those roll-with-it moments where he wants to see what kind of information he can get before revealing his cards.

Either way, I'm not having any of it. "We don't know where Ben is." I say the words deliberately, clearly, so there's no room for any confusion. "That's why we broke you out."

"He didn't send you to get me?" Elijah says, then he looks at Barclay. "You better start fucking talking."

Barclay shrugs and leans back in his chair. "We don't know where Ben is, but we need to find him."

Elijah doesn't say anything. "Do you know where he is?" I ask.

"I might have an idea."

"He's been convicted of human trafficking, unauthorized interverse travel, and treason," Barclay says. "The order for his execution has gone through, and IA is going to execute everyone he cares about in three days if we don't figure out who's behind the trafficking ring and come up with the proof we need to take them down. So we need to find him."

"Oh, that's it?" Elijah laughs and the bitterness makes me shiver. He shakes his head. "We've got bigger fucking problems than that."

My breath catches in my throat. Breaking out Elijah was supposed to find us more answers, not more problems. We have enough of those.

"About three months ago, IA grabbed both me and Ben and brought us in, threw us in that prison," Elijah says. I almost interrupt and tell him we know this part. But I bite my lip and let him finish. "A couple guards brought this guy in, Constantine Meridian, or something pansy like that, and he told us he could get us out if we worked for him."

Constantine *Meridian*. I picture the guy I saw outside of Derek's cell. His military-green button-down with blood spattered on the front. His shaved head and the barbed-wire tattoo on his neck.

"The choice was join up or get your shit kicked in. When that didn't work"—he pauses and looks at me—"it was join up or watch them kick the shit out of people you care about."

I swallow. I'm not surprised. I saw what Derek looked like and the shape Elijah was in.

"I held fast," Elijah says. "*Me*. I told them I didn't give a shit about anyone including myself." I know it's a lie. No matter what he was like in my world, Elijah cared about getting home, he cared about getting back to his family. And he cared about Ben.

But what he says next is even more wrong.

"Ben, fucking Ben. He said, 'Sign me up.'"

# 03:01:11:36

"There's no way he would do that," I say, my voice firm. I'm relieved there's something I can be sure about. Ben isn't a bad guy. He would never help them. I look at Barclay to validate what I'm saying, but he just sits there. No disagreements. Worse, there's no surprise on his face, nothing to suggest he didn't know this was coming.

I shake my head. "Ben wouldn't do that," I say again. I know Ben. I know what he went through—how guilty he felt—when he was in my world. He would never use what he could do to smuggle people—to make people slaves. Not for anything.

Elijah touches my hand.

I look from Elijah to Barclay. "You know he wouldn't." I'm practically pleading with him to agree with me. Elijah's been tortured and locked away in prison for months. He's delusional. But Barclay is rational. And we've talked about Ben. He told me he didn't believe that Ben was involved—that Ben was just some kind of scapegoat for the dirty IA agents to cover their tracks.

But when Barclay looks down and avoids my eyes, I know.

This is what he expected to hear.

Which means I'm missing a huge piece of the puzzle because I can't think of anything that would make Ben join a human-trafficking ring. Of all people, Ben knows what it's like to stumble out of his world and end up somewhere else—somewhere he doesn't belong. He would never inflict that on anyone else.

I turn away from the table and look around the café. It's the first time that I notice there's another Seattle's Best right across the street. Apparently Seattle's Best is this universe's Starbucks. I'm trying to grasp some kind of normalcy, something I can latch on to, something that will tell me that I'm not losing my mind. But everything is wrong.

"Tenner, take a seat," Barclay says.

I can't sit down and discuss anything with Barclay. I can't even look at him because I know he's lied to me. Again. I know he's kept this from me, that he brought me here, made me go through hell to break Elijah out, and he knew that Ben had done this. He knew that if we made it this far, I would find out. And he made me find out this way.

I can't believe I trusted him, that I didn't see this coming, that I sat on the couch in his mother's house and listened to him tell me stories about his life and I thought we were friends.

The rage from that idea boils somewhere deep inside me. It burns deep in my chest, because I can't believe he's put me in this position—and worse, I can't believe I was this stupid. I clench my hands into fists to keep them from shaking, and I wrap that anger around myself, because I didn't ask for this. I didn't want to come through a portal and chase after bad guys. I didn't want to watch Ben walk out of my life, or find out the best friend I have left was abducted. But I have to do something about it.

"Tenner—"

I turn back to the table, reach out, and slap Barclay across the face. Hard.

A few people at nearby tables gasp. The force blows his face to the side, and Barclay's skin is already red by the time I pull my hand back. It stings as I sit back down.

He sits paralyzed for a moment, his head to the side, mouth slightly ajar. Whether he's shocked, ashamed, or actually hurt, I don't care. He deserved that, and if he didn't know it before, he knows it now.

I take a deep breath, swallow back the flood of emotions. "You said we'd keep each other in the loop. You promised me that I would know everything I needed to."

"You didn't need to know this," he says as he turns back to face me. "You needed to stay focused."

"You don't get to be the judge of what I need," I say. "Anything that concerns Ben or me or my family, that's stuff I need to know. Got it?"

Barclay doesn't answer. He just rubs his jaw.

If he thinks he's going to get away with not answering, he's wrong. "I've had a pretty rough night. In fact, ever since you started following me around, things have gone to shit. Before I go any further, I want to know everything that both of you know."

Elijah shrugs. "No fucking problem here."

Barclay hesitates. He looks up at me with those big, stupid blue eyes, and I try to ignore the way something in my chest twists at the hurt I see in them. He has no right to feel hurt right now. "I don't have all the answers," he says. "I've got some suspicions, sure, but I need them confirmed by either Elijah or

Ben or maybe someone else. I don't know what else to tell you."

It's a shitty apology—if it even is one. But it doesn't matter.

Because he's right about one thing. We have a source at this table, someone who can give us concrete information about what the hell has been going on.

I look at Elijah.

He must know what I'm thinking because he says, "What do you want to know?"

"Everything."

He nods, raises his mug to his lips, drains the last of his tea, and puts the cup back down. Then he tells us everything that's happened in the last few months. Everything that's happened since he and Ben portaled back to their world and left me in the canyons behind Park Village with Alex's body.

And it's worse than I could have imagined.

# 03:00:47:36

When Ben, Elijah, and Reid tumbled through the portal and ended up in my world, they were ten years old. They spent every free moment afterward trying to find a way to get back to their world, back to their families. Back to where they belonged.

But when they finally did, seven years had gone by.

And seven years in the wake of a national tragedy, it turns out, is a long time.

They expected to walk back into their world, back into their families, back into the lives they left behind. Only, the world they left behind wasn't there anymore. In its place was a world much different.

Seven years ago, Elijah's father, Nathaniel Palma, was the North American prime minister in their world, and when his firstborn son was "abducted" from a birthday party, it became a national tragedy. Every law-enforcement agency in the country was tasked with looking for the missing kids, and nothing was to stand in their way.

Anyone suspected of knowing anything related to the case was brought into custody and questioned, even tortured and imprisoned. Ben's parents, and Reid's too, were thrown in jail for being at the birthday party and not having the right information. Ben's brother was sent to foster care.

The longer the boys were missing, the worse it got. Until people couldn't stand it. There were protests, talk of revolution.

A little over two years after they went through the portal, Nathaniel Palma was assassinated and a revolution overthrew the government. The leader of the rebellion established himself as a military dictator and is still in power today.

Elijah's mother remarried a wealthy businessman. Ben's parents were released from prison, and Derek, Ben's brother, got out of foster care, but any joy from that was short-lived. Their family wasn't quite the same.

Two years after the boys went through the portal, Ben's parents got divorced. His mother threw herself into work, and his father got remarried and started a new family.

Seven years after they went through the portal, when they came back, it was to a very different homecoming than they expected. Half the country seemed to have forgotten about Ben; the other half blamed Elijah for his father's tyranny and the resulting crumbling of society. While his mother and Ben's parents and especially his brother were thrilled they were finally back, the world had gone on without them.

They had expected being home to calm the restless feelings inside them, the ones that screamed they didn't belong in my world. But once they were there and reunited with their families, neither one of them felt like they fit in *there*, either. The more Elijah thought about it, the more he realized he fit in better on the earth they'd left behind.

My earth.

He realized he could have made a home there. He didn't have his parents, but he had Ben and Reid. Only now Reid was dead, and Ben was an emotional wreck.

Elijah decided Ben was his real family now, and it would be best for both of them to turn around and go back—back to the universe they'd left behind, back to Eastview and foster care, and everything.

But Ben couldn't do it yet. Derek was so glad to have him back, and Ben felt guilty—for tripping and falling into the portal, for pulling Elijah with him, for taking too long to get back. He felt like it was his fault that everyone else's lives became so messed up.

But Elijah couldn't just sit around with his mother's new family and feel sorry for himself. So he started focusing on the abilities the hydrochloradneum gave him. He stopped drinking like Ben always told him he should.

Then he started opening portals and traveling through them, to different worlds. Technically he knew the portals were unstable, but to stay under IA radar and avoid Wave Function Collapse, he moved through worlds quickly and efficiently. He didn't return home after each jump. He portaled in, took notes on what was different from other worlds and what was the same, and then he portaled somewhere else.

Meanwhile Ben's depression was making him paranoid. He started to suspect people were following him, that they were out to get him.

When Elijah found a deserted world with no signs of people, he went home and took Ben there. They decided it would be a great safe zone, and if they ever ran into any trouble, that's where they would go to meet up.

But trouble caught up with them too quickly. Eleven weeks ago, a little over a month after they got back, they met to touch base. Elijah was excited about all the worlds he'd visited, but Ben was looking over his shoulder, even more paranoid than he'd been before. He insisted someone had broken into his and Derek's apartment, that some of his things were missing.

Elijah urged him to think about going back to the universe they'd left behind. Back to me. Ben said he was thinking about it, that despite how much he loved Derek, he just didn't belong here anymore. Elijah agreed. Not only did he want to go back with Ben, but he thought they could probably bring Derek with them. They'd just need to get their hands on some hydrochloradneum to keep the radiation from frying him.

Ben liked that plan and promised him he'd talk to his brother about it. No matter what, he knew he couldn't stay where he was.

But IA busted them, took them to Prima, and threw them in prison. Elijah was sure it was because he'd been universe hopping, and as a result, he'd somehow gotten Ben in trouble too.

But it was worse.

Their abilities had been recorded in Barclay and Brandt's original case report. Two young men who could portal in and out of any world without being tracked by technology were exactly what a human-trafficking ring could use, especially a ring that was currently attracting heat from the IA's wonder-boy agent, Taylor Barclay.

While Ben and Elijah were in prison, Meridian broke into their apartments and confiscated their belongings. He found the notebook where Elijah kept notes on the different worlds he'd visited. Meridian praised what Elijah could do, the notes he'd taken, and promised him money, power, women—anything he wanted.

For a second, it was tempting—not for the money, power, or women, but for the freedom to go from universe to universe and discover what was out there. That was something Elijah wanted.

But this was slavery, and Elijah knew what it was like to be taken from your family and your world, and he wasn't about to do that to anyone else. So he refused.

That's when the threats started. They threatened his life and his body—and they beat and tortured him to prove they could follow through. Still he refused. So they threatened his mother and everyone he cared about.

He bluffed, shrugged, and told them to go ahead.

So they took some of his blood and beat him for good measure, but left him in his cell.

He didn't see Ben—not since they were first arrested. They were in different cells and weren't allowed to see or talk to each other, but some nights Elijah could hear Ben scream.

And he heard him scream the last night Ben was there—the night before he agreed to help them. It was when Meridian and IA threatened people they cared about. They threatened to bring in his parents, his brother. And then they did. They brought someone in—beaten and bloody—and told Ben he could watch them die, or he could help.

That's when he gave in.

# 02:23:49:27

"And that's it. I've been rotting in that cell, eating sloppy mush and waiting for him to come back and get me out of there." Elijah cracks his knuckles and looks at Barclay. "So, you gonna call in the cavalry or what? I'm ready to beat some asses."

"Why did they take your blood?" I ask, ignoring his question. He just got shot; he's not going to beat anyone's asses, and there's no cavalry to call in. We're it.

"To do tests and shit." He rolls up a sleeve and shows me the needle marks.

For a minute I don't get it, then Barclay says, "If you were running a human-trafficking ring between universes, wouldn't you want to somehow replicate what he and Ben can do?"

A shiver moves through my body. Criminals with the power to move through the universes—go wherever they want—without a quantum charger. They'd be virtually untraceable. And who knows what kind of damage all those unstable portals would do to the multiverse.

"Tell me more about Meridian," Barclay says.

Elijah describes him—six feet, lanky, sandy-blond hair shaved close to his head, scruffy facial hair, light eyes, barbed-wire tattoo—and Barclay jots down notes, adding a few questions here and there, and I recognize this for what it is—a gentle interrogation. It's the way you question a victim about their attacker. Quietly, nonthreatening, slowly.

I watch Elijah when he answers. He speaks deliberately. He's calmer than he was in my world, more thoughtful. He still swears a lot, but it's more habit than swearing for some kind of effect. I can't imagine what he's been through, not just in the prison, but in the months before it. He spent seven years waiting to get home, and when he finally did, he found out it didn't exist anymore.

And that makes me think of Ben.

As horrible as this is, I find myself wishing it hadn't been Elijah in that cell, that I hadn't gone in to break *him* out. I wish it had been Ben. Because I have a fierce urge to lay my face against his chest and breathe him in until the world makes sense again.

Only I can't, because I don't know where he is. At least not yet.

"Why did you think Ben would come back for you?" Barclay asks.

"I couldn't keep good track of time," Elijah adds. "I think the bastards only fed us once a day. Four or five days, or maybe a week ago, the guards and Meridian came back into my cell. They wanted to know where Ben would go. Where he would hide."

"They'd lost him?" I ask. He must have had a plan—he must have agreed to keep his family safe, while at the same time coming up with some kind of plan to get away from them, to get out of it.

Elijah nods. "But it was worse than that—for them, I mean. I got the impression he took someone with him."

# 02:22:51:42

I tell Barclay about seeing Meridian at the prison—about him torturing Derek. "What do you think?"

He doesn't respond right away, and I'm tempted to reach over and slap him again.

Then he says, "Constantine Meridian is bad news. If he's the one behind the trafficking, it makes sense—it's clearly an organized, multi-universe operation, and he's got the manpower and the money to back it."

My shoulders relax a little, and I take a shaky breath. I'm suddenly less mad, because this is good news. If Barclay knows something about this guy, it means we're a huge step closer to finding him—finding Cecily—than we were just minutes ago.

"Good," Elijah says. "Glad I was able to fucking help. I'm ready to beat the shit out of him too, if you need me."

Barclay shakes his head. "It's not going to be that easy."

Of course it's not, but I don't like the expression on Barclay's face. He looks . . . defeated. "What are you leaving out?"

His eyes flick to mine. "Meridian's been on our Most Wanted list for the last seven years, and if he's been in and out of the

Piston, it means he's got a lot of inside help. Maybe more than I suspected."

I bite down on my lip. We need more good news—less things for us to try to do ourselves. "We just need to prove that he's behind it all and Ben's not."

"Ben *is* part of it, or he fucking was," Elijah says. "IA's not going to just forgive that. Hell, who knows how many of them are fucking in on it?"

Barclay puts a hand on Elijah's shoulder. "Meridian is bad news. He grew up in the underground. He's one of those guys with a juvenile file twenty pages long. Breaking and entering, theft, larceny. He smartened up when he was an adult, but that doesn't mean he's been any less active. His predecessor, Crewe Fielding, ran all the organized crime in the underground. Then suddenly he's dead on the floor in front of one of the elevators, mutilated so badly he's unrecognizable. It was the worst thing I've ever seen."

"Even worse than that house?" I say and I cringe involuntarily. An unstable portal killed everyone with high levels of radiation. It made them look like their skin was melting off their bones.

Barclay doesn't need me to elaborate, but he nods. "This was worse.

"Eric and I had a case last year, drugs coming from other worlds and spreading through the underground. A lot of kids ended up overdosing. We had four deaths, a couple of people in a coma, and one of the dealers in custody. We suspected Meridian was responsible, but before we were able to prove it, we were reassigned, and our case moved to a different department that just sat on it. Eric thought someone might have been using Meridian as an informant, keeping him on the Most Wanted list in order to keep up pretenses but using him for information about other cases—bigger cases."

"So what the fuck are we going to do about all this?" Elijah asks. "I'm sick of just sitting here."

"We need Ben," I say. It's what I need—to see him, to wrap my arms around him, to hear what's happened to him in the past few months in his words, to tell him we'll get through this. But it's less selfish. If Ben worked for this Meridian guy, he also has more information than the three of us. We need that information before we can save Cecily and come up with the proof that will expose anyone involved.

I look at Elijah.

"I know where he is, or at least where he should be," he says.

"How are you feeling?" Barclay asks.

"Better than I was before," Elijah says with a shrug.

"Good." Barclay stands. "Think you can portal us to wherever you think Ben is?"

Elijah stands up. "Abso-fucking-lutely."

"Won't it be unstable?"

Barclay nods. "We'll have to open it and go through quickly. No standing around and staring at it. Unstable portals attract attention and become dangerous the longer they're open and the more they're used. Once we're all together, we'll use the charger." He looks at Elijah. "No more world hopping."

"I make no promises," Elijah says. "Not with your IA thugs after me."

Barclay looks at me. "Let's go."

There's a fluttering in my stomach, and I drain the last sip of my mocha latte to keep my hands from shaking.

After waiting for so long, suddenly I feel a little nervous.

So much has happened in the months that we've been apart. Ben's been through so much—at home, in prison, working with the traffickers. What if he's different?

I think of the guard I killed. The life draining out of his eyes. What if I'm different?

# 02:22:42:52

**B**arclay pays the check and we leave the coffee shop and walk back toward the motel. When we pass a deserted alley, we turn down it, and Elijah holds his arm out in front of him.

"How do you do it?" I ask without thinking.

Elijah looks back at me.

"I mean, how do you open the right portal?"

He smiles. "I think of the place I want to go. The more details I have right, the better, but ultimately I just feel the molecules in the air, reach for the nothingness, and try to pull it apart, expand it. The whole time, I think of where I want it to take me, and it does."

"It sounds so easy."

He nods. "It is. Ben was right. All it takes is a clear head and a lot of practice."

*It also sounds wrong.* But I don't say that. It is wrong. Taking a couple of precautions doesn't change that. Opening too many portals is what destroyed my world.

But it doesn't change the fact that we need a portal to take us to Ben. Elijah and I can argue over his extracurricular activities when this thing is behind us. If we're both still alive, that is.

Elijah turns around again, stretching his hand out. The air in front of him shimmers a little, and a small black hole opens up right in front of his fingers. Elijah squeezes his eyes shut tighter, and it starts to expand. Slowly at first, and then faster, until there's a full-size portal in front of us.

Barclay nods to me before he moves through, and I suppose if he can trust that Elijah is going to get us where we need to go, I can too.

My palms touch first, and the rest of my body slams against the ground a split second after. Dust from the road springs up around me and I cough it out of my lungs as I take stock of my surroundings. At first glance, it seems like we've landed on the outskirts of a normal suburb. There's a strip mall with a dry cleaner, a hair salon, and a grocery store. Beyond them is what looks like apartment buildings. I can see someone's wash hanging on the balcony, flapping in the wind.

But there's something off.

There are buildings everywhere—high-rises, strip malls, concrete parking structures, and even a park. But the leaves are missing from the trees, the grass is brown, and as I look closer at the buildings, I can see that they're crumbling a little under the weight of the vines that are growing up around them.

I push myself to my feet and take a more in-depth look around. And I listen, but I can't hear anything.

"What is this place?" I ask. It's not the same as the abandoned world Barclay has taken us through a few times, but it looks like that's the way it's headed.

"Someplace no one will be looking for us," Elijah says.

"Oh shit," Barclay says, as he looks around.

"What is it?" Maybe this place isn't as safe from the IA as Elijah thinks. It wouldn't be the first time he's been wrong. I reach for my gun. It can't hurt to be ready.

Barclay shakes his head. "IA doesn't come here," he says, and there's something about the way his says it, like whatever we're about to face is going to be worse.

Still looking around, he brushes a hand through his hair. "This is Earth 36552." His voice is drowned out by the wind that picks up, but I can see the expression on his face. Lips slightly ajar, eyes wide, he looks horrified.

I'm not sure why.

But I don't have time to ask. The history lesson can come later.

"This way," Elijah says.

I follow him, but Barclay grabs my arm. "Take this off." He grabs at my hoodie, yanking it off my shoulders.

"Why are you trying to undress me, you creeper?" I shove him off.

"Nuclear war destroyed this world," he says, giving my arm a sharp jerk.

# 02:22:39:00

"I don't know where we are, but the radiation . . ." Barclay says. "Don't breathe this air unfiltered." Pulling his own jacket off, he ties part of it like a scarf around his neck so that it covers his nose and mouth.

I do what he says and copy him, even though I'm not sure it will do much good. If he's right, and all the people in this universe died from the radiation fallout of a nuclear war, a layer of cotton between me and the air I'm breathing isn't going to save me.

"Stay in the middle of the road," Barclay shouts at me, and I nod. Radiation sits on the soil, on the grass, in the water, and in fruits and vegetables, like apples and mushrooms. It isn't retained by asphalt.

We pass something that might have been an apartment building. There's a wooden sled discarded on the lawn. It looks like it might have once been painted red, but the paint has long ago peeled off, and it's back to being just the color of wood and rusted metal.

I turn around to look at Barclay. He's wrapped up like some cross between a cowboy and a ninja. "How did this happen?"

Rather than shout over the wind, he jogs to me. "About sixty years ago, the former Soviet Union wanted to have missiles in range of the US, so Khrushchev moved them to Cuba. To compensate, the US armed missiles at their base in Turkey. It's not exactly clear who started what, since there isn't anyone left to tell the tale and IA didn't have anyone stationed here. But the basic idea is that no one would back down, someone fired first, someone else struck back, and they started World War III."

We pass a building that looks like a school, only the trees are growing unchecked and their roots are starting to overturn the foundation of the building.

"Nuclear war," Barclay repeats. "About eighty percent of the population died off within the first year from the bombings and the actual war. Everyone else was gone within the next five years because of the radiation levels."

So this is what the Cuban missile crisis could have looked like.

We go into a building slightly overrun by vines and plants. It's an old hospital. The once cream-colored walls are gray in places and chipped in others to reveal the concrete underneath. There's a small tree coming up through the floor in the lobby, and there are cockroaches skittering around in dark corners. I'm not surprised. The level of radiation lethal to a cockroach is over a hundred times that which is lethal to a human, and now, without people to kill them, they must be rejoicing.

"The elevators don't work," Elijah says.

He doesn't bat an eye at the way either Barclay or I are dressed and covering our mouths. Which means he knows there's a radiation risk here. Either he or Ben figured out what could have caused this at some point in their exploration. But he doesn't make a move to shield his own breathing, which means he's been here enough that he's not concerned about the levels of radiation hurting him.

I reach up and pull my hoodie away from my face. It's probably not doing anything anyway.

Barclay grabs it and shoves it back in my face.

I gesture to Elijah. "Doesn't look like we're about to drop dead yet."

"He drank a pure source of hydrochloradneum," Barclay spits. "He's practically immune to radiation. You've only had one shot."

I roll my eyes. "Stop being such an alarmist." But I do what he wants. He knows a lot more about this shit than I do.

"Do you see anyone *living* around here?" he says, shaking his head. He mutters something else, but it's lost underneath the jacket covering his mouth.

We're wasting time. We need to find Ben, get somewhere safe, figure out what he knows, and come up with a plan. Every second that goes by is a loss—and we don't have that many to lose.

I turn to Elijah, and he must sense what I need.

"I'm not sure which floor he'd be on," he says. "But if he's here, this is where he'd be."

"Why here?" I ask, my breath shallow.

"It's a hospital, Tenner. There are empty beds, blankets and shit." Elijah smirks. "And I stashed food and medicine here, in case we need it."

I suppose it's as good a reason as any. I just hope Ben is here.

I'm not sure if I can stand to come this close and then wind up empty.

We climb the stairs. They're sagging and crumbled in places, but we climb them anyway, and to make Barclay less nervous, I try to keep from touching anything.

When we get to the fourth floor, I hear something.

Correction. I hear some*one*.

I can hear him singing.

# 02:22:09:47

The singing is gravelly and slightly off-key, and it feels like my heart has skipped a beat. I don't have to think twice to know that it's Ben. I don't bother with Elijah or with Barclay. I just run toward the sound. It's the only noise there is—other than the wind outside—which means there's nothing to throw me off.

I recognize the song, and it brings a smile to my face. It's "Iridescent" by Linkin Park, complete with sound effects for the guitar riffs. It's a song we heard on the radio when he picked me up for our first date. He glanced at me, turned the volume up, and we drove with the windows down, the sun on our faces, and the ocean breeze moving through the car.

He's thinking of me.

I race through the empty hall. He's in the last room on the right. The door is ajar, and I barrel through it, only to stop short a few paces into the room.

Because I see him.

He's sitting on the edge of a bed, wearing a gray, long-sleeved thermal, jeans, and white socks. His Chuck Taylors are discarded on the floor a few feet away. His hair is a little longer than when

I saw him last. The brown curls droop into his face past his eyes. His lips, curled into a smile as he sings, falter slightly when he looks up and sees me.

He pushes his hair out of his face, grabbing the ends, and I'm breathless at the sight of it, because even something as simple as a familiar gesture matters. Because it's familiar—to both of us.

Ben's mouth drops, abruptly cutting off the song, and the surprise and confusion on his face are clear.

For a split second, I wonder why he hasn't jumped to his feet and rushed toward me. Then I remember what he's been through—and what I must look like with my burned hair pulled back into a bun, and my hoodie wrapped around half my head. I pull the hoodie off and smile.

Around us it's almost quiet.

Almost because I can hear Elijah's and Barclay's clunky footsteps as they chase after me.

And because I hear my own voice whisper, "Ben," before I can stop myself.

Before he says, "Janelle?" his voice raised in question, before he looks down at the bed next to him, and before I realize he's not alone.

# 02:22:07:18

My gaze moves to the bed. Under the once-white blankets is a girl. Her brown hair, highlighted with blond streaks, is thick and long, and it's strewn over her pillow in messy waves. Her eyes are closed, but her olive skin has faint bruises that look like they could be a few weeks old. Her arms are curled around the blanket, and as I take a step closer, I realize the oversize black hoodie she's wearing is Ben's.

But that's not what makes my own breath feel like it's choking me.

I take another step closer, unable to take my eyes off her. Her heart-shaped face, the long eyelashes, and the Italian nose—even the bone structure of her cheekbones and jawline.

It's like looking in a mirror.

# 02:22:07:12

"I never would have believed this shit," comes Elijah's voice behind me.

I knew there might be other *me*s out there. Of all the universes, there have to be others where my father and my mother both existed, and they married and had children. And this isn't the first double I've seen. Only a day ago, or maybe two, I had to sit across from someone who wasn't Struz even though he wore the same face, and answer questions. But I didn't expect this. I wasn't ready to see another version of myself.

Because the girl lying in this bed is me.

Me with highlights.

I want to turn around, to look at Elijah and Barclay—to see the expressions on their faces. To confirm that I'm not dreaming or crazy. But I can't. My body is frozen in place, captivated by her—by me.

I wasn't prepared to face this, another version of me with the guy I love.

I tear my eyes away from her and look at Ben.

The whole world feels like it's just vanished. My eyes are

glassy, my face is too hot, and my hands won't stop shaking. My throat feels so thick it hurts, and it's a good thing I don't have anything to say because I'm one word away from losing it.

While we're standing there staring at each other, the girl who looks just like me—I don't even know what to call her—reaches up and puts her hand on Ben's arm. It's a casual, careless gesture. Her eyes are still closed. She hasn't seen me. It's the kind of gesture that suggests familiarity. Probably something she does all the time.

The sight of her touching him like that—like I should be touching him—makes me physically ill. I have to clutch my stomach with one hand and cover my mouth to keep myself from gagging.

I didn't used to be like this. I didn't believe in love and romance and swooning. My default setting was bitch.

Then Ben came along and changed that. He made me believe. And I thought love was black-and-white. That I loved Ben, that I belonged with him, that somehow *that* would always be enough. Despite everything stacked up against us, I believed we would overcome it—maybe not today or tomorrow, but at some point in our future, we'd end up together.

I thought we were special, that what we felt for each other would be powerful enough to take down human traffickers, save the world, span universes.

I thought we had the kind of love that could do anything.

I can feel the tears threatening me in the burn behind my eyes and the tightness in my throat.

Because right now, looking at that girl—the one who looks just like me—with her hand on his arm, I suddenly don't know who I am or how I fit with anything in this world. I've seen too much. I was supposed to be a normal high-school junior dealing with mean girls like Brooke Haslen and cocky guys like Kevin Collins. Instead I've dealt with death and the fate of the world on my shoulders. I've seen worlds that shouldn't exist.

And it's finally just Too Much.

I turn around and head for the door. I don't look at Barclay or Elijah on my way out. I push past them and walk into the hallway.

No "I missed you."

No "I love you."

Nothing.

I ran this moment—seeing Ben again for the first time—over and over again in my mind. I imagined a thousand different scenarios. But not one of them was like this.

Not one of them was silent.

## 02:21:55:32

After I leave the room, I just walk past Elijah and Barclay. I don't particularly know where I'm going, but I know that I need to get away. My legs move like they're on automatic, and I end up down the hallway, in a hospital room not much different from theirs. White plaster walls, two twin beds, a curtain between them. I sit on the bed farthest from the door and pick up a discarded stuffed animal on the floor. It's a bunny.

I look out the window at the ghost town below and let myself just fall apart.

From this angle, the city looks quiet, sleepy almost, as if all the people are tucked away inside.

I'm in over my head, up against people more organized, more connected, and more dangerous. I'm beat up, bruised, worn out, and exhausted, and we're quickly running short on time. I'm in a strange and abandoned world, and I feel like someone has reached into my chest and ripped my heart to pieces.

Right now in this moment, I don't know who I am anymore.

All I know is that I should.

The door opens and my heart lurches. I stand and turn,

expecting Ben, but it's just Barclay.

I wipe my eyes. "Great. What do you want?"

He shuts the door softly behind him and doesn't bother to look insulted. "You shouldn't be this upset."

I can't keep in the snort that is my response. "Why, because it's no big deal?" I almost warn him that if he comes any closer I might punch him. But I don't because it might feel good to hit something.

"No, because you're better than this," Barclay says, as he moves toward me.

"Oh, that's so original." I roll my eyes. "Do yourself a favor and don't try to do comforting and supportive. It's not your forte."

Barclay chuckles, a smile breaking over his face. "No, I guess it's not. But be serious. Why are you upset?"

I realize my tears have actually stopped. Typically, Barclay had managed to piss me off quickly enough to make me stop crying. But now, thinking about Ben and the way he looked, leaning over and caring for someone else, my eyes sting and I feel the pinch in my chest all over again.

Barclay takes another step closer and reaches out, putting a hand on my arm. He's not tentative, he's not afraid I might hit him like someone else would be. I've hit him enough that he should be, but he's not. He's just here. And Barclay as a normal, caring human being is what makes the dam break.

"The way he was looking at her." My voice sounds foreign, too high pitched, like it belongs to someone else, some other girl stupid enough to get her heart broken.

"She looks just like you," he says, pulling me into him. His arms are strong behind my back. "You have to be able to see how this could have happened. IA grabbed another version of you, maybe she was even already in custody. They put her in front of Ben, said she was you, and threatened her if he didn't help them."

"I never would have wanted him to help them in order to save me. I would rather have died."

"Tenner, come on. You think that matters?" Barclay whispers, his hand rubbing my back. "He wasn't thinking about what you wanted. He was just thinking about you—about the fact that he thought you were being hurt, and it was his fault."

"And now?" I say. "Why didn't he save Elijah, and his parents—his brother?"

"I don't know what he was thinking," Barclay says. "But you'd better believe we're going to ask him. We'll figure this out."

The words fall out of my mouth—the ones I've been keeping inside since we got here. "He didn't say anything. When he saw me . . . nothing."

Barclay doesn't tell me I'm crazy. He doesn't make excuses for Ben, and he doesn't agree with me either. He doesn't even point out the most likely truth—that Ben was in shock and confused. He just lets me be upset.

I don't know how long we stand there like that, but after a while, Barclay clears his throat. "There's something I didn't tell you."

I'm too exhausted to do anything but slump a little in his arms.

"Here, sit back down," he says, lowering me back onto the bed. "And get rid of this stupid rabbit. Who knows what kind of radiation it's got."

I let him take the stuffed animal from me and toss it back

onto the floor, but I notice he's not wearing the scarf around his face anymore. As if he knows what I'm thinking, he says, "I used the charger to check the radiation levels, and we should be pretty safe if we're only here a few days, but try not to touch everything."

I nod. "What do you need to tell me?"

Barclay takes a deep breath. "Weeks ago, Hayley told me she'd heard someone say they had you in custody," he says. "It was hearsay, and I couldn't get the clearance to get into the prison and find out whether it was actually true."

I think of the way Hayley looked at me when we were at Barclay's mother's house—like she recognized me. "You knew this might be a possibility?"

"No," he says with a shake of his head. "I hacked into the database and there was no arrest record, which meant she had to have heard it wrong."

"And it would just be in the file?" Bad guys don't always keep records of all the bad stuff they're doing. Or at least the smart ones don't. What better way to get caught than to have all your secrets on a server?

"After Eric died, I went to your world, I looked around, and I saw you passing out bottles of water and bags of food with a couple of poor excuses for soldiers. You were there, doing whatever it is you were doing, which meant you couldn't possibly be in an IA prison."

I nod, but I don't know what else to say. Sure, I can be pissed Barclay didn't know that this is what we might find when we found Ben, but it isn't his fault. He checked the files and then he checked in on me and saw I was fine. Why would he think IA would grab someone else and pretend it was me?

Well, they're certainly shitty like that, but for some stupid reason Barclay hasn't quite grasped that yet.

And really, what hurts the most *isn't* that my doppelgänger is involved. It's that Ben didn't recognize her for what she was.

It's the realization that I'm replaceable.

Barclay must know that, because he sits next to me and pulls me into another hug.

The odds are stacked against us, and we don't have enough time. I don't know how things managed to get so colossally messed up or confusing, and now, I don't know what this means for me and Ben, if we manage to live through the next three days.

I thought we would find a way to be together, but how do we come back from this?

It's when I feel Barclay's heart thumping under his shirt that I realize I've stopped crying again. I push away from him, feeling strangely better and numb to everything—Ben, human trafficking, another version of me in the other room.

"Good," Barclay says, and for a moment I wonder if I've spoken out loud. "We have something important we're going to have to address."

"You mean other than taking down a human-trafficking ring?" My voice is hoarse from too much emotion, and I realize I'm exhausted.

"That girl in there, we don't know who she is," Barclay says.

I want to laugh. "Actually, we do. She's me."

He shakes his head. "Just because she has the same face doesn't mean she's you. Remember she wasn't in the database. There was no arrest record. She could be a victim, she could be someone who just got dragged into this, or she could be some kind of IA plant. No matter what, we can't trust her."

"If IA beat her, I doubt she's working for them." The last thing I need is another reason to not be able to look at her.

"The question is, *did* IA beat her?" he says. "We still need to talk to Ben. But we also need to know exactly what happened in that prison and what he saw."

He's right about that, at least. If we trust the wrong person, we're going to end up dead. "Okay, let's talk to Ben without her, then we can talk to her, see if we can put all the pieces together."

Barclay smiles. "Good plan, and no matter what happens, remember who you are, Tenner."

"What do you mean by that?" I'm not sure whether I'm supposed to be offended.

"After I graduated from North Point and went through IA training, one of the first things they drilled into us was to always remember who we were," he says, and I realize why it's important even before he keeps going. "There's always the chance you're going to run into another version of yourself. It doesn't happen that often, but it does happen."

"Have you ever seen another version of you?" I ask, repressing a shudder. Barclay is annoying enough and there's only one of him.

He shakes his head. "But this girl isn't you. She's had different experiences, she's grown up in a different world."

So I have to remember who I am—and that she's not me. "So who am I?"

Barclay smiles. "You're Janelle Tenner, the only chick I've ever asked for help."

I can't help but smile at that, even though we both know he didn't really have a choice.

He keeps going. "I mean it. You're tough. Whatever happens, tonight, tomorrow, even the rest of your life, remember who you are and why you're still alive."

He squeezes my arms. "Think about everything you've already been through. Remember what you've done and use that. This is just another day at the office."

My laugh doesn't sound as bitter as I'd expected. "Just another day fighting crime and saving the world?"

"Exactly." He smiles. "Tenner, you're the girl who saved your world. Now you're going to help me save mine."

"Does that mean I get a piece of your monument?" I ask.

Barclay pauses for a second before letting out a dramatic sigh. "I suppose I could be persuaded to share it with you. But you'll have to earn it."

I take a deep breath and wipe my face with the ends of my sleeves. I wish I could go back somehow, go back and restore my own innocence, go back and un-know the secrets that I've been carrying with me every day since I uncovered the truth about the multiverse. But short of getting a lobotomy—which really isn't in my plans—there's nothing I can do except forge on. Cecily is out there, scared and alone, and she still needs me.

We've only got three days left and so far we haven't actually uncovered anything all that useful.

"We better get to work then," I say, because really, what else can I say at this point? I need to refocus. Now that we've found Ben, we need to figure out what we're going to do next.

Barclay smiles and opens the door. I look at him, really take him in, the hair that's too long, the cocky grin, the striking eyes and the angular jaw, the stance that says he knows just how badass he is. He's a guy in his early twenties with the world at his feet—or I guess, really, the fate of the world on his shoulders. He's a real-life superhero.

For the first time I wonder if Barclay is what my dad was like

278

in his twenties—or Struz when he first started with the Bureau. I wonder if this is what Alex would have been like in five years if he hadn't died.

I press the heel of my palm to my chest, pushing back against the pain on the inside.

I've lost enough people in my life. I refuse to lose more.

I have to see this through. I have to get Cecily back and go home. For my dad, for Alex, for Jared and Struz—for me.

# 02:19:32:16

Barclay convenes a meeting on the seventh and highest floor of the hospital in what looks like an old staff lounge. My doppelgänger is the only one not invited. When Ben comes in, he heads straight for me.

"Janelle," he whispers, and I'm reminded of the day I died. It's the way he says my name—I don't know how he manages to put so much feeling into one word, but it makes me shiver.

I don't respond. I don't know what to say, but I glance his way. His eyes are soft, the lines on his face tell me he's worried, but when he reaches for me, I flinch away.

"Are you okay? Are you hurt?" Ben asks.

"I'm fine," I say, trying to look at him as little as possible.

We sit at a round table, drinking stale Pepsi Elijah stashed here before IA grabbed him. "We need to know everything," Barclay says.

Ben looks at me like he wants to say something, but instead turns to Barclay. "Half the things I thought I had figured out an hour ago have just been turned on their head."

Because he's anything but subtle, Elijah says, "Who's the girl?"

Ben kicks one of the legs of the table, and the whole thing jerks.

"It's as good a place to start as any," I force myself to say.

Ben pushes a hand through his hair and I see his eyes. They're bloodshot, like he's trying to keep from crying. "We've been here almost five days," he says with an audible swallow. "I brought her here because we'd be safe. She was in really bad shape, bruised, beaten up, all that. I've been taking care of her."

"So you don't fucking know who she is," Elijah says, leaning back in his chair.

Ben shakes his head and looks down. "I thought she was Janelle," he whispers.

I look at the ceiling to keep from tearing up again.

"She *is* Janelle," Barclay begins. "But another version of her."

Ben doesn't say anything.

"That can't be a bad thing, right?" Elijah says before looking at me. "Don't let that go to your head. It's not that I think you're that great or anything, but you're not half bad for a chick."

"You're not exactly a party either," I say, because trading insults with Elijah is something I can handle. He must feel the same because he flashes me a grin.

Barclay shakes his head. "Look, it's important for all of us to go into this with our eyes wide open. In IA, we call ourselves 'originals,' and the other versions of us are 'doubles.' There are cases of doubles so similar they were practically identical to their original—and cases where the only similarity was physical appearance. Right now we need to get up to speed, and then we need to talk to her, figure out exactly who she is, how she got into this, whether we can trust her—and if she can help us."

"I think she's suffered some head trauma," Ben says. "Or I

thought she had because she . . . she doesn't remember me. But I guess she shouldn't."

I think of Ben's double, the guy I saw at the yard sale with Cecily. I knew almost immediately he wasn't mine.

It might be unfair, it might be a demand I have no right to hold against Ben. But I do.

He should have known she wasn't me.

# 02:18:29:54

Seeing a break in the conversation, Elijah jumps in. "I told them about everything I could. How we got back and it wasn't the same, how I went world hopping and you were being followed—"

"Come on, Eli," Ben says. "Can't you see now that I wasn't paranoid? They're trying to use me as a scapegoat and execute me."

"They're trying to execute all of us, asshole," Elijah says. "The question is, what are we going to do about it?"

I cut in. "We still need to know what happened to you," I say, looking at Ben. "They picked you up, brought you into IA custody, threw you in prison, and then what?"

He just stares at me and doesn't respond, so I add, "We need to know," for good measure. Because we do.

Ben nods. "I'm sorry, J, I . . ." He swallows. "This guy came to see me—"

"What guy?" Barclay asks, I guess to make sure we're after the right one.

"His name's Constantine Meridian," Ben says. "He's tall, thin, light hair shaved close to his head, gnarly barbed-wire tattoo. Kind of looks like a skinhead."

Barclay nods.

"He's a bad guy," Ben says, and I'm surprised at how shaken he looks. "He caught one of the guards sleeping when he was watching the security cameras. He got all of us together, woke everyone up who was asleep, called back the guys who were out on an assignment, and told us, 'Carl's tired. We need to make sure he gets more rest.' Then he injected him with something. Killed him on the spot."

I think of the way Meridian looked at me in the prison, the blood on his shirt, Derek telling me to run, and I feel cold.

Ben tells a story similar to Elijah's. Meridian was impressed with his abilities and offered him a job. When Ben refused, they beat him up and threatened the people he cared about.

"I held on as long as I could," he says, and for a moment, I think that's all he's going to say. He's looking down, hair flopping in his face, his Adam's apple moving as he swallows down the guilt he must feel.

Then suddenly, he pushes up from the table and walks toward a window. "When they brought her in," he says, his voice cracking, "her face swollen and bloody, that was it. I couldn't bear to see what else they would do to her." He lowers his voice, but not too much. We all hear him. "I thought she was you."

He stops then, and we all let him. I've been wrapped up in what I'm going through, so I haven't exactly bothered to ask him how he's dealing with all this. He thought he'd done something noble and brave—something for me—and it turned out that he made the wrong choice.

I can't blame him for that. I've killed a man, and I'm going to carry that around with me for the rest of my life. But just because I don't blame him doesn't mean things will ever be the same.

Ben turns around, leans against the wall, and folds his arms across his chest. "I worked with them for about three weeks," he says, his voice raw with regret. "I did whatever they asked, and then when they'd started to relax around me, trust me a little, they brought her to see me again as a reward. That's when I ran."

I suppose I should be thankful that he valued me over Derek and his parents—that I was more important to him than taking down Meridian and saving the people he grabbed. But it just makes me feel worse. It weighs on my chest and makes it hard to breathe. I wonder how many people out there are injured or dead because of me.

"What can you tell us about their operation?" Barclay asks. He hesitates a little as he says it, like he's choosing his words carefully, and I realize, even though we're all on the same side here, he's still treating Elijah and Ben like outsiders, like suspects. He might not tell me everything, but at least he doesn't lie to me or play games.

"While I was working for them, I lived in the world that's their base of operations . . . it's hard to describe, sort of like a movie, where everyone there is a bad guy. There's a processing center for everyone they bring in," Ben says.

"The slaves?" I ask, because I don't want to get confused about who we're talking about, and I don't want to mince words or pussyfoot around something because it makes us uncomfortable. We need to call it what it is. These people who are being trafficked, they're slaves.

Ben nods. "We called them the Unwilling."

# 02:18:24:44

I can feel the hair on the back of my neck standing on end, and a shiver moves through me. "They have Cecily," I say. I explain everything I know. How my world fell apart—the shortages of food, water, electricity, medicine, everything. I recount the first missing-persons case, the high count of people who vanished from Qualcomm, and the last abduction, when Cecily was taken too.

In the end, I add, "We need to get her back."

Ben swears. "I . . ."

"We'll get her back," Elijah says. "We'll get them all back, and we'll take these fuckers down." He reaches out, grabs Ben's shoulder, and gives it a shake. "What do we need to do?"

"We need to know everything about the operation," Barclay says. "We need to know how it worked. How did you know who to grab and where and all that?"

Ben takes a deep breath and repositions himself on his chair. It's like I can see him pulling a hardened shell around himself. He's overcome—I know the feeling—but he's with us. He isn't about to let these guys get away with this. "It was different depending on the assignment. I guess Meridian had people who were doing scout work, I'm not sure. In the beginning, I had to work with a partner. We'd get a location and a type of person they wanted. It could be vague, like gender and age range, or sometimes it would be more specific, like hair or eye color or something."

Like shopping. If my stomach wasn't so empty, I'd be fighting to keep from throwing up.

"The last couple of jobs I did were different," Ben continues. "I was on my own, and I had a specific person they wanted me to grab: name, age, height, weight, appearance, sometimes even a picture or files, like someone had been keeping tabs on them."

"So they sometimes were targeting specific people?" Barclay asks, and I know from his tone he wasn't expecting that.

Ben nods. "When I brought them in, they didn't stay at the processing center. Someone else portaled them out that night. Usually one of Meridian's main guys."

I take a deep breath and blow it out slowly. I'm not sure why these targeted people are different, but they are and I know that's important. It's another piece of the puzzle. Whenever I think I've gotten a handle on this situation and what we're up against, I'm surprised by the horror of it. How can this be real?

Barclay is still calm. "So you lived at the processing center in this world. Could you take us there if you needed to?"

Ben nods.

"And you'd get a job, portal out, grab whoever the job was, and portal them back to the processing center. Then what?"

Ben shifts on his feet and blows out a steady breath. I wonder if he lay awake at night, unable to sleep because of the guilt, how he justified to himself that saving me was worth so many other lives, and if he's started to think about what he did—for me—and how it wasn't actually for me at all.

His eyes find mine, and I know what I'm seeing in them. Because what Ben is feeling, I am too. I don't know how things got so messed up, how we went from belonging to two different worlds—something that already seemed impossible—to wherever we are now, with my double in another room, human traffickers and IA agents looking for us, and countless people whose lives we're both responsible for tearing apart.

"Come on, we need to focus," Barclay says.

Ben nods. "There was a guy in charge of the processing center, and I'd report to him."

"What's his name?"

"Basil something. A lot of the guys there called him Razor or Raze."

"You're fucking kidding me," Barclay says with a snort. He pushes back into his chair and runs his hands through his hair. The gesture looks so much like something Ben would do.

Trying to concentrate, I lean forward. "What? What does that mean?"

"Basil 'Razor' Lehrman is a smuggler and a rapist. He got his nickname when he was fifteen and killed his parents by cutting them up with a razor blade. But he's . . ." Barclay's eyes widen and he lets out a bitter laugh. "They've set up their processing center right under IA's nose on the Black Hole."

"The Black Hole?" Please let this not be what I think it means. I am not up for space travel.

"It's a world that was demolished thousands of years ago," Barclay says. "Someone in IA found it when we were first making a map of the multiverse, but it's got no sustainable plant or animal life anywhere. We even tried to set up a colony, but plants shriveled and died after a few days, and people would get sick. It's like something happened to the atmosphere."

"What does IA use it for?" Elijah asks.

"They built an underground prison there like fifteen years ago and stationed some IA guards there—you know, the guys who fucked up beyond repair. It's where they send the worst of the worst, the criminals who are so bad, they want them on a different world."

"Guys like Basil Razorblade?" I ask.

Barclay nods. "Guys who have a lot of ties to other bad guys, guys who IA is never going to let see the light of day outside a prison again. They exile them to the Black Hole and put them underground."

It's unfathomable to me that the IA would execute me in three days, but someone like Basil gets to live out his life in prison.

"Why not just execute them?" Elijah apparently has the same thought.

"A lot of these guys have big secrets, and if they die, whatever it is they know is going to die with them," Barclay says. "If those secrets are information that could be valuable to IA or the government, then why not put them in a hole in the ground for ten years and then see if they're willing to give it up?"

"But if it's an IA prison, that can't be where the base of operations is," Ben says.

But I see where Barclay is going with this. If you were organized and had the technology to set up anywhere—get in and out of any world—which Meridian obviously does, it would be the perfect place to set up operations. As long as Meridian and his guys could come and go undetected, there's virtually no risk.

It's essentially an unmonitored world—no unwanted IA agents are going to just drop in, and if you kill or pay off the guards, everyone else who's there would be cheap labor. After all, Meridian can smuggle in things they want, make their lives better in almost every possible way, and maybe even offer them a way out after they've done enough for him. Talk about incentives.

Which means the prison has probably been converted to the processing center, and the inmates are probably now in charge of the slaves.

I look at Barclay. "This is bad. How many guys are in this world?"

He sighs. "I don't know. The universe has been stripped from the records. It doesn't even have a name. We just call it the Black Hole because that's what it is, and you've got to call it something when you're talking about it. There could be a dozen guys or there could be five hundred. I have no idea."

"It's more than a dozen," Ben says. "As a guess, I'd say there are about forty guys who are working for Raze, and then twenty more who take turns smuggling the Unwilling in and out. At least, I think. There could be a few more, but I met twenty of them. They've only got eight of the devices that open portals. I got the impression they used to have a few more, but they've stopped working or something."

So they're working in shifts. "How many jobs did you do a day?"

He doesn't look at me when he answers. "Anywhere between eight and twelve."

That number makes me go cold, all the way down to my fingertips.

If he was there three weeks, it means he grabbed somewhere

between 168 and 252 people. And that's just Ben. If there are twenty guys bringing back that many people . . .

"Holy shit," Barclay whispers, and I know he's just done the math in his head too.

"What?" Elijah says, looking from Barclay to me.

I press my palm against my chest. Ben did this because of me and that makes those people he grabbed my responsibility. It hurts to say it out loud, but I do anyway. "That's like an average of fourteen hundred people a week."

# 02:17:01:14

"It's a huge operation," Ben says. "And that's just the processing center I was working with. They've either got others set up or they're working on it." He looks at Barclay. "This thing is only going to get bigger. Meridian's got someone trying to replicate the formula for the hydrochloradneum that Eli and I drank. If he can give that to all his guys, they can stay under the radar better and work around the clock. He can even recruit more guys to help. They'll be more efficient."

The laws of supply and demand apparently don't discriminate.

Barclay leans forward. "Okay, let's go back to the processing center. After you brought in the slaves, then what?"

"Raze would have someone take the Unwilling and place them in the cell that designated where they were going."

Thinking of Cecily, I ask, "How long did they stay there?"

"I'm not sure," Ben says. "I didn't have much to do with the transfers out. But I think it depended on a couple things, like how cooperative they were and what kind of orders there were."

"Orders?" Like a purchase order—I can't understand how human trafficking can be so emotionally detached.

292

Ben nods. "It's organized. They've got a couple computers where they keep all the records. It's coded, I think, but they've got files on all of the Unwilling, where they came from, where they're going, whether it was a specific order or not. They've even got files on big customers who are doing bulk orders."

"This shit is so fucked up," Elijah says, and I'm glad we're on the same page.

"We need those files," Barclay says. "That's our proof."

I agree with him completely. Something like that would be black and white—no one would be able to jump in and say they didn't believe us. It's enough to make me wonder why bad guys would keep a record of the illegal things they do when it's so obviously the thing that could sink them.

But these guys have an organization that seems like it would rival a major corporation, and if Barclay's right, they've got someone in IA in their pocket, and they've been operating for years now. They're pretty sure they're not going to get caught.

"So we break in and grab that shit," Elijah says. "Let's do it now."

Barclay squeezes the bridge of his nose, and I know why. It's not going to be that easy—and we still have a big problem. Ben has just given us a lot, but nothing that exposes who in IA is involved, and Barclay needs actual concrete proof of the operation that he can take to IA, *and* he needs to know who he can take it to so that it won't get swept under the rug. He isn't sure how high the conspiracy goes.

"Just tell me what to do. How can we fix this," Ben says, and I can't tell if he's talking to me or Barclay.

I don't know what to say or if this can be fixed, so I let Barclay do the talking.

"Going back to Janelle's double," Barclay says. "Did you ever actually see them hit her?"

"I didn't have to. She was beat to shit."

"I just think it's important to note, you didn't actually see anyone hurt her," Barclay says, his voice quiet but stern.

"Her injuries aren't fake, if that's what you're saying," Ben says.

He might not know her, but he's certainly willing to defend her. I can't bear to hear any more of it, so I add, "That's not what he's trying to say."

Elijah suddenly leans into the table. "Are you saying you think someone else could have beat her up?"

Barclay shrugs. "Maybe someone else beat the crap out of her, and someone in IA offered her some kind of deal. A 'help us, and we'll take care of your problem' kind of deal."

Elijah stands up abruptly, knocking his chair to the ground. "If she's working for them, she could lead them right to us."

"I know," Barclay says. "Which is why we need to talk to her."

# 02:16:49:43

**O**n my way out, Ben moves in front of me and blocks my path to the door.

When I look at his face, I see him singing to her—her hand touching his arm. It's enough to make my throat constrict, to make my eyes watery. I'm not ready to talk, so I try to move around him.

"Please," he whispers. "I just need to know you're okay."

Barclay and Elijah disappear down the hallway.

I'm tempted to say, "We don't have time for this," or to make some other excuse. To ask him how any of us could possibly be okay in this situation. We're on the run from IA, trying to take down human traffickers. I escaped from prison and killed a man. Cecily has been abducted into slavery. And I just saw the guy I love with another version of myself. None of that is in any way *okay*.

I'm some kind of glutton for punishment, so I look at Ben and tell the truth.

"No, I'm not okay."

His lips press together, a grimace passing over his face, and he reaches for me. I can't handle that, though, and when he sees me flinch he lets his hand fall to his side.

"I'm sorry," he says, his voice a little shaky.

"Is that it?" I ask because *sorry* doesn't fix this.

Ben shakes his head. "I just . . . I don't know . . . it never occurred to me that she wouldn't be you, and . . ."

He shifts his weight on his feet, and I feel like I should say something—something to bridge the gap between us, or at least something to help him do that.

But I can't. I just can't—it's like I'm waiting for this tidal wave of emotions to crash down over me and carry me away from this conversation.

"Do you remember the time sophomore year when you had that old truck?" he says. It was my first car, a 1968 Ford F-250. "It was in October, I think, and I didn't have work. I was headed up to Black Mountain Park, and I saw your truck, empty, with steam pouring out of your engine."

The thing was a manual transmission and it sucked going up hills, even the ones that were lame. It was always stalling out or locking up. I was constantly leaving the truck on the side of the road. That afternoon was one of the reasons I convinced my dad to get rid of it.

"I went over to check it out and see what was wrong," he continues. "I don't know what happened, and you had obviously stormed off, so I checked it out. The radiator hose had a leak, so I fused it back together. I even waited a little for you to come back. I told myself I was actually going to talk to you, start a conversation, but then Elijah texted and asked what was taking me so long to get to his house, and I lost my nerve."

I remember that day. I thought the engine was going to

explode, the way the steam was pouring out from under the hood. But when I made my dad take me back that night to check it out, he ruled that it just needed more coolant.

"You fixed my truck?" I ask. It's weird to think I was so *present*, for lack of a better word, in his life, when he didn't exist in mine. "Why?"

"I wanted to help you," Ben says. "You pulled me out of the ocean and you saved my life. I owed you, and then I realized you were smart and tough and different from everyone else, so I liked you."

I look into his eyes. They're dark and sad.

"The decisions I've made, they were always about getting home or helping you," he whispers. Then he adds, "I thought they had you."

He doesn't need to add anything else. I get it. I would have flipped out and done something crazy if I thought he was in danger. I did—I followed a guy I barely knew through a portal and into another world.

But that's the logic of it, and that doesn't help undo the fact that I was alone and he was comforting someone else.

I think about saying just that, but I don't get the chance. Ben straightens up and takes a deep breath. "I don't expect you to forgive me, but I just needed you to know." Then he steps aside so I can get through the door.

Something about how resigned he is almost breaks me. I feel it in the hollow place in my chest where my heart should be. I want to tell him that of course I'll forgive him or that we fell in love in the middle of a situation that was worse than this.

But I don't want to lie.

# 02:16:38:51

**M**y doppelgänger is awake when I enter her room.

It was Barclay's idea that I interrogate her, and no one can really argue with him. He's the one with the investigative knowledge and experience to call the shots—not that I'd admit it.

Elijah is talking to Ben somewhere else in the building, and Barclay is outside the door in case I need him.

It's my job to find out who she is and what she knows about all of this. Since I know myself better than anyone else, supposedly, I should be able to assess her best. I need to determine who exactly she is—how alike, how different.

At least, that's the plan.

Right now, all I can do is stare at her.

Her hair is a shade lighter than mine, but the highlights are growing out and the roots are the same dark brown. Her face is the same shape, with an identical nose and mouth, and I'm looking into the same eyes, which is something I don't think I'll ever get used to. Her eyebrows are different—like someone paid more attention to shaping them than I ever did to mine.

The bruises on her face, around her left eye and her jawline, are faded and yellowed, definitely in their last stage of healing. I have no doubt they were nasty when she got them, and I don't envy her. I've been lucky. I've been in a few fights but none left me with a beating like that.

Pulling a chair up to her bed, I sit down and give her the time she needs to get used to what I am. I want to let her speak first. What she says will tell me a lot.

Her mouth slightly ajar, she takes in my features. I wonder what she sees. With the burns and bruises around my neck, I'm not exactly at my best.

When she's done examining me, she looks down at her fingers and picks at the chipped red polish on her nails.

I want to ask her so many things, and not just what she knows about Ben and the case, but about her family. Is her dad still alive, does she have an Alex and a Cecily who are safe and well, did her mother stay sane? But I remain silent and wait for her. If she's anything like me, she's dying to find out who I am too.

After about half a minute, her bottom lip starts to quiver, and I'm left thinking that they must have broken her back in that prison.

Turning her watery eyes to me, she says, "So I guess you're the one he meant to save?"

I don't respond. Not because I'm still playing the silent routine—her first words just told me a lot—but because I remember Ben sitting on her bed when I first saw him, and my throat feels too tight to speak.

She sniffs and looks up at the ceiling to keep from crying, and the familiarity of it catches my breath. I do that. It's a gesture I've become entirely too familiar with over the last five months. "I knew it was too good to be true."

"What was?" I ask, using my best quiet, nonthreatening voice, which probably isn't all that good. I've never done meek well, and I've had a pretty rough past few days.

"Ben." She looks to the door and the waterworks start. Her face crumples and the tears fall down her face. Her body rocks with the sobs. "He kept telling me that I was safe now, that I'd remember when I got better, that everything would be okay."

I want to reach out and offer her some kind of comfort—and maybe if I was friendly, I'd get more information out of her. Besides, if she's another version of *me*, I should identify with her, empathize or something. But I just can't make myself do it.

Touching her would somehow make her more real.

"I wanted to remember," she says, wiping her eyes, though it doesn't do any good. She's crying too hard to stop. "He saved me, and he's so perfect. I love the sound of his voice and how gentle he is . . ."

The crying gets worse, to the point where she can't talk. So I sit there silently next to her, my insides tight and burning, but I refuse to let go. We don't have time for me to sit and cry and feel bad. We don't even have time for me to figure out what's going on between Ben and me.

We've got bigger issues, and a little less than three days to solve them.

"How could I have forgotten someone who loved me like that?"

Someone who loved *me* like that.

I know Ben did all of this for me. He didn't come back to me because he was being followed and he didn't want to bring danger to me—and later, he thought he was saving me. That should count for something.

But I don't know what.

Because here she is, this girl who isn't actually me, with a stylish haircut and a chicken pox scar on her forehead, and now she's crying over being dealt a bad hand.

I've cried more than I care to admit, but I get over it and come up with a plan to right whatever new catastrophe has just blown into my life. Then I do it.

Shouldn't he have seen differences in her—as someone who loves me, shouldn't he have known she *wasn't* me?

"We're not okay either, are we?"

I shake my head. "No, we're not." I'm not really one to mince words.

She nods, like she knew it deep down, but it only makes her cry harder.

She knows I'm her double. Based on her reaction to me, it's doubtful she ever saw her double before, but she knows that's what I am. Which means she's from a universe that has widespread knowledge of the multiverse.

And she's either the best actress I've ever seen, or she's in way over her head and scared shitless, which would make her a terrible plant. So I'm going to give it to her straight. "Janelle," I say, rolling the word around my tongue and trying to ignore how awkward it feels. "I need to know how you ended up in that prison. It's important."

She nods, but it takes her a while to actually calm down enough to talk to me.

But when she does, she tells me everything.

I walk out of that hospital room knowing two things for sure.

She's not an IA plant.

And once you get past how much we look alike, she's nothing like me.

# 02:16:00:11

The *other* girl named Janelle Tenner was born and raised in Prima.

Instead of going to West Point, spending six years in the Army, and then joining the FBI, *her* father worked in Homeland Security, where he excelled through the ranks.

The creepy part is that he met his future wife the same way my parents met—at a group dinner party with mutual friends. She was a graduate student who thought she knew everything and had too much to drink. He thought she was obnoxious and jumped in to correct her when she made a broad generalization about international policy, which turned into a heated debate. She got his number and took him out for coffee the next day to apologize.

They had two children, Janelle and Jared, but any similarities other than our names seem to end pretty soon after that. Because her dad and mine made two very different crucial decisions when their wives got sick.

When "Janelle's" mother was diagnosed with bipolar disorder, her father didn't try to work it out on his own and then just let it go. He had her committed to a mental institution, and hired a nanny to take care of his children.

"Janelle" and "Jared" were raised by the nanny and the housekeeper until they were old enough to be sent to expensive boarding schools. "Janelle" hated school. She wasn't into sports, and she wasn't particularly into classes, and as a result, she felt sort of aimless—she didn't know what to do with her life. At her first school, she fell in with a bad crowd, drank a lot, and ended up getting expelled for breaking too many rules.

At her next school, she tried to study and play the good student, but she met a guy, thought he loved her, and spent all of her time with him. Then she spiraled into a depression after he slept with her and moved on to someone else. She ended up failing too many classes and got kicked out again.

When she enrolled in her most recent school, she already had a reputation, and instead of feeling sorry for herself, she embraced it and decided she would drop out instead of waiting to be expelled. Only this time, when she slipped in with the wrong crowd and fell for the wrong guy, he was a lot worse than some prep-school jock.

And she had no one to save her.

Three years earlier, her father had remarried. He and his new wife had a baby. Then a year ago, while on a case, her father was killed and left everything to his new wife, who didn't want anything to do with his nothing-but-trouble daughter.

So "Janelle" moved in with her boyfriend, who lived in the underground. She knew he was a bad drunk with anger issues, he was cheating on her, and he was involved with some pretty bad guys, but she didn't know where else to go.

One night he asked her to take his car and drive to the docks to drop off a package—probably drugs—to a friend of his. She did. Only some idiot rear-ended her and was screaming about how it was her fault. It wasn't, but she'd had a beer and she had a DUI last year, so when the cops came, she fled.

And accidentally left the package in the car.

Her boyfriend beat her up when he found out what happened—she thought he might kill her. But the next thing she knew, she'd been arrested and handed off to a couple of prison guards and taken to a solitary cell where she was being used as leverage for a guy she didn't even know.

I don't know how to feel about this—or, more accurately, I feel too many different things that don't really mesh with one another, and I don't know which one is right.

We have the same parents. We share the same DNA. This girl is supposed to be my double, but our lives have been so different. And it's sad.

I don't exactly think my life has been a cakewalk, but hers . . . hers has been a lot worse. She doesn't even talk to her brother anymore and she never had anyone like Alex, who would listen to her no matter what, or someone like Cecily, who was determined to make her smile.

And she never had someone love her like Ben loves me.

It makes me wish my dad was still around—or that there was at least some way for me to apologize to him. I was so hard on him when he was alive. I felt like it was his responsibility to do something for Mom so that I didn't have to take care of her. I felt like it wasn't fair that I had to grow up so quickly.

A rush of guilt throbs in my chest. Not just because I spent so much time feeling mad at him and now he's gone, but also for my mom. She's been missing and presumed dead since the quakes, and the most prominent feeling that left me with was relief.

My parents deserved better from me, and now they're gone and it's too late for me to tell them I loved them or to thank them.

If they had made different choices I would have turned out a lot different.

And as crazy as it sounds—even though I'm burned and exhausted, even though I might be executed in three days—I'm glad I'm me.

# 02:16:00:10

Barclay is waiting for me when I come out of "Janelle's" room. I repeat what she's told me, but I keep my reflection to myself.

"Who's the boyfriend?" Barclay asks. I'm not sure what he's thinking, but the focus in his eyes and the concentration in the lines of his forehead tell me he's got something that might be the beginnings of a plan. I can practically see the wheels turning in his head.

That he's coming up with our next steps makes me breathe a little easier.

"Joe Tarancio?" I say. Obviously the name means nothing to me, but it might mean something to him.

Barclay smiles, and the tension in my shoulders starts to drain. His prison-break plan worked—against all odds it worked—so I'm willing to follow Barclay just about anywhere right now.

That thought almost makes me laugh.

Barclay must notice I'm losing it. "What?"

"Nothing," I say with a shake of my head. "What do you know about the boyfriend?"

"She might be able to help us," he says. "Tarancio is one of

Meridian's right-hand guys. Between whatever she knows and what Ben has told us about the operation and how it works, we should be able to get the proof we need to the right people at IA in order to get us all in the clear."

"And we can get Cecily too, right?"

He rolls his eyes. "Relax, Tenner. I'm not going to go back on my promise."

"In less than three days?" I ask, thinking of the deadline and the people I had to leave behind in that prison.

Barclay nods.

"So what's the plan?" Elijah says. I turn around and see that he and Ben are down the hall. I can tell from here that Ben's eyes are bloodshot, and there's a pang of regret that moves through my chest. No matter how I'm feeling, I don't like seeing him this way.

"We need food and sleep and a concrete plan of what we're going to do," Barclay says, scratching behind his head. "Not exactly in that order, though."

"We can get food," Ben offers, looking at me. "What do you feel like?"

"Hell yeah, food," Elijah says. "Let's get pizza. It's been entirely too fucking long since I've had melted cheese."

"Is pizza okay with you?" Ben asks me. I nod. Pizza is fine.

"Good. Get food," Barclay says. "I'm going to talk to Janelle's double and get some more information. Then we'll eat and talk about how the hell we're going to pull this off." He looks at me. "After that we'll sleep and then we'll go after Cecily."

# 02:15:22:04

The radiation levels in the hospital are higher than those in your average nuclear-disaster-free city, and if we stayed here permanently we might die before our time. But according to the tests Barclay did with his quantum charger—yeah, those things can multitask—the next two and a half days aren't going to hurt us.

And after that we'll either be headed home or dead, so it's not a problem.

The food is pepperoni pizza, my favorite kind, and I'm pretty sure Ben did that on purpose. It comes from a different world. I don't ask how he and Elijah got it since it's pretty obvious. We don't exactly have a ton of money on us, and there isn't a common currency in the multiverse. Two guys who can portal in and out of everywhere can steal what they need pretty easily.

The plan, however, is more complicated.

After he's demolished two slices, Barclay opens his backpack and spreads the contents on the table. He's apparently been carrying an armory around with him since we left Prima. I touch the gun I've had with me, and think of the prison guard and the way I could pinpoint the exact moment when his life slipped away.

I take a deep breath and try to tell myself that I didn't have a choice.

"We're going to be outmatched," Barclay says. "I can't be sure exactly *how* outmatched, but it will be bad. Our advantages are the element of surprise, their arrogance, and him." He gestures to Ben, who's sitting next to me. I look over at him, and our eyes meet for a second before I look away.

Then Barclay lays out his plan for taking down the biggest interversal criminal operation anyone's ever seen.

We can't go back to the Piston and get Ben's family out. IA will expect us, and we'll probably never be able to get out again. We just have to hope they can hold on another day or two and that we can get the proof we need to convince IA that Ben is innocent and his family shouldn't be punished.

Step one is the Black Hole. We'll portal into the processing center. Ben draws us a map of what he remembers—where the guys slept, where they portaled in, where they kept the slaves, and where the control room and surveillance are located. Lucky us, they don't have any hydrochloradneum shields in place.

"We can go straight into the control room," Ben says. "There will be a couple guys on duty, but we can surprise them and subdue them pretty easily. The computers are there, so we can copy the files we need. From there we'll be able to open the cells and get any of the slaves in holding. There will probably be somewhere between twenty and thirty, and we can bring them back here with us."

Barclay thinks it's as good a plan as any.

Step two is Cecily. We'll find out where she is and rescue her.

Hopefully her location will be in the files we steal in step one.

Step three is dealing with IA. We'll have proof about Meridian and his operation. If this was a normal case, Barclay would file the paperwork, put together a task force, and they would bust everything up. But it's not. Which means we need to take the proof to someone high up, who we can trust isn't involved.

And right now, that's a really short list.

We need the files at the processing center to help us with that.

As Barclay goes over the minor details, we all lean toward him to make sure we get it right. A couple of times Elijah asks questions and makes Barclay repeat his idea in different words. Other times, he offers his own suggestions—like how we should break into IA and search through their files to find out who's dirty, or go after Meridian ourselves, both of which get shot down.

After a while, I realize Ben is so close to me we're almost touching. We're barely an inch apart and every time he moves I'm sure he's going to reach out and brush my arm or my thigh. The air in the space between us is electrified.

But no matter how many times my heart skips a beat, or lurches forward, he doesn't touch me.

Worse, I don't know if I want him to.

# 02:11:17:49

I'm on the roof of the building when Ben comes to see me.

We've hashed out the plan as much as we can. We're leaving around three a.m. because the middle of the night will be our best chance of getting in and out alive.

Despite what I've said about my double and the fact that she's unlikely to go anywhere else, Barclay doesn't trust her enough to leave her alone. Not even while we're sleeping. He's promised he'll figure out somewhere for her to go before we leave. But for now, he's pulled three more beds into her room so that all five of us can lie down and sleep before we leave.

None of this is her fault, and I don't blame her for whatever's going on now between Ben and me—at least, logically I don't. But I don't exactly want to spend any more time in the same room with her than I absolutely have to. Not even an extra minute.

She makes me feel . . . crowded.

When I'm in that room with her, it's like I can't move without touching someone or bumping into them—it's like everyone is in my personal space.

Her presence is stifling.

Instead of sitting there and pretending it's normal, I wander around. But empty hospital beds, peeling paint, and the absence of anything alive is the last thing I need.

Then I find the roof.

I never realized there could be so many stars. The only other light is the full moon and some faint red lights off in the distance.

I'm sitting on the edge of the roof, my legs dangling over the side, when I hear the hinges of the door creak. "Don't let it swing shut," I call, assuming it's Barclay. "It locks from the inside."

"Got it."

It's Ben's voice, and I freeze at the sound of it, my heart picking up speed, thumping harder against my chest, as if it's straining to know whether he's going to come over or just fade back inside.

I hold my breath as I wait.

And suddenly he's beside me, sitting down next to me. We're not quite touching, but I can feel the warmth of his body next to mine.

"I was wondering where you went," he says.

"I just needed some air."

He nods. I feel the movement next to me.

I don't say anything, and Ben seems comfortable with the silence. I'm not sure how much time passes like that—the two of us, side by side, yet somehow so far away.

When he finally breaks the silence, he says, "Those red lights out there . . ."

"What about them?"

"They're trees."

"Trees?"

"I checked it out a few nights ago," he says. "They're really close to one of the nuclear power plants that got taken out. The fallout from *that* is actually probably what ended up destroying this whole area. The radiation there is still so bad, like three hundred thousand times what could kill a person, or more, that the trees glow in the dark because they've absorbed so much of it."

I don't ask why he knows that. I kind of like that he does, because it reminds me of the guy who sat next to me in AP English just a few months ago, the guy who crashed my AP Physics class because it would be a good place for us to hang out.

But this isn't what I want him to say right now. It's a start, but I just want something . . . more.

More real. More meaningful.

Just *more.*

But he doesn't say anything, and again we lapse into silence. It's not a comfortable one, not like we could have shared before all of this. It's awkward, like two people who want something from each other but don't know how to express it.

It's like we're broken, and I don't know what we can do—if anything—to fix that.

"We're going to make it," Ben says, breaking the silence.

I nod, even though I'm not sure I believe it. We're one IA agent and three teenagers, and we're up against some of the worst criminals in the multiverse.

"I love you," he adds.

And I realize he's not talking about whatever is going to happen at the processing center. He's talking about *us*—about him and me. He thinks we're going to make it. That we're going to be okay.

It's what I thought I wanted to hear. More than that, it's what I've been waiting to hear from him since I first realized I was falling for him. Just a few hours ago, what I wanted more than anything was for him to tell me that what Elijah said was true, that he was planning to come back. That if IA hadn't grabbed him, he was going to come back to my world and to me.

But now he's saying that and I can't help but think about the consequences. If he does come back with me, then what? Sure, it might be great for a little while, but in five years or in twenty? What if he regrets his decision, what if he decides to leave then? I feel like I can't take that chance.

For four months I looked for Ben. For 120 days, I thought about him. Every time a door opened or I walked into a room, I looked for him. I was jumpy and on edge, and . . . *waiting*.

I'm just not willing to put myself through that again.

For a long time I don't say anything. Then I feel Ben's hand cover mine. His skin is rough and calloused like I remember it, and it takes everything I have to ignore the wave of sheer yearning that sweeps over me. I want so desperately to lean my head against his shoulder and pretend we're just stargazing and not two people looking out into the end of the world.

"After all this, I'm going to come back with you," he whispers. "I thought about you all the time."

I squeeze his hand, because I'm not sure I can form words.

Ben turns toward me, and even in the dark, I can see the tragic beauty of his face, his deep-set eyes and hard jaw, the way his hair is too long, how it flops into his face and covers his eyes.

Flushed and breathless, I lean into him, our foreheads touching, our noses brushing against each other, his breath warm against my cheek.

And right when I think he's going to kiss me, I say, "We can't be together."

314

## 02:11:06:14

He reels back and I see the surprise in his face and the hurt in those brown eyes, and somehow that makes it worse. It's not that I want to hurt him. I just need to save myself from getting hurt again.

I push to my feet and start walking away.

"Wait," Ben says, and I can hear him following me even though I don't look back. "Why are you running away?"

I turn around, but keep walking backward. "You have a family and a life in your own world, and I have one in mine."

"And I'm saying I want to be a part of yours."

"But you can't!" I shout. "Look what happened today. I walked in on you with another version of me. I can't even begin to explain how messed up that is."

"I know, and I should have known," he says. "I'll make it up to you, I promise. I'll—"

I shake my head. "It's not about that. It's . . . If I needed a sign from the multiverse that we're not supposed to be together, that was it." I take a deep breath and ignore the way my eyes sting. "How we feel about each other doesn't matter. We're from two different worlds and being together has only hurt us—both of us."

"You don't really believe that," he whispers.

"I do," I say, my voice cracking. "My world is falling apart, and we're both wanted criminals. You abducted people from their worlds, and you did it for *me*. And I broke out of a prison and became a fugitive and a murderer."

I press the heel of my palm to the center of my chest to try to hold on to some semblance of self-control.

"I killed a man."

Ben's voice comes out quiet, calm, and even, everything that mine is not. "That wasn't your fault."

"I shoved a piece of glass into his neck and felt his life bleed out all over my hands," I say, and hearing the words out loud makes them more true. And that makes my eyes burn and my throat constrict because those words shouldn't belong to me.

I have to pause and catch my breath. "We've both ruined people's lives in the name of being together."

I turn around and head to the door. I don't look back. This time, he doesn't follow me, but as I'm pushing it open, he says something. It's quiet, and I can't quite make out the words so I'm not sure if he meant for me to hear them or not.

When I turn, I don't ask him to repeat himself. But he does anyway. "So you think we're doomed?"

"Aren't we?" I whisper.

"How am I supposed to forget how I feel about you," he says, and it's not a question.

"I don't know," I say. It's the truth. But I also don't know how we can be together. So I say something stupid, something that I've heard other people say because they don't get it. The wrongness of the words makes me stumble over them. "It won't feel like the end of the world forever."

And then I slip through the door, careful not to let it latch behind me.

# 02:06:00:00

I'm not sure I've ever been so in need of coffee.

It's three a.m. I tossed and turned through the couple of hours we had to sleep and I can't be certain if I nodded off at one point or just lost track of time. I'm awake, dressed—not showered, but as ready as I'll ever be.

I have Barclay's 9mm HM USP Match and an extra magazine in case I run out.

We're all here.

"Earth 49873 is going to be the safest place for you," Barclay says. "It's got civilization, unlike this place, but it's one of the universes that barely has any IA presence."

My double shifts on her feet. She's wearing jeans, a long-sleeved T-shirt, and Ben's hoodie—and even though I shouldn't care about that, it bothers me. "Why can't I just stay here?"

Barclay doesn't tell her that he doesn't want her to somehow lead people to us, that he wants to be able to come back here. Instead he says, "What if we don't make it back? Who knows what effects the radiation could have on you if you're here too long. You'd probably be dead or out of your mind within a week."

She frowns. "All right, I guess I'm ready."

"Just remember what I told you," Barclay adds. "The industrial revolution never happened, so things will be really different. You need to learn the culture and assimilate—and quickly."

"Sounds like a blast," she says, the sarcasm dripping off her in waves.

Barclay's nostrils flare a little in annoyance, and in another situation, I would want to smile. I like that she can push his buttons.

"I'm serious. If you stand out, they'll notice you, and you'll end up dead," he says.

She doesn't look at him when she says, "Yeah, I got it."

The inherent sadness of what's about to happen weighs down on me, and I take a deep breath to try to balance myself. Barclay is going to open a portal, and this girl who's lost everything is going to walk into another universe where she won't know a soul, and she has no idea what to expect—other than the fact that if IA finds her, she's as good as dead.

I wonder what's going through her mind, if there's any interest, even a spark, at the idea of seeing not just another world, but one that's practically a window into the past. If she's scared. Looking at her, she just seems bitter.

"Let's get this over with," she says.

Barclay points the quantum charger at the ground, but as he's about to open the portal, I give her a chance.

"Wait," I say, reaching for her.

She flinches away.

"You don't have to go," I say, ignoring the way Barclay is looking at me. "You could come with us—help us."

"Go . . . go with you?" She shakes her head. "Why would I want to do that?"

"Because of what they did to you." They beat her, made her pretend she was someone else, and then when she'd played her part, they left her to rot in a prison cell.

She either doesn't remember or she doesn't care. She just stares at me with a doe-eyed expression I can't imagine on my own face.

"You can help take them down, make right the things they've done, help get them put away."

Her lips turn into a sad smile. "Or I could end up in the same place I was in six months ago—or worse. Better to run now. Maybe I'll luck out and they'll think I'm dead."

Maybe she doesn't get it. I'm not sure why I can't drop it—why I can't just let it go. But I can't. She's got as much stake in this as any of us—maybe more. "But if you run, you might not ever be able to go home."

Her laugh is harsh. "What home? Prima? I don't have anything waiting for me back there." I open my mouth, but she doesn't let me say anything else. "Look, I'm not willing to die yet. I'll do what I have to—you do the same."

And with that she turns to Ben. "Thanks for getting me out."

His eyes flick to me, but I look away.

She doesn't look at any of us as she closes her eyes and steps into the portal, but I can't take my eyes off her as she disappears through it.

"Glad that's fucking over with." Elijah looks at me, his lips turned up in a smirk. "Also glad you're the version we got. Someone should have gotten their money back for that one."

I smile, but I don't feel it.

# 02:05:44:22

When we portal in, we'll walk right into the main office of the processing center.

Before Barclay opens the portal, he grabs my arm. "Don't hold your breath."

I nod and shift my grip on the USP Match. I think of the guard I killed. Then I remind myself that there's no other way, that in two days and five hours we could all be dead. The portal opens and Barclay goes through. I follow immediately behind him, gun raised and trying to breathe normally.

Freezing-cold air whips into my lungs, then it turns warm—too warm, and I feel like I'm breathing fire, but I refuse to let myself tense up.

And then we're there.

I relax my knees and let them give a little to keep myself from stumbling. True to Ben's description, there are six guys hanging out in front of the computer monitors in the processing center, which is a large circular office with glass walls that overlooks the six lower levels of the prison. They're all startled and fumbling for weapons.

"Arms behind your head," Barclay is screaming. "Get down on the ground!"

I train my gun on the guy who looks like he's in charge, a big bulky brute of a guy in a T-shirt and cargo pants, as Ben and Elijah come through the portal behind me, guns raised and spreading out with their backs to the window—just like Barclay instructed.

My grip on the gun is relaxed, my arms slightly bent at the elbows. The safety is already off, and my finger is on the trigger. The pounding of my heart echoes against my eardrums. I tune out the sounds around us, as if I'm at the shooting range—as if the men in front of me are targets. I know from experience that if I fire off ten shots, all ten of them will be fatal.

They're not outnumbered, but they are out-gunned, and apparently that makes up for it. All six guys reluctantly raise their arms, some of them more hesitantly than others. Barclay moves to the first one, and I flank him just in case the guy tries to do something stupid.

But he doesn't. He lets Barclay restrain his hands behind his back and lower him facedown on the ground, something Barclay repeats with every guy in here. I follow him, keeping my gun aimed at their heads. I speak evenly and tell each one that if he makes the wrong move, I'll put a bullet between his eyes.

My voice is so cold, I barely recognize myself.

When we get to the last guy, I see his eyes dart around, as if he's looking for a way out. His hand twitches and I nod toward the gun at his hip. "You'll be dead before you get your hand on it."

Barclay smirks and grabs the guy's left arm, folding it behind his back. "Better not try her, Basil. She almost shot me once."

Basil doesn't find that as funny as Barclay apparently does, but he stays still and lets Barclay restrain him. Then he looks behind me at Ben, with nothing but pure hatred on his face.

"You drink my beer and tell me about your girlfriend and your dog, and how much you miss them, and you listen to me tell you about my family, and now you come back here and point a gun in my face?" he says. "I kept you safe here. I thought we were comrades."

I risk a glance at Ben. His face is flushed. His gun raised, his hand quivers as he points it at this supposed *comrade*. "You rape the Unwilling and put out your cigarettes on their skin," Ben says.

"Don't," I say, moving toward him. I don't care what this guy has done, how awful he is. We're here to save the slaves and get the proof we need. I think of the guard I killed and the way his eye looked when he was gone, how his blood spilled warm over my skin when he died. I'll defend my own life and the lives of everyone here, but we need to get through this without killing anyone else if we can.

That's what I'm thinking. What I say is, "Remember what it is that makes us the good guys."

Barclay rolls his eyes, but he lets my decision stand, and Ben lowers his gun.

With all six guys subdued and restrained, Barclay and Ben move to the computers. I look out over the prison. In the underground facility, we're six stories up, essentially in a glass cube. Surrounding us are four walls, each one with ten holding cells in a row and six floors high. It means there are 240 cells in this place.

"Shit," Ben says, and I turn around.

"What's wrong?"

Barclay shakes his head. "The flash drive doesn't have enough space to hold all the files. We'll have to copy them from the network to the computer and take the whole damn thing with us."

"Elijah can do it," I say. He's got the ability to portal in and out, and he's moving slower than the rest of us on that leg of his.

"You fucking do it," Elijah says. "I've got vengeance to wreak."

"What does that even mean?" I say.

Barclay ignores us both. "When the transfer is done, shut this down so it can travel," he says to Ben. Then he looks at Elijah. "Take it back to the hospital. Portal straight in where we left and set it up in the room where we slept last night." He leans in and says something else, then he looks at me. "Are you ready?"

I am. I know what we need to do next, and it's not going to be easy.

Barclay opens the portal back to the hospital, and with a CPU under one arm and a monitor under the other, Elijah steps through and disappears, while Ben types into the keypad on the wall.

We're officially one man short.

The holding cell doors open, the alarm goes off, and all hell breaks loose.

## 02:05:38:29

Ben opens another portal. We need to get to a different location in the prison to get people out. If we're lucky, we'll be able to save them before any of the traffickers can pull their act together and stop us.

Barclay presses the intercom button and his voice travels through the prison, over the alarm. "This is IA. If you have been abducted from your world and put in a holding cell, do not panic. We're here to save you. Exit to the end of your row and then head toward the tunnel exit."

Barclay puts the intercom down and the elevator dings. He raises his gun toward it and looks at Ben. "Get all of the Unwilling out of here," he says, and he pushes me through the portal.

Ben and I hit the ground hard in the northwest corner of the prison. I'm so off balance that my head snaps back and hits the pavement. Stars cloud my vision, but Ben is there, pulling me up. "Are you okay?" he's asking.

He whispers my name, and for a second I forget where I am. I think I'm back on Highway 101 and seeing him for the first time. And then I wish it was true, because we'd have another chance, a chance to start over and fix whatever is broken between us.

The sound of gunshots and flashes coming from the processing center office above us snaps me out of it, though—that and the mob of people who are running toward us.

"I'm okay," I say to Ben, even though it's not true. I can sleep off my headache later.

"This way!" Ben yells to the mob of people, and he pulls me up the exit tunnel. According to Barclay, this long hallway will actually lead to the surface of the world, a place that we don't want to go, since the atmosphere can make people sick. But we can't just open a portal and expect people to follow us through it. That's how they got here—someone grabbed them, stuck them with a needle, and pulled them through a black hole. Despite the logic of the situation, these people are traumatized, and logic will be overruled by their emotions and their aversion to going through another portal. And we don't have time to convince them that we're better than the people who brought them here.

So we decided before we got here that to do this fast, we would have to trick them.

Ben runs ahead of me as I wave and shout to the Unwilling. "This way! This leads to the surface!" I keep shouting it over and over again, and they come toward me.

I try to keep track, to count them somehow as they run past. But there are a lot, and the higher up we get into the corridor, the darker it gets.

At thirty-seven, I lose count.

Because I see Cecily.

# 02:05:32:49

She's still in her pajama pants and her I ONLY DATE NINJAS T-shirt, and her milky-blond hair hangs loose down her back. In her arms is a little boy.

I'm about to run toward them when the woman a few paces behind Cecily grunts and collapses to the ground. The little boy hides his face in Cecily's neck and she visibly picks up the pace. But about ten yards behind her is a guy in boxers and commando boots and he has a gun pointed at them.

Ben has a portal open up ahead in the darkness so that no one can see it—they'll run right through it and end up in the hospital on the dead world—but with this guy shooting people, they'll never make it.

"Drop your gun or I'll shoot!" I scream, pointing my gun at him.

I know he shot that woman, and I don't know if she's stunned or dead, but she's not moving, and I'm not about to let that happen to Cecily.

He swings his gun toward me.

I don't think. I just pull the trigger.

But he does too.

I'm lucky that I'm farther into the darkness, because my aim is better. He goes down while something clips my shoulder, sending me reeling backward. My head runs into the wall of the corridor and again, all I can see is stars. I doubt I hit anything that hard, but my head has taken a beating in the last twenty-four hours.

"Janelle? Oh my God, what are you doing here?"

Cecily is next to me, using her free hand to try to pull me away from the wall. I see her blond hair and watery blue eyes, and focusing on her clears my vision.

"I'm okay, Cee," I say, trying to ignore the way my shoulder is on fire. "We have to run, go!"

"But, you—" she says.

I push off the wall and start running with her. "I have a gun, you don't. Keep running."

She does what I tell her, but she turns to look back at me.

"I'll be right behind you," I lie.

I turn around and raise my gun, moving backward up the corridor on the lookout for a threat. The last few trafficked slaves limp past me. "Go!" I say. "You're almost there."

Below me, in the light, I see another guy with a weapon.

And he's not alone.

# 02:05:30:06

There are a little more than half a dozen of them.

I turn and start running up the corridor, because I can't fight all these guys off. I don't even have that many bullets.

I spray a few shots behind me and hope that will slow them down, maybe make them a little more careful since they're headed into the darkness. But I know the only real solution is for us to move faster.

I run to the slowest of the slaves. She's limping, trying not to put any weight on her right foot. I grab her arm and throw it over my shoulder. "They're coming," I say and she gets the message.

In front of us is only blackness. I can't actually see the portal, but I can smell the salt and open air from it so I know we can't be that far off.

I hear gunfire behind me, and I point my own gun back without looking and fire. It's not like in a movie, where it's easy. I'm shooting with one hand, while trying to run forward, and I'm already off balance to begin with. The kickback from firing doesn't help. In fact, it's slowing us down.

"Janelle!" It's Ben's voice, and it's strained. I don't know how long he's been holding open the portal, but it's probably too long. We need to get there before he runs out of energy, or we won't have a chance.

"We're coming!"

And suddenly we're in the light.

The girl I'm supporting gasps and falls to the ground.

White floor, white walls all around us. People are everywhere. They're crying, consoling one another, looking around for someone to explain something. And then Ben crashes into me, and I tumble to the ground with him on top of me.

I have a moment to see his face, flushed and covered with a thin layer of sweat. Then the portal closes behind him, and he lays a warm hand against my cheek. I lean into it a little and the world goes fuzzy.

In my pain-induced sedation I dream about the night Renee Adams went missing—about the look on Cecily's face when she asked me, "Where are they all going?"

I dream about Ben, about how he was the first thing I saw when I came back from the dead, silhouetted against the sun and hovering over me with his hand over my heart. Except this time, Barclay is there too.

*Can't you do something to fix her?*

*I've tried, but I can't. I held that portal open too long. I've got nothing right now.*

Barclay throws his hands up. *What good are you?* And then he's gone.

Ben leans closer, his hair tickling my face.

*I'm sorry,* he whispers. *I'm so sorry. I should have known she wasn't you.*

And I dream about Alex and my brother. It's before the world fell apart, and we're in the driveway of my old house. We're playing the basketball review game Alex made up to trick Jared into studying. Jared runs toward the basket and Alex fires a question at him. If he answers right, Alex will throw him the ball and he'll shoot. Once he gets ten baskets in a row, they trade places.

It's kind of a lame and unoriginal game, but when Jared was in middle school and preoccupied by his "basketball is life" philosophy and failing English, it was brilliant.

Only instead of vocabulary words, Alex keeps asking questions about the case. He asks things Jared couldn't possibly know—where Meridian is, how many people still need to be rescued, who in IA is involved.

Jared just stands in front of the basket, confused and frustrated with bloodshot eyes and a scowl on his face. It makes me think about what a terrible sister I am.

Then Alex asks, *"What if Janelle doesn't come back?"*

Jared surprises me. He looks up and turns to where I'm watching them, and he says, *"She's so tough, it's frightening. That girl will outlive us all."*

# 01:13:27:41

When I come to, the sun is already setting, and the room I'm in is dark.

I shoot upright—who knows how much time we've lost while I was unconscious—and I can't help letting out a startled screech at the pain that shoots through my shoulder and head. Stars move through my vision, and I close my eyes and take a deep breath.

When he shifts, I realize someone is next to me.

Ben sits up, his eyes bleary, his hair pointing every which way. For a split second, he's just confused, and then he sees me looking at him and a wide smile overtakes his face. He reaches for me, his warm, calloused hands coming to rest on each side of my face, and he whispers, "Janelle."

I glance around the room. It's empty and we're alone, but next to my bed is a bowl full of some kind of strange berries. They're a bright, almost electric blue, and they look like a cross between blackberries and raspberries.

Ben clears his throat. "Barclay banned me from the room earlier. He thought I was hovering, and I didn't know what to do with myself, so I portaled out and picked up some of these. I don't know what they're called, but they're sweet, and the first time I had them a few weeks ago I knew you'd like them—"

"You brought me berries?" I say. In the middle of a crisis, he ran out and got fruit. It doesn't make sense.

He blushes and shrugs his shoulders. "I thought about getting flowers but they're generic, and what would you do with them here, but I messed up and you were hurt and I didn't know what to do. I thought we could eat these together . . ." To make his point, he grabs a berry and tosses it into his mouth.

I suppose it's not like he could go to Roberto's and grab me a burrito and a grape soda.

I pick up one of the unknown berries and turn it over between my fingers. It's soft and smells amazing so I go ahead and eat it. And Ben is right, it's sweet and sugary with a little bit of tang, and I do really like it.

"Thank you," I say, and I can't help but smile. It's not exactly the *I'm sorry* gift I imagined getting from a guy, but nothing happening right now is in line with anything I would have imagined.

Suddenly he says, "You are the most beautiful thing I've ever seen."

I roll my eyes, not because I don't like hearing that, but because he's clearly still asleep and we have a lot we should be doing right now. I try to move, but he holds me in place.

"I'm serious," he says. "I've thought of you every single day since I left, about the way you look up and pinch the bridge of your nose when you're thinking really hard, the way your lips curl into this tiny smile when you've figured something out, even the way you roll your eyes. I remembered every moment we spent together. I replayed them over and over in my mind. Every morning when I woke up, I would forget that we weren't together, that you were a world away."

He takes one hand and slides it down my arm until he has my fingers, and then he presses them against the center of his chest. I can feel his heartbeat underneath the rough thermal material of his shirt. "Even though I wasn't there, you were always with me. Always."

His face is so earnest, and his eyes are so dark. If I look at him like this for another second, I'm going to cry again. I lean into him, pressing my forehead against his, and I close my eyes.

"And now here you are, and I didn't do you justice. You're even better than I remembered." One of his hands moves through my hair, and the other massages the back of my neck. "You're beautiful and strong and fearless, and I'm so afraid for you. Not because this is bigger than you, or too dangerous for you. I know you can handle anything, but I . . ." His voice cracks. "If anything happens to you, because of me . . . *I* can't handle that."

I clench my fist around his shirt, holding him next to me. I can't speak. There's a lump in my throat that won't let my voice out, but I don't want him to go anywhere.

"When you walked into the hospital room with your jacket tied around your face, I knew. I knew I had screwed up."

"It's okay," I say, my voice thick and raw with forgiveness. It hurts, it makes my body ache, that he didn't know who I was— or who I *wasn't*—but I still love him. More than anything.

But I feel him shake his head. "I should have known," he whispers, his breath warm against my cheek. "You don't need anyone to save you. You're the one who does the saving."

I want to protest and tell him that's silly, but I think not just of Ben, but of Elijah and Cecily, and all the people we just portaled out of the processing center, who must be around here somewhere, and hot tears spill over my eyes and run down my cheeks.

Once upon a time, I would have said that I could save myself.

But I open my eyes and see Ben's long, dark eyelashes and the perfect curve of his mouth, and I say, "We save each other."

And then I disregard everything I thought just a few hours ago—all my intentions of staying away from him get tossed out the window, and I press my lips against his and savor the way we seem to melt into each other.

# 01:13:19:21

Cecily looks like death.

She comes in when I'm in the middle of changing my shirt to something that isn't bloody and sweat stained. Her skin is pale, her hair in disarray, and I can see the circles under her eyes from here.

"How're you feeling?" Her voice is tentative.

I feel like crap. My head is pounding, my arm aches, and my whole body is sore whenever I move. But it doesn't matter. I would gladly feel worse if it meant getting her out of there. "Probably about as bad as you look," I say. "You would think you'd been kidnapped or something."

She rushes toward me and throws her arms around me. "You came to save me," she says, so I know someone, probably Ben or Elijah, has filled her in.

And then she bursts into tears.

I hold on to her as she cries it out. For all that we're different, Cecily is a lot like me. It's why we're friends. She's tough—she lost both her parents a couple of years ago and got uprooted to San Diego to live with her aunt, and she didn't go emo or become withdrawn. She joined the cheerleading squad, won the annual Physics Day challenge, and befriended everyone she met.

She's like me, just nicer and peppier—and better at science too.

When she's finished, we sit on the bed and I tell her everything that happened before the quakes—the day I died, Ben healing me, my dad's case and the UIED, the portals, the multiverse, and Barclay. Then I tell her about what led us here.

When I tell her there are different universes, she snorts. "I've kind of figured that one out."

"Sorry I didn't tell you sooner."

She shrugs and wipes her eyes before changing the subject. "Eli told me all about how you broke him out. I hadn't realized you were so badass."

"Lame. I thought you knew me."

Cecily smiles. It's small and a little sad, but it's enough. She's not actually mad at me. I relax a little. "What about you?" I ask. "Are you doing okay?" I don't need to add that she's been through a lot.

"I'm not sleeping well and I don't like to be alone," she says with a shrug. "I'll probably have to be in therapy the rest of my life, but I'm not dead and it could have been worse. It was only a few days. It felt longer, trust me, but this whole thing was only a few days."

I wait to see if she'll tell me more. I saw a few of those specials on *60 Minutes* about human trafficking and how girls are drugged, beat up, and worse until they're broken.

She senses what my silence is about. "Maybe I'll tell you about it when we're home."

"I can have Barclay take you home now," I offer.

Cecily shakes her head. "I can't leave everyone, not until we know where they're going too. Some of them are from our world, but some of them aren't."

"You don't have to take them on as a responsibility. Your aunt—"

"Will still be there in a few days," she says. "I was an Unwilling and so are these people. We're in this together."

Despite how much I think she's wrong, that she should let us send her home, I nod. She deals with things by helping other people. I know that; I've seen her at Qualcomm.

"Janelle," she says, grabbing my hand. "I'm going to be okay. We're all going to be okay."

I don't have the same kind of blind faith, but I hope she's right.

# 01:13:06:41

"That can't be it," Barclay is saying as Cecily and I enter the room where they've set up the computer and hooked it up to a generator. "Let me see that."

Ben is seated in front of the computer and Barclay is looming over his shoulder. It's the kind of thing that would be driving me crazy, but apparently Ben has more patience, or he's pretending he does.

Elijah is slumped in the corner with his back against the wall and his eyes closed. Without opening them he says, "Fucking Christ, what's wrong now?"

Ben taps a few keys on the keyboard and analyzes the screen. If anyone knows more about computers than they should, it's him. But neither he nor Barclay respond, and I don't like that. It implies that *a lot* has been going wrong since we got back.

"It's taken a while to break down the encryption on the computer," Cecily says next to me. "And by a while, I mean like all night. The three of them haven't slept and at least twice they almost came to blows over something ridiculous like who was going to press 'enter' or something."

I clench my jaw. What a time for me to succumb to a concussion and pass out. I can't exactly picture Barclay and Ben getting along—although I couldn't really picture *me* getting along with Barclay either, and we've actually worked pretty well together. But still, Barclay went to Ben's house, accused him of opening the unstable portals, and pulled out a gun. If I hadn't gotten there and complicated things, Barclay would have killed him.

I'm not surprised there's tension, and I doubt throwing Elijah into the mix helps much. Confrontation follows him wherever he goes—he's just like that.

"What is it?" I say, because I can't just wonder how bad the situation is.

Barclay turns around, gestures to the computer, and answers just a little too loud for the close quarters we're in. "We finally cracked it but it doesn't have anything we can use against IA."

"We'll figure it out. Let's just all calm down." Ben's fingers press on the keys a little harder than they should.

"We'll come at it from a different angle," I say, because we have something even if it didn't come from the computer.

"One that involves less testosterone in one room," Cecily adds under her breath.

"What other angle is there?" Barclay throws his hands up in frustration.

"Don't fucking yell at her," Elijah says, pushing off the wall. "This wasn't her plan. It was yours." He raises his voice and mocks Barclay. "*Break Elijah out, find Ben, go to the processing center, grab their computer.* All that's managed to do is add to our injuries."

"Yelling at each other isn't going to help anything," Ben says, his voice calm but also unnoticed by Elijah and Barclay.

"Want me to take you back to the Piston?" Barclay says. "I could probably get you executed right now if you don't want to wait another day and a half."

Elijah crosses the room, and for a second I'm sure they're going to come to blows right here, and I'm not sure what I'm going to do about it. Sure, I'll end up jumping in, probably with Ben, to break it apart, but it won't be pretty. I'm beat to shit, I feel like I've been run over by a truck—I know what that feels like—and my morale has taken a beating.

We're injured and low on time. If we fight each other we're going to end up dead.

But then Cecily is between them, her hands on Elijah's chest.

"This is stupid," she says. "How many times do I have to say that this room is entirely too small for brawling? We have plenty of space outside if you really want to start training for UFC."

I jump in. "Barclay, the three guys in your apartment—they have to be involved, right?"

"Good idea," Ben says. "We'll start there."

"And do what?" Barclay says. "We don't have time to stake them out and see who they talk to."

My chest tightens. I can tell from the tone of his voice there's an insult in there. There's a comment on how Ben and Elijah stalked Eric back when we thought he was the bad guy. Because I'm frustrated, I say, "So what, you're just going to give up?"

Only it's a bad time to push Barclay. Instead of responding to me, he shakes his head and walks out of the room.

And because I'm me, I follow. We are not done with this conversation.

"Barclay," I call after him.

He doesn't turn around.

But other people do. The hospital is crowded with Unwilling. We rescued more than forty people, most of them women, and a lot of them young. Someone—probably Cecily—has set them up in different rooms on the floor we've taken over, and when they hear me yell at Barclay, they come to their doors.

"Barclay," I call again. He still doesn't turn around and even though it's childish, I add, "You're being an asshole!"

He just keeps walking. I debate running after him, but I'm not sure what good it's going to do. I look at the faces in the doorways. Wide eyes focused on me. Hope is practically dripping from their expressions.

They're counting on me. No matter what Barclay says, we have to get them home.

I head back into the computer room.

"We need a plan," I say, because apparently I like to state the obvious.

"We need to fucking disband IA, maybe blow the shit out of them or something," Elijah says.

"Somehow I doubt that will get you off the Most Wanted list," Cecily says with a smile.

Elijah shrugs, but I see a smirk on his lips.

Ben ignores them both. He puts a hand through his hair and takes a deep breath. "Barclay is right. If we don't know who in IA is involved, we don't know who to trust. We could hand over the evidence to the wrong person, and my family will still be on the execution block, only the rest of us will be right there with them."

"I know," I say as I move to his side.

We've also blown our element of surprise. We broke into the processing center, stole their slaves, tied up their guards, and I

342

shot at the people coming after us. And now it's taken entirely too long to break into the computer and come up with a plan. Anyone who's working for Meridian will know Barclay is trying to take them down.

Which means they're hunting us. With their resources and manpower, we don't have long before they succeed.

There's only a day and a half before Ben's family will be executed. But we may not even have that much time anymore.

"What do we have?" I ask, looking at the computer.

"A whole lot of nothing," Elijah says.

"Eli, since you want to be so helpful, you can come with me to see the Unwilling," Cecily announces. He looks at her like she's crazy, but whatever it is about Cecily that makes people listen to her, he sees it.

Cecily looks at me and smiles. "We'll be back and ready to come up with a plan." Elijah is in for some kind of terrible lecture about staying positive and upbeat, I know it—I've gotten those lectures before.

He must have already gotten one too, because he rolls his eyes and mimics her, but he follows her out of the room anyway.

When they're gone, Ben takes my hand and gives it a squeeze. I breathe a little easier. We may not have a lot of time, but no one here is going to give up either. If IA takes me down, it's going to cost them something.

"Here, let me show you what we've got," Ben says, opening a software program on the computer. He gives me the rundown of how to read it, and somewhere in the middle of it, I realize what he's showing me is the ledger with the identity of everyone they've ever stolen. Where they're from, where they were sent— and for what.

"We already knew that most of the Unwilling are coming from underdeveloped worlds and being taken to the wealthiest ones," Ben says. "And we probably could have guessed that most fall into two valuable commodities."

A wave of nausea moves through me. "Girls and kids." Sex slaves and forced labor.

"We did find something new in the data, though. A couple years back the rate of teenage boys and young men who were trafficked skyrocketed."

That doesn't make sense. Men might be strong, which would make them good candidates for forced labor, but they're also the least likely to go quietly. They're trouble. Women and children will bend easier under the will of someone stronger in order to survive; men lash out and end up dead. Rebellion and dead slaves aren't really good for business.

Ben sighs and puts a hand through his hair, "I think they might have used them for soldiers."

I feel sick at how inhumane all this is, and I press my hand to my stomach. Essentially, wealthier countries going to war could use Unwilling to fight wars for them, probably promising the teenage boys they'll be able to go home if they win the war and all that. But they'd be put on the front lines because they're the most expendable, which would make them the most likely to die, and if they did live, then it wouldn't be that hard to sell some of them off once the war was over.

"How long is the list?" I ask.

Ben looks down. "Longer than it should be."

He's right. It's too long—much longer than I had been expecting.

Because Meridian hasn't just been grabbing people for the past few months or even the past few years. He's been grabbing people for over two decades.

From the records, the turnaround wasn't quite as big in the beginning—he was trafficking about twenty-four people in eight-person increments every few months during the first few years, mostly young women. Then five years ago, the number jumped to ten people every few weeks, which in itself is a major operation, but it continued to grow—steadily—after that, then spiked again about five years ago and skyrocketed from there.

As I look over the numbers, I do the math in my head, and then I do it again, because it can't possibly be right.

Because if it is, Meridian's responsible for abducting and selling 131,824 people into slavery last year.

# 01:12:40:07

"That's . . ." Ben takes a deep breath and stares at the computer screen. He swallows hard, like he's trying to digest the information, trying to convince himself it's somehow not that bad.

But this isn't exactly the kind of data that you can spin.

A hundred and thirty-one thousand people is a city. There's no upside here.

"It's not your fault," I say, because if I were him, that's exactly what I would be thinking.

"I should have done something," he says, his voice gritty with emotion.

"You did." I don't mention that he could have tried to do something sooner, because really I don't think that's true. If he had tried to do something sooner, maybe we wouldn't have the information that we have now.

Ben doesn't respond, and I can tell from the hard look on his face that he doesn't believe me.

"I'm serious. Look how far back this goes." I start scrolling back to the first records, which of course are only the first records that they wrote down in a computer. Who knows what they were doing before that?

In the ledger, 1995 was the first year that the trafficking ring recorded the Unwilling. Even though they referred to the people they took by number—took away their names and identities—they've listed the universe each person came from and where they were sent.

And I see a listing for my earth—Earth 19402. Someone was trafficked from my world to Earth 04032. And in the next column, where there are sometimes notes, it says, "Female, seventeen, blond."

It makes me feel sick.

# 01:11:59:31

That's when the plan comes to me.

I'm looking at an entry of a girl stolen from my world—and I realize we've been going about this all wrong.

Five and a half to six years ago, the human-trafficking operation more than doubled and became something much bigger than a crime organization—that's when it started operating on a corporate scale.

Which means, that's the point things changed, when they had more resources and fewer concerns about being caught.

That must be when Meridian started recruiting people in IA.

Whether he was paying them off to look the other way or involving them deeper—maybe getting old quantum chargers from them or something—either way, that's when things really changed.

But we don't need to know who in IA is involved. We don't even need to know who's *not* involved. We just need to get it in the hands of the right people at IA.

So why not just get it into the hands of *everyone*?

My plan is pretty simple—we're all going to Prima.

We'll copy the files from the ledger to a couple of zip drives—Barclay or Ben can portal somewhere and grab however many we'll need. Then we'll break into IA headquarters, upload the files to its intranet, and email them to everyone with an IA address.

Then everyone in IA will have the files. They'll have proof of the operation. They can take down Meridian, search the processing center, find and bring back the Unwilling who are slaves, and root out their own conspiracy.

Even if we're caught, someone is going to recognize this operation is bigger than IA has been letting on—and bigger than Ben. They'll see what Barclay saw and what I see. That there are people in IA who are dirty.

"How are we going to get into IA headquarters?" Barclay asks after I lay out my idea.

"Being a dangerous criminal makes everything more difficult," Elijah says, and Cecily laughs a little.

"Elijah and I can just portal right into an office," Ben says.

"We can even go tonight."

Barclay shakes his head. "This is IA headquarters we're talking about. You'll never get through the hydrochloradneum shields."

"I'll go," Cecily says. I shake my head, but she doesn't let me talk over her. "You guys are all wanted by the government or whatever, but nobody knows anything about me. I'll just go to Barclay's office and use his computer."

Suddenly Barclay smiles. "We'll all go." Then he looks at Elijah. "Not you, you'll stay here."

"Why the fuck do you think I'd stay here?"

"If we don't make it, we need someone who can portal the Unwilling back to their worlds," Barclay says. He doesn't say that Elijah's leg is messed up or that he's been shot, but he doesn't need to. We all know that.

"We'll go in as two teams. Janelle and I will approach IA from the front entrance," Barclay says. "Ben and Cecily from the back. We'll each have a route, and everyone will have to memorize a few passwords, but it gives us two solid chances. I can even set up a com link between us."

Cecily must see the look on my face and know what I'm thinking. "Don't even, Janelle. If you think I'm just going to sit here and wait for you to either pull this off or end up dead, you're out of your effing mind."

"Cee—"

She shakes her head. "Don't even try to placate me. I was minding my own business, and some asshole with terrible breath grabbed me, stuck me with a needle, and pulled me through a black hole. *A. Black. Hole.* And then they put me in a cage. There are portals and other worlds, and an Interverse Agency, and all I want to do is go home.

"But I'm not going to feel safe there if I'm always worried about someone else grabbing me and abducting me into *slavery*!" She takes a deep and shaky breath, blowing the air up into the strands of hair that fall into her face. "I am a part of this whether you think it's safe or not."

I look at Barclay because he's the one everyone is going to listen to—at least usually.

Our eyes meet briefly, then he looks at Cee. "I say she's in. She's right, but more than that, we need two teams. It'll throw security off and give at least one of us a fighting chance. And Elijah should stay here."

"She's never used a gun," I say.

"Neither had Ben or Elijah until recently," he says. I open my mouth to say more—that she's never run from the law or had to do something this dangerous—but Barclay cuts me off. "Look, I'd rather have three agents with tactical training and experience at my back, but I don't. I have three people who have a lot to lose, and it might not be ideal, but it's going to work."

Now that he has a course of action and a purpose, his determination is back.

I look at Cecily and my eyes sting. This was never supposed to happen to her. She should be planning more movie nights, taking care of people in Qualcomm, bossing Marines around and making them fall in love with her.

But she's here now, and I don't have the right to take her choices away from her. She's smart and she knows how dangerous this is going to be. The best thing I can do is make sure she's prepared.

"All right," I say, and I'm not sure who I'm saying it to or what

I'm talking about. But it's what everyone needs to hear.

Barclay takes a deep breath. "So here's how we're going to do this."

He knows IA headquarters inside out. Now he just has to teach it to us.

Before time runs out.

# 01:02:38:27

We're up the rest of the night, going over the specifics of the plan, anticipating how we're going to deal with the various things that could go wrong, and memorizing the layout of IA headquarters.

When we break for a few hours of sleep, sunlight is peeking over the corners of the horizon. I wander the halls aimlessly. Time has been draining away, we've only got about a day left, and if things go wrong when we break into IA, I won't make it out alive.

Maybe none of us will.

I've only made it about ten steps when I turn down a hallway and find myself face-to-face with a teenage girl about the same age as Jared, with long, wavy blond hair and big green eyes.

She's startled at first, and she flinches away from me.

The sight of her—doe-eyed and flinching—makes me feel like I've just been punched.

"I'm sorry," I say, and I want to add something else, but I don't know exactly what I'm apologizing for. For startling her, for not being able to get her home, for this happening to her in the first place—it's all a blur.

I give up and move around her, still muddled in my own thoughts, and when she's safely behind me, I hear her say, in a soft, tentative voice, "Thank you."

I look over my shoulder to see if I heard right or to say "of course" or ask "what for" or something—I'm not sure what— and I realize her eyes are glassy and she's smiling.

Her face is flushed, and she hugs her arms around her body. "I thought I was going to die in that place."

She's not, but she might end up dying here if we can't figure out how to get her home.

As if she knows what I'm thinking, she adds, "No matter what happens, anything is better than that place. I'm glad you got us out."

"Me too," I say, and I mean it.

Looking into her face, I'm struck by how many *more* people like her are out there. It's what I need. Energy manifests in the pit of my stomach with that realization and starts to spread throughout my body. I stand up a little straighter, I seem to lose some of the weight pressing down on me.

We have to succeed tomorrow. We don't have a choice.

If we don't shut Meridian down, thousands more people will become Unwilling.

# 01:02:30:27

I head up to the roof and watch the sunrise. The sky is a mix of orange, gray, blue, and black. The world is still and quiet, and even though it's completely different, it reminds me how I felt when I would go to the beach and stare out at the ocean.

I tilt my face to the sky and close my eyes, feeling the wind brush past my face and through my hair. I think of my double and how she chose to run away rather than help us, and of my dad and Alex, who are gone.

I wonder what Jared is doing right now—if he's still sleeping late and complaining about how we don't have milk for cereal, still walking younger kids to school, still reading and playing board games each night. I try not to think about how mad he must be that I'm gone, and I hope he isn't sulking and giving Struz the silent treatment.

I need to get back to them.

I don't belong here on this lifeless world. The wrongness makes my bones feel heavy and sluggish. Something about the stillness has made me numb, like I'm now this unfeeling person who's running around with a gun, but that's not who I am. It's not who I want to be.

I want to go home and hug my brother and never leave.

But the thing is, I'm standing here, surrounded by what should be a waking world, and it hits me that this may be it. Shivering from the cold, I close my eyes.

I might not make it home.

On my way down, I find Ben.

There are a million and one things I could say to him right now. I could tell him I'm scared and restless about what we're about to do, that I'm worried about losing more people I care about, that I'm afraid I won't keep my promise to Struz. I could tell him that I've thought about him every day since he left, that I can't picture the rest of my life without him, that I don't want to be replaceable.

But I don't say any of that. Instead I just reach for him.

My hand touches his shirt and I feel the heat of his body radiating underneath.

He pulls me to him and whispers, "Are you okay?" His breath is warm on my cheek.

I tilt my face to his, look up past the dark curls and long eyelashes, into those bottomless eyes. I almost tell him the truth—that I haven't been okay since he left. But I can't bring myself to speak.

Instead, I look at his lips and raise up on my toes so they're only a millimeter from mine, then I lift my eyes to his.

His lips part. Under my hand his chest rises and falls faster than it should, and his heart pulses through his whole body and reverberates into me.

One of his hands slides behind my back, the other he lays

over my fingers, and we stand there suspended in time, in the dark, with only the warmth of our bodies, and the sounds of our breaths.

"I'm sorry," Ben says, and then his lips are on mine.

They're soft, and he tastes minty, and the familiarity of it just feels so right. I kiss him back with everything I am, opening my lips, touching his tongue, remembering every inch of his mouth.

And everything that's wrong seems to fall away. It's like we're somewhere else—like we're back at Sunset Cliffs, kissing for the first time. My skin burns with his touch and my heart is slamming against my chest, and it's like my whole body has just come alive.

The nervous energy we're both holding inside morphs into something different, something more active, something a little dangerous. We grab at each other, a force behind our kisses that we can't quite control. We're not gentle or careful—we're not thinking.

His arms pull me in tighter so there's no room for anything between us. His hands slip under my shirt and are warm against my back, and a shudder moves through me.

"I love you," Ben breathes between kisses. "Let's never be apart again."

I pull his lips back to mine and force him to kiss me. That's all I want right now.

My thoughts are scrambled, my blood is tingling, and it feels like my skin is on fire. We're just lips, tongues, hands, and skin—two people who have everything and nothing to lose at the same time.

I'm tired of the never-ending fear I can't shake.

I don't want to be afraid anymore. I don't want to be numb. And I don't want to die.

But somehow in Ben's arms, when he kisses me, none of that matters.

Because I'm not alone.

# 00:18:20:05

"If it's not tight, it will be hard for you to move fast," Barclay says. I'm wearing jeans, sneakers, my bra, and a bulletproof vest that Barclay is helping me tighten. It's lighter and thinner than anything my dad ever wore, and instead of having Velcro, it laces like some kind of crazy weapon-resistant corset.

But he's right. Once the laces are tight and it's fitted against my body, it moves with me, like it's a part of me rather than something that will get in the way. I don't tell him that, though. He's got enough of an ego.

I do understand why I'm wearing it. The likelihood we're going to get shot at while we break into IA is . . . well, it's more of a certainty. Barclay grabbed both these vests—his and Hayley's—from his mom's house, along with the zip drives he used to copy the files. Wearing them, if we get hit, we'll be bruised and achy, but we won't be bleeding or dead.

I suppose that reduces the risk a little. I can pretend it's like playing paintball and less like running from the law.

Unless, of course, someone shoots us in the head.

Someone clears his throat, and I look up to see Ben in the

doorway. He isn't looking at me, though. He's looking at Barclay.

Barclay hands me my shirt and takes a step back. "See you in a few minutes," he says, and he can't fully suppress the smile.

"Did you get your earpiece?" I ask Ben as I pull my shirt over the vest.

"Yeah, Barclay showed me how it works," he says.

Barclay only had two of them, so he and Ben will wear them. It will let us communicate with each other in case the plan changes or things start to go wrong.

Ben grabs me and pulls me into a hug, crushing me against his chest. "You don't have to do this," he says. "It could just be me and Barclay."

Shivers run up my spine, and my legs feel too weak to support me. Here, in Ben's arms, with the smell of mint and soap in my nose and the beat of his heart underneath my face, my resolve falters slightly. The thought of running away flickers through my mind. We could be together, on the move, living an adventure most people don't dream of. But it's nothing more than a momentary hesitation, an image conjured up by the fear that's taken root in my mind. I don't mean it.

Because no matter how scared I am, I *do* have to do this.

It's the best plan we have.

Because we've got less than a day left.

"We can do this," I say to Ben. Because I have to believe it. Because it's our only option.

"I love you," he whispers, and my heart flutters.

Knowing it deep down and hearing it out loud are still two very different things.

"If we make it through this . . ."

I shake my head against his chest. "*When* we make it through this, we'll talk about it then."

"But—"

I look up, my nose brushing against his cheek. "Remember when the world was ending?" I whisper.

He nods.

"We didn't say good-bye or make promises then, and we're not going to now." It's not that saying good-bye will be like admitting we might die. I know the odds we're up against. I know we might not make it out of this. It's more complicated than that. "I need something to look forward to."

He doesn't say anything, so I push back in his arms and look at his face. His eyes are glassy.

"Don't worry about me. I have a lot to live for," I say, and I mean it. Right now, it's the truest statement I can make.

He nods, and I lead him, our hands intertwined, to the roof of the building.

Barclay is waiting for us. Cecily is there too. She's showered and pulled her hair back. The circles under her eyes aren't quite as dark, and I'm relieved that even though she was angry with me, she was at least able to get some sleep. She smiles at me. "Let's get this party started."

I give her a sideways glance. She's a little too excited for someone wearing a bulletproof vest.

"Oh c'mon, J," she says. "We are going to nail these guys."

"Yeah, just try not to end up dead," Elijah says as he comes in.

"Didn't you see the sign?" Cecily says. "This room is positive-thinking only."

Elijah just snorts.

"Enough of the bickering. Are we ready?" Barclay asks. I look at him—he's wearing a small smile and cracking his knuckles, his body weight shifting on his feet. He can barely stay still from the adrenaline, and even though I can't exactly describe what it is that he's feeling, it's contagious.

It starts as a nervous fluttering in the pit of my stomach, and it spreads through my body, becoming a restlessness in my limbs.

I take a deep breath and squeeze Ben's hand.

"Ready," I say, stepping to Barclay's side. He nods and holds his quantum charger in front of him, pressing a button. That brief, high-pitched electronic sound hits my ears, and then the cool, empty air of the portal is in front of me.

My heart beats a little faster. This is it.

In an hour, this could be all over.

Or we could be dead.

# 00:17:59:55

It's just Barclay and me now. Cecily and Ben are in a different position, planning to enter the building from a back entrance. They're the backup plan. They have a zip drive with the files and if Barclay and I fail, they have to get the files into IA's system.

I push my worry for them to the back of my mind. I can't let that distract me.

Barclay and I have the more dangerous position. We're standing in front of the only entrance into IA headquarters—for the second time. Now, the dozen concrete steps loom in front of us, and the oily glass skyscraper seems more sinister than it did only a few days ago.

"You agreed you'd take orders from me—you'll remember that, right?"

I turn to Barclay. I don't like that he's bringing this up now. "I did agree to that, why?"

He looks at the doors, where there are no less than six armed guards who at worst could have a *shoot on sight* order for both of us. Our only hope is they're caught by surprise, that no one expects us to walk in the front door. "If it looks like we're going down, I want you to run."

"You want me to leave you?" I don't worry about how incredulous I sound.

"If I'm caught, they won't execute me, at least not right away."

I'm not sure either of us believes what he's saying. He's worse than me, after all. He's the guy who was on their side, and is now committing treason with the enemy.

A traitor is always the worst thing someone can be.

But we don't have time to argue about it now. I've made a lot of promises to people I care about. This one is no different. "I'll follow your orders."

"Good," he says with a nod.

And we climb the stairs.

# 00:17:58:52

We go through the center glass doors side by side. This time I don't pause to take note of the marble floors and the corporate business decor of the lobby. I don't linger on the airport security–style body scans.

My eyes find the armed guards.

Of the six guards, four are focused on the people coming into the building, operating body scans and giving directions. One is about fifteen feet in front of us, in the direction we want to go—he's standing by the elevators. The other is standing off to the side—the same guy we approached just a few days ago.

And lucky him, he has to deal with us today, too.

We're just a few feet from him when he takes notice. His face is all business, like he's about to regurgitate the company line, tell us we can't enter this way, and go through the motions. Then his face changes. His lips part, and his eyes widen slightly, shifting from Barclay's face to mine. The recognition is clear.

Everyone is looking for us.

When he reaches for his radio, I relax a little. The orders aren't *shoot on sight*. They clearly still want to bring us in alive.

Everything happens so fast—it's over in a split second—but I'm ready for it. I know what Barclay is going to do. I know what *I* have to do.

The guard has time to press the button on his radio, but no sound comes out because with one swift move, Barclay knocks him out with an elbow to the face. Before he hits the ground, we've both disarmed him. Barclay has the machine gun, and I'm pulling the sidearm from the guard's hip.

Barclay turns the machine gun on the armed guards at the body scanners, and I raise the sidearm, pointing the barrel at the face of the guard by the elevator.

"Drop your weapon!" I yell, advancing on him. My grip is tight on the gun, and my arms burn from the tension. "Drop it or I'll put a bullet between your eyes." I won't actually do it, because I'm too tense and too far to be that good a shot, but also because we don't want to hurt anyone. I'm bluffing—and I'm bluffing big because I'm outgunned, and if he thinks too long about it, he'll realize that.

His surprise and my threats outweigh any inclination to try to be a hero, and he lays his machine gun on the ground. My heartbeat kicks into overdrive, and I kick the gun farther away so he can't make a lunge for it. "Hands up, behind your head."

Behind me, I have a vague sense of Barclay going through the same motions. But more because I know the plan and less because I'm paying attention to him. I've put my trust in him and his ability to guard my back, but I know he's yelling and making threats, telling the guards—and the people in line—to get rid of their weapons and lie flat on the ground.

With his hands over his head, the guard in front of me drops to his knees, and I relieve him of the sidearm and the backup gun at his ankle. I take both of them for my own and keep my gun trained on him the entire time.

"Facedown on the ground," I say, taking a step back to give him room.

He does what I say, and I turn to Barclay. The room is remarkably quiet—no sobs, groans, or even gasps. It's a creepy sort of silence, the kind that comes before a storm, and I hope that we're ready for it.

Barclay has everyone on the ground, and he's stripping the last two guards of their weapons, dismantling them easily, breaking the pieces apart, buying us just a little more time.

When he's finished, he starts toward me. He still has the machine gun pointed at the guards and the crowd, and he reminds them, "Stay on the ground. Don't make me shoot you!"

He continues backing up.

Someone from the crowd calls out right as Barclay is about to reach me. I can't see who because he stays down. He says, "You don't have to do this, Taylor. Whatever's going on, there are people you can turn to."

Barclay's expression is stone-faced when he answers. "Tell that to Eric."

# 00:17:54:51

When Barclay reaches me, I run for the door to the stairs and pull it open. We need to get to the fifth floor, and taking the elevator is too dangerous. Barclay follows me.

But before he does, he pulls the fire alarm.

It blares around us as we run up the steps. It's so loud that it drowns out the pounding of my heart and most of my thoughts. I'm on automatic, pushing myself up the stairs, following Barclay as closely as I can. We pass the second floor, then the third. People who think this is a drill start to flood the stairwells and pass us on their way down to the lobby. A lot of them are analysts or administrative staff and a lot of them either don't know—or know of—Barclay or me. They're too wrapped up in their own jobs or they don't expect anyone to be crazy enough to break into IA headquarters.

Whatever it is, they don't give us a second glance as we pass them.

But they still put me on edge. My legs quiver with each step, the burn spreading throughout my body from my hamstrings to my chest.

Barclay passes the fourth floor a few steps ahead of me, and in between us the door opens. I know the second I see his face that this guy coming through isn't like the rest of them. He knows something is up, and when he sees me running toward him, his eyes narrow in recognition.

The air seems to freeze in front of me, and I can't get a breath, but instead of going for me, he looks up the stairs at Barclay.

It takes me even less time to see what's in his right hand.

"Gun!" The scream is automatic, and thankfully Barclay hears me over the fire alarm and reverses direction, heading straight for the guy.

But he's going to be too late.

I do the only thing I can. It doesn't take any thought. I just react. I throw myself up the remaining stairs and against this guy I don't know, effectively ramming him into the wall.

His right arm is pinned momentarily before he gets over the surprise and knocks me off him.

The distraction is enough, though. Barclay is there, and the heel of his palm comes up directly into the guy's nose. Blood rushes from his face, and Barclay brings down his gun on the back of the guy's head, knocking him out.

I knew Barclay was good with hand-to-hand combat—he'd have to be. But even I'm impressed.

People are staring at us now. This whole incident, only seconds long, has managed to attract a lot of attention. Barclay grabs a passing guy—he's skinny, his tie is crooked, and he looks young, little more than a kid. "Get him out of here," he says, pointing to the unconscious body. The authority in his voice is unmistakable. This is a command, delivered with urgency, the kind people don't question, not when there's a fire alarm blasting in their ears. "When you're outside, get him in restraints and have him detained."

Skinny Kid nods, and as I head up the stairs after Barclay, a couple of people are helping him lift the unconscious guy up.

We keep going, to the fifth floor. Barclay grabs the door and holds it open for me.

The fifth floor is empty. Everyone has either cleared out or they haven't reported in to the office yet to begin with. I follow Barclay as he makes his way through the floor, past the cubicles to the empty corner office. I don't ask where he's going. I know the plan.

The corner office belongs to Special Agent Ian Bachman, who is clearly someone important. And someone who works the night shift, so he's not here right now. He's also the guy with the gruff voice who broke into Barclay's apartment. Or at least Barclay seems sure that it's him.

We're going to email the proof to everyone from Bachman's computer.

I slide open his desk drawers, pulling out their contents, scattering his papers on the floor. I'm sure there's nothing he'd keep here to imply that he's in on the conspiracy, that he's working for Meridian, and even if he did, we wouldn't have the time to go through it all without getting caught, but we want to make him—and anyone else who's involved—think we're on to them. If they're scared, they'll be more likely to make mistakes.

While I'm destroying his desk, the zip drive is in the computer, uploading the files, and Barclay is prepping for our escape, with the one step that I don't want to think about—despite how necessary it is.

He's using a small, handheld heat laser to cut through the glass of the corner window.

There are only two exits in this building—the one we came through and the one Ben and Cecily used—and there's no way we can get out of either now. Which means we have to make our own.

Breaking the window is something Barclay has assured me will register on IA's building security system. It will bring security running to this floor—this office. Which should let Ben and Cecily get out easier the way they came.

Only it requires that we slide down a rope for five stories.

The cool air from the broken window flows through the room, rustling the papers I've littered across the floor.

Because, of course, a five-story drop from IA headquarters is actually a lot more than that. It's five stories to the platformed walkways, then a hundred feet to the street of the underground. Which means we're a lot farther off the ground than I'm comfortable with.

Barclay ties the rope to the desk. A desk he's assured me is bolted in place.

I look at the computer. "It's almost done," I say.

Barclay pulls up the email program and addresses it to the "All IA" mailing list. He types a short note.

**Eric Brandt was murdered. Because he uncovered this.**

And then he attaches the files.

While we wait, he says into the com link, "We're uploading now. Abort and get out of the building."

I breathe a little easier, knowing Ben and Cecily will be able to follow the crowd of people evacuating the building because of the fire alarm.

From the hallway, I hear the elevators ding.

# 00:17:42:57

"It's going to be fine," Barclay says as he wraps the rope around one of his hands and one of his feet.

Across the floor, I can hear the shouts and orders of some kind of task force coming for us. They're fanning out, advancing on us so there's no way back to the stairs.

I look at Barclay and the iridescent sky peeking through the window. The wind moves through my hair and chills travel down my spine.

"Tenner," Barclay says, his voice calm. "We have to go."

I know we do, but it's like everything in my body is refusing to move forward. Climbing out a window this high off the ground—the real ground—just isn't natural.

But I take Barclay's outstretched hand, and he pulls me the few feet to him. From behind, I wrap my arms around his chest. I'm holding on to him, he's holding on to the rope, and the rope is attached to the desk, which is bolted to the floor.

I tell myself Barclay knows what he's doing, that he's done something like this before.

"It'll be over before you know it," he says.

And we go down the side of the building.

# 00:17:42:02

The air is cold, and it burns as it whips past my face.

But worse is the feeling of gravity. The sensation of jumping only lasts a split second, and then I can *feel* gravity take over and begin pulling us down. My heart lurches in my chest at the lack of control, and my feet start to cramp from the fear.

My ears pop, something stings my shoulder, and I look down in time to see the white platform rushing toward us. I open my mouth to let loose a scream, but I don't have time.

Barclay does something to the rope, and we lurch, not to a complete stop, but slow enough that the sounds of the world—people, traffic, general noise—come rushing back to my ears, and I can breathe again.

We're about five feet off the platform when Barclay says, "You have to jump."

Instead, I let go of him and just sort of fall to the ground. I keep my legs loose so that when I hit the concrete platform, my feet sting from the contact, but my knees bend, and I end up in a crouch with my hands on the ground to steady myself.

I don't wait for Barclay, though I know he's right behind me.

I just start running. We have to get away from IA headquarters—as far away as the city will allow.

I think of the map Barclay drew for me last night, and I head in the direction we planned, essentially to the opposite end of the city.

We slid down the building in full view of the cameras, so IA will know where we're headed, but at least that will help Ben and Cecily slip out unnoticed.

I push past people on the platform, ignoring the gasps or the way they stumble after I knock into their shoulders. I don't have time to do too much dodging or weaving. I'm moving fast, and they need to get out of my way.

When I knock into the shoulder of a girl around my age, she swears and yells after me. I glance back out of habit and realize she's with a bunch of friends, all dressed in matching white polo shirts and plaid skirts—a school uniform for sure. One of them gives me the finger and the rest of them start to laugh.

I don't spare them another second—I need to keep running—but something pinches in my chest. I should be with friends, laughing and being stupid, not running from the cops.

Barclay catches up with me, pressing his palm into my back. We're about to hit a crossroads at the platforms. Right would lead us back around the way we came, and in front of us is some kind of upscale mall.

I go left because that leads away. The alarm from IA headquarters is still blaring in the background.

"Shit!" Barclay swears.

"What is it? Is it Ben and Cecily?" I ask. Just the question tempts me to turn around and head back.

"Keep running," Barclay says.

We turn left and run through the people on the platform. Barclay is in front of me now, and I keep my eyes focused on his back and push myself to keep up.

I know IA has teams of people following us—they have to— but they won't shoot at us since we're surrounded by civilians, and everything else, all of the details we pass, are a blur. My feet pounding against the pavement, my lungs pulling in air, the way my whole body throbs with the burn of too much exertion, and Barclay's back in front of me—are obvious. The rest of my attention is focused on looking for a threat and being ready to avoid it.

# 00:17:34:18

I'm not sure how much time has actually passed when we hit the major monorail station that will get us on the train out of the city and to safety. It feels like we've been running for hours, and my legs are aching with exhaustion.

But I don't slow down or stop.

I know that once I do, I'm going to collapse.

The station, completely made of glass, looms in front of us, reflecting the bright sun. Running up the stairs makes pain shoot up my hamstrings, and I feel like my legs might not continue to hold me.

Barclay glances over his shoulder and calls for me to hurry.

The plan is to get on the train. If we were fast enough, we've timed it right so that the train doors will be open, and we'll be able to get on before they close. But anyone trailing us won't.

Only Barclay stops short in front of me.

I barrel into his back.

The train isn't there.

I'm too short of breath to ask what we're going to do, but I don't need to. Barclay grabs my arms and pulls me toward the edge of the platform.

Behind us, I hear the shouts of pedestrians, and I know IA is close on our trail.

"Ben and Cecily?" I ask, because I can't help it.

He shakes his head, and for a second I can't breathe. My hands are shaky and I feel unsteady from the panic rising in my chest.

"What happened?"

"We don't have time for this now," he says.

"Barclay!" There's no way I can do anything without knowing what's going on.

"They got caught in the hallway. They ran into the deputy director, and he recognized Ben. They're in his office telling him everything right now."

I feel something inside me relax. They've been caught, but they're alive. They have the proof on them, and Barclay got the email out. I remember the faces of the two little blond children on Struz 2.0's desk. He might be better dressed than my Struz, but he'll hear Ben and Cecily out.

He has to.

The bell signifying the coming train starts to ring, and an announcement comes over the loudspeaker saying that everyone should step back from the edge of the platform.

But there's another announcement too.

People behind us are screaming, "Get down on the ground!"

I look over my shoulder and see that the order isn't necessarily directed at us—it's directed at everyone else, and behind the throng of commuters are guys with guns. They're IA agents and security forces, dressed like the guards at the front of headquarters, and there are some guys in regular clothes, too—agents who've joined the chase.

The oncoming train is approaching, but by the time it gets here, IA will be on top of us. Even if we get on the train, we'll just be giving ourselves less room to run.

We're essentially backed into a corner.

Closest to us is a guy in his late twenties with a military-style crew cut, khaki pants, and combat boots. His gun is trained on Barclay. "You got nowhere to go, Wonder Boy," he says, and I recognize his voice as the guy who couldn't stop chuckling when he broke into Barclay's apartment.

It's over. We're trapped.

We can only hope the proof we emailed is enough.

Right as I'm about to raise my hands and surrender, Barclay's fingers dig into my shoulder, and I hear him say, "Trust me!" but I don't have a chance to say that I do or ask what that means.

Because he pushes me.

I stumble off the platform and fall onto the thin rail track.

My legs throb from the impact. The track vibrates with the approach of the train, and below me, all I can see is air.

Over the roar of the train, I hear a few shouts across the platform, and suddenly Barclay is next to me, pulling me up to my feet so we're both standing on the track. He winces and clutches his side, and I hope the vest has kept him from actually getting hit.

He says something to me, but I can't hear him. The train is too loud, but he throws himself forward, his hands catching the edge of the opposite platform, and I know that's what he wants me to do.

I hesitate. If I jump for the wall and slip, I'll fall over a hundred feet down to the underground. And I won't have anything to break my fall.

But a rush of warm air envelops me—the heat of the train bearing down on me—and my palms are slick with sweat. I do what he says.

I jump.

My hands hit the concrete platform edge, and my whole body—even my face—slams against the wall with a thud so painful it's almost blinding, and then the heat from the train is singeing my back as it pulls into the station and screeches to a stop.

Next to me, Barclay presses himself straight up. I try to imitate him, but I just don't have the strength, and the train is too close to me, restricting my movement. My fingers feel slippery, and the fact that there's nothing below me except sky makes the arches of my feet start to cramp.

I don't want to die this way.

But Barclay is there, grabbing my arms and pulling me up.

Once my knees hit the cement, I scramble to my feet.

Another train is pulling into the station. It's headed in the opposite direction, and it's at least a hundred yards away. And I know the new plan before he even says anything.

Barclay grabs my arm. "We have to get on that train!"

We run.

All around us, I can hear people yelling. The IA agents are shouting orders. They know what we're going to do and they're trying to get to the platform and its train before us. The ordinary people trying to go to work scream when they're caught off guard by the sheer amount of guns and excitement.

My whole body hurts. My ankles sting in pain every time one of my feet hits the ground, my shoulder and back throb from where the bullets are lodged in my vest, and my lungs feel like they're ready to burst because I'm not getting enough air.

Heart pounding with the same furious rhythm as my legs, I narrow my focus on the open train doors. Like I'm in a tunnel, leading only to those doors, I block everyone else out. Getting there in time is the only option.

I push harder, move my legs faster, and when we're about ten feet away and the bell sounds to signify the doors are about to shut, I hold my breath.

Barclay reaches the train just before I do, as the doors are sliding shut. His hand pushes against one of the doors, leaving a six-inch gap and giving me an extra second.

Out of the corner of my eye, I see Chuckles coming down the stairs to this platform, several agents behind him.

The bell sounds again, and the doors push against Barclay.

I throw myself into the train and collide with Barclay, throwing both of us into the back wall. A metal pole runs into my shoulder, and I groan at the pain because that's definitely going to leave a bruise.

The doors are closed. I release the breath I was holding, and suddenly I feel dizzy with relief. Barclay smiles at me, pulling me to my feet, and we stare at each other, breathing heavily.

Then I see Chuckles.

He's barely ten feet away, running toward us at full speed and screaming at someone—probably the conductor of the train. If the doors open again, he'll be able to get on. I turn and grab Barclay's arm, trying to pull him toward the next door. If Chuckles gets on the train, we can get off. But Barclay stands his ground, smiles, and gives Chuckles the finger.

And the train starts to move.

# 00:17:31:25

Barclay's face is flushed from running, and I can't help it, I throw my arms around him. Because we made it. We're still alive.

Barclay hugs me back, his arms tight, pressing me into his chest. I know he feels it too.

"Ben and Cecily?" I ask, pulling away.

"He believes them," he says. "He's asking a couple questions now, but . . ."

He doesn't need to say anything else. The weight of this conspiracy has just been lifted off our shoulders, because it's over now. We'll portal back to the hospital, gather up the Unwilling, wait for IA, and then we'll be able to go home.

We've won.

It's enough to make me come undone. My eyes sting, my shoulders droop, and my body starts to quiver. I'm so relieved that all I can do is cry.

"Good plan, Tenner," he says, but then I see his smile falter.

For a second I wonder if someone's behind me, if one of the agents managed to make it on the train. If we're not really safe.

But Barclay raises a hand to his earpiece, and I realize it's something else.

It's something happening with Ben.

"What is it?" I say as I lean into him, trying to hear.

At first, I can't make out anything. Barclay's body is tense next to me, and I realize he's holding his breath. I don't know what he heard, but he's coiled like he's waiting for an attack, which means it's bad.

I wonder if the deputy director will still punish Ben for his involvement and if he's not going to grant him immunity for his previous crimes, like working with the traffickers to snatch people from their worlds until he could save the other Janelle.

And then I don't have to speculate anymore.

Because I hear something from Barclay's earpiece.

A gunshot.

# PART THREE

*But already my desire and my will*

*were being turned like a wheel, all at one speed,*

*by the Love which moves the sun and the other stars.*

—Dante

# 00:17:26:17

efore I even have a chance to register what's going on—or what I'm doing—I grab the earpiece and pull it from Barclay's ear. He lets out some kind of yelp from surprise and pain, but I'm not paying attention.

"Ben, are you okay?" I say, pressing the button. There are several more shots, and I can hear Cecily screaming, "No!" and "Don't!" and "Ben!" Then there's some kind of thud. Then nothing.

"Ben?" I say again. I'm shaking my head, because this can't be happening. Not after everything. He has to be okay.

Barclay grabs my hand, pulling it off the button. "If they're in trouble the last thing he needs is you talking to him in the middle of it."

I open my mouth to argue, to tell him that he doesn't understand, but I don't say anything. I know he's right. Instead I take a deep breath and listen. If ears could *strain*, that's what I'd be doing right now. I'm listening for anything that's going to fill me in.

It's like time—or the world—slows down, and all that matters is what I'm hearing from the earpiece. My eyes are closed, and I wait to hear Ben's voice again, for him to say something, anything. And every time my mind starts to conjure an image of him lying in a pool of blood with a bullet wound in his chest, I squeeze my eyes tighter and push it away.

I want to shout that it's not fair, that this should be over, that I shouldn't have to lose him, too.

I don't register anything else until I realize my face is flushed, and the taste of blood is on my tongue. I let out the breath I've been holding and steady myself against the wall of the train as stars cloud my vision. Barclay reaches over and wipes the blood from where I've bitten deep into my lip.

And still I try to listen.

But I don't hear anything except the echo of my pulse in my ears.

Not a thing.

Not the commotion that would result from fleeing the scene, not labored breathing from someone who's injured, not screaming or shuffling around. There's nothing.

"Ben, are you there?" I ask, my voice cracking. There's no response, which shouldn't surprise me because deep down, I know he's not. "Ben?"

"Tenner, we're approaching the next stop." Barclay tugs on my arm, his voice an urgent whisper.

The image of Ben is back. It's all I can see. There's blood everywhere, soaking through the front of his clothes, pooling underneath him, coating his dark brown curls. My chest constricts, and I can't breathe. This was my plan. It's my fault—I'm the one who sent him into IA.

It's like Alex all over again.

Suddenly I'm so angry, I want to scream as loud as I can at

the sheer unfairness of all this.

This wasn't supposed to happen.

"Janelle."

I take a wheezing breath and turn on Barclay, pounding my fists into his chest and arms. "What happened? What happened to them?"

At first he just takes it. He stands there and lets me hit him. He doesn't do anything to stop me or to minimize the damage I want to do, and for some reason that just makes the anger worse. Because I'm so insignificant—I can't change anything. Everything we've done has been as effective as throwing ourselves against a wall.

But something in Barclay changes, and he reaches up, cupping my head in his hands while I hit him. His voice comes out, steady, even, and calm, but there's a certain gravity to his tone as well. "Janelle, we need to get out of here."

It snaps me out of it, as I remember where we are.

Our train is half full with commuters on their way to work. They're all squeezed in next to one another at the other end of the car, pretending not to stare at us with masks of indifference, their body language saying, *I don't see anything*, as if they're trying to blend into the background. As it is, the waves of panic coming from that end of the train add a tangy scent to the air.

"Let's go," I say, my voice raw.

Barclay nods and pulls out his quantum charger.

When the portal opens, I go through it first. I don't even register how it feels or what I'm doing when I go through. It's just another portal, and after everything else I feel numb to the fact that I'm slipping through a black hole and ending up in a different world.

I'm waiting for Barclay, on my feet in his abandoned overgrown jungle of a world, when he comes through behind me.

"Hey, you went through relaxed," he says. "I knew you'd get it eventually."

I don't care about that. "Tell me what happened," I say. "I need to know everything."

"It might not be as bad as it sounded, Janelle," Barclay says, but even I can tell that this is him playing hopeful and optimistic. He doesn't believe what he's saying.

"Just tell me."

Barclay recounts what he heard. He starts at the beginning with the parts I already know, but I don't stop him. I said I wanted everything, and I do.

If these are the last moments of Ben's life, I want to be able to picture it all. I want to commit it to memory.

Ben and Cecily went into IA headquarters on cue—they headed up the back stairwell to the second floor and waited for everyone to leave after Barclay pulled the fire alarm. They didn't make it to their computer, but as soon as Barclay told them he'd gotten the email off, it didn't matter. They kept their heads down and walked out with the crowd, allowing the people around them to dictate how fast they moved and where they went.

Only they ran into Deputy Director Ryan Struzinski. He seemed surprised but not alarmed when he recognized them. Of course, both Cee and Ben recognized him, too, so they went into his office and he promised to listen to them.

Cecily told him everything. She started with her abduction and didn't leave anything out. And then Ben filled in what he knew.

The deputy director was impressed but skeptical. He asked to see the drive with the evidence from the processing center. He put it in his computer and looked shocked at what he saw. He praised Ben and Cecily for everything they'd done, and Ben sighed in relief and said he was so glad he could trust Struz.

Silence followed.

Then the deputy director asked if they had been worried about who to give the information to. Cecily said, "You have no idea," with a laugh, and all three of them chuckled.

Then the deputy director asked, "So you mean you haven't shown this to anyone else?"

That's when Barclay stopped. Because he knew that wasn't right—*that* shouldn't be the next question.

Ben didn't say anything, but Cecily started to answer.

Barclay isn't exactly sure what happened, but it was clear to him that Ben had the same sudden realization that he did. The deputy director wasn't on our side. "You know the rest," Barclay says. "The next thing I heard was the gunshot, you ripped the com out of my ear, and now no one is on the other end."

My body feels heavy, like it's already dead and is just waiting for me to notice. I can't keep fighting—keep moving forward, keep trying to win against something like IA, not after everything. Barclay never should have come to me for help. We're up against something that's too big, too powerful.

Now both Cecily and Ben are gone.

## 00:16:51:44

I think of Cecily on the back soccer field, standing with her hands on her hips, her hair lit up with the sun, as she looked at Ben, as serious as a heart attack, and said, *Who's your favorite superhero?*

Ben stepped back like he'd been wounded, and laughed. *That's it? That's all you got? That's easy.*

And then he looked at me. His eyes dark, his lips curled into a slight half smile as he said, *Wonder Woman.*

Cecily threw a grin in my direction before grilling him on his choice, and Alex offered his two cents about the wonderfulness of her costume, and I just felt light-headed—in the best possible way.

It feels like it could have been yesterday. I remember it all so clearly.

*How did we get so far away from that moment?*

# 00:16:51:43

Now they're gone. All of them.

And it's my fault. My stupid plan. We should have left them at the hospital with the Unwilling. Barclay and I should have just gone in ourselves. I should have fought harder to keep Cecily out of it—I should have fought harder to keep them alive.

More tears spill over my eyes. I can't hold it together anymore.

"We don't know what happened," Barclay says again.

"What, you think they got out of IA headquarters, away from a guy with a gun who was shooting at them? You and I both know that office layout, tell me how that's a possibility."

He doesn't say anything.

I hold a hand over my eyes and try to will the tears to stop, but they seem to have a mind of their own.

"This isn't over," Barclay says, grabbing my shoulders.

I don't say anything. I have nothing to say.

"Look at me," Barclay says, giving my shoulders a jerk that shakes my whole body.

I look at him.

"Pull yourself together. We don't know what happened."

I shake my head because I can't get the words out.

"Those shots could have been fired at the air," Barclay says. "Even if they're hit, it might not be fatal. I'm not going to sit around waiting for IA to find me, and neither are you. We have a limited amount of time before they start doing a multiverse sweep or someone realizes that the best place to hide is in a world where no one is looking."

"We don't have anything left," I say, because wasn't *this* our Hail Mary play? How can we win if the conspiracy goes as high as the deputy director of IA?

"There's always something left."

# 00:16:48:09

"This is just a setback," Barclay says.

"A setback?" I could punch him. "Ben and Cecily could be dead, and if the deputy director is involved, couldn't he be making an announcement to IA that you're crazy or something? Can't he bury this?"

Barclay shakes his head and starts pacing. "I mean, he could try, sure, but the order to disregard an investigation would have to come from the director."

Suddenly his eyes widen and he turns around, grabbing me by the shoulders. "I know what we need to do."

I wince and remember that I have at least two bullets lodged in my vest. Even though they didn't do the damage they could have, they're still a throbbing pressure against my skin.

"We'll go straight to the director's house and talk to him," Barclay says, letting go of me.

"How do we know he's not involved?" I'm starting to feel like the whole multiverse is against us.

"Don't you see, I knew someone high up had to be involved because of the way that paperwork got erased or rewritten. But

Director Franklin is older. He's about to retire. He's been giving a lot of his responsibilities up to Struzinski."

"That doesn't make him innocent," I say. I don't want to rain on Barclay's plan, but I can't help myself. We're in a colossal mess right now. "If the deputy director is involved, who says the director isn't? All of IA could be involved!"

"They're not," Barclay says through gritted teeth. He's clearly trying to keep from getting emotional, and I'm impressed with his willpower. "We just need to get to the director and he'll help us."

I can't listen anymore. "How can you possibly think that!" I yell.

"Because I don't know who else to trust!" Barclay screams back. He turns his back on me and walks a few paces away. "This isn't just happening to you, you know."

"I know," I say, my voice thick. I haven't really been thinking about what he's going through—if he's scared for his family or if he's worried he'll never be able to go home.

"We'll go to the director's house, we'll get a task force set up—"

"How can you still have faith in them?" I ask.

He turns and looks at me, his eyes glassy. "I have to," he says. "I'm still good. Nothing would make me sell out. Eric was still good."

I don't remind him that Eric's dead, that they killed him.

"This was my dream, as a kid, to be IA and to make a difference." His voice cracks slightly, and he takes a deep breath. "There have to be people left who are like me."

"What if there's not?" I say. It's callous, but I have to say it. We can't walk into a trap because Barclay is feeling sentimental.

"Janelle, there are terrible people out there, in every world," he says. "Trust me, I know that just as well as you do, but for every one of *those* people, there are people like you and me."

I wish I believed him.

But right now I can't. The two of us running around playing heroes can't last much longer.

"I can go alone," Barclay says. "If you don't trust me."

I kick the dirt. "You can't go alone." I have faith in Barclay. And I do trust him, whatever his misguided and romanticized feelings about IA are. "I don't have any better ideas, anyway."

We have to go to the director's house. We'll need to try to convince him of what we've seen. We know enough of the operation on the processing center and we have witnesses. That should get an IA task force into the Black Hole and working on the files. That should get the Unwilling back to their homes.

"How do we get into the director's house?" I ask.

# 00:15:40:37

**W**e portal into the director's backyard and end up hiding out behind a hydrangea bush.

This is by far Barclay's least complicated plan, and part of me is glad for it.

Anyone who's anyone in IA has hydrochloradneum shields around their house, which means the director most likely has a really good security system. There's no way we'd be able to break in, and we don't want to seem like a threat anyway. The plan is to just go up and knock on the front door.

So that's exactly what we do.

My fingertips tingle with anticipation as we approach the house. The sun is beginning its descent, and the lights inside the house, set against the graying sky, make it look a little like it's glowing.

An older woman opens the door. She's probably in her sixties, but I can tell she was classically beautiful in her day, with thick blond hair that falls to her shoulders and washed-out blue eyes. She's wearing a long-sleeved black dress and high heels.

This is clearly the director's wife. "Can I help you?" she asks.

Her tone says she's confused as to why two bruised and beat-up people in dirty clothes are standing on her doorstep, but she doesn't look alarmed.

Some of the tension coiled inside me gives a little and my shoulders relax slightly.

"Mrs. Franklin," Barclay says. "I'm so sorry to bother you, but I'm an agent with IA, and I have something urgent I need to discuss with your husband."

I don't say anything. I'm just along for the ride.

She opens the door wider, her confusion turning to a knowing smile. The director is apparently the kind of guy who brings work home. More tension uncoils—I know a few guys like that.

"Of course," she says. "Let me just . . ." She turns, and I see a man approaching the door. He's in his sixties as well, with distinguished gray hair and lines etched into his face, but he's built like someone who is still in the kind of shape he was in when he was thirty. "Keith, one of your agents—"

She doesn't get a chance to finish, because that's when Keith Franklin, director of the Interverse Agency, recognizes us.

# 00:15:32:19

He's got his phone out of his pocket and to his ear so fast that there's no time to tiptoe around the issue or make apologies. The door's wide open so I cross the threshold.

"You don't want to do that," I say. My voice shakes a little despite my conviction. This has just all been too much.

It's not what he's expecting. A bad guy would go for the phone or pull a gun on the innocent wife. Plus Barclay is the one everyone thinks is running this operation. I'm just some girl from another universe who's caught up in it.

The director's gaze shifts from Barclay to me, though not for long. He's not stupid—he knows who he needs to be watching out for.

"Look, I know what you've heard. That Barclay's a traitor, that I escaped from prison, and that Ben—" My voice cracks. "That Ben Michaels is operating a human-trafficking ring. The truth is that's all a lie. It's a cover-up, because there's something a lot bigger going on."

"Director Franklin, sir," Barclay says. "Please just hear us out.

Let me explain everything that's happened. If you still think we're guilty, we'll willingly go into custody."

I don't look at Barclay. I don't want to give away the fact that I know that's not at all the plan. We have an escape route he's mapped in case the director is involved or doesn't believe us.

But he doesn't need to know that.

I watch the director as he decides what to do.

On one hand, Barclay trusts him, likes him even, and on the other, he's the guy who signs the paperwork to execute people—I can't believe that this guy, who's willing to execute innocent people because of their association with someone who isn't even proven guilty, can be one of the good guys. There are supposed to be some lines you don't cross.

I try not to think about that, though. Otherwise I'm going to dwell on the fact that we're here, trying to get his help, and I don't understand how we can really be putting our faith in this guy.

He puts his phone in his pocket and looks at Barclay. "Come inside, Taylor."

I hear voices from another room, someone laughing and then calling, "Keith! Annamarie! What's keeping you?"

I look at Barclay, and I'm not surprised to see the shock in his eyes and the confusion on his face. Because I recognize that voice. It takes me a minute to place it, but then I remember—she invited him to lunch at a restaurant with the *best air in the city*.

It's the governor.

"Dinner guests," the director says to us. He's been entertaining while my friends have been dying. Looking at his wife, he says, "Could you tell Hanna and Macon that I'll be a few minutes?"

"Of course," she says as she gives us a wary glance and moves through the house.

I hope a few minutes is enough time.

# 00:15:28:19

The director takes us into what's either his library or home office, and he closes the door behind him.

He folds his arms across his chest. "You have five minutes."

Barclay tells him everything.

And when I say everything, I mean he doesn't leave out any part of it. He starts with the case he was on when he met me and Ben—how we helped him figure it out, sort of. He explains how he stumbled on the trafficking ring and how it was a lot more complicated than one girl getting nabbed from her universe. He details his suspicions about Eric's death and IA involvement.

Barclay doesn't even leave out the things the two of us have done that are clear violations of the law. Like the fact that we've each killed people.

It takes longer than five minutes, but the director doesn't stop Barclay or look at his watch. Instead, he takes a seat while Barclay is telling him about the three guys who broke into his apartment.

After Barclay explains everything we found at the processing center, he pauses.

"And you have this computer?" the director asks.

"I emailed the files to everyone at IA, including you," Barclay says.

The director gets up and moves to his computer, turning it on. As I wait for him to open his email and read the files we've sent, I can't help holding my breath. This is it—the moment we find out if he's going to listen to us or not.

His eyes widen as he reads. "Taylor, this can't be right . . ."

"It is, sir," Barclay says, leaning over him and pointing a few things out on the computer. "The records begin in 1995 and continue up until yesterday. This is a fully formed operation."

The director takes off his glasses and rubs his eyes.

Barclay nods. "But there's more. And sir, it's worse."

The director raises his eyebrows. "Worse?" he asks. "How does it get any worse?"

Barclay swallows, and I know what he's about to say. He's about to point fingers at the director's right-hand man. "Today, Ben Michaels went in with the proof. He brought with him a girl who had been abducted as a witness. They spoke to Deputy Director Struzinski. They told him everything, and they showed him the evidence we'd gotten from the traffickers."

"And he shot them," I say before I can stop myself. The best friend I had left and the guy I loved are gone. I'm not about to sugarcoat it.

The director looks at me, his eyes slightly widened, lips parted. Now he's surprised. "This happened today? When—"

"An hour ago," I say.

"At headquarters?" He looks at Barclay. "No one called."

"Deputy Director Struzinski is involved," Barclay says. "He was going to bury the proof. I heard it all on the com chip I was wearing."

The director looks down. He's shocked, and his brain is trying to process what he's just heard. But he isn't telling us to get out or arresting us, which means some of his memories are waving red flags, telling him that this actually makes some kind of sense, that there have been signs about Struzinski, signs that point to this.

"Sir, please," Barclay says. "I urge you to handpick people for a task force. We need to move tonight while we still have a chance to get into the Black Hole and find the proof we need before someone destroys it. We can't afford for them to move the operation."

The director has his phone out again. He dials quickly and holds it to his ear.

I look at Barclay. I'm not sure what this means. The phone call could be because he believes us, and he's going to follow Barclay's suggestion and set up a task force, or it could mean that he's about to have us arrested.

I'm frozen, holding my breath. I can't take it if another person we thought we could trust turns on us. If the director is involved, we're done. There aren't any more surprise moves or last-ditch options.

Worse, if he's involved, we're trapped.

Which means if we're going to run, we need to do it *before* other people get here.

# 00:14:43:54

The director calls Special Agent Robert Barnes and puts him on speakerphone. He asks Barnes to open Barclay's email and tells him he's going to run point on the operation. They'll need a task force set up to go into the Black Hole and shut it down. They'll need a team of tech people who can go through the computer files Barclay has recovered and sort out the evidence.

Then he tells him Struzinski and other people in IA may be involved.

Over the line, Robert Barnes swears. "Struzinski has been out of touch since the shooting this afternoon." He goes on to recount what everyone in IA was told happened. Two suspects broke in, attacked the deputy director, and fled.

"They fled?" I interrupt. My heart feels like it's in my throat, and my voice comes out a little breathless. I'm afraid to hope. "Does that mean they're still alive?"

"A team went out after them but didn't recover any bodies," he says.

Barclay jumps in to explain what he heard through the com link. I can barely listen to the words, though. Ben and Cecily are alive. The relief is staggering. They're probably back at the hospital waiting for us and wondering where we are.

"Sir, may I also suggest looping in Hayley Walker," Barclay adds. "I know her well, and I can vouch for the fact that she isn't involved."

"I authorize her reassignment," the director says. "Make the calls, get everything set up, and let's meet in the briefing room at 0600."

"Ben's family," I say, jumping in before he hangs up. "They've been put in prison. They're supposed to be executed tomorrow morning, but they're innocent."

"It's true, sir," Barclay adds. "There were orders for people to be detained and executed."

The director nods and speaks into the phone. "And Robert, you'll put a stay on the executions slated for tomorrow and check out the transfer orders for anyone Struzinski sent to the Piston."

A knot in my chest unfurls. I think of the way Derek's face looked, bruised and swollen when he told me to run, and about how I promised to get him out when I knocked on his door.

I've made good on that, as long as it isn't too late.

"Taylor, you should have come to me in the beginning," the director says after he's hung up the phone. "You're one of the best agents we have. I would have listened to your suspicions."

"That approach did Eric a lot of good," I say, because let's be honest, that's why he's dead.

Barclay tenses, and I know I should feel bad. Maybe I shouldn't have brought up Eric—maybe I should be thankful the director believes us, but I can't help it. I don't like him. And even though it appears he's not dirty, I still don't *trust* him. Did he not know Ben's family was wrongfully imprisoned? Or did he not care because the ends justified the means? Either way, it's wrong. He's stupid or he's immoral—both are qualities that make him unfit to be in charge of IA.

Barclay takes a deep breath. "I didn't know who was involved, and even if I did . . . If I came to you with suspicions but no proof that your deputy director and a number of other people I can't even name were involved in a smuggling ring, would you have believed me? Jumped in to investigate?"

The director leans back, and I can see that he's thinking about it and has decided that we're right, that he wouldn't have believed that of his own people—that he still can't, despite what Barclay is telling him and despite the fact that he knows it's true.

"Well, we're going to investigate it now," he says.

For a second, I think this might really be it, that even though I don't like this guy, we might be able to portal back to the hospital, find Ben and Cecily, and go home.

We might have won.

But it's not even close to being over.

# 00:14:41:27

The door opens.

The governor comes in, a glass of wine in her hand, flanked by two of her bodyguards. Her cheeks are flushed and her eyes glazed, and she almost seems giddy, like she can't keep from smiling. The bodyguards seem disinterested, like most bodyguards should.

"Keith, what have you been doing back here?" she says. "Can't you possibly take a night off? We've already opened the Bordeaux."

"Hanna, this will just take a few more minutes, if you could excuse us," he says.

Then she sees Barclay.

"Oh, Taylor, have you come to dine with us?" she says.

There's something wrong about it. Even if she's a lightweight, how much has she really been able to suck down in an hour? Plus, unless she's losing her mind, she should be able to see that there's some serious shit going down in this office right now. If she wanted to know what was going on, she could just ask. I don't understand what her game is.

As I'm trying to sort out the thoughts in my head, I hear a car engine, and we're briefly washed in blinding light from headlights pulling into the driveway.

I know what's wrong.

But I'm too late, and I know it.

I'm reaching for the gun at my back, but both bodyguards have their guns out already, and they're pointed in my direction. "Don't even think about it, sweetie," the governor says, her demeanor completely changed. She's hard now and stone-cold sober. The transformation makes her look like a completely different person, and I realize how wrong I was to underestimate her.

"Hanna? What's . . ." The director is apparently a step even behind me.

"Listen very carefully and do whatever I say," she says. "Macon has a gun in poor Annamarie's mouth, and he's never liked her much. Put your guns on the floor." She's looking right at me, so I do it first. Maybe she'll overlook someone else. She turns to Barclay and he removes the gun at his back and drops it on the floor. She kicks it away from him and adds, "All of them."

He pulls the other gun from his ankle holster. Whatever advantage we might have had, it's gone now.

The governor bends down and picks up Barclay's gun. As she stands, she smiles at him. "I always knew you were one to watch, Taylor." Then before I can realize what's happening, her grip on the gun changes and she fires three shots.

Straight into Director Keith Franklin's chest.

He's dead before his body crumples to the ground.

# 00:14:38:25

It's like all the air has just been sucked out of the room. I'm frozen, staring at the body of the director on the floor next to me. Of all the possible scenarios I'd worked up when we headed here, *this* was one I hadn't seen coming.

The front door slams, and whoever is in the car that just pulled up has joined the party.

My eyes flick to Barclay, but he's clearly as shocked as I am—he's just staring at the governor.

I look at her, ready to dare her to make her next move, but she isn't looking at me. Her bodyguards still have their guns trained on us, but she's looking at the door, and the man coming through.

I've seen him before.

He's tall and lanky, but with a defined build. His clothes are nothing flashy or dark, nothing to say that he's anything but an average guy. His face is hard, and something about him gives me the same chills I got when I first saw him. His light hair is shaved close to his head, and it intensifies the effect that he's been in his fair share of fights, and he's not the kind of guy to mess with.

When his eyes zero in on me, he pauses, staring me down, but no emotion crosses his face, and a shiver moves up my spine.

I don't need the introduction. I know who this guy is.

Constantine Meridian.

Last time I saw him, he was having guards pull Derek Michaels out of his cell and there was blood splattered on his shirt.

Several guys come in behind him. They're more of the same, a little scruffier maybe, but not as scary.

"It's about time you got here," the governor says. "I've been trying to get ahold of you all day."

He ignores her and gestures to one of his men. "Get them processed."

The governor starts talking to him, but I'm not listening to her. He's going to make us Unwilling. That thought fights through the cloudy shock in my brain and wakes me. I'm not about to let that happen. I'm probably going to end up getting shot if I try to fight these guys, but I can't let them take us. I move a step toward Meridian—even though I'm not sure what I'm going to do.

I just know I need to do something.

"Don't," Barclay says under his breath.

But I don't listen. Instead, I take another step, and now I'm close enough for Meridian to notice I've moved.

"Thought you'd be long gone by now," he says.

For a second, I'm thrown off. I don't get what he's saying, and then I remember. He knows my double. He's never looked closely at her or paid enough attention to her to recognize that I'm different. And maybe that makes sense—she left rather than stay and try to take him down. But he doesn't know how different I am.

I can use this. I can do something unexpected, catch him off guard.

"You thought I'd be dead?" I say.

He shrugs. It's noncommittal. He doesn't care—he just thought she wouldn't be here.

I haul off and punch him in the face.

# 00:14:34:19

My fist connects to the left side of his face, and it feels like I've just slammed my hand into a brick wall. Pain shoots up my arm, but I don't stop. I ram my knee into his crotch and reach for the gun at his back.

Glass breaks behind me, several shouts move through the room, and Meridian grunts. And when my fingers brush past the gun, I think I might have it, but then I feel the sharp pain in my head, and a rough hand coiled around my hair pulls back, then pushes me down to my knees.

I feel cool metal against my temple and smell the gunpowder.

Meridian reaches down and grabs my chin, forcing my face up to him. The guy with the grip on my hair doesn't ease up, and I can feel some of it ripping out of my head.

Meridian shakes his head, his hand falling away. "Not who I thought you were," he says quietly.

Something about the calmness in his voice makes me flinch. Having his attention directly on me turns my stomach and makes my skin feel uncomfortable. I don't want him to touch me again.

He doesn't. Instead, I see his hand coming down.

And pain explodes in the back of my head.

# 00:09:06:30

When I wake up, I have the worst headache of my life—shocking.

And my face itches.

I'm facedown on a beige carpet, and my hands are restrained behind my back. I can't tell how long I've been out, but I don't think it's as bad as some of my other injuries from this week. For one thing, my hands haven't gone numb, which means they haven't been in this position all that long.

"If we don't find them, we'll draw them out," a female voice says. "Surely you understand the concept." It's the governor.

From where I am, I can't see her—I can't see much of anything.

For a split second, I debate whether I should move around, test my restraints, take stock of where we are and possibly give away the fact that I've come to, or just keep lying here. The second option feels a lot more appealing to my aching head. It also feels safer. I'm less likely to get hit again, less likely to get outright shot, less likely to attract attention.

But what is that going to get me in the end?

No matter what happens, I'm probably going to end up in the same place.

Dead.

I shift a little and turn my face to the side so I have a view of the room. I'm still not ready to go down fighting. Through my blurry vision, I manage to make out bookshelves lining the wall. Behind me is a desk. Across the room is a door. It's partway open, and a girl—probably my age or a little older, with brown hair—is sitting at a desk, a high-tech computer in front of her. Her nose is crooked and half her face is black and blue with relatively fresh bruises. She looks like she either got hit with a fly ball or punched in the face. I don't have to be too creative to assume it's the latter.

Next to my feet is another guy, who's restrained, conscious, and sitting up with his back against the wall. He's been beat up pretty badly—his face is covered with blood, some dried and some fresh. He snorts, blowing a spray of blood out of his nose, and I realize it's Barclay. He's not quite close enough for me to touch him.

"It's your job to handle this, both of you," a male voice says. I think it's Meridian, but I'm not entirely sure.

I can't see him—or any of the people talking to him in hushed tones. Unless I've damaged my ears, they must be at least a room away from us, because I can only hear them when their voices are raised.

The girl at the computer looks at me. Our eyes meet, and she knows I'm awake.

# 00:09:01:21

She looks at the door and then back at me. She's thinking—trying to make a decision about something. I can see it on her face, the way her lips are pressed together. I just don't know what she's planning.

My pulse speeds up. It feels like it's pounding directly in the ear I have against the carpet. I look at Barclay to see if I can get his attention, but he's got his eyes closed. He's either passed out or hurting too much to concentrate.

The girl gets up from her desk and moves to the door that separates our rooms. She's in jeans and a white sweater. If she didn't have the bruises, she'd look so normal. It makes me wonder what she's doing here. How she got roped into this.

She hesitates and looks at the door to the hallway—the direction the voices are coming from.

No one is in view.

She rushes to my side, putting her hands under my shoulder and hip as she turns me a little—just enough so I have a better view of what's coming, and then she presses a ballpoint pen into my hands. "I don't have anything else," she whispers, her attention still on the doorway.

"How many of them are there?" I'm not sure what I can really do with a pen, especially if I'm still in restraints, but if I'm going to do anything, I need to know that much.

"Right now?" she says, biting her lip. "They always have four guys who are like Secret Service or something. The governor and her husband, I mean. Tonight her cousin is here. He had a few people with him, but he sent them out. They'll probably come back, though. And then this new guy showed up."

"So at best there's eight of them," I say. Not good odds. "At worst, maybe twelve?"

She nods.

"Where are we?"

Her head tilts just slightly and she says, "Governor Worth's house."

I'd already guessed that much. "No, I mean, the layout of the house, where are we?" Our best chance may be trying to escape while they think we're still knocked out.

"Second floor," she whispers. "Near the back of the house."

Not what I wanted to hear. In the condition we're in, the three of us aren't going to be able to do a second-story drop and then get up and start running, and we're obviously too far from a door.

"I think they're coming," she says, and as she stands up, her left hand moves past my face. She's wearing a gold ring on her ring finger, and she's missing most of her thumbnail.

The words pass my lips before I think too much about it. "What's your name?"

She glances back and smiles. "Renee," she says, and then she's through the doorway and back at her desk, looking at the computer.

Brown hair, early twenties, half of a fingernail and a ripped sheet at the scene, Renee.

Cecily said Renee Adams worked with computers somewhere downtown, but according to the stalker files we found on her, she worked an assortment of temp jobs during the day and otherwise spent a lot of time at home on her computer.

Assorted temp jobs at big companies—ones with big databases and information that potentially could be worth something. If I wasn't restrained or lying on the floor, I would be looking up whether those companies ever filed suits about information being stolen. I'd be looking into Renee Adams's bank accounts and seeing what kind of major deposits were being made.

I watch her type something into the computer, and I hear someone say, "How are you possibly going to fix this?" And I try to ignore the fact that I'd know that voice anywhere.

It might be a stretch, but I wonder if Renee Adams is some kind of computer hacker.

The bigger question, of course, is what kind of work she's doing for the governor.

But I don't get a chance to ask, because she was right. Someone was coming.

Now they're here.

# 00:08:55:26

It's Meridian, the governor herself, two of her bodyguards, and Deputy Director Ryan Struzinski.

I push the ballpoint pen into my restraints, but they're wire, not rope, and a pen isn't going to do anything. I slip it into my sleeve. It still might be the only weapon I'll get my hands on.

Through heavy lids, I track Meridian and the governor's movements. Based on the positioning—the bodyguards are flanking her, and evil Struz is trailing them—they're the ones in charge.

They're also arguing. "Take care of the girl, and I'll handle Taylor," the governor says.

"I can use her. She's pretty enough—not anything special— but still. Someone will pay something for her. This one . . ." He kicks Barclay's foot. "He'll just be trouble."

My throat constricts as I realize what exactly they're arguing about.

What to do with us.

Specifically, whether they should kill us. If my options are death or slavery, I'm not sure which one I'd vote for.

They're both unacceptable. I'm not ready to die—I promised *my* Struz that I would come home to my family. And I'm certainly not going to get shipped off to some other world where my free will would be stripped from me in whatever manner works best.

I try to move my hands a little in the restraints. The wire bites into my wrist, but I have a little leeway. I have small hands—if I can compress them, make them a little smaller, I might be able to slip one of them out.

"I can control him." The governor laughs. "He's just like Ryan, smart, ambitious, and hungry. We just have to find out what he wants."

"You've done such a bang-up job so far," Meridian says.

There's a pause, and they must expect Struz's evil twin to weigh in on the decision, because he says, "Don't look at me." His voice is low, gritty, and tired. "Just do whatever you're going to do."

Meridian laughs. It's not maniacal evil laughter or anything, but it's cold, like he's laughing because he's supposed to, not because he understands humor. I shiver and focus harder on the restraints. I'll try to get my left hand out first—the wire will undoubtedly slice it open in a few places, but it'll leave my right hand—the hand I need—unscathed.

"You play the innocent card so well," Meridian says. "Especially for someone experimenting on kids."

"I never said I was innocent," the deputy director says, the resignation in his voice coming out like disgrace.

"Enough." The governor crosses the room, toward Renee Adams and the computer. "Taylor wasn't a problem until he met her. The girl is a bad influence. Just kill her and I'll handle him."

Silence.

I'm tempted to sit up and call bullshit. Tell her I was just a normal high-school junior with a bad attitude until Barclay showed up—that it was *Barclay* who came to my world and asked me for help. I don't even want to be here in this stupid world with its ridiculous skyscrapers and people who spend their lives a hundred feet off the ground, like they're better than everyone beneath them.

But I stay still, and I let my indignation wrap itself around me—let it steady my hands and still my body. I hold on to it so it keeps my fear at bay.

As bad as slavery would be, I'd still be alive.

The silence stretches out. None of the men in the room make any protests, as if the argument is over.

And why wouldn't it be? Meridian might think it's a waste to kill me, especially if he can get some money for me as a slave, but I haven't proven to be all that weak and he's probably already got enough money.

I shift my eyes to Barclay, wishing I could reach him and try to wake him somehow. But when I see the blue of his eyes through the bloody and swollen skin, I realize we're in the same boat. He's also been listening and faking being passed out.

I try to communicate with him. I try to tell him, *It's now or never* with my eyes. My only hope is that he's figured out how to get out of his restraints as well.

I'm not sure if he gets the message or not. He gives a slight shake of his head, whatever that means.

"Well?" the governor says.

"How about I just kill them both?" Meridian says.

She makes a pouting noise, but she doesn't object.

My hands are sticky and warm from the blood, but I think I can get them out. If I'm going to do anything, it's going to be right now. I'm not about to let Barclay or myself die without making some kind of move.

"Get her up," Meridian says, and one of the bodyguards is in front of me. "What? You want me to shoot her while she's passed out?" He snorts. "Where's the fun in that?"

# 00:08:50:59

The bodyguard slips his hands under my armpits. With my eyes closed, I picture the room and everyone in it.

Farthest from me, about six or seven feet away, are the governor and one of her bodyguards. Renee Adams is behind them in the other room.

Struz's evil twin is lingering by the door, about five feet away.

Meridian is directly in front of me, no more than a few feet, but just out of my reach.

As the bodyguard lifts me up, I hold my breath and yank my left hand through the restraints.

The pain is more than I would have imagined possible. At least three layers of skin from about half my hand come off, hot blood pours from my wrist to my fingertips, and I let out some kind of terrible yelp.

But my hands are free.

# 00:08:49:57

I open my eyes.

The bodyguard is trying to lean me against the desk. Meridian is behind him, his face blank.

I shift my right hand and let the ballpoint pen drop out of my sleeve and into my fingers.

I take a deep breath and think of my dad, of the lengths he would have gone to keep me safe. I think of Alex and how he looked at me when I asked him to take self-defense classes, how he said, *I'm in. We won't let anyone ever hurt you again.* I think of Cecily and how she insisted on coming to IA with us, how she said, *I was minding my own business, and some asshole with terrible breath grabbed me, stuck me with a needle, and pulled me through a black hole.*

Meridian draws his gun and taps it against his thigh.

I think of Ben, of his family who might still be executed tomorrow, of how he might be dead or bleeding out somewhere.

And I tell myself that it's my life or this guy's, and I have every right to do anything in my power to make sure it's not me.

I shift my grip on the pen, so the point is facing out.

I tell myself that no matter what I do right now, it doesn't make me as bad as them.

The bodyguard turns to look at Meridian. His lips part like he's about to say something, but I don't give him a chance. While he's not paying attention, I swing my right arm around and drive the pen straight into his right eye.

# 00:08:46:56

The bodyguard screams, drops me, and grabs for his eye. I move with him, using his body as a shield while I reach for the gun under his jacket.

Over the screaming, someone shouts—or several people shout at one another, but I have no idea who's saying what and I don't care.

My fingers close on the metal grip of the handle, and I pull the handgun out and turn to aim. I haven't thought through exactly who I should be aiming at. But I don't need to.

Some kind of survival instinct drives me.

Meridian is the target. The governor only thinks she's in charge—he's the most dangerous person here.

I hear the shot as my finger squeezes the trigger.

But my right arm suddenly stops working. It drops to my side, and the gun slips from my fingers.

Confused, I look down at my arm. When I see the blood welling through the shirt covering my upper arm, I feel the pain.

Someone swears, and I look up and see I'm not the only one bleeding. I got a shot off, but it was a bad one. It looks like all I did was graze Meridian's shoulder.

He grabs me by the throat and pushes me against the wall. Hard.

But he doesn't stop there. He relaxes his grip and slams me back again and again. Too many times to keep count. The pain each time my head hits the wall feels like something is exploding against me. I try to kick or claw at him, but it's like my body is useless. I've done too much damage to myself, and I don't have any leverage. All I succeed in doing is wiping some of the blood from my left hand onto his face.

With his fingers pushing into my throat, and the weight of his hand over my windpipe, I'm out of air fast. Blackness edges my vision, like I'm about to pass out, and despite how weak I am, I reach up, wrapping my fingers around his hand, trying to pull it off my throat.

Suddenly he stops, his grip relaxes slightly, and as the air rushes back into my lungs, my vision clears, and I realize the bodyguard is still screaming.

Meridian raises his hand, and without a word, he fires three shots into the guy's chest, and the screaming stops.

"What—" the governor screams.

"Keep making noise and I'll shoot you, too," he says.

She snaps her mouth shut, but she's not about to take threats from him either. It looks like she's about to say something.

But she doesn't get the chance.

A shout comes from downstairs, then a spray of gunfire.

# 00:08:41:27

Two men bring in Elijah and Ben. My breath catches at the sight of them. I don't have time to wonder what they're doing here together or why Elijah left the hospital. I'm just so relieved to see Ben alive that it floods through my body and makes me feel weak and warm.

Their hands are restrained behind their backs. I wait for someone to bring Cecily in too, but she's not there. I'm not sure what that means. She could be safe at the hospital; she could be somewhere else in the house; she could be injured somewhere or worse.

I look at Ben.

The position we're in—that we're both likely to be killed—doesn't matter. He's not bloody or unconscious or in an IA jail, and seeing that gives me hope.

"We had a situation." The guy who speaks looks like he's in his sixties, and he's not wearing the same *Men in Black* bodyguard uniform. He must be the governor's husband.

"Did we lose anyone?" the governor asks. Her husband nods.

The governor gestures to the bodyguard who's been here. "Go

with him," she says before she turns to the new one. "You stay."

The governor's husband and one bodyguard leave the room, leaving Meridian, the governor herself, one remaining bodyguard, and evil Struz, who has been strangely quiet. If I wasn't about to die, I'd be focused on the fact that we have even numbers.

I look at Ben. He's staring at me, and I think about what he said—how most of his decisions revolve around me. He must have burst in planning to save me, but he made a fatal error.

He hadn't prepared himself for the fact that if he was going to barrel in here, he'd need to pull the trigger first and ask questions later, and that means he portaled in here with a life-threatening disadvantage. And he got caught.

"What is this?" Meridian says.

The governor's bodyguard clearly doesn't get that the question is rhetorical. He starts to tell us that Ben and Elijah came out of nowhere and started attacking them. He doesn't have a chance to finish.

Meridian points his gun at Elijah first, and then he fires.

Elijah grunts, stumbles back, and slumps to the ground. The bullet went into his bad leg. Blood wells up and coats the fabric of his jeans.

"Ben!" I yell. I don't know what I'm trying to do, if I said his name to warn him that Meridian's aim has shifted to him, to tell him to run, or something else entirely.

But it doesn't matter.

I don't have the chance to finish the thought.

Meridian pulls the trigger twice, one bullet for each of Ben's legs. He grunts with each impact and falls to the floor, his face twisting with the pain.

My breath catches in my throat. I have to think of something, otherwise we're all going to die here.

Meridian tosses his gun to the ground.

I can't breathe again, only it's not because of Meridian. Tears sting my eyes, and I gasp for air. All of the relief at seeing Ben alive and the hope that we might make it out, that we were so close—it's gone now. And the emptiness it leaves behind is crushing. Now Ben is only going to get himself killed.

"Wait!" Ben says, as the governor's remaining bodyguard grabs his hands, pulls them behind his back, and wraps the wire around them. "Let her go. Kill me instead," he says. "I'm the one you want."

I start to shake my head, since that's a terrible idea.

I'm not the only one who thinks so. Meridian says, "Why would I do that? I have you both."

He tightens his grip around my throat, and I renew my struggle against him as he pulls something that looks like a hunting knife from his pocket.

"You caused me a lot of trouble," he says to Ben. "Now you can watch her die before I kill you."

He lifts the knife to my neck.

# 00:08:36:27

With my back against the wall and the steel blade biting into my throat, there's nowhere to go. My eyes take in the room one more time.

To my right stands the governor with her arms folded across her chest, waiting for me to die. Behind her through the doorway, Renee Adams is cowering behind her computer monitor. Across from me, the dead bodyguard is on the ground, slumped on his side, one hand still holding his eye where I stabbed him. The other guard is standing next to Barclay, who's got his back against the wall, a grimace on his face. Elijah is on the floor, blood staining his pants. He's breathing normally, though, and glaring at Meridian. He doesn't look like he's going to die just yet. Struz's evil twin is still loitering in the doorway.

And Ben.

Ben is across from me, on his side, his lips slightly parted, his eyes wide, struggling against his restraints. He looks too pale, but I can't see how much blood he's losing. I try to tell him with my eyes that this isn't his fault, that it's okay.

If I move the wrong way, I'll cut open my own throat, and

my ankle is still sore from Barclay pushing me into the subway. There's no need to try to calculate my odds of escape, so I force myself to stop.

I meet Meridian's eyes with my own. This close, I can see they're a muted green with flecks of gold—not the color I would have imagined for someone so cruel.

"Are you going to try to bargain for your life?" he asks. "Offer to switch sides?"

I don't answer. I hold myself straight and set my jaw.

This is it.

# 00:08:36:17

I've heard that some people accept their death when it comes—that it's their time. I never understood that until just now. It's not that I'm giving up or lying down. It's that I'm going to make the choice to go proud.

This time when my life flashes before my eyes, it's not my optic nerves firing, it's not death, and it's not Ben Michaels.

It's me.

I remember my mother on the beach, pregnant with Jared, our discarded sand castle next to her.

I remember the summer I turned thirteen, when the local video store had a special on old movies: four movies, four days, four dollars. Kate and I let Alex pick four action movies with no plot, and we laid out our sleeping bags in my living room and watched all of them in a row. We let Jared watch with us until he fell asleep and then we drew aliens on his forehead in permanent marker, ate popcorn and pizza, and drank Sprite until Alex puked from eating too much. Then we rode our bikes to Black Mountain Park and watched the sun rise.

I remember coming back to life on Torrey Pines Road, with

Ben's silhouette leaning over me, his hands warm on my skin. His first memory of me flooding my mind—when I was ten, in my pink flowered bathing suit, pulling him from the water, like I was some kind of angel.

I remember Jared's birthday this year. It was just me, Struz, and two of Jared's friends, a cake from a box with soymilk and egg substitute and frosting from a jar. We sat outside and passed around a flashlight telling the creepiest horror stories we could think of until the batteries died, and then Struz surprised Jared by getting one of the helicopter pilots to take him up for a quick midnight spin.

I remember my first date with Ben. When he took me to Sunset Cliffs and we ate takeout from Roberto's and watched the sun set over the water. The warmth of the sun, the smell of the ocean, and the sound of the waves—the taste of Ben's lips against mine for the first time.

I remember my dad. The way he used to come in and read to me as soon as he got home from work, the way he managed to make it to all of my swim meets despite his job, the way he looked at me every day—like he was radiating pride.

And I remember that day at Disneyland. The smell of popcorn and funnel cake, the bright colors, the balloons, and little kids on vacation laughing and screaming, Jared and I gorging ourselves on chili bread bowls and Mickey Mouse ice cream, waiting in line for Space Mountain and the Tower of Terror twice, then watching the Jedi training show and the fireworks at Cinderella's castle.

I don't even blink as I tilt my chin up and think of everything I'm about to leave behind—in my own world and here in Prima. Something warm trickles down my neck. I've left my mark on the lives of all the people I saved—the ones Ben and Barclay and I set free, the ones IA will be able to free once they take Meridian down.

I was here.

I lived.

I mattered.

This is a good way to go.

"It's a shame I have to kill you," Meridian says.

He readjusts his grip on the knife, and right before he drags it across my throat, I pretend I can see Ben in front of me, smell soap, mint, and gasoline—

# 00:08:36:16

Everything seems to happen at once.

I don't actually register it at first. It's just a series of noises.

A grunt and a sort of gurgling noise.

Then a gunshot, and something warm sprays my face.

Shouts, a struggle, the pressure against my throat gone, and another gunshot.

And another.

I touch my face, and my hand comes away covered in blood. I lean forward and put my face in my hands, feeling around, but I can't tell if I've been shot. Someone grabs me by the shoulders and turns me to face them, shouting something at me, but I can't concentrate on their words.

Fighting to get my bearings, I focus on the room.

It doesn't make sense at first. There's a body on the ground next to Ben, lying in a pool of blood, something sticking out of his throat. The governor is lying facedown in a crumpled heap on the floor. So is Meridian, in front of me, and his face is gone. A bullet is lodged in the wall a few inches above my head. The man who is not Struz stands in front of me, a gun in his hand.

For a second it looks like it's pointed at me, but then I realize he's just holding it, holding it like someone who's just used a weapon and done something he didn't think he was capable of, and now he's at a loss for what to do next.

When I see Barclay on the floor, a gun in his hand, blood pouring out of the hollow of his throat, Elijah crawling toward him, I know what happened.

# 00:08:36:09

Barclay rescued me.

He must have been in the process of trying to escape when I made my run for it too early. *That's* what he was trying to tell me—what he wanted me to know.

I was just too focused, and too arrogant to pay attention.

When I was reliving the moments of my life, with Meridian holding the blade to my throat, Barclay finished breaking out of his restraints. He grabbed the ballpoint pen from the dead bodyguard's eye and drove it straight into the jugular of the live one, while in the same movement reaching for the guy's gun.

And before anyone could react, he shot Meridian in the back of the head.

But that's as far as the element of surprise could get him. The governor had a gun too, and as he turned on her next, she shot him.

Barclay killed the governor's bodyguard and then Meridian. The governor shot Barclay—

And someone shot *her* in the back.

# 00:08:36:08

As I look at him, Deputy Director Ryan Struzinski lifts his gun.

I make a dive for Barclay, grabbing the gun from his hand, and point it at the last threat in the room.

He might be in shock, but he's not stupid. His gun is on me a split second before mine is on him, and my body tenses involuntarily, like that could somehow stop the bullet.

But he doesn't shoot.

At least, not yet.

We're frozen, both of us pointing guns at each other. At this range, neither one of us would miss a shot to the head, and the effect would be fatal, no question. Even with delayed reaction time, either of us firing would likely end up with both of us dead.

"You don't have to do this," I say, though I'm not sure why. I have nothing to bargain with. Sure, his two main conspirators are dead, but with us out of the way, he could still patch this up. And I'm not going to bother even trying to lie to him about keeping his involvement quiet. He would never believe me.

Struzinski's eyes meet mine. He looks a little sad, like he doesn't want to do what comes next, and I can feel the muscles in my right arm starting to spasm under the tension.

"It's over," he says.

Then he turns the gun on himself and fires.

# 00:08:35:01

For a split second, I'm paralyzed with shock.

Then my own gun drops from my shaking hands, and I reach for Barclay. I'm not about to just let him die on me.

The blood is everywhere.

I try to stop it, to put pressure on the wound, to somehow keep that blood in his body, but it pulses against my hands, warm and thick.

I want to tell him he's an idiot or slap him across the face. That has to have been the dumbest thing he's ever done—jump up like that and take on four people with weapons. And Barclay of all people should have known his odds. He should have known he didn't stand a chance.

But as his eyes flick toward me, I know he did. He knew all that, and he made his move anyway. He sacrificed himself.

To save me.

It's almost too much to handle in a long line of things that should have been too much. My throat constricts, my eyes sting, and I shake my head. All the times that I've been hard on him and called him an arrogant asshole, there's never been any question that Barclay has been a good guy. Without him, Cecily and the other Unwilling would be slaves for the rest of their lives. Without him, I'd be in the Piston, waiting to be executed.

But it's more than that. He believed in me. He did things to protect me to make sure I'd be okay. And now I may never be able to pay him back.

I try to will my hands to stop shaking so that I can actually be of some use, and I look over at Ben, who's crawling toward us, his blood leaving a trail on the carpet.

Elijah has his hands over Barclay's abdomen. Halfway up his forearm he's covered in blood. "I can't fucking heal him!"

Then Ben is beside me, thrusting his hands into the fray.

I lean over Barclay, my free hand reaching for his face. The blood on my hands smears across the cool clammy skin of his cheek, and the faint beat of his heart thrums against my skin. I suck in my breath. His eyes are unfocused, his skin pale, and his lips are starting to turn blue. He's got seconds before he bleeds out, and if Elijah can't heal him—

"Tenner," Barclay grunts. "The gun . . . the door."

"Nothing is fucking working," Elijah says.

"The door," Barclay repeats, his voice strained.

I do what he says, ignoring the protest in my muscles. The last thing we need is to be caught unaware. I remember what Renee said about the guys Meridian sent on an errand.

"Is it working?" I look at Ben.

He shakes his head.

We've been here before, and I refuse to have the same outcome. I don't care how tired and beat up they are, we just need to give Ben enough time to heal Barclay so we can all get out of here.

Then it hits me. They won't be able to heal him. Not in this building.

"The hydrochloradneum shields," I say. "You can't open portals or heal him while we're inside."

"We have to get him out of here," Ben says.

I jump to my feet. "We just have to get far enough outside the house—"

"Tenner!" Barclay coughs. "I'm fucking dying."

"Don't worry, we've—"

"I said I'm dying, Tenner. You can't."

"You're being stupid," I say, dropping to his side so he can see me.

"The window," Ben says, reaching under Barclay's shoulders. "We just have to get outside. We'll do it anyway."

But Barclay reaches up and grabs my arm. "Don't play God, Tenner," he says.

"Don't be a dick," I say back. Because I've just started to like him and now he's determined to die on me.

"We can still do it," Ben says.

Barclay coughs in response and blood coats his lower lip. It seems too dark to be real.

I open my mouth to say something else—to try to convince him somehow—but my throat is closing up. The only thing that comes out is "please."

But I know I've already lost.

I look at Ben, and he takes the gun out of my hand.

Barclay smiles. "The bullets," he says.

I glance around. I have no idea what he means.

"Hydrochloradneum . . ." His voice trails off.

I'd forgotten. Even if we got him outside the shields, IA

standard-issue ammunition is hydrochloradneum-plated bullets, which create wounds that can't be healed by their powers. Elijah found that out the hard way when Eric shot him last fall.

"We made a good team, Tenner."

I want to say, *One of the best*. I open my mouth, but I can't get the words out.

Barclay reaches out and I clasp his hand. "I couldn't have done it without you." Tears spill out of my eyes, and they burn as they roll down my face.

He coughs again, his time more blood coming up. He's pale, ghostly, even, and I squeeze his hand as if contact with the living will keep him with us just a little longer. His fingers move slightly, and then his hand is dead weight in mine.

"Janelle . . ." he says, his eyes having a hard time staying focused.

"I'm here," I say, adjusting his head so he's looking at me. "Right here."

"Make sure." His eyes close.

"What?" I say, shaking him a little.

"My monument."

And then I'm laughing and crying at the same time. "I'll oversee it myself if I have to."

And then I know. He's gone. Whatever made Taylor Barclay the conceited asshole, determined and driven to the point of obsession—whatever it was that made him my friend—that person is gone. He's just a body now.

# 00:08:28:57

Ben pulls me to him, and the warmth of his body around mine is just too much to handle. We've both been shot, and we're both bleeding, but we're still here.

We're alive.

"I thought you were dead," I say, and I taste the salt from my tears.

"Yeah, so did he," Elijah says.

"I would never leave you," Ben says, his voice whispering into my hair.

"Cecily?" I ask.

"As chipper as always," Elijah says. "And back with the Unwilling."

"What happened?"

"I took a risk," Ben says. "I ducked when I saw the gun, and the first shot missed me; the second grazed my arm. Two more ended up lodged in the vest. I grabbed Cecily and ran us through the closest exit: the window."

"But the drop . . ."

"He thought it would be a good time to test these

portal-opening powers," Elijah says. "As they were falling, he thought of the hospital, opened a portal, and they fucking fell right through. You believe that shit?"

"You went back to the hospital?" I say. We should have gone back there—we should have regrouped, but I just didn't have faith. "I thought you were dead."

"The landing was brutal, and we were both knocked out cold on the hospital floor."

I squeeze Ben tighter. I'm still expecting him to disappear, to wake up and realize I'd only imagined that he's still alive. "How did you find us?"

"The guy was desperate to find you," Elijah says. "It was pathetic."

"I didn't know where I wanted the portal to go, but I knew I had to find you. Instead of thinking of the location I needed to go, I opened a portal, thinking of just you. I wasn't sure where it would take me, but we ended up in the backyard of an estate. It brought me as close to you as we could get. We tried to sneak inside but got caught by the guards downstairs. You know the rest."

I can't believe it. Against all odds, we might get out of this room. We've managed to save each other—again.

"I hate to break this up, but we have to get the fuck out of here," Elijah says.

I nod against Ben's chest. Who knows if or when Meridian's guys are going to come back here?

Remembering Renee, I push back and turn in her direction. She's crouched under the desk with her eyes closed, and I think she's praying.

"Renee," I say, approaching her. "Come with us, we'll get you out of here." I want to ask her what she's been doing for the governor, but now's not the time, and the governor is dead anyway. We have plenty of time to discuss that later.

Her watery brown eyes look up at me, and she looks younger than early twenties and older at the same time. I suppose being abducted can do that to a person.

"We'll get you home."

She stands up. "Home," she says, and something about the way that she says it, I know she's not talking to me. I know she didn't think that word would have meaning for her.

I grab the gun Barclay used to kill Meridian, and check it—four bullets left. "Grab a gun. We might need it."

"Whatever, J," Elijah says. "This is the second fucking time I've gotten shot when I was with you. I don't think we can be friends anymore."

For some reason, the fact that we are friends makes me want to smile.

Ben pulls the quantum charger from Barclay's pocket.

I almost tell him that we don't need that. For some reason, I don't want to rob Barclay of something that is so intrinsically his. Ben doesn't need it to open portals, and I don't know how to use it.

But then I remember that both Ben and Elijah have been shot, and are likely pretty exhausted, and I certainly know how to learn. Having a charger is the smart thing to do. Besides, Barclay would want me to take it.

Elijah carries Ben, piggyback style, and we move through the house, quickly and quietly, in a single-file line. I go first, ignoring the throbbing pain in my arm and the exhaustion moving through my whole body. I hold the gun in front of me, and I'm ready to fire if I need to. I don't know where the governor's husband is, but I keep reminding myself that we just need to get outside. Then we can portal to safety.

Renee is behind me, and Elijah and Ben are behind her. The details are a blur.

All I know is that when we get downstairs, I see headlights—headlights that belong to too many cars for me to count—but instead of panic setting in, all I've got is anger.

It rolls through me like fire—anger that I've been shot, that I almost died twice tonight, that I'm beat up, exhausted, and in more pain than I thought possible. This needs to end, here and now. I'm not running anymore.

And that's my only excuse for doing possibly the stupidest thing I've ever done.

I walk straight to the door. I don't hear a thing Ben tells me. I throw open the door and walk out into the floodlights, gun at my side.

Because of the angle and the lights, I can't see anything, but I hear people shouting for me to drop the gun and put my hands up. It's so different from whatever I expected to happen that it's like someone has thrown cold water on me.

A silhouette moves toward me. Her arms are raised, her hands are empty, and she's talking to me.

I drop the gun and put my own arms up, as Hayley Walker's discernible features come into view. I focus on her lips. At first all I can hear is the blood rushing through my ears, but then I realize she's asking, "Janelle, are you okay?"

I'm not okay.

I'm not sure if I'll ever be okay again. So I just say, "They're all dead." Because that pretty much sums it up.

The questioning lasts for hours.

The silence that follows is even longer.

After Hayley and the IA cavalry descended upon the governor's house and found us, they took *everyone* back to IA headquarters for medical attention and debriefing. I was separated from Ben, Elijah, and Renee immediately. The bullet wound in my arm was looked at, treated, and deemed superficial at worst, all on the drive in. Once my left hand was bandaged, they sat me down in a windowless room with a cup of coffee and demanded to know everything.

So I told them.

Then I told them again. And a third time.

I even talked to a sketch artist about people like Chuckles and the guys I saw in the Black Hole.

But somewhere between my fifth and sixth cup of coffee, when I'm not sure how many minutes, hours, or even days have gone by, I start to put together the missing pieces:

I owe my life to Hayley Walker and her partner, Jimmy Mason.

The director never made it to the briefing room at 0600 like he was supposed to. While Special Agent Robert Barnes briefed everyone else, Hayley knew something was wrong. She grabbed her partner and they drove to the director's house. When they got there and saw both he and his wife were dead, Hayley called it in.

Barnes already had an emergency task force raid the Black Hole, confiscate all the equipment, and arrest anyone who was there. So he put Hayley and Jimmy in charge of forming a task force to look for us.

The director kept an organized calendar, even for his social plans. That the governor had been there for dinner with her husband and neither of them had bled out on the floor meant they were either part of it, or they'd been taken.

Lucky for us, the first place Hayley and Jimmy looked was the governor's house.

According to Hayley and Jimmy, IA found and arrested the governor's husband. He was the link between her and Meridian. He took his wife's name when they were married, which apparently wasn't that unusual on Prima. Macon Meridian became Macon Worth, and the governor found herself connected to Meridian by blood.

As Prima's longest-serving governor, she lied, cheated, paid people off, and used the Unwilling to stay in office. Renee Adams was the latest in a long line of computer hackers—the best in their respective worlds—that had been special ordered and delivered to the governor. She put them to work breaking into private accounts to spy on and destroy political rivals.

Hours after I've told them everything, including the location of the Unwilling we saved from being processed, the door opens. I've been awake so long, the muscles in my right eye are twitching.

Hayley comes in first. Her eyes are bloodshot. She's probably been awake as long as I have, and now that exhaustion has set in, she can't hide the sadness that's weighing on her shoulders.

I hope Barclay knew how much she loved him.

Robert comes in behind her. He's in good shape for a guy in his mid- to late forties, but his whole appearance is disheveled—tie loose, shirt untucked, hair sticking up in odd places. He yawns and tries to excuse himself, but his words are lost in a mishmash of syllables.

"Sorry about that," he says, sliding another cup of coffee across the table.

I shake my head. "I think I've hit my limit."

"You sure?" he says. When I nod, he shrugs and takes a sip from it himself.

"What else do you need to know?" I ask. There's no point in

asking when I can go home. They know I want to, and asking isn't going to get me there any sooner. They'll send me home when they're good and done with me.

"Not much," Robert says, glancing at the door.

"You've been amazing, Janelle," Hayley says, offering me a genuine smile. "We'll get you out of here soon."

"We've got all our computer specialists working on those files," Robert adds. "We've also been working on finding their other facilities. We're going to find all those people and get them back."

I can tell from the tone of his voice and the sincerity on his face that he's not lying. It makes me breathe a little easier.

Neither of them says anything else.

I know a lot of strategies designed to make people talk. As soon as I turned thirteen and my dad realized I didn't tell him everything anymore, he started using all of them on me.

One is silence.

They must be thinking there could be questions, questions they don't even know they should be asking. If they're silent, maybe I'll just volunteer the information.

Only there isn't anything left to tell.

Instead, I decide to ask *them* a question. The thing I don't understand, the piece of the puzzle that's still bothering me. "The deputy director," I say, trying to choose my words. "What do you think . . . why did he do it?"

He had to have everything anyone could ask for. He had almost unchecked power within the IA. He could travel to any world. I'm sure he made a high salary. Why get involved with a human-trafficking ring, and then shoot yourself when it goes south? It doesn't make any sense.

Robert runs a hand through his already mussed-up hair and slides into the chair across from me. "Ryan was an incredible agent," he says. "Fifteen years younger than me, and he was my boss. The governor took notice of him. He was promising, smart, and ambitious. At the time, people thought she saw that in him, and supported him because of what he could do for IA."

But it turns out she supported him because she saw something in him she could use.

"We looked into his bank records and talked to his wife," Robert says with a sigh. "It looks like he might have caught on to Meridian about five years ago. Based on some of the correspondence on his personal computer at home, we think he may have stumbled onto the human-trafficking ring when it was smaller, and that the governor convinced him to cut a deal and look the other way, and then ultimately to support the operation."

I shake my head. "But why?"

"He has two children. They're eight and six," Robert says, and I think of their pictures—smiling faces with blue eyes and curly blond hair. "Both of them have variant genetic Creutzfeldt-Jakob disease."

"What is that?" I ask. It's nothing I've heard of.

"It's a degenerative neurological disorder," Robert says. "Prima has medicines that can prolong their lives, of course, but at significant cost—and a lot of them are experimental. They can have side effects that severely damage quality of life."

I'm cold all over, and I can't suppress a shiver. I don't even need to know the rest.

Because I know the lengths my Struz would go to keep Jared and me safe, to keep us alive.

"We have records of some of the travel he did. He was trying to meet with the best doctors in the most advanced worlds, but not many of them were open to interverse travel. They wanted him to bring his kids to them. But as you can imagine, that's dangerous for a sick kid. It looks like he may have brought in some of the specialized doctors, and then maybe even some kids."

I let my breath leave my body in a sigh. I don't want him to say any more—I don't want to think anyone is capable of what he's about to say.

"The kids may have been human test subjects for a new experimental procedure," he says, and I lean forward to feel the cool metal of the table against my skin. Anything to keep me grounded in this reality.

I wrap my arms around myself to fight off the chills. I know exactly why he shot himself. Each step he took would have been small—maybe he abducted a doctor because the doctor could help his kids, maybe he intended to send the guy back. The thing is, once a desperate man takes one small step, he'll take another and another, until he's nowhere close to his starting point.

I don't have time to ask anything else. The door opens and two impeccably dressed people come in. Robert stands and introduces them.

Charles Swanson and Ella Manderlay are both probably in their late thirties, maybe early forties, and they're two of the highest-ranking officials in Prima's aristocratic government.

"You must be exhausted," Ella says. "Director Barnes tells us you've been here almost forty hours."

Putting a number to my time here seems to add weight to my limbs. I glance at Robert. He must be the acting director right now.

"We wanted to personally thank you," she continues. "For everything you've uncovered. The risks you took were extreme, and we can't thank you enough."

Charles clears his throat. "But we'd like to try. What can we do to thank you for your service?"

This is not exactly the line of questioning I was expecting.

In fact, it's so far off base that I don't know what to say.

And then I remember something.

"Taylor Barclay," I say, and my voice cracks on his name. "We never would have uncovered anything if it wasn't for him. He's the one you should be thanking, but he gave his life for this. You should put up some kind of monument for him."

Ella nods. "That can absolutely be arranged."

"And I want something else," I say, an idea coming to me. "IA has the ability to help the people in other worlds who need it. My universe was stricken with disaster when it almost collapsed. We need supplies and disaster relief."

"Janelle, there may be some things that we can't do," Robert says.

But Ella holds up her hand. "I'm sure something can be arranged."

Charles nods. "We'll have a team put together in order to offer aid."

"And I just want to go home," I say. I might as well ask now, if they're offering to give me whatever I want.

"Of course," Robert says. "But before you do, I'd like to offer you an opportunity. We don't do this often—hardly ever really—but we'd like to offer you a job with IA."

I snort. "No thanks."

All of them look shocked. So much so that I feel the need to explain myself.

"IA is corrupt. What kind of agency that's sworn to protect imprisons and threatens to execute the innocent?" I ask. "I mean, has Ben's family even been released from prison yet?"

"They have," Ella says.

"Look," Robert says. "A lot is going to change. There are some extreme ideas in place that I don't agree with."

Charles and Ella both nod, echoing his thoughts.

"The corruption is wider spread than just IA," Charles says. "We have people working on tracing where the Unwilling have gone, and several members of the government have been implicated."

"I want to change IA," Robert says. "And I'm offering you the chance to help me. There are a lot of people who may have been involved in this conspiracy—or others—and I need good people to seek them out. I'm offering you the chance to finish what you've started.

"You would report directly to me. You'd work with Hayley and Jimmy and a few other people I've hand-selected for the team. After everyone has been jailed or cleared for their involvement—or lack thereof—you can attend North Point and become a full-fledged IA agent."

For a second I think about it. I believe what he's saying. I believe that he wants to make a difference. I admire him for wanting to try, and I'm flattered he thinks I can help.

But I just want to go home. Be with my family. Curl up and cry about everything that's happened these past few days.

Maybe not worry about dying.

"Thank you for the offer," I say. "But my own universe needs me."

Robert nods, but Ella reaches out and touches my arm. "Please think about it," she says. "We need more people like you."

I look at Robert, then at Hayley, who says, "Taylor saw something in you, something he didn't see in most people."

My eyes water and I look away. I can't imagine I'll change my mind, but I owe it to Barclay to at least consider it. "I'll think about it."

A few hours later, when I'm released, Hayley nods toward two agents who have just portaled in with a woman. "We've already started to retrieve some of the Unwilling," she says.

The woman is older, probably in her thirties or even forties. She's thin with dull blond hair and eyes that look a little sunken, and she walks with her head down and her shoulders turned inward.

"She's one of the older ones," Hayley says. "From your world, actually. She was abducted back in the nineties."

"And she's still alive?" About 80 percent of people abducted for human trafficking are dead within a few years, be it from violence, drugs, or despair—they just don't usually make it.

"She might look meek and timid now, but she must have been strong when they grabbed her to have made it this long." Hayley bumps my shoulder. "She probably never thought she'd make it home." She doesn't have to say *because of us*; it's implied in her mannerism. Despite how broken up she feels over Barclay, she's proud of what we've accomplished.

I guess I should be too.

"What's her name?" I ask.

Hayley pulls out her charger and scrolls through it. "Bauer, I think. Emily Bauer."

My breath catches in my throat. The girl from my father's case. Warmth spreads through my body and I feel my lips curve into a slight smile. My dad would be proud.

Because of me, Emily Bauer is finally coming home.

Because of me—and because of Ben.

I see him. He's in different clothes—clean and fresh—and he's got bandages on his neck and one of his arms. His face is serious and closed off, his eyes hidden behind the waves of his hair. It's like the air flees my lungs when I see him. I love him so much that it physically hurts.

He's not alone. Standing next to him is his double. And I mean that in the traditional sense, a guy who looks a lot like him—almost identical but not quite. This guy is an inch or so taller, he's a little thinner, and his hair looks a little shorter. But they're clearly brothers.

Derek Michaels sees me first. His nose has been broken, and the skin around his eyes looks almost black with the bruising, but he's cleaned up. And he's alive.

He takes a step toward me. He's slow; the movement is a little jerky, and I know there may be some long-term damage under his clothes. "It's nice to finally meet you," he says. And something about his voice has weight to it.

"You too," I say, and I turn my eyes to Ben's. I want to

memorize every line of his face so that I can conjure up his image months from now.

Next to me, Hayley smiles. "We should give you two a minute."

"Go on," Derek says with a laugh.

We're just outside IA headquarters in a closed-off area where people can portal in and out. The sun is peeking through the clouds, bathing us in light, and there's a frenzied energy, an unbridled excitement around us—it's the feeling of knowing you've just broken a big case.

This is just the beginning, though. Who knows what the energy will be like when they start cleaning house?

I feel more than see Ben move beside me. "Did you take the job?" he asks.

I laugh. "They offered to put you in IA too? After everything?"

He shrugs. "I think they want to keep a close eye on me."

"I just want to go home," I say.

"Me too," he says, and I hear it in his voice. No matter how much he might miss me—no matter how much he might think he wants to come back to me—he can't come. Not now—not when Derek is here and his parents have been sent to a hospital in his home world.

And if I'm honest with myself, maybe not ever.

It's not that he isn't going to choose me. It's that there might always be *something* that says he needs to stay.

He must read the thoughts off my face, because he reaches out and squeezes my hand. "I believe in us," he says, his voice thick. "I do."

My throat is tight, and I can't speak, so I don't.

"From the moment I portaled into your world, you've been the best thing to ever happen to me," he says. "I love you more than anything. But my family: They've just been released from prison, and they were there because of me. I need to make sure they're okay. I need to—"

"I know," I say quietly. I look back at the IA agent who's lingering with a quantum charger behind us. "Open his portal," I say.

A split second later, he does.

Looking across the chasm into the nothingness of the portal, I can't help but feel a sense of déjà vu. The air around me, charged with the energy of the portal and the weight of my emotions, is cold against the warmth of my flushed skin.

I feel the rough calluses on Ben's palm and try to memorize them. I want the feel of his fingers imprinted on my senses.

He squeezes twice. "Janelle." His voice cracks.

For a moment I do nothing. I just wish I could close my eyes and let this moment melt away. I'm not ready for it.

I'm not ready to say good-bye again.

But no amount of closing my eyes and wishing is ever going to erase any problems. And even if that did somehow miraculously work . . . well, I'm just not like that.

So I squeeze back.

It's all it takes. Ben pulls me into him, and for a moment I give in to what I want to feel. His arms tighten around me, and I just let myself lean against him. Relish the feel of him holding me. The tension in my shoulders disappears. With my face pressed against his chest, I feel the pounding of his heart.

The rest of the world is gone.

It's just Ben and me, the beat of his heart in my ears, the texture of his thermal against my cheek, the strength of his arms around me, the smell of minty soap on his skin, the feel of his lips against my hair.

When he whispers, "I love you," I know it's the truth. I know how much he means it. And that makes what I'm about to do so much harder.

My throat constricts and my eyes burn, and I wish there was some other way.

But there's not.

I can't watch him walk through another portal and out of my world again, not if I'm still holding on to the hope that he'll come back.

I can't spend the rest of my life waiting for the ghost of a chance. I don't want either of us to go through life dead but breathing.

My body shakes as I push him away from me. The tears sting as they slip down my skin.

"What's wrong?" Ben asks.

This whole situation is what's wrong—portals, other universes, human trafficking, conspiracies, dead bodies piling up around us.

*We're* what's wrong.

I take a deep breath and force my voice to come out steady. "You shouldn't prolong it. You should go."

"J—" He reaches for me, but I step back and shake my head.

"Don't." My voice breaks, and I swallow back the lump in my throat. "Maybe someday . . . maybe we'll see each other again; maybe then it'll be different."

"I want to come back with you. I just—"

"I know," I say, my voice barely above a whisper. "Just give me this moment. No promises." Because I want to remember what we're like together, right now.

His eyes are red now, and the tension in his body makes something pinch in my chest. He takes a step toward me, and I hold up a hand to keep him at a far enough distance. He grabs it and holds it against his chest.

I can feel the throb of his heartbeat.

"I love you," he says again.

I know he does, and I love him, too. More than anything. But does that really mean he's willing to give up seeing his family for me? Even if his world wasn't what he was expecting, even if he didn't belong there anymore, it's a little more complicated than just checking to see if they're okay and promising to visit them next Christmas. Plus there's everything we've just been through, the lives we've taken—directly or not—and the people we've lost.

"Maybe love isn't enough," I say, and I wonder when I started believing that was true.

Ben shakes his head. "I don't believe that."

Underneath the fabric of his shirt, I can feel the warmth of his skin. My own pulse seems to thump at the same rhythm as his, and when he leans in, I can smell the soap from his shower, the mint on his breath. I bite my lip and concentrate on the physical pain to keep the throb in my chest from overwhelming me.

We've seen worlds where we don't belong—too many. And

**468**

nothing will ever change the fact that his home is actually a world away from mine.

"You need to go home," I whisper as I pull away. And I turn around because I can't watch him walk out of my life again.

As I head down the hallway to find Hayley and demand we leave this instant, I wish this was some romantic movie, and he'd chase me down, turn me around, kiss me so hard it hurts, and tell me something romantic, something I'd have to believe.

I know the moment he's gone. I can't explain how, but it's like something changes—the air, the temperature, the energy, or maybe it's just me—I feel a little emptier than I already did.

I think of the last time he left, when I sank to the ground, alone in the rain. I didn't think it was possible that anything could feel worse than what I felt in that moment.

But I was wrong.

This is worse. I'm not sure how, but I know that it is.

It's just past dawn when we portal back to my earth. As my feet hit the grass outside our apartment on Miramar, a rush of emotion barrels into me and knocks me to my knees.

I've kept my promise.

I've come home.

"Where are you going to live?" Cecily says as she reaches down to pull me back to my feet. She's not talking to me.

"Fuck, I thought I'd live with you," Elijah says.

"Oh, I'm sorry," she says. "We have language limits at Qualcomm. You can only say the F word once a week. You'll have to join the Marines. I think they're more your type." Her face is washed and her hair is pulled back into a ponytail. She doesn't have to tell me she's happy to be home—she has a bounce in her step that I haven't seen since our last class at Eastview.

Elijah nods. His face is serious, like he's really thinking about whether he could make it a week and only swear once. I don't know why he's even considering it—we all know he couldn't do it. "What if I promise to light that sweatshirt on fire?" he says.

Cecily looks down at the I ♥ NEW PRIMA sweatshirt she has

on and when she lifts her head, her smile has overtaken her face. Her eyes look almost squinty because of it. "I know exactly what we're going to do," she says. "We'll have a bonfire party, maybe near Scripps Pier. We'll have to clear away the debris, but that would be the perfect place. And we can make s'mores. Or maybe just toast marshmallows, there are a ton of those lying around. . . ."

Elijah jumps in and he's just as bad. He wants to have fireworks and sparklers and maybe even an explosion or two.

"Wow, so is this normal for them?" Hayley says.

I shrug. "Cecily does like to plan parties. I think Elijah just likes to attend them."

I'm not sure what's normal for any of us anymore. We've seen too much—too many different worlds, too much violence, too much death, too much grief. That's something we'll have to get through together.

Right now, holding on to some piece of normalcy is the only way to cope.

The front door opens easily, and I think of my dad and how he never locked our door. Struz is just like him.

I wonder if things would have turned out differently if their doubles had been friends.

Cecily and Elijah fall silent as the four of us walk into the kitchen. Hayley has paperwork for Struz to sign, and a million details to go over with him.

I have food.

The apartment is sleepy, like the rest of San Diego right now, and as I mix up the pancake batter, slice the fresh strawberries, and brew the gourmet coffee I brought with me, I revel in the small space, the pile of dishes, the discarded Monopoly board and its fake money on the living-room floor—and the fact that there are seven more-than-half-empty glasses of water on just the first floor and only two people asleep upstairs.

It almost seems like I never left. Like nothing has changed.

Nothing here, at least. There's no denying that *I've* changed, that in less than seven days, the world threw everything it had at me, so many things tried to break me, and a lot of them beat me down.

But I made it through.

And now I'm home.

Cecily breathes in the scent of the coffee. "You might end up waking the whole base with this," she says.

As if on cue, a sleepy and unobservant Struz—with his eyes half closed, his hand rubbing his hair—comes down the stairs. He's wearing a white T-shirt, gray sweatpants, and mismatched socks.

I'd secretly been worried about seeing him again. After everything with his double, I was afraid I'd look at him in a new light and wonder what he was capable of. But now I realize all I can see when I look at him are the differences between them. I see the mussed-up hair, the clothes that don't fit right because he's too tall and too thin.

My heart thuds harder in my chest, and I take a shallow breath.

His eyes snap open with alarm, and then he sees me. "Holy shit," he says, and he's taking the stairs three at a time.

I hand the pancake batter to Hayley and move around the island into the living room, in time for Struz to wrap his arms around me.

He sees the bandages on my left hand and right arm, and I sense his demeanor change—he's taking me in, the same way Barclay taught me to take in a room.

"I'm okay," I say. "Just a few scrapes."

He just hugs me again, and I can feel his whole body shaking.

"Jared!" Struz shouts, letting me go. "J-baby is back!"

Never in his life has my brother gotten out of bed so early and so quickly. It's like his feet don't even touch the stairs. He just flies down them, and before I realize what's about to happen, he launches himself into my arms, like he used to when he was a kid—when he was smaller than me—and he tackles me to the ground.

He fires questions at me, but there's no need for me to respond.

"Where have you been? How could you leave without telling me? If you ever do that again, I swear I'll . . . I'll do something you really won't like," Jared says. "And it'll be worse than messing up your clothes in the laundry."

When Jared lets me up, I introduce him and Struz to Hayley and finish making pancakes. We all sit around the kitchen table and Struz regales us with dramatic stories about what I've missed—everything from his terrible attempt at cooking to moving everyone out of Qualcomm. I give an abbreviated and censored version of what I've been through, Cecily tells us about the Unwilling she met, and Hayley shares a funny story about the night she and Barclay first met. And Elijah eats.

Suddenly everything is the same as it was. The only thing different is me.

After Hayley has gone back to Prima to prepare the next shipment of supplies, and after Cee has taken Elijah to a new evac shelter on a "trial basis," I sit on our living-room floor next to the discarded Monopoly board. Struz is at another meeting off base, and Jared has already gone to bed, and I wonder if I'll ever be able to sleep again.

If I'll be able to close my eyes and see nothing, rather than seeing the faces of the people I've lost.

If I'll ever forget the curl to Ben's hair or the way his half smile always looked like a secret he shared with only me. If I'll ever be able to remember him without feeling that ache in my bones and that throb in my chest—if I'll ever get over missing him and the way I felt when his arms were around me. And if I want to.

Then I hear it.

The high-pitched tone of something electronic powering up—or someone opening a portal.

For a split second, it's like someone has drained all the air from my lungs, and I think Chuckles or someone else has not only caught up with me but traced me back to my family. But then I remember who I am and what I've just accomplished.

I stand up and reach for the iron poker next to the fireplace.

The portal is there, a black hole in our living room, and the cool, wet, never-ending scent of possibility moves through the room and raises goose bumps on my skin. I tighten my grip on the poker.

The portal ripples a little, like a pool of ink. But no one comes through yet. It hangs there, suspended by nothing, and I'm struck by the enormity of just how incredible this is. The idea of something that seemingly violates every law of the natural world being not only possible but also something that's become ingrained in my life.

Right when I think it's about to flicker out of existence, Ben steps through.

He looks exactly like he did when I last saw him.

"What are you doing here?"

He smiles, probably because my voice sounds so breathy, and then he says, "I missed you."

I don't know what to say to that.

Luckily, I don't have to say anything, because Ben eyes the poker. "You expecting someone else?"

I put it down on the kitchen counter and almost say, "I wasn't expecting *you*," but I don't. Because what I was expecting doesn't matter. He's here. Right now.

Instead, I wait for whatever it is he wants to say.

"You know what I love most about you?" he says as he shoves his hands in his pockets.

I smile. Even if I did know, I still want to hear him say it. "Probably not."

His smile widens. "Don't get me wrong, I love your face, and your hair, and your eyes, and I love the way you laugh a little too loud and the way you scare me a little when you're angry, but . . ." Ben runs a hand through his hair. "I love listening to you—your voice, the things you say, everything."

I'm warm, and a little light-headed, and I wonder again what he's doing here.

But I try not to hope.

"Do you remember when we went on our first date—I guess our only date?"

I do. I remember it so well, it feels like it was just yesterday.

We sat on a blanket on the edge of Sunset Cliffs. Below us were only rocks and white water crashing against them. We watched the seagulls as they flew in to their rock in the middle of the ocean, landed, and squawked at one another before taking off again. Ben was close enough that he could lean into me, that the heat of his body could keep me warm as the wind from the ocean washed over us. The sun, starting its descent, hung like a huge golden globe near the edge of the water, casting red, orange, pink, and purple streaks in the sky.

It felt like we were the only two people in the world.

I nod. "I do." How could I really ever forget that?

"The world was falling apart around us, but it didn't matter. I didn't care." His voice cracks a little under the weight of emotion, and I take a step toward him. I want to wrap him in my arms and make him promise to never leave me again. "At that moment, I knew I wasn't alone anymore. Because I had you. This world may not be my home, but four months ago, when I went back to my world, that wasn't home either."

His eyes are glassy with tears, and his hand reaches out to cup my cheek.

"Janelle, you're my home."

I pull him to me, feel his lips as they touch mine, and I'm not sure if I should laugh or cry.

Ben seems to know what I'm thinking. I feel him smile against my lips.

Everything else in the world seems to fall away. The space between us evaporates. One moment we're a foot apart, the next every inch of Ben's body is pressed into mine. The soft scent of mint and soap—the smell of Ben—fills my senses, and I hold on to him tighter, pull him closer, kissing him, tasting his tongue as I feel his hands on my back and tangling in my hair. The strength of his arms around me makes my heart beat faster; I'm feverish and I can't tell where I end and he begins.

Nothing has ever felt so *right*.

Everything that tried to stand between us doesn't matter now. We might have broken a little.

But now we're stronger in those broken places.

And we're going to face whatever comes next together.

# ACKNOWLEDGMENTS

Writing my sophomore book was a much different experience than writing my debut. This book would never have been possible without the slew of amazing people who brainstormed ideas, kept me on deadline, and still managed to make me laugh. Special thanks to Dan, Joanna, and Sarah.

I'm insanely grateful to the team at Balzer + Bray who have put so much faith in Janelle and Ben's story, especially Kristin Rens and Sara Sargent, who read the monstrous five-hundred-page first draft. Because of them, this book is a complete novel with no plot holes, and it's shorter. I also owe huge thanks to the marketing and publicity teams, who were so fabulous and supportive: Caroline Sun, Alison Lisnow, Emilie Polster, Stephanie Hoffman, Molly Thomas, and Stephanie Macy.

I'd also like to thank everyone else at HarperCollins who worked behind the scenes. Special thanks to Alison Donalty and Alison Klapthor, who designed the amazing covers; Caitlin Garing with audio; Jean McGinley in subrights; and everyone at HarperCollins Children's in the UK and Australia: Nicholas Lake, Rachel Denwood, Alison Ruane, Sam White,

Lara Wallace, and Elizabeth Ryley.

As always, a huge thank-you to Janet Reid, Pouya Shahbazian, and Steve Younger. And to my family and friends who have been so supportive, and all my former students, who are some of the best people I've ever met.

Most of all, thank you to everyone who read *Unraveling*.